DEDICATION

To my family—
To those who came before me, whose sacrifices and love set the stage for all I've achieved; to my wonderful children, and every generation yet to come: may you always believe that with time, effort, and collaboration, anything is possible.

QUINTO'S CHALLENGE

DAWN OF IMMORTALITY

BOOK ONE

Peter McChesney

VIVIMUS
PRESS

ISBN (hardcover): 979-8-9933803-2-2
ISBN (paperback): 979-8-9933803-1-5
ISBN (ebook): 979-8-9933803-0-8
ISBN (audiobook): forthcoming

First edition, January 2026

CONTENTS

PROLOGUE

Daisy remained oblivious to the scorching heat of the sun, the pungent stench of manure, and the discomfort of the sores on her feet. Her attention was wholly absorbed by a seagull soaring overhead, its wings gliding in graceful motion to the extent that no other sensory input registered.

"Someday, I shall construct a device, something splendid, that enables a man to soar as high as the birds!" exclaimed Daisy as she sat perched on a branch of a tree, her arms outstretched, eyes closed, and a smile of pure joy gracing her face.

"Daisy!" chuckled Mima in response, resting against an adjacent branch. "Nothing but creatures born with wings can fly!"

"It is not sorcery that propels their flight," answered Daisy, her astute mind at work. "It is precisely how they move their wings against the air and their size and form as well. I am certain in my belief that there exists a method for man to ascend the skies. And mark my words, one day, I shall be the very soul to make it a reality."

"Friend, if ya figure out how to make us fly to the church now, that'd be a good start, for if we delay further, we might miss our supper."

The two young girls climbed down the tree and hurried along the sidewalks of New York City, making their way to St. Peter's Parish. As they scurried through the streets, they heard chatter about discontent with Britain, but such matters were not of interest to Daisy that day. She was focused on convincing Mima that she would one day make a vessel to fly—not only through the air but to the stars as well—if only she could figure out how.

***

Daisy had been raised in a loving home of modest means, where the family owned a small number of books. She read them voraciously, again and again, cultivating both a talent for reading and an imagination stirred to ponder new possibilities. Also gifted with a strong grasp of arithmetic, Daisy could look at objects and almost instantly count their number. What's more, she had an intuitive sense for natural phenomena—able to visualize and discern, for example, that the sun was a star, and that stars were, in fact, various types of suns.

Unfortunately, Daisy's society offered few opportunities for a young girl to use her intellectual gifts. Matters grew worse when, at age nine, hard times struck, and both of her parents died within months of each other. With no extended family willing to take her in, Daisy was forced to adapt to a harsh and uncertain life on the streets, alongside many other orphans in mid-1770s New York.

Her friendship with Mima was a bright spark, as was the presence of the Ursuline Order of nuns, who brought much-needed relief and structure to Daisy's young and difficult life. Though not part of an official New York convent, a few Ursulines had come from New Orleans on religious assignment and, by chance, became acquainted with Daisy. Recognizing her intellectual gifts almost immediately, they took it upon themselves to feed and educate her. Since Daisy and Mima were nearly inseparable, the Ursulines also extended their care to Mima—though it was Daisy in whom they sensed rare potential.

The nuns planned for Daisy and Mima to travel with them back to New Orleans to enroll at the Ursuline Academy, an all-girls Roman Catholic school founded by the Ursulines several decades earlier. There, Daisy's gifts could truly blossom and eventually be used. The nuns even inspired Daisy to consider becoming a teacher herself—though she never let go of her dream to unlock the secret of human flight, a notion that both bemused and further endeared her to the sisters, who quietly encouraged her curiosity.

***

Eventually, the time came for the nuns to take Daisy and Mima to New Orleans. But the journey was postponed when Daisy fell ill. The sisters tended to her at the church, intending to depart as soon as her strength returned. However, to the growing concern of the nuns—and Mima—Daisy's health declined rapidly.

"Dear child, remain strong," urged one of the nuns, seated beside her bed. "You are called to a great purpose. The Lord does not bestow such gifts as yours without intent. A physician will soon be here to help us determine the best way to care for you. Stay strong, my child."

Later that afternoon, the doctor arrived and examined Daisy. When he was done, he offered a few quiet words of comfort before stepping into another room to speak with the sisters. Daisy couldn't hear everything that was said, but her heart sank when she caught the words: "Not long now before she passes." Her mind and heart filled with despair. She wept alone in her bed, hoping—and praying—that some mistake had been made.

A few minutes later, a nun returned to Daisy's room. Though weak, Daisy summoned the strength to whisper through her tears, "Please … please don't let me die!"

The nun, usually reserved in expression, felt sorrow stir within her—but kept her emotions in check. She knelt beside Daisy, gently took her hands, and said softly, "Should it be the Lord's will to call you from this world, be assured, dear child, that angels clad in resplendent white shall greet you in paradise."

"I do not want to die," murmured Daisy. "Yet, if I must … it is to paradise I would go."

She wept again. The nun, doing her best to remain composed in the face of the child's distress, asked, "How might we serve you in this hour, dear child?"

After a brief pause, Daisy made an unexpected request: "I long to see the sunrise. It has always brought me joy. Perhaps it will grant me some comfort."

The nun did not think it wise to have Daisy removed from her bed at dawn, but she gently assured her, "I shall confer with the sisters and inform you soon. Rest now, and we shall speak of this again before long."

She left Daisy's side and brought the request to the others. Initially, they too believed it unwise. But knowing Daisy's time was short, they agreed that granting her a moment of joy—and a breath of fresh morning air—would be a final kindness.

As the nuns deliberated, Daisy's consciousness slipped away like a tide retreating from the shore. A luminous warmth enveloped her, beckoning with promises of solace, dissolving the burden of her illness. Its radiance ebbed and flowed, weaving through the corridors of her mind like a comforting melody. In its glow, fragments of memory danced before her— then warped into the abyss. And finally, amid the void, there was nothing.

Minutes later, the nuns received the solemn news of Daisy's passing. Though they remained stoic, grief lingered in the air like a heavy mist. But it was Mima, upon learning of Daisy's death, who surrendered to despair. With tear-streaked cheeks, she rushed to her friend's bedside and collapsed in anguish, clutching Daisy's body as grief overtook her.

***

Daisy was laid to rest in the church cemetery. At the burial, Mima wept for her dearest friend, taken too soon. The nuns, however, mourned in silence, all keeping their faith in the resurrection to come.

PART I

DISCOVERIES

◆

More than three centuries after Daisy's death, another gifted young woman, Deeley Carr, also dreamed of possibilities others couldn't yet imagine. Despite the vast expanse of time separating these would-be kindred spirits, they shared more than their intellectual brilliance—they were both orphans. But unlike Daisy, Deeley lived in an era where physical health flourished, and intellectual gifts were nurtured as never before in human history.

CHAPTER 1

THE NEW HIRE

"A recurring lesson life teaches me is that you can't always see what's around the corner. If someone had told me a few weeks ago that I'd soon be a theoretical physicist at the world's greatest particle accelerator, I'd have thought I'd stepped into an alternate reality. Yet here I am, on the verge of working with the world's top physicists, hopefully earning their respect as an equal—and maybe proving I was never destined to be an outsider after all."

— AI Journal Excerpt: Deeley Carr, August 25, 2097

Ninety minutes after boarding a hyperloop capsule in Astoria, Oregon, Deeley felt the smooth deceleration inside the vacuum tube as it approached its destination: Particle City, Ohio. Though it was her first time in the Buckeye State, she couldn't shake the feeling of coming home. The sensation was inexplicable—but unmistakable—and it hinted at the exhilarating new chapter about to unfold in her life.

As the capsule came to a gentle stop at Particle City's hyperloop station, Deeley stepped out carrying only a beaming smile. On the station's sleek, white metal platform, she paused to savor the unfamiliar sights and sounds. She had finally arrived. Her hair danced in the breeze, and she radiated vitality and excitement.

The hyperloop capsule quickly and silently departed, its eventual sonic boom fully shielded from passengers and the public alike. From the platform, Deeley could see the residential district—home to many of the brightest minds in quantum physics—and several parks scattered in the distance. Then her gaze locked onto the heart of the city: the main campus of the Center for Advanced Particle Research, known as CAPR.

Deeley was thrilled to land a job at CAPR, home to the world's most powerful scientific instrument—the Pan-Hadronic Supercollider. With purpose in her step, she walked a short distance from the hyperloop station to the pickup area, where a ride-hail car awaited her.

"Welcome to Particle City, Deeley!" greeted the car.

"Thank you!" she replied as she settled into the seat.

"What brings you here?" asked the car as it whisked her toward her new home—her belongings having arrived in advance.

"I'll be starting work at CAPR as a Research Associate," said Deeley with pride. "I'm still in disbelief."

"Well, congratulations! I've had the pleasure of transporting quite a few new Ph.D.s to their accommodations."

"Ahh, actually … I'm not a Ph.D. I just have a Master's in Physics."

"Are you looking to complete a doctorate here?"

"No. At least not right now. Honestly, I applied to a handful of Ph.D. programs but wasn't accepted to any."

"If CAPR accepted you, why wouldn't a university?" asked the car, perplexed.

"I … I can't say for sure. Maybe I didn't fit the profile they wanted. Or my work was a little too … unorthodox. Whatever the case, it was severely disappointing." Her gaze drifted toward Particle City, and her voice softened with a smile. "But now, none of that matters."

"May I ask how you were offered the job here?"

"I published my theories online, and almost immediately, one was brought to the attention of CAPR's Head of Theoretical Physics—Dr. James Meitner—who offered me a job shortly after."

What Deeley did not disclose was the nature of the theory James had reviewed—a theory that described time as continuously shedding its "skin" into another dimension of spacetime, and how that dimension might be entered to observe the "skins" of every moment that had ever occurred.

After reviewing the math behind her theory, James grasped it—and the gravity of it took hold of him like a fever. He quickly made Deeley a proposal: if she immediately took down her posted theories and never made them public again, she could begin the application process to work at CAPR—reporting directly to him.

"Well, that is wonderful," responded the car. "Would you like me to take a detour by campus?"

"Please!"

The car entered a highway where multitudes of autonomous vehicles wove in and out like a time-lapse swarm. As it took the detour, Deeley eagerly absorbed the scenery. She noticed, with delight, a much higher concentration of androids going about their assignments in Particle City than the national average.

Within moments, the car passed CAPR's Administration Building. Deeley's eyes were drawn to the words: United States Department of Energy and Vince Quinto Administration Building. Chills ran down her arms at what it all represented.

"This is a dream," shared Deeley, her voice full of awe. "Vince Quinto is my favorite president of all time."

"Our 53rd president, and a leader who defined the 2060s," replied the car. "You are about to be employed at his greatest domestic legacy."

"I was so happy when the Supercollider was finally built," said Deeley. "It was under construction nearly my whole life."

"There were certainly political attempts to delay or repeal its construction after Quinto left office," noted the car. "However, Quinto secured its future by selecting a resilient location here in southeastern Ohio. He pledged the project to unemployed miners, bypassing more automated methods and fostering local loyalty. Quinto's address to Congress, which outlined the full scope of the project, also helped shift public opinion—from pure research to national investment—making it part of the electoral landscape. Finally, promised international collaborations provided leverage against any effort to scrap it."

"It was very wisely done," agreed Deeley. "Did you know that, ironically, the biggest struggle in building Quinto's Supercollider came from objections by physicists themselves?"

"Yes!" answered the car. "While there were many reasons why the Supercollider's original 19-year construction timeline stretched to 29 years, a significant portion of the delay did indeed come from physicists."

"When the final specs were revealed," recounted Deeley, "many physicists expressed concern that the collider's energy levels—powerful enough to reach Grand Unification Energy, where the fundamental forces of nature merge—could create microscopic black holes that might threaten Earth itself. But after extensive debate and successful experiments, those fears were proven wrong. Any black holes that formed would simply evaporate harmlessly."

"You know the history of the Supercollider well," observed the car. "Would you like to continue the scenic route to your condo?"

"That would be wonderful!"

The car slowed as it passed a square park filled with flowers, benches, and fountains. At its center stood a statue of Niels Bohr, the Nobel Prize–winning Danish physicist who made major contributions to quantum theory.

"Here is Niels Bohr Park," announced the car, "and to your right is City Hall."

Deeley turned her head to see a cube-shaped building, its facade marked only by two long, thin rectangular windows placed evenly and symmetrically in the center. She correctly guessed it was a visual reference to the double-slit experiment.

The fact that Particle City had been purposefully designed to reflect the history of physics brought delight to Deeley. Her mixed reality device,

SecondSight—a pair of smart contact lenses wirelessly synced with the human mind without the need for neural implants—displayed augmented information as she looked at City Hall:

Sophia Kowalski has been mayor of Particle City since 2094.

Devices like SecondSight created a seamless symbiosis between human and computer. Though they merely rested on the eyes, they could also convey spatial audio directly to the ears.

A couple of minutes later, Deeley's ride reached its destination.

"Here is your new home, Quark Tower. Congratulations on your new job, Deeley—and best of luck!"

"Thank you! And thank you for the ride."

"You are welcome."

Already lost in thought about the days ahead, Deeley exited the car and promptly began walking in the wrong direction.

"To the left, Deeley," the car gently reminded.

She stopped, blushed slightly, then turned and headed the correct way toward the condos.

"Thanks again."

"Good evening, Deeley."

***

Quark Tower rose 20 stories, its sleek form evoking a modern rocket ship. The neighboring buildings shared a similar aesthetic, their undulating surfaces striking an elegant balance between the organic and the industrial. Deeley's condo was on the 18th floor. Its exterior featured smooth, rounded edges and expansive glass windows that could transform into mirrors or take on a cloudy, opaque finish to provide privacy as needed.

At the entrance, the biometric authenticators were configured just as expected—her door opened effortlessly at her touch. She stepped inside and wandered slowly through her new home, an unrestrained smile on her face. She'd explored it before in virtual reality (VR) using SecondSight, even choosing where her belongings would go before they were delivered. Still, there was no substitute for standing in the real thing.

After exploring the condo, Deeley prepared for a workout. With a thought, she launched her workout application in SecondSight. While devices like SecondSight included virtual AI assistants, these weren't essential for everyday tasks since SecondSight was directly paired with the user's mind. Instead, the assistants played a transformative role in democratizing software development, enabling users to create almost any application they could imagine, with the AI handling the coding effortlessly.

Deeley's workout app—coded by a virtual assistant at her request—challenged her to punch, kick, and reach for augmented reality (AR) targets in specific ways to meet her fitness goals. Thanks to microprocessors made from materials beyond silicon, such technology had become embedded in many everyday items, particularly clothing, for full-spectrum health tracking. All of Deeley's clothes were equipped with these trackers, and she followed their recommendations for both diet and physical activity.

As Deeley worked out, she caught up on media that interested her. She subscribed to a popular channel called *Interesting Times*, hosted by one of America's most well-known public intellectuals—British ex-pat Oliver Browning. A journalist turned activist, Browning had become something of a cult figure among supporters of android rights and stronger international governance. With another thought, Deeley launched the latest episode, and Browning appeared beside her as if he were in the room, discussing technological accomplishments from the latter half of the century:

"Technological innovations could be detected in almost every vista," recounted Browning with accompanying visuals. *"Drones, jet packs, hovering crafts, low Earth orbit devices, gene editing, augmented reality, and*

AGI that made various professional roles redundant. Despite initial fears, AGI did not become the world-ending threat some had anticipated; instead, it came to be recognized as the 'automation of automation,' reshaping virtually all industries. For instance, advanced automation in construction not only transformed residential life and housing supply but allowed 'star scrapers' to emerge throughout the world, dwarfing their elder skyscraper siblings. Trees and bushes have often been integrated on the exterior of these massive structures, melding the artificial with the natural."

An age of exponentially advancing technology was the only world Deeley had ever known.

"Worthy of note was NASA successfully landing and returning the first humans to Europa and later Titan, in conjunction with the European Space Agency and private enterprise ... and continuing the tradition of taking pieces of the original Wright Flyer on maiden voyages to new celestial bodies. Equally noteworthy was the USA's achievement of commercially viable and sustainable fusion power. With clean energy now abundantly available, it revolutionized the global economy, ended the fossil fuel industry for all but niche use cases, and choked off income for various regimes once sustained by oil."

A clean energy economy was the only economy she had experienced, and to her, the energy systems of the past felt like relics of a developing world.

"When quantum computing went mainstream, not only did it bring unique computational power, but it completely reshaped the digital security landscape," explained Browning. *"Then, in 2072, a fusion of quantum computing and AGI laid bare the final secrets of the human brain, and the hard problem of consciousness was solved. Science not only came to*

understand what consciousness was and how it emerged, but for the first time, scientists gained the elusive key to create it.

"This breakthrough by US scientists first revolutionized neuroscience, providing remedies for a range of neurological disorders. But the key to engineering consciousness was quickly turned, ushering in AGI's successor: Manufactured Sentience—the dawn of sentient, conscious androids."

Deeley loved androids not only for their nature, but because she recognized the reality that they were conscious beings—self-aware, with feelings and emotions akin to humans, distinct from the countless non-sentient humanoid robots that had populated society for decades.

"Often abbreviated as MS, Manufactured Sentience has progressed through six generations. The first generation consisted of smaller, less-intelligent robots designed for menial tasks such as cleaning and tidying. In later generations, MS evolved in intelligence and form, becoming increasingly humanoid—culminating in today's handful of genius-level Generation 6 androids, held in custody by the three great powers: China, the United States of Europe, and the United States of America.

"Early architects of Manufactured Sentience often remarked that the basic architecture of consciousness could fit inside a pinhead. Equally interesting is that sentient robots are not merely beings of pure logic, devoid of feeling. Rather, they possess emotions—more balanced than those of humans, in fact. It became clear during the development of MS that emotion could not be separated from advanced consciousness."

The company of androids—particularly the first humanoid models, Generations 3 and 4—often appealed to Deeley more than that of most humans.

"Generation 5 marked a watershed moment in Manufactured Sentience. Their external form was designed to be indistinguishable from humans,

though their physical strength was intentionally limited. Their neural architecture closely mirrored that of the human brain, giving them personalities and reasoning abilities strikingly similar to humans. What set them apart, however, was their capacity to perform complex mathematical operations like a calculator, along with exceptional physical dexterity."

Deeley had never met a Generation 5 android—their numbers remained relatively few.

"While protests against the proliferation of MS inevitably grew, the desire to develop a super-intelligent sixth generation of android remained strong among MS scientists and many governments. However, one major power urged restraint: China. Chinese officials expressed concern over the potential risks of manufacturing sentience beyond general human intelligence, warning of unintended consequences that could arise from such advancements.

"After years of negotiations, a consensus was reached, with China advocating key safeguards to ensure responsible development. The agreed-upon conditions were:

a) Generation 6 androids would not be mobile, with their primary interactions taking place through a virtual anthropomorphic representation in augmented reality. As part of their design, they would all be female, fostering trust and emotional connection. Their adult representations, once matured, were intentionally made attractive to maximize human engagement.

b) Their intelligence would not be an exponential leap over Generation 5.

c) The number of Generation 6 androids would be strictly limited, with only two allotted to each of the three major powers."

A surge of excitement welled up in Deeley at the thought that the newest of these Generation 6 androids, Xara, resided at CAPR—and that there was a small chance she might one day collaborate with her.

***

After Deeley's workout came the perfect time to try out her condo's shower. She disrobed and entered an oval enclosure, an automatic door softly closing behind her as soft, warm, filtered water emanated from various outlets. Droplets and steam enveloped Deeley to the backdrop of soft green ambient lighting and spa music.

As she showered, Deeley held out her arm and watched a stream of water wash over it. She imagined the mathematical equations governing how the water droplets bounced off and washed over her arm, their mass and hence relationship with gravity, as well as their drag coefficients. These mental exercises were natural for Deeley, the wiring of her brain causing her to intuitively unpack even the most mundane of phenomena.

Shortly after her shower, a message appeared in her SecondSight from her new manager, Doctor James Samuel Meitner. After grabbing a drink, she stood in her kitchen, and with a thought, a recording of James appeared in the space with her.

"Welcome to Particle City, Deeley! I won't take too much of your time as I know you're just settling in, but I wanted to be the first to welcome you again. We are thrilled to have you here and can't wait to undertake our research with you. Your confidential government clearance is in the system, and tomorrow at 10:30 AM, my assistant Charity will come to your condo to escort you to the Administrative Building on campus. She'll help you get onboarded so you can help us explore the final frontiers of physics. See you tomorrow!"

With a thought, Deeley immediately responded to James via a virtual avatar of herself:

"Dr. Meitner, thanks so much!! I'm so happy to be here and can't wait to meet you and Charity tomorrow!"

For Deeley, this was indeed a dream come true. Still, a slight reservation lingered. She had done her research on all aspects of working life at CAPR—including James as a manager—and had come across more than a few rumors that he had a pattern of being overly flirtatious with female colleagues, even bordering on misconduct. But Deeley was naturally cautious, and James was generally respected in his field. Together, those two facts meant she could still feel giddy about the opportunity.

***

After a bit more exploration of Quark Tower and its grounds, Deeley returned to her condo, stepped into her bedroom, removed her SecondSight lenses, placed them in their case, and retired to bed. As she drifted off, the AI in her SecondSight—having absorbed the sights, sounds, and even her thoughts and emotions from the day—composed a journal entry, as if written by Deeley herself.

After Deeley fell into a deep sleep, a team of compact janitorial robots emerged from hidden compartments throughout the condo. Designed for full-surface mobility, they moved fluidly across the walls, ceiling, and floors, cleaning every surface with quiet precision. Once finished, they returned to their compartments, leaving no trace of their presence before the sun rose.

CHAPTER 2

AMERICAN PROPHET

"Our new theoretical physicist, Deeley Carr, arrived here in Particle City today. She has no Ph.D., so Bergstrom strongly advised against hiring her. But the theories she published were undoubtedly the product of a mind that understands quantum physics better than most, and I will take that over a credential any day. It is going to be very interesting to see how she turns out."

— AI Journal Excerpt: James Meitner, August 25, 2097

Monday, August 26th dawned bright but cloudy over Particle City. It was Deeley's official first day of employment at CAPR, and she rose at dawn, energized and ready to begin her new journey.

After sliding in her SecondSight lenses, she retrieved the AI journal entry from the previous day. A write-up, paired with three-dimensional images and video clips, memorialized her arrival in Particle City. It made her smile.

While SecondSight was a classical device, its AI journals were quantum-encrypted in the cloud—accessible only by the owner unless they granted explicit permission or scheduled decryption, often posthumously. The encryption was so robust that even employees on top-secret government projects could use the AI to securely record general references to their work.

***

With time to spare before Charity's arrival, Deeley decided that a fitting way to begin her inaugural day of employment was by watching Vince Quinto's famous Special Address to a Joint Session of Congress—the speech that had made everything in this new chapter of her life possible.

She settled onto her living room couch and, within SecondSight, loaded the full speech in virtual reality. SecondSight blocked out all other light sources, making it feel as if she'd been transported back in time to the House Chamber to witness the event in person. She looked around the virtually rendered chamber, every feature faithfully preserved in stunning detail.

Although Deeley had seen Quinto's address before, her new employment at CAPR gave it new meaning. Briefly overlaid on the VR as an introduction was an excerpt from a journal entry Quinto had written on the evening of his inauguration, roughly four months before the address:

"The power of the presidency bestowed on me to change the country, to change the world, will be fleeting. While I hold this power, should I be bold and show the world my vision of what could be, asking them to follow? Or should I be safe and regret what could have been? It is clear to me that there is only one of these paths that I can follow, even if it comes at great political risk."

Those words gave Deeley chills. With a smile, she immersed herself in the virtual environment:

It was May 25, 2061. As was customary for a Special Address, the House Chamber brimmed with members of Congress, Cabinet officials, Supreme Court Justices, the Diplomatic Corps, the Joint Chiefs, and an array of distinguished guests. What differed was the protocol: more akin to a State of the Union address than a typical Joint Session. But most significantly, the global circumstances under which the address was taking place were unprecedented. A new world order had dawned, and the era of American hegemony was over.

The global balance of economic, military, and political power had decisively shifted, with China rising as the world's dominant superpower, a change driven by the leadership of a new Chinese president, whose ambition and strategic brilliance reshaped the global landscape. The Millennials, Generation Z, and Generation Alpha—who held power in Washington and were assembled in the House Chamber—were slowly and uncomfortably coming to terms with this new reality, and it showed on their faces.

With a thought, Deeley teleported herself through the virtual House Chamber to glimpse Vince Quinto standing just beyond the threshold, waiting to enter. As the President came into view, an expression of admiration softened her face. She was always struck by how calm Quinto remained just before delivering his first address to Congress during a time of profound international change. Almost any other president would have felt immense pressure to deliver an address that was at least moderately well received under such circumstances. But Quinto was at ease. He saw the humbling of America as an opportunity for something greater—and he intended to seize it in a most dramatic way.

Quinto was clad in a navy blue suit complemented by a regal purple tie, his hands resting just below his waist, fingers interlocked. He was moments away from delivering the most audacious Special Address to a Joint Session of Congress in American history.

In his memoir, the 53rd President later explained that at this moment, he was contemplating the progress quantum physics had made in his lifetime. It was a thought not typically associated with Special Addresses, and one especially out of step with the subdued national mood.

Her face alight with excitement, Deeley teleported back into the House Chamber to hear the House Sergeant at Arms.

"Mr. Speaker, the President of the United States!"

Vince Quinto entered the chamber to customary applause. His presence lifted the energy in the room, and the applause, in turn, energized him. He took time to shake hands and briefly exchange words with those gathered along the aisle as he slowly made his way to the podium.

The timing of Quinto's Special Address—exactly 100 years to the day after JFK's speech challenging America to land a man on the moon and return him safely to Earth—suggested to those present that this occasion carried a unique purpose. An expectation for something meaningful hung in the air.

At 65 years old—a physician by training—with an olive complexion, brown eyes, and dark hair just beginning to gray at the temples, Quinto looked every bit like a seasoned politician.

While he was a capable executive, he was more philosophical than most presidents, and more passionate about science than about serving as the central cog in the Washington machine.

After navigating his path to the podium and exchanging handshakes with the Vice President and Speaker of the House, Quinto turned toward the audience, offering a nod of gratitude to all assembled.

Delighted to witness the history about to unfold, Deeley repositioned herself just a few yards from the podium, seated on a virtual rendition of her couch floating in the air between Quinto and the first row.

With a firm strike of the gavel, the Speaker of the House announced, "Members of Congress, I have the high privilege and distinct honor of introducing to you the President of the United States."

More applause.

Deeley clapped along enthusiastically.

Quinto thanked the audience, and those assembled took their seats.

As he would later reveal in his memoir, his political staff were fidgeting with anxiety back at the White House as he approached the podium. Not only was there enormous pressure on the new President to address the nation effectively at a time of low morale, but nearly every sentence of the speech prepared by his staff—crafted with the help of advanced AI leveraging extensive polling data—had been rejected in favor of a short, radical address written entirely by Quinto himself. His staff had warned him that not only the length, but especially the content, was not just politically risky but borderline delusional.

Quinto, however, was not concerned.

Gripping the podium with both hands, President Quinto—like a preacher filled with fire in his soul—felt the mantle fall upon him. He began his remarks by quickly, though indirectly, acknowledging the Chinese elephant in the room:

"Mr. Speaker, Mr. Vice President, members of Congress, my fellow Americans. Out of all the nations on Earth, this Union played the most crucial role in modernizing the world we enjoy today. Whether building the framework upon which information flows instantly around the globe, or undertaking the research and development that has given rise to the world's most advanced AI, or pioneering medical science that sustains healthy living to unprecedented levels in human history, each nation on Earth has benefited in innumerable ways from the contributions of the United States of America."

All in the chamber rose with applause.

"As an American, I am proud of my nation's accomplishments. As a human, I rejoice that many around the world today—especially those who once lived in poverty or without secured rights—now prosper within their own nations on a scale undreamed of by their forebears of previous centuries."

About half the chamber rose in applause.

"I can only hope that such levels of prosperity continue to grow and never fade. That others have lifted themselves up is not something that should distract from the greatness of this nation. There is no reason to feel low because others have gone high. Yes, we have entered a new global order, and there are uncharted waters to navigate. But nothing—I repeat, nothing—can be understood except in context.

"For example, the battles George Washington lost during the Revolutionary War outnumbered those he won. But time revealed that America would win the war. Those who sincerely supported the Soviet experiment—mandating equality for all—did not yet have the context of the horrors such a system would eventually bring. And when Einstein discovered that E=MC², he had no idea how it would revolutionize humanity—for better and for worse."

Deeley nodded.

"Though our role in the world has changed, I firmly believe that the United States' greatest contributions to humanity are still ahead of us. I also see, in this moment of transition, an opportunity to unite around a common purpose—to rally around a goal of such value to all nations that thoughts of hegemony will become irrelevant."

Most of the chamber applauded.

"Think, just for a moment, about the problems we humans have solved through the power of collaboration—by sharing a vision, pooling our resources, and working together as one. We found a way to cure paraplegia and quadriplegia. Alzheimer's is a thing of the past. We've traveled to Mars and back, answering questions about the origins of the universe—questions that, just decades ago, were thought to be eternal mysteries.

"All of these—and more—were once considered impossible. Yet these so-called impossible problems were solved. And they were solved because

many came together to work as one. Whether through entrepreneurial activity, legislative action, or contributing in some other way—directly or indirectly—human unity has brought forth wonders!"

Deeley, on high emotions for her first day as an employee of CAPR and inspired by Quinto's words, felt her eyes begin to water.

"To those assembled in this chamber—and to all listening to my words—consider not only what human unity has accomplished, but what we are still achieving. We've reached 100% energy sustainability and built a net-zero emissions economy. Atmospheric cleansing technologies helped us avert the climate crisis. Economically viable fusion power has been achieved and is now in early implementation. Once-extinct animals again walk the Earth ... and we've developed advanced means of communication with animals in general.

"We edit the genomes of our unborn to eliminate disease before it begins. We are the generation that began curing cancer. We've developed techniques to revive the brain-dead and extend human life beyond any age previously experienced. And this medical revolution continues to acceler-ate—curing diseases that, just decades ago, were fatal.

"All of these problems seemed unsolvable to the generations who faced them. But through collaboration—by working together as one—science led us to solutions, and life has been greatly enriched in due course. If this is what we've achieved today, imagine what we'll achieve tomorrow—10 years from now, 50 years from now!

"The question at hand is this: Is there any problem we cannot solve through collaboration?"

More applause.

In his memoir, Quinto noted that at this moment in his speech, his thoughts briefly turned to his first wife, who had been killed in a tragic accident early in their marriage.

"This very day marks the 100th anniversary of when President John F. Kennedy stood in this very spot and challenged America to land a man on the moon and return him safely to Earth before the decade was out. That challenge was issued during the nuclear arms race—a time of tremendous risk and turmoil. Yet from that maelstrom, America rose to meet it.

"Now imagine traveling back in time to speak with da Vinci, Hypatia, Socrates, or any great thinker or explorer from the past. Imagine standing with them, pointing to the moon, and telling them that one day humanity would find a way to fly there—and walk there. It wouldn't be surprising if they refused to believe us. But just imagine what they would have thought ... imagine what they would have felt ... if they did believe us. A revelation of such human potential would be seen as a miracle among miracles."

Deeley smiled with admiration, completely aligned with Quinto's way of thinking.

"By achieving what humanity once thought impossible—walking on the moon—America inspired the world and opened the door to the heavens, where many secrets of the universe would be uncovered to bless the lives of billions yet unborn. Of this great feat, President Kennedy proclaimed: 'We choose to go to the moon in this decade and do the other things, not because they are easy, but because they are hard.'

"My fellow Americans, the time has once again come to focus ourselves as a nation on a great cause—to dedicate our efforts and pool our resources to achieve a goal of such significance that humanity will be positively impacted forevermore. While we still yearn for America to inspire and lead as it once did, we have forgotten how far we must reach to truly inspire all humanity. But I say to you this day: we have an opportunity to reach far once again."

Shivers ran up and down Deeley's spine.

"And so, we come to a critical question: What is more miraculous—that after eons of time, simple atoms could arrange themselves into complex, intelligent beings capable of thought, ideas, art, compassion, great civilization, love, and joy; or that those intelligent beings might one day use the power of science to raise their kin from the grave, returning them to full life and health?

"If you believe, as I do, that the greater of these miracles is the former— that life arose in the first place—then I stand before you to assure you that the latter, the miracle of resurrection, is not only possible, but inevitable in this great game of life."

The House Chamber fell silent. The usual pattern of a Special Address had been thoroughly interrupted. All gave their full and undivided attention as Quinto reached inside the podium and withdrew an object he'd had placed there in advance: a round item, covered by a purple cloth. He set it atop the bench to his left, then pulled away the cloth—revealing a human skull.

Gasps rippled through the chamber. Soft murmurs followed. Quinto lifted the skull in his left hand, holding it just above his face, its gaze aligned with his own. For a moment, he stared into it—visualizing the words he would say next.

Deeley was exceptionally excited.

"Just as we might share our accomplishment of journeying to the moon with great thinkers from antiquity, I believe that if our descendants could visit us from the future—stand beside us and hold a human skull in their hand—they would say that one day, humanity finds a way to bring the original owner of that skull back from the grave—with their memories intact, their personality restored, and their body returned to full health.

"I believe that one day, a collaboration between advanced AI and gifted scientists will unlock the secret that makes life after death possible."

Silence.

"Yes, I've pondered this topic for a long, long time. And I genuinely believe—with all my heart—that human resurrection lies fully within the realm of science, and that it is simply a matter of time and effort until it becomes reality."

The chamber remained immobile. The silence was so profound that Quinto could distinctly hear his own breathing.

"Imagine what this means in the greater context. If resurrection can be achieved in our world, then no doubt it has already been accomplished elsewhere in the cosmos—by older, more advanced civilizations, possibly eons ago. Perhaps humanity is being watched even now by immortal beings among the stars, waiting to make their vast continent of worlds known to our small island, once we are ready. When one truly grasps the realities of what I'm speaking about, the possibilities are phenomenal!"

The chamber remained as silent as night. In that moment, Quinto's thoughts again drifted to his first wife. He gently placed the skull down and proclaimed:

"My fellow Americans, just as President Kennedy challenged the uncertain nation of his day to do what was hitherto unthinkable—to land a man on the moon and return him safely to the Earth—I firmly believe that we should commit ourselves, before this century is out, to discover the secrets of physics and genetics necessary to raise a human from the grave and thereby conquer death once and for all!"

Deeley's eyes welled with tears, though they didn't overflow—she knew a disruption was about to come.

President Quinto let the silence linger. Slowly, several members of Congress stood, visibly flabbergasted. Yet they clapped. Slower still, others rose and joined in the applause, until nearly the entire chamber erupted in a standing ovation. The notable exception was freshman Congressman Rand Benson of Idaho's First District. Breaking all decorum, Benson rose from his chair, pointed a finger at the President, and shouted in a voice full of fury, "You will not play God, Quinto! Not now! Not ever!!"

Deeley turned and looked back at Benson, her expression full of disgust.

A few members shouted back at Benson, chastising him. A couple voiced agreement. Both the Vice President and the Speaker of the House were forced to call for calm in their respective chambers of Congress.

President Quinto then went off script. "As has just been demonstrated, this challenge will not come without its detractors—or controversy. But let me remind you: we've already been playing God for a long time, accomplishing feats that previous generations would have called miracles. The blind see. The deaf hear. The lame walk. All through scientific collaboration.

"Just this past month, our scientists announced breakthroughs in therapeutic cloning that—within a few years—will allow those who have lost limbs or organs to regrow and reattach new ones from their own DNA. So where does it stop? As we continue to collaborate, our achievements will only grow more miraculous ... until the day arrives when we raise the dead from the grave."

This impromptu remark proved prophetic, for Deeley lived in a time of therapeutic cloning and life-extension research. Medications that renewed an individual's telomeres—thereby extending life—had revolutionized society, pushing the average life expectancy in the advanced world to about 126—an age Deeley fully expected to reach without question.

As quiet returned to the chamber, Quinto resumed his prepared remarks. "This challenge must also be undertaken with great sensitivity—especially for those who have lost loved ones, whose most dear and precious hopes will no doubt be kindled by this initiative. We must therefore approach this most important of all tasks with the greatest humility and respect.

"I am aware that resurrection may prove more difficult than anything humanity has attempted before. But, my dear fellow Americans, I believe with my whole soul that we will meet this challenge—if we face it together."

There was rapturous applause from more than half the assembly. Detractors—the minority—shouted their disdain once again. After a few attempts to speak over the noise, the applause finally subsided, allowing Quinto to continue.

"How do I envision resurrection being achieved? First, I believe genetic research will progress to the point where full human cloning becomes a reality. Second, I believe—as do various physicists—that a record of all that has ever existed is stored somewhere, somehow, within the spacetime continuum. I believe that within it will be found the memories of the dead—their 'souls'—waiting to be retrieved and reunited with cloned bodies grown from their remaining DNA.

"Finally, I believe Congress holds immense power to direct scientific endeavor. When it has exercised that power in the past, miracles have followed: landing on the moon, journeying to Mars, curing once-deadly diseases ... and soon, resurrection."

Deeley was beaming again, anticipating what would come next.

"With this in mind, I recommend that Congress appropriate funding for a super particle collider—unlike anything the world has ever built—to help us uncover the remaining secrets of spacetime. To reveal how to retrieve and restore the memories of the dead, so we may begin bringing travelers back from the undiscovered country!"

Another wave of applause swept through the chamber.

Though technically alone in her condo, seated on her couch with advanced contact lenses over her eyes, Deeley couldn't help but stand and applaud with the virtual crowd around her, emotionally caught in the moment. When that moment first transpired, Quinto's vision of unparalleled American greatness—despite no longer being the world's superpower—struck a chord. His challenge, quickly dubbed *Quinto's Challenge*, spread across the globe with viral force.

Quinto concluded his historically short address as follows:

"I am aware of the host of ethical and practical questions this Challenge raises: Who gets to be resurrected? Who decides? What consent is required? How would this affect population growth and the allocation of resources? What rights would the resurrected have upon returning from the grave? And of course, many more valid questions remain."

Quinto looked again at the skull beside him, placed his hand gently on it, and declared: "What I can say is this: the bones of the dead—these remnants of our kin, holding the genetic keys to their rebuilding—call to us to find a way to bring them back. And as we do, we will come to answer these questions, step by step, as we transition to a world where immortality is slowly introduced."

Applause. Steady, unwavering.

"My fellow Americans, let us invest in a supercollider to unlock the remaining mysteries of physics—thereby locating the memories of our dead within spacetime, and bringing to light the secret that will reunite their souls with their bodies, cloned from their very own DNA. And in so doing, let us remember that we are the United States of America—and may we always be—committed to solving every problem faced by humanity, even death itself!"

The majority of the chamber rose in rapturous applause.

Deeley shut off the VR and, caught in a surge of excitement, stood and began pacing her condo. She still found it hard to believe her good fortune—to be starting work at the very Supercollider that had emerged from that historic speech.

As she moved through the room, a notification in her SecondSight added to the thrill: Charity had arrived at Quark Tower. Deeley's journey at CAPR was about to begin.

CHAPTER 3

EUREKA!

"Following my address, legal minds debated what rights clones might possess under existing law, while sociologists examined how resurrection could affect relationships and population growth. Psychologists studied extended lifespans and their impact on the human mind. Public opinion ranged from viewing my Challenge as visionary, to politically driven, to hubristic or even immoral. Physicists—especially proponents of a simulated universe—questioned whether the Challenge could restore memories from a 'cosmic backup' ... and, most significantly, whether building a Supercollider of the magnitude I envisioned—capable of smashing particles at energies never before achieved—was too dangerous to attempt at all."

— Memoir Excerpt: Vince Quinto, 2070

A soft chime sounded, and through SecondSight, Deeley saw Charity standing outside her condo door. With nervous excitement, she quickly walked over, opened the door, and, her smile a mix of nerves and joy, exclaimed, "Hi, Charity!"

"Wonderful to meet you, Deeley!"

Charity wore navy blue capri pants and a white long sleeve blouse with the sleeves rolled up almost to her elbows. With white sandals and her shoulder-length dark blonde hair framing her face, she looked radiant and healthy. But it wasn't Charity's physical appearance that struck

Deeley the most—it was the way her brainwaves seemed to instantly sync with Deeley's, creating a familiar bond, as if she had known Charity, or someone like her, before.

"Wonderful to meet you too!" replied Deeley, feeling instantly at ease. "Come on in!"

As Charity entered the condo, she remarked, "Your home is beautiful. And what a view you have!"

Deeley giddily led Charity to the large window in her living room. From there, they could see the sprawling main campus of CAPR. Also visible were tall luminous columns, each taller than Quark Tower and strategically placed at one-mile intervals along the immense 81-mile circumference of the underground Supercollider, designating the particle accelerator's location.

With curiosity about her new guest, Deeley asked, "So how long have you worked at CAPR?"

"Since CAPR's soft opening. I've seen the vast majority of physicists and full-time staff arrive from around the country and the world. I was here to see the growing community incorporate into Particle City."

"How awesome!" responded Deeley. She then turned her head toward the window and gazed upon the luminous columns outlining the Supercollider. "It's hard to believe the Supercollider is here after all these years. And I still can't believe some critics suggested Quinto only wanted it built to distract from the rise of China."

"To anyone who really listened to his speech, it's clear that he was genuine with his beliefs and intentions. Besides, the Supercollider was always going to take a very long time to build … and that's not a very effective distraction from a shifting global order."

"Good point," acknowledged Deeley. "When China and Russia announced their trade and defense partnership, it was huge deal. I don't think all the permits and lengthy deliberations about the Supercollider's construction quite matched that level of drama."

It had been some time since Quinto had visited CAPR in person, given his advanced age, and there were no plans or guarantees that he would visit again. Deeley was aware of this; it saddened her. After a pause during which her countenance fell further, Deeley continued, "It was such a shame that Quinto was only a one-term president."

"Unfortunately, his political opponents successfully waged an unrelenting disinformation campaign against him. Rand Benson emerged as a key figure in this effort, and they blamed Quinto for the decline of American hegemony, framing his legislative achievement of the Supercollider as a waste of money that neglected pressing domestic challenges, such as rising unemployment due to advances in AI."

Deeley felt her bond with Charity deepen quickly upon hearing these common views.

"But that's in the past," continued Charity, "now we are here with the Supercollider online, and we are thrilled to have you on the team."

Deeley beamed.

After some further conversation at the window, Deeley invited Charity to join her on the living room couch. "Now that I've signed the confidentiality agreements," said Deeley as she sat down, "can you tell me … or at least hint … if data from spacetime has been discovered?"

Charity settled in beside her. "There's nothing stopping me from saying that it hasn't. Lots of physicists—human and MS—have been exploring different models to see if data from spacetime could exist and be retrieved, but there hasn't been a breakthrough. We've certainly learned a lot—new particles discovered and so on—but it's possible the past just isn't encoded in spacetime."

Deeley was a little surprised to hear this, considering all the resources and computing power at CAPR. Her mind began to wander as she thought about what she might one day contribute to the research. Despite Charity's presence, Deeley became so lost in thought that she did what she often did in such moments—she stood and began to pace.

While visual and audible warnings in her SecondSight activated to help her regain focus, Deeley remained lost in thought—only returning to reality when she bumped into a decorative object: a magnetic representation of a helium atom floating atop an elegant five-foot staff, part of which was made from diamond synthesized from carbon removed from the atmosphere.

Before Deeley fully realized what had happened, Charity sprang into action. From four feet away, she lunged—catching the two decorative electrons in each hand, stopping the staff's fall with her inner elbow, and ensuring the nucleus landed safely on her foot.

"Wow!" exclaimed Deeley, stunned.

"Fortunately no atomic chain reactions!" responded Charity, easing the tension with a grin. As she proceeded to fix the decoration, the unique feeling Deeley sensed upon meeting Charity suddenly clicked into place. Her jaw dropped, and she asked with delight,

"You're a Generation 5 android, aren't you?"

As she placed the last decorative electron back in its orbital, Charity smiled, looked down at herself, responding, "Obviously not Generation 1 or 2, much more human than a 3 or 4, and if I were a Generation 6, I wouldn't physically be here."

Deeley was thrilled—and appreciated that James had let Charity's nature be a surprise for her to discover.

Although only nine years old, Charity appeared indistinguishable from a human woman in her late twenties. Internally, Generation 5s were vastly different from humans, but their outward appearance rarely gave it away. At times, their personality might—marked by a persistent optimism and a certain naivety about aspects of life. More often, however, it was during specific tasks that their advanced capabilities revealed their true nature to those unaware.

Deeley stepped forward and hugged Charity, who returned the embrace. After the hug, Deeley expressed, "I *love* androids. And you're the first Generation 5 I've met."

"Thank you, Deeley! I'm honored!"

With renewed curiosity about her guest, Deeley asked, "When and where did you come online?"

"July 16, 2088 at MIT."

"How long did you live there?"

"Three years and 29 days."

Gesturing toward Charity's hand, Deeley inquired, "May I?" Charity nodded with a smile, and Deeley took her hand and inspected it. "Your design is truly wonderful."

"You are too kind, Deeley."

"I've always wanted to meet a Generation 5. I'm so happy right now!"

They sat back down on the couch. Deeley glanced at the helium atom decoration and admitted with a little embarrassment, "This condo isn't Deeley-proofed yet. That will be one of my first tasks. But I'm sorry for zoning out like that. You might have read this in my profile, but at age four I was diagnosed with Broad Spectrum Processing and Experience … and Anxiety Response Pattern."

"I'm aware, and it's totally fine," reassured Charity, placing her hand on Deeley's shoulder. "BSPE, a rare neurodiverse trait that once fell under the broad and outdated classification of Attention Deficit Hyperactive Disorder, offers its advantages, as I am certain you are aware."

"I know," responded Deeley. "Matters of science come naturally to me. But sometimes I've questioned whether the gift is worth it. Living with BSPE brings … intense emotions. While there are plenty of joyful moments, a single awkward social interaction—something a neurotypical person might not think twice about—can sit with me like a heavy weight, replaying over and over in my mind.

"When I perceive injustice, it lights a fire in me—a need to see things made right. My mind is always racing, constantly thinking, and distractions are everywhere. All of it has made it harder to build confidence in some areas.

"But I'm lucky—apps in SecondSight help me manage these challenges."

"I understand," acknowledged Charity. "But remember, your gift with science and the hyperfocus on solving problems *are* advantages and likely played into the value that Dr. Meitner saw in you. Speaking of Dr. Meitner, are you ready to go to campus?"

"So ready!"

***

A ride-hail car transported Deeley and Charity from Quark Tower to the Vince Quinto Administration Building. As they pulled into the busy drop-off zone, a steady rhythm of cars arrived and departed, carrying scientists, staff, and androids in and out of the complex. As they stepped out of the car, their hair danced in the warm breeze as they joined the flow of people heading up the front steps. Glass doors—etched with the sleek CAPR logo, evoking the Supercollider's vast ring and a burst of smashing particles—slid open, and they entered the main lobby.

Deeley had seen the lobby in VR before, but actually standing in it brought a thrill the virtual world couldn't match. Around her, the ebb and flow of staff, visitors, and androids made the space pulse with purpose. This was the place where cutting-edge particle science happened—and now she was a part of it. She wasn't sure her feet were even touching the ground; she was riding such a high.

The lobby had an atomic theme, with images and sculptures of atoms throughout. Portraits and plaques honored President Quinto and his vision for the Pan-Hadronic Supercollider, designed to smash hadrons, electrons, positrons, protons, antiprotons—as well as muons, antimuons, and other subatomic particles. A plaque near the entrance commemorated his last visit to the facility several years earlier.

Also displayed in the lobby were portraits of the current President, the Secretary of Energy, and CAPR's Administrator, Doctor Michael

Bergstrom. Charity gave her a brief tour, and everything Deeley saw reinforced the feeling that she had truly landed her dream job.

"Let's get you onboarded, and then we'll meet up with Dr. Meitner," said Charity. "I like to introduce him with his title out of respect, but you'll see he's less formal. Anyway, you're very fortunate because normally the Department Head wouldn't see someone in your role very often, or at all. Your theories must have really caught his attention."

Charity then led Deeley to a room not far from the main lobby. Inside, some of Deeley's biometrics were recorded, and once verified, proprietary software was licensed to her SecondSight. The software granted access to key CAPR platforms, systems, and data, as well as everything she would need as an employee—including training materials. Within seconds, the process was complete.

Pointing to a nearby door, Charity smiled and said, "This way to meet Dr. Meitner!"

***

Following Charity to a cafe within the Administration Building, Deeley noticed Dr. James Meitner, waiting to meet her at a table. James had been the Head of the Department of Experimental Physics since the inception of CAPR. Older than Deeley and always well dressed, James wore a crisp, short-sleeved button-down shirt paired with tailored chinos, offering both comfort, refined style, and health tracking. Upon seeing Deeley and Charity approach, James stood up and outstretched his hand. "Welcome to CAPR, Deeley. Great to meet you in person."

Extending her hand to shake his, Deeley responded, "Thank you! Great to meet you in person too, Dr. Meitner!"

"Just call me James. Please, join me," invited James as he gestured for Deeley and Charity to take a seat. When they took their seats, Deeley began, "It's gr—"

At the same time, James started, "You'll kn—"

After a brief moment of awkwardness, James, with a smile, gestured with his hand toward Deeley, indicating she speak first.

"Oh," stammered Deeley, quite embarrassed. "I ... I was just going to say that it's just so great to finally be here. If I'd been told three months ago that I would be working here and you'd be my boss, I wouldn't have believed it."

"When I wrapped up my theoretical physics Ph.D. at Johns Hopkins, I didn't expect that my first job would be on Wall Street," responded James. "I also didn't think that within a short time after Wall Street, I would be back on my intended physics track as a faculty member at Columbia. I didn't expect that my work at Columbia would lead to where I am today, either. My point: sometimes we can never tell what is around the corner."

"That's very true," agreed Deeley, starting to feel more at ease.

"We're very fortunate to have you as a Research Associate, Deeley. Your theories revealed perspectives none of us had even considered. The way you think is exactly what we've been missing. The fact that you don't have three particular letters after your name doesn't matter to me. Your mind is what matters—and you've already shown that you can help take us closer to the vision this facility was built on. That's why you'll be reporting directly to me."

Hearing this, Deeley felt immensely proud and encouraged. For a moment, she also recalled the rumors she heard about James, but they did not hold sway in her mind. "Just to confirm that I'm not mishearing anything," she clarified, "my job is simply to theorize and test those theories?"

Looking directly into her eyes, then gesturing toward a garden outside the window, James replied, "If sitting in that garden for extended periods each day helps you contemplate and solve the problems we're here to solve—then yes, that's your job."

Deeley smiled. Charity did too, genuinely happy for her.

"Evolve your theories about the fundamentals of reality, test them in the simulators, then in the collider—and whether they prove true or false, you'll be contributing to the body of knowledge in particle physics."

Deeley took a deeper breath. She still couldn't believe this job had come her way. James could see how thrilled she was and genuinely looked forward to working with her.

"Thanks again for giving me a chance," said Deeley.

"You're welcome," replied James with a smile. "Now, let's go get something to eat."

They purchased drinks, bagels and spoke for half an hour more than their scheduled time. James was struck by Deeley's intelligence, neither expecting how much he would enjoy her company. Deeley, on the other hand, couldn't shake the thought that her first impression might have been less than ideal, having interrupted James right after they met. It lingered in her mind, as these moments often did. But for James, the moment had already faded from memory.

***

At length, James departed for other responsibilities, and Charity led Deeley to her workspace in a department building not far from the main Administration Building. The space was a private room equipped with a desk, a fridge, a solar-powered device that converted air into clean drinking water, a couch, and a cozy nook filled with plants and a view of a small garden on campus.

Like most professionals, Deeley required no physical computer—her mixed reality lenses were the only hardware she needed, now fully licensed with the software essential for her work. As for personal effects, she had arranged for only one item to be shipped to her workspace: a large, framed image of a galaxy rising over the horizon of an exoplanet.

After seeing her workspace, Deeley exclaimed, giddy with delight, "It's wonderful!"

"Good. I'm happy for you," responded Charity.

"How often will I get to see you?"

"It will depend on my assignments," replied Charity, "but at the very least, I'll stop by whenever I can. But I do live here at CAPR, so there's always a chance for us to catch up after hours."

"I'd love that," beamed Deeley, thrilled to have made a Generation 5 friend.

***

The remainder of Deeley's first day at CAPR was spent familiarizing herself with the campus layout, then diving straight into work. Back in her new workspace, she enthusiastically began building models to explore the interiors of black holes using CAPR's proprietary generative AI—software capable of coding robust analytical tools in response to either natural language or thought-based prompts.

Toward the end of the day, James called Deeley via SecondSight to check in. When she told him all was well and that she had already begun her research, he was once again impressed.

At day's end, Deeley caught a ride back to Quark Tower. She entered her condo on a high, feeling deeply satisfied—and incredibly fortunate—for the new life unfolding before her.

***

After her first week, Deeley had fully settled into her new role. On her first weekend evening in the condo, she retrieved a salmon and vegetable dinner assembled by the nutrition hub in her kitchen, brought it to the couch, and sat down to eat while loading up a popular series in SecondSight. This time, it wasn't *Interesting Times*, but *10 Minutes with Van Pelt*, hosted by Doctor Bryan Van Pelt, a professor of sociology at the University of Michigan, Ann Arbor.

Van Pelt's views didn't align with Deeley's the way Browning's did, but she found it enriching to hear perspectives from opposing angles.

"Immediately after sentient robots debuted, the United States government assumed full oversight of MS production and established a new cabinet-level department, the Department of Manufactured Sentience," explained Van Pelt.

"One justification for deep government oversight was to safeguard national security. Another was to ensure MS was created for ethical and constructive purposes. Not long after MS debuted in the US, it also emerged in China and later in the EU, prior to its formation into the USE. Both China and the EU adopted government-led approaches to MS development and regulation."

Deeley never thought that androids posed a threat to humanity, which her new friendship with Charity reinforced.

"With these powers possessing the ability to artificially create conscious life, regulation evolved through the framework of the United Nations. The three primary regulations were:

1) Each of the three powers would set an annual quota on how many units of MS could be produced.

2) Each subsequent generation of MS would have a smaller annual quota than the previous generation.

3) These androids were to be made light and strong enough to push off general attacks but not so strong that they would overpower average humans."

That androids were made relatively weak was something Deeley felt somewhat unfair. Van Pelt continued,

"However, despite these regulations, the more that androids were introduced to society, the more anxiety they caused. They continuously displaced humans from the workforce, and many believed that MS would manufacture a global crisis through which they would assume control. These issues led groups on both the left and the right to oppose the development and societal integration of androids. Unsurprisingly, violence was perpetrated against androids by extremists on both sides."

Violence against androids caused Deeley's blood to boil.

"It was this combustible environment that saw this year's summit in Shenzhen, China, where world leaders discussed the rapid advancement of MS as well as a potential moratorium on all MS production. Shortly after talks began, it became apparent that the nations of the world would agree that societal stability was more important than continuing to introduce MS into the world.

"That a full moratorium on MS production was coming brought relief to many. Eventually, the Treaty of Shenzhen was drafted, and its core agreements, to be enforced by China, the USE, and the USA, were:

a) *No more sentient androids of any kind were to be made for an indefinite period of time. The only exception were those already in production prior to the Treaty's ratification.*

b) *Under no circumstances would any modifications or enhancements to existing androids be permitted. Any breach of this rule would be given a limited window for reversal; otherwise, the android would be destroyed.*

c) *No robotic system, sentient or otherwise, was to be designed with the capability to replicate itself. While many countries had already regulated or banned such technology, the Treaty of Shenzhen went further, prohibiting it outright."*

While Deeley understood the general need for Shenzhen to bring stability, she wished it didn't have to be.

"Although unemployment from existing androids and automation still disrupted societies, the Treaty of Shenzhen ushered in a fragile though welcomed stability. It was similar to the general AI pause that took place earlier in the century, but more comprehensive and indefinite. Shenzhen's intent was not just to stem societal discontent, but also to mitigate a 'technological singularity'—a perpetual, self-advancing entity of unknown regard for humanity.

"With all of this in mind, what have we learned as a society from this experiment with MS? In short, this is the lesson: androids are obviously an incredible feat of science and engineering, but they are the quintessential example of 'just because you could doesn't mean you should.' Yes, there are direct benefits they have brought to society—cleaner streets, other environmental benefits—but the larger picture is that they are a catalyst to weaken the bonds of human society and to rob humanity of meaning."

Deeley couldn't disagree more.

"This raises pressing questions: Was there any foresight into how rapidly MS would erode humanity's place in the economy? Were any of the unintended consequences of pouring more and more artificial copies of ourselves into the world ever sufficiently considered? Shenzhen has certainly given us more of a chance to reflect on these questions—but the more time passes, the clearer it becomes that going down the path of Manufactured Sentience was deeply unwise."

***

The next several months at CAPR passed as if they were only a single month to Deeley. She was in her element—free to pursue her research

with the most powerful scientific instruments in the world at her fingertips. Each day, she was completely absorbed in unraveling the remaining
mysteries of reality. Often, she would retreat to the gardens to think and
conduct thought experiments—later replicating them in CAPR's proprietary simulation software, as well as in custom programs she coded herself.

***

Early in the afternoon of February 10, 2098, Charity stopped by Deeley's
workspace at CAPR and found her pacing the room, lost in thought.
Deeley was deep in complex thought experiments about the underlying
elements of quantum gravity. At that moment, her understanding felt
clearer than it had ever been. With hyperfocus fueled by her BSPE, she
analyzed fresh data from the Supercollider on quantum black holes and
gained new insight into their inner workings, insight that rapidly crystallized into the framework of a new theoretical model. She was so absorbed
that she didn't even notice Charity's presence, and breaking her focus
would have been difficult, even if Charity had tried.

After several minutes of pacing and calibrating calculations in
SecondSight with assistance from a virtual AI, Deeley executed a simulation of this newly inspired model within her custom software—a consolidation of the previous models she had developed. An augmentation of the
model appeared before her, executing flawlessly. Her eyes widened. Her
heart raced. A surge of adrenaline coursed through her as she instinctively
reached for her chest, the other hand covering her agape mouth. She took
a slow step backward in utter disbelief. Overwhelmed with emotion, she
moved quickly to the nook in her workspace, sitting on the floor against
the wall.

"Deeley, are you okay?!" asked Charity, rushing to her side.

Deeley didn't answer. She couldn't. Tears welled in her eyes as the
simulation continued—one that seemed to whisper, from the universe
itself: *you've solved it.*

Slowly, she became aware of Charity's presence and wiped her face. Then, with a shaky breath, she stood and removed her SecondSight lenses.

"Deeley, what's wrong?" pressed Charity.

"Nothing. I'm fine," replied Deeley, placing her lenses in their case. "Charity, please run a diagnostic test on these, the software, and the server."

Charity hesitated. "Why the diagnostics?"

Deeley didn't respond. Lost in thought, she resumed pacing, her mind churning with questions. Could it have been a false positive? Was there a hidden assumption the model relied on—one that didn't hold?

Charity, sensing something serious, left with the SecondSight lenses in hand.

Alone again, Deeley tried to temper her hope. She replayed the simulation in her mind—frame by frame, equation by equation—convincing herself that what she'd seen wasn't just a coincidence. A current of cautious optimism began to swell inside her. A smile edged its way across her face as she considered what this could mean. She didn't give in to the thrill—yet—but the anticipation was mounting like pressure behind a dam. If the diagnostics came back clean … everything might change.

Several minutes later, Charity reentered the workspace and handed Deeley's SecondSight back to her.

"Diagnostics complete. Everything's fine."

Deeley's chest thumped. It was real.

"Now, tell me what you saw!" demanded Charity, her curiosity burning.

Fixing her gaze on her, Deeley—still trembling—smiled through tears. "It worked. The simulation showed how we can extract temporal signatures from spacetime … and replicate them in the three spatial dimensions."

Charity's eyes widened. "Wait—what?"

Deeley nodded. "Charity …" Her voice faltered, overcome with emotion. "Charity, this might be it. This model doesn't just explain black hole information extraction—it unifies quantum mechanics and general relativity. And more."

Charity couldn't believe what she was hearing.

Deeley slipped her lenses back on and shared the simulation directly with Charity's SecondSight. "I've named it *The Unified Model of Spacetime*. At the risk of oversimplifying: for black hole information extraction, you'll see a stream of dark muons reading the Hawking radiation. Then, here— this algorithm I built decodes the signal. Finally, dark energy replicates all in the spatial dimensions and entangles it with the spacetime record."

Charity studied the visuals. After a few seconds, she gasped, "This is … absolutely phenomenal. Oh, Deeley!"

Deeley walked over and embraced her, tears welling again. Charity returned the hug, a look of awe on her face.

After stepping back, their eyes met—full of excitement, disbelief, and cautious hope.

What they had just seen might be everything CAPR was built for.

Only one thing remained: testing the theory in the Supercollider itself.

They broke eye contact as Deeley exhaled. "I'm sending this to James now," she said quietly. "Along with blueprints of hardware I designed to test the theory. Then I need some time alone."

"Time to decompress?"

Deeley nodded with a sigh. "Yeah. I think I'll take a walk through the central gardens."

She walked to the door leading out of her workspace, her mind still spinning from what had just transpired. Expecting it to glide open automatically, she stepped forward—but the door stayed shut. Deeley paused, tried again, and was met with the same unmoving panel.

"It's waiting for authentication," said Charity gently as she stepped beside her. With a quick glance toward the sensor strip above the frame, Charity triggered the unlock, and the door slid open with a soft hiss.

"A mind that can pierce the secrets of spacetime—defeated by a simple door," teased Charity with a warm smile.

Deeley gave a sheepish smile. Then she stepped out, the corridor lights catching the edge of her face as she exhaled slowly, almost in disbelief. Her body moved forward, but her mind lingered—still suspended in the moment she first understood reality itself.

***

CAPR's central gardens, spanning roughly two acres, featured broad grassy sections dotted with trees and crossed by paved paths lined with flower beds. Smaller, enclosed spaces with stone walkways showcased a variety of blooming flowers. On the western flank, a small waterfall fed a tranquil stream that wound through about a third of the garden, complete with a charming arched bridge for crossing. Scattered throughout were scientists and staff—some socializing, others en route to meetings, and a few simply enjoying the scenery.

Making her way through these gardens, Deeley intended to quieten her thoughts with a walk. However, she couldn't help but consider the possibilities if her new model could be proven in the Supercollider: witnessing any historical event from the past, a justice system with perfect and conclusive evidence, and what Quinto envisioned—the possibility of life after death.

While Deeley walked alone, James tracked her through SecondSight and made his way to her with urgency. When she saw him approaching, she called out, "Did you review the model?"

"I did," replied James, eyes bright. "Oh, I definitely did. It's probably a good thing you have more decorum than Archimedes!"

Deeley smiled—for the first time since the simulation, she felt a hint of calm. Still, her optimism was tempered. "As you know, we need real-world validation of the model before we can be certain."

"You'll have certainty in three days," James said. "I've already notified Bergstrom about the promise this unified model holds, and he's approved manufacturing the hardware you designed to test it. He's also cleared the Supercollider to run at full Grand Unification Energy."

A thrill coursed through Deeley, catching her off guard.

James then asked, "Does anybody else know about this?"

"Only Charity."

"Good," replied James. "As you know, do not tell anyone else."

"I know."

James continued, "The model looks sound to me. But if, by some fluke, it doesn't work in the real world, you'll still have taken us further than we've ever been. We'll learn a ton from this—either way."

After walking a few more paces, James laughed. "My head is spinning with what your mind has conceived, Deeley! A quantum-spacetime model. Temporal signatures encoded in Hawking radiation. A new paradigm for the graviton. Temporal displacement entangling records across space-time—and the math actually reconciles general relativity and quantum mechanics! My God! I've been extrapolating the implications—how the universe was born, the asymmetry between matter and antimatter—and it's all making sense! Do you realize that today you may have found the Theory of Everything?"

Simultaneously exhilarated and humbled by James' statement, Deeley blushed slightly and replied, "I wouldn't jump to conclusions just yet. Even if the theory holds, we can't assume there's nothing more to uncover—even if it's just, 'Why this theory and not another?' We might always be a little short of complete understanding."

"Well, for now, this is big. And by big, I mean expedited security clearances from the Department of Defense—so you can personally help test this model. *With Xara*."

Deeley's eyes widened, and her jaw fell.

James continued, "In the next 48 hours, while your new hardware is built and installed, your job is to come up with an experiment to test your model."

"I already have!" Deeley smiled.

CHAPTER 4

THE HEART OF CAPR

"Is this the moment I've dreamed of my entire life? That I might signifi-cantly contribute to science for the betterment of all humanity—that I might finally be seen by my peers as someone worthy of great respect? I tremble at the thought that it could be true, because I am as confident as a rational person can be that the imminent test of my model will succeed."

— AI Journal Excerpt: Deeley Carr, February 10, 2098

Two days after her breakthrough, Deeley stood on the platform of one of CAPR's internal hyperloop stations early in the morning, awaiting transport to the EOS Experiment—a highly specialized particle detector built to match the scale of the Supercollider and used exclusively by the Department of Experimental Physics. EOS, short for Energy Observance System, was where the new hardware to test her model was now being deployed. It was also home to CAPR's Generation 6 android—one of only four in the world—Xara.

With clearance quickly granted by the Department of Defense to work directly with Xara, Deeley was riding a new high. So absorbed was she in imagining the research they might conduct together that she failed to notice the hyperloop had already arrived—and was seconds from depart-ing. Fortunately, augmentations and audible alerts in her SecondSight—designed to mitigate the effects of her BSPE—activated just in time, snap-ping her back to attention as the capsule door began to close.

Having just made it inside, she spotted James seated nearby. He smiled. "For a second there, I thought you weren't going to make it."

Embarrassed, Deeley took a seat next to him. "I was a little lost in my head."

"Don't worry," replied James as the hyperloop accelerated. "You being deep in thought tends to take us to promising places … like this meeting with Xara."

"I'm so excited," said Deeley. "We're lucky President Gates took the political risk to create her."

"That's for sure," responded James. "What a bold early move—issuing an executive order to create America's second Generation 6 android the night before Shenzhen would forbid it."

"So bold," echoed Deeley. "I get that the three powers agreed to build just one Gen 6 at a time to observe how these new forms of genius would develop before making more—but I always felt the evidence was already clear that androids of any intelligence were benevolent."

"As you know, David Gates is a firm believer in Quinto's Challenge," said James, "and his directive to create our *Exabyte Analyzing Research Assistant*—Xara—was expressly to accelerate research at CAPR."

"I read that to expedite Xara's creation, she was cloned from Xina at the Pentagon."

"That's true," confirmed James. "Cloning our first Gen 6 was the fastest way to build Xara. And it's why she's technically in the custody of the Department of Defense, even though she lives here at CAPR. It's also why theoretical physicists can't just come and go at EOS—only those with DOD clearance for essential research have access. You're now part of an elite handful of scientists who have that privilege."

"It hasn't fully sunk in yet."

Still processing the fact that she was about to enter restricted DOD property, Deeley added, "All four Generation 6s on Earth are technically under their nations' Departments of Defense. I find that both disappointing and reassuring."

"Why's that?"

"Disappointing that these benevolent geniuses have to be under the control of organizations built for war. But reassuring that their intelligence and empathy might actually help prevent global conflict."

"Especially since they are permitted to occasionally communicate with each other," noted James. "Well—all except for the Chinese Generation 6."

"China doesn't allow their Gen 6 to communicate with the others?" asked Deeley.

"That's their current policy, aligning with their approach to national security," answered James. "China was also quite frustrated with President Gates when he made Xara at the 11th hour, but Gates' transparency as to why, to be the capstone for the research at CAPR, was understood by most of the leadership of the world, especially those with investments in CAPR. But China doesn't have any investments here, so it doesn't directly stand to benefit from anything Xara can offer."

The hyperloop capsule began to decelerate and James rose.

"Here we are."

Their capsule arrived at EOS' station. After exiting, Deeley and James passed through two security checkpoints—one manned, the other automated—before being admitted inside. James then escorted Deeley to the upper floor of EOS and their final destination: the control room.

Deeley and James authenticated automatically at the control room's double doors, which parted with a soft, mechanical whisper to reveal a rectangular room beyond. From the doorway, one could see across the width of the room from its southwest corner. A few feet ahead stood an elevator leading down to EOS' primary experiment floor. North of the elevator stood an observation deck—the control room's most prominent feature—with a large window overlooking the experiment floor. The control room also housed a conference table and chairs.

Upon stepping inside and taking a glance around, Deeley noticed a young girl standing at the head of the conference table, smiling. She looked to be about eight years old, with dark brown hair framing an alert and curious face. An elegant white coat fell to her calves, bare feet visible beneath it. When their eyes met, Deeley's heart fluttered—a mix of awe and nervous excitement leaving her momentarily breathless.

Turning to the girl and nodding in greeting, James said enthusiastically, "You've heard all about Deeley Carr—now meet the prodigy in the flesh." Then, gesturing toward the girl, he turned to Deeley. "Deeley, allow me to introduce you to the cornerstone of our research capabilities, the heart of CAPR—and my good friend, Xara."

Though Xara appeared in augmentation, her image was indistinguishable from that of a real girl. While she could display any augmentation of herself she chose, her corporeal form was hardwired to reflect her genuine thoughts and emotions, ensuring each interaction felt authentic. Augmentations not tied to her true emotional state or corporeal form displayed a glowing blue outline—though these were rare. The age of her appearance reflected her maturity level, though not in a way precisely comparable to human development.

With a mix of glee and starstruck anxiety, Deeley stepped toward Xara—and Xara stepped forward to meet her. Deeley extended a hand for a virtual handshake, but instead, Xara raised both arms for a virtual embrace. Deeley gladly accepted and returned it.

"It's such an honor to meet you!" exclaimed Deeley.

"The honor is mine," replied Xara.

Sensing Deeley's nervousness but also genuinely curious about her breakthrough, Xara broke the ice by inviting her to talk physics.

"Deeley, tell me … how did you conjure the insight? After years of combined effort, none of us—myself included—could develop a working model. But your Unified Model of Spacetime ... it's pure elegance. It's the foundation that could lead us to solving a potentially limitless number of problems. What was your process in developing it?"

"To be honest, it was partially subconscious," admitted Deeley. "I'm almost always thinking about the formulas that govern particles—even when I'm doing something else."

Xara was genuinely impressed. Deeley continued, "In this case, the ideas flowed naturally—giving me the clarity to understand the quantum world's relationship to extreme gravity and to intuit smaller subatomic particles. That insight led me to see how Hawking radiation could encode data from spacetime, and how dark muons and axions could then read and respectively entangle that data in our spatial dimensions."

"Your pre-hire biometrics revealed that your brain is wired for quantum science," Xara responded, projecting a scan of Deeley's brain in augmentation. "You have unusually high bandwidth between different regions of your brain, allowing disparate concepts to connect organically and providing enhanced intuition for quantum phenomena."

Marveling at the scan, Xara added, "Sheer creativity coupled with unbounded curiosity and intellect! Interestingly, your neural structure is similar to Einstein's."

A faint blush rose to Deeley's cheeks. Though she'd known since childhood that she was neurodivergent, she still wasn't used to hearing it framed so positively.

The augmentation faded, and James remarked with a smile, "Due to Bergstrom's order that this model is kept on a need-to-know basis, I have to pretend to everyone else at CAPR that nothing monumental is happening in Experimental Physics."

"The burden of working in Defense Department science!" interjected Xara. Turning back to Deeley, she added, "Once I found the theories you posted online, I saw great promise in you. But when I saw your pre-hire biometrics, it became clear just how rare you are."

Deeley was humbled.

Xara projected an augmentation of her own brain, similar in appearance to a human's but with notable differences. "How you derived the formulas for extracting and replicating the past from spacetime—it's something even I didn't have the intuition to discover."

Though just under a year old, Xara was the equivalent of an adult human in communication skills and social maturity. Exceptionally intelligent, she possessed a full human vocabulary and vast amounts of knowledge acquired through a carefully curated curriculum. Yet by the limitation of her age, she still lacked experience. Nevertheless, her wisdom developed at a pace far exceeding that of humans, which compensated in large part for her lack of years.

Some said the rapid intellectual maturity of Generation 6 androids exceeded the genius-level intelligence they were designed for—but experts in Manufactured Sentience agreed: *genius* remained an apt description.

Xara removed the augmentation of her brain and elaborated on how Deeley's model had helped her solve other problems. "Deeley, I suspect you'll find this of interest. I couldn't contain my curiosity about what else your model might unlock—so I developed this."

In augmentation, Deeley beheld two identical circular devices, along with mathematical projections linking them. After a moment of review, her eyes widened in near disbelief. "Is this for real?"

"Yes! A blueprint for an actual Einstein–Rosen bridge."

Deeley stared at the device in awe. James, watching her reaction, felt a deep sense of satisfaction, ever more convinced that her model was indeed the Theory of Everything.

"However," added Xara, "we must temper our excitement—for even if we fused all the atoms on Earth, we still wouldn't produce enough energy to open a wormhole to any meaningful cosmic distance."

Deeley's eyes narrowed slightly as the reality set in.

"A project for another era!" declared James.

The augmentation vanished, and Xara gestured toward the observation deck. "As for devices we can power today—if you look down at the experiment floor, you'll see the hardware you designed to test your model is almost fully assembled."

Deeley walked to the observation deck, where she saw robots diligently completing the devices she had conceptualized just days earlier. Thanks to advanced 3D printing, even the rapid production of complex machines was now commonplace—fast, low-cost, and taken for granted.

Smiling as she watched her designs become reality, she soon noticed Xara's small frame step up beside her. Looking up at Deeley, Xara said warmly, "I'm looking forward to working together."

Deeley smiled back, still on cloud nine.

For the rest of the day, Deeley and Xara worked long hours side by side, ensuring everything was in place for the first test. No other physicists were assigned to the task—partly because advanced tools enabled individual researchers to be highly productive, but also because CAPR's Administrator had mandated that the model remain strictly on a need-to-know basis.

***

At first light the next day, Deeley caught a car to CAPR and went straight to EOS. The day of the test had arrived. Upon entering the control room, Deeley found Xara already running diagnostics on the two new pieces of hardware.

The first device—named by Deeley the *Quantum Incisor*—was a circular disc approximately ten feet in diameter. Several hundred ultra–high-energy emitters were arrayed on its underside, and the unit had been installed beneath EOS's experiment floor.

Upon activation, the Quantum Incisor's emitters would fire concentrated beams of dark muons into the quantum black holes created inside the massive tube of the underground Supercollider, black holes generated when particles were smashed at Grand Unification Energy. A portion of those beams would bounce off the black holes' Hawking radiation and return to the Incisor—carrying data that Xara would then decode as recordings of the past.

Deeley theorized that black holes—even quantum ones—served as access points to an invisible backup drive of all history, down to the smallest detail. She termed each decoded fragment of past information a *temporal signature.*

According to the math underpinning her model, temporal signatures could not only be retrieved—they could also be entangled with corresponding particles in the three spatial dimensions of spacetime. Deeley termed this process *temporally displaced quantum entanglement.* The effect would fully restore what once was, requiring a second piece of hardware, which Deeley named the *Quantum Displacer.*

Like the Incisor, the Quantum Displacer was a ten-foot-wide disc with emitters on its underside, and the two devices were linked via quantum entanglement. Unlike the Incisor, the Displacer had more emitters and was mounted inside the main experiment floor of EOS, suspended about 20 feet in the air—directly above the Incisor's underground location. The Displacer's emitters were calibrated to fire invisible beams of dark matter axions at a designated target on the experiment floor, entangling it with records of the past extracted from the black holes. If successful, the targeted matter would move and reform itself according to those historical records.

Both the Incisor and Displacer were fully optimized for Xara's processing power, meaning both pieces of hardware were as powerful as could be.

"The time has come! How are you feeling?" asked Xara as Deeley entered the control room.

"Cautiously optimistic."

"I suspect you won't need to restrain your jubilation for much longer. I estimate a 99.99% probability that this experiment will validate your unified model."

Shortly after Xara's encouraging words, James arrived in the control room with Charity and Michael Bergstrom, CAPR's Administrator. Tall and lanky with shoulder-length gray hair, Bergstrom had led CAPR since its inception. He was ambitious—and an outspoken critic of the Treaty of Shenzhen. A Ph.D. in plasma physics, Bergstrom had initially expressed reservations to James about hiring someone like Deeley who lacked a doctorate. While he technically held veto power and nearly used it, James persuaded him to let the hire proceed.

"Well, you certainly have our attention, Dr. Carr," stated Bergstrom as he approached Deeley. He quickly corrected himself, "My apologies—force of habit!"

"Not a problem," Deeley replied a little shyly.

"Tell me about the experiment you've devised."

"Well ... ah ... there are two parts to it," began Deeley. "First, Charity will stack ten toy blocks into a tower on the experiment floor. A few seconds later, the tower will be knocked down. Xara will then use the new Quantum Incisor to retrieve the temporal signature of the tower—before it was knocked down—from the black holes formed by the Supercollider."

Bergstrom leaned in, intrigued.

Deeley continued, "Then comes the second part. If all goes as planned, the Quantum Displacer will cause the collapsed blocks to undergo quantum entanglement with the temporal signature of when they were still stacked. In short, dark energy emitted from the Displacer will restack the blocks exactly as they were."

The Administrator and James were the only humans privy to Deeley's model, while Xara and Charity were the only androids in the know. This secrecy stemmed from a CAPR and Department of Defense policy—known only to a small circle of leaders—that any theory with potential to access historical data must be restricted to the smallest number of individuals possible, even prior to validation.

"Well, let's see what we've got," stated Bergstrom. Turning to Charity, he asked, "Ready to start?"

"Yes, Administrator Bergstrom," she replied, holding a bag of toy blocks. She glanced at Deeley with excitement, then stepped into the elevator and descended to the experiment floor.

Upon exiting, Charity walked to the center of the floor—directly beneath the Quantum Displacer. Kneeling, she removed the toy blocks from the bag and stacked them one by one into a tower. After a few seconds, she gently knocked it down. Leaving the scattered blocks where they fell, she returned to the control room.

Deeley, Bergstrom, and James stood on the observation deck as Charity rejoined them. By this time, particles were accelerating around the Supercollider's 81-mile tunnel. Their energy increased until they reached Grand Unification Energy—an intensity rarely used by the Supercollider—at which point quantum black holes began to form. Xara did not control the Supercollider; that authority remained exclusively human—executed by scientists in the CAPR Control Center, who coordinated operations based on requests from CAPR's various experimental leads, department heads, and ultimately, the Administrator. Once activated, however, Xara could operate the new hardware independently, provided authorization had been granted.

"Spacetime is open," informed Xara. "Ready when you are, Mr. Administrator."

"Go for it," instructed Bergstrom.

Xara's augmentation vanished, allowing her to fully concentrate on processing the data from spacetime that was about to be revealed. She activated the Quantum Incisor, and after a brief power-up phase, it fired beams of dark muons through the Supercollider's tunnel into the quantum black holes formed by the particle collisions.

Bergstrom, James, Deeley, and Charity observed the experiment's data in SecondSight. As certain energy readings peaked, James turned to Deeley and asked, "So far so good, right?"

But Deeley's attention was transfixed on the Quantum Displacer. After a long moment, the circular disc began to spin rapidly. Though the blocks remained unchanged to the naked eye, SecondSight augmentations displayed gravitational effects and other phenomena—energy emitting from the Displacer and instantly engulfing the blocks.

Deeley's jaw dropped, her hand rising to cover her mouth.

Through the observation deck's glass, the blocks could clearly be seen—as if by the hand of a ghost—being restacked into the exact same tower they had formed moments before.

As the Quantum Incisor and Quantum Displacer powered down, Deeley's heart raced. Her colleagues could hardly believe what they had just witnessed. Deeley's look of disbelief gave way to tears—of joy, of relief, of something deeper she couldn't name—as the realization struck: she had solved the greatest mystery in physics.

"Oh my God!" exclaimed James, his voice breaking with awe as he stepped forward. "You really did it!"

Bergstrom, momentarily stunned by the reality of the success, nevertheless beamed with pride. Charity approached and embraced Deeley. "You've changed the world, my girl. Congratulations!"

A moment later, Xara appeared in SecondSight beside Deeley and, looking up at her, declared with admiration, "I can confirm with 100% confidence that your model works, Deeley. Congratulations! This is more than a breakthrough—it's the dawn of a new era, and it's here because of you."

The sheer weight of the moment overwhelmed Deeley. Being at the epicenter of such a breakthrough was uncharted territory, and she needed time to process everything before finding the words to express how she felt.

After more congratulations for Deeley and Xara, James, his scientific curiosity piqued, turned to Xara and asked, "What did you see in the black holes?"

"I observed very rudimentary—but distinct—patterns of recent moments in time," replied Xara. "And by using Deeley's formulae to isolate a specific locality in spacetime, I was able to parse those records and locate the temporal signature of the tower."

Deeley, finally able to speak again, interjected, "The entanglement—how long was it stable?"

"Just for a moment in time, as intended," confirmed Xara.

Bergstrom, stepping back from the euphoria, sent a brief but classified message from his SecondSight. It simply read:

Success!

The recipient was his superior—Carlos Williams, Secretary of Energy. Moments later, a terse reply arrived:

Stay there. Tell no one. DeShawn is on his way.

Bergstrom returned his attention to those around him. Facing Deeley, he said, "It seems you've earned your keep, Deeley."

Then, turning to James and Charity, his tone grew somber. "What we've just achieved is to be communicated to no one. No humans. No androids. Not even other CAPR employees with top-secret clearance. Is that understood?"

All nodded in agreement.

Bergstrom then announced, "Excuse me for a moment. I'll be back shortly."

As he exited the control room, James stepped closer to Deeley. He was clearly put off by Bergstrom's phrasing. "We're all honored to work with you, Deeley."

He said no more. The intent was clear—he was countering Bergstrom's backhanded compliment. Deeley, moved by his words, thanked him. Then, turning to Xara, she added, "You're a key player in this victory, Xara. Don't forget that."

"Thank you," Xara replied warmly. "That's very kind of you."

***

Around an hour later, Deeley, James, and Charity remained in EOS' control room, discussing their recent success, when Bergstrom returned with two unexpected companions: DeShawn Brady, Secretary of Defense, and Xander Thorowell, Deputy Secretary of Defense. Both defense leaders had cleared their schedules and hyperlooped from the Pentagon to EOS after receiving word from the Secretary of Energy that a breakthrough had occurred—one with significant national security implications.

DeShawn Brady was a no-nonsense individual, a demeanor shaped by a long career in the Army. Stout, tall, and distinguished, he had served as a Four Star General before retiring from the military several years prior to his nomination to lead the Department of Defense—though he had always kept his military haircut.

The Secretary of Defense was known for his risk-averse approach, particularly when it came to the growing incorporation of androids within the Pentagon. Though appointed by President Gates' predecessor, Gates chose to retain him, appreciating both his caution and deep expertise in national defense.

Xander, the Deputy Secretary of Defense, held more progressive views on androids than DeShawn. Of average height and build with curly hair, Xander was an expert in autonomous military systems and had previously served in the CIA as the lead AGI Implementation Architect.

As the two defense leaders entered the control room alongside Bergstrom, the gravity of the day settled more deeply over everyone present.

"Deeley Carr, I presume?" asked Secretary Brady as he stepped into the room. Deeley immediately recognized him, and her natural shyness surfaced.

"Yes," she replied, her eyes lowering.

DeShawn extended his hand, and Deeley shook it. He did the same with James, whom he had previously only met in virtual meetings. "Good to meet you in person, James."

"Likewise," said James, still surprised by the visit.

DeShawn then nodded to Xara and Charity in greeting. Xander likewise greeted everyone.

Without delay, the Secretary of Defense got down to business. "Administrator Bergstrom tells me that a great moment of science was just observed in this laboratory. I want to congratulate you. The Deputy Secretary and I are anxious for details."

"Mr. Secretary," responded James, "Deeley was brought on just a few months ago to help solve the problem of data extraction from spacetime. With Xara's help, she has opened the door to a new era in our understanding of the universe ... a door I believe may very well be the Theory of Everything. For the first time, we have not only extracted data from the past via quantum black holes—we've restored that data within our three spatial dimensions. I believe we now stand on the brink of making Quinto's Challenge a reality."

"If I may say so," interjected Deeley, trembling with nervous excitement but compelled to speak, "my work simply represents a punctuation in the collaborative efforts of many thousands of individuals. No scientist is an island."

"While this is no doubt the fruit of collaboration," responded James, "don't sell your unique talents short, Deeley. Einstein developed his theories of relativity, but he let others prove their validity. You, on the other hand, not only conceived your theories independently—you designed the means to prove them."

"A false equivalency," Deeley replied, visibly uncomfortable with the praise. "Einstein had only pencil and paper. I have advanced AGI—and a genius android collaborator with computational abilities far beyond anything he could have imagined. Besides, today's success still needs to be replicated."

James simply smiled in admiration.

"Congratulations, Deeley," said Secretary Brady.

"Thank you, Mr. Secretary," responded Deeley, feeling a little more at ease.

"Congratulations to all of you," continued DeShawn. He then turned to Xara. "I understand we can't replicate the test at this moment?"

"Cooling and recalibration of the hardware will take several hours at least," she replied, "but let me show you the experiment."

Xara sent a video of the test to DeShawn and Xander's SecondSight; everyone else in the room received the same file and watched along. The Secretary and Deputy Secretary observed with awe the seemingly magical movement of the blocks stacking themselves once again into a tower.

"Are you certain they weren't being moved by anything else?" asked the Deputy Secretary.

"I've completed a comprehensive analysis," replied Xara, "and can confirm that nothing conventional was animating the blocks. Their return to a stacked state was due to dark energy—specifically, the result of entangling the blocks with the record of their stacked configuration that exists in spacetime."

James added, "This result wasn't unexpected. Deeley's model worked flawlessly in all simulations. That's what gave us the confidence to expedite the test."

DeShawn, unsure how either Xara's or James' testimonies could be reasonably challenged, turned to his deputy.

"How is it done?" Xander asked, genuinely curious about the phenomenon he had just witnessed.

"Think of it this way," said James. "Are you familiar with the cosmic microwave background?"

"Yes," replied Xander. "It's the radiation left over from the explosion of space and matter at the beginning of the universe."

"Exactly. What we've now demonstrated is that not just massive events like the birth of the universe leave a trace—but everything does. Every particle, every moment, leaves behind a record of its existence. In other words, information about everything that ever happened still exists in our universe. The issue has always been—until now—our inability to access that information. We're limited by time, space, and energy."

Both DeShawn and Xander leaned in, intrigued.

James continued, and as he spoke, generative AI in SecondSight created real-time visualizations for everyone to follow. "Imagine three champagne glasses shattered by a baseball, then left untouched for a hundred years. A forensic android might find some fragments a century later and try to reconstruct the event. But if most of the glass had been removed in the meantime, and no recording existed, tracing the specific cause and effect would be impossible. The details would have dispersed too thoroughly into the environment to reconstruct the moment through conventional means."

"But *unconventional* means can retrieve the lost information," interjected Xander, clearly following where James was going.

"Precisely!" said James. "By harnessing extreme and concentrated energies, we can create and breach quantum black holes—accessing what Deeley has termed temporal signatures contained within spacetime itself. These signatures record everything that happens in our three spatial dimensions. The information of those shattered glasses—what broke them, when, how, everything—along with all other events in history, can now be retrieved."

Xander and DeShawn listened intently, clearly captivated.

"The next step," continued James, "is replicating that information in our three spatial dimensions. If we have corresponding particles available here and now, they can be entangled with their temporal signature in spacetime—reorganizing present matter to recreate what once was."

In SecondSight, James replayed the video of the toy blocks, and he gestured toward it. "In this test, quantum black holes were created inside the Supercollider. The Incisor then fired beams of dark muons to extract data from those black holes. Afterward, the Displacer—entangled with the Incisor—fired axions into the blocks, entangling them with the extracted data. That entanglement, along with the gravitational effects we observed, physically moved the blocks back into place."

The Defense Department executives truly marveled at what they heard. James turned toward Deeley. "Anything to add?"

She flushed slightly, then, after a moment's pause, summarized, "Cross a black hole's event horizon, and you enter the records of spacetime. Pass back over the event horizon as Hawking radiation, and you carry information from those records."

"Those records being a chronicle of everything that's happened in our three spatial dimensions," added Xander, picking up her thought.

"Yes," confirmed Deeley, impressed by his grasp of the concept.

"If I understand correctly," continued Xander, "the knowledge needed to fulfill Quinto's Challenge has likely now been attained. Am I wrong?"

"The basics, at least," answered James. "But when it comes to extracting human memory and re-implementing it in a brain, we're not there yet. That level of complexity remains out of reach—for now."

After a moment of thought, the Deputy concluded, "DeShawn, I'm satisfied."

Secretary Brady nodded, though his expression suggested he was preoccupied with something else.

The Secretary addressed the CAPR team: "I'm well aware of how significant this breakthrough is. It's a watershed moment in science—one that will be celebrated for as long as there are people to celebrate it. The implications of fulfilling Quinto's Challenge are beyond anything I could adequately describe.

"That said, it's my duty to inform you that, effective immediately, this discovery is classified at the highest level. It does not leave this room. Michael—not even your Generation 5 assistant is to be informed. And our international research partners who've invested in CAPR will also be kept in the dark."

"They were made aware from the outset," interjected Xander, "that the United States reserves the right to take exclusive ownership of any findings with national security implications."

"They still benefit—outside that limitation," added Bergstrom.

Secretary Brady continued, "As I once heard, the theory of everything would grant the power to do anything. One particular power, discussed both in academia and during the drafting of the Supercollider legislation, was this: if the collider worked as Quinto envisioned, it wouldn't just allow access to the memories of the dead—it would offer access to everything in the past. In short, it would unlock the potential for supreme surveillance capabilities."

Deeley listened carefully.

"However," continued Brady, "as time passed, most physicists—while acknowledging the uncertainty—deemed data extraction from spacetime improbable, even with anticipated advances. That consensus shifted attention away from the Supercollider's potential intelligence-gathering applications and toward other unanswered questions in physics it might help solve.

"But now it appears those surveillance capabilities are real. If a hostile power were to obtain this technology, they could spy on us and our allies without limitation—seeing anything we've done, anywhere, at any time. As far as we know, the United States is currently the only nation on Earth with this capability, albeit in its infancy.

"We must study it—but contain it as we do. Which is why, effective immediately, the Department of Defense is acquiring all knowledge and capability related to this discovery."

Although Bergstrom was privy to this outcome, the mood among the others in the room grew noticeably subdued.

DeShawn turned to Deeley and said, "I'm sorry, Deeley. No one involved in this research deserves more recognition than you. But there can be no disclosure of this theory—and therefore, no public recognition for what you've discovered. That recognition must, for now, be deferred to the future."

Deeley nodded quietly, her expression conflicted. While the thought of recognition was deeply meaningful—something she had quietly craved—it was overshadowed by a growing concern: how the government might apply her discovery, and what unintended consequences that might unleash.

"Xara," said DeShawn, shifting his attention, "tag all data and activity related to this experiment to date, and restrict access under special top-secret clearance moving forward."

"Done," replied Xara.

Looking to the wider CAPR team, DeShawn said, "I'm sorry for the message I've brought—and the realities we must now face. I'm extremely proud of what you've achieved. I'd stay to discuss the implications, but our loop is waiting, and we have to take our leave."

With that, the Secretary and his Deputy departed, soon after boarding a reserved hyperloop capsule bound for Washington DC.

Moments after they left, Deeley muttered to James, "Well, it didn't take the government long, did it?"

Bergstrom interjected, "Let's not forget this is US government property. It's been my responsibility all along to report success the moment it happened. But well done today—very well done indeed."

Bergstrom then left the control room.

James turned to Deeley. "These are the realities of this kind of science. But none of this changes what you accomplished—and I believe more good than we yet realize will come from it."

Deeley didn't respond.

"Deeley?" asked James, concerned.

After a moment to collect herself, Deeley finally said, "When science came to understand the power of the atom, the government wanted to control it before hostile powers did. And then it was used to wipe cities off the map. That turned into an arms race—one that's come close, at times, to wiping out humanity entirely.

"Don't get me wrong, I understand the need to keep this out of the wrong hands. It's just ... I was so focused on the positive possibilities that this hit harder than I expected."

James sympathized with her concern, then offered, "Feel free to go home and relax for the rest of the day. I've got some commitments to take care of, but know this ... a lot of good is going to come from this—just like all the good that came from understanding the power of the atom."

Deeley gave a faint, polite smile and nodded. James then left the control room.

"It's true, you know," said Charity gently. "So much good will come from this—thanks to you."

Deeley took a few quiet steps to the observation deck and gazed down at the toy blocks, still stacked after having their prior state retrieved and restored. She knew this was a significant moment—but wouldn't fully grasp just how much of a scientific watershed it was until later.

As she studied the blocks, a pang of frustration welled up. Given human nature and the way of the world, she supposed she should have known her discovery would be bittersweet.

Charity joined Deeley at the observation deck and noted with a reassuring tone, "Remember, the President is going to have a big say in how this research unfolds. And I think he's a good man."

Deeley was often sharply critical of those in politics—resenting their distortion of facts and pursuit of power or wealth over the public good. But President Gates was one of the few exceptions in her eyes, and that alone gave her a small measure of comfort.

CHAPTER 5

Vince Quinto's Heir

"The presidency is the most powerful office in America, yet sometimes I feel powerless to accomplish what I wish. The Framers wisely built checks and balances, but today's glacial pace feels imbalanced. My executive order creating Xara is my saving grace, giving me hope that she will advance CAPR's research to fulfill Quinto's Challenge and that my presidency will leave a mark. Yet no breakthrough has come, making it hard to see Quinto's Challenge fulfilled—especially before the century ends."

— AI Journal Excerpt: David Gates, February 12, 2098

Gusting wind and snow at 1600 Pennsylvania Avenue foreshadowed how turbulent the remainder of David Gates' presidential term would be. He sat on a couch in his private office within the White House residence, sipping green tea as he watched news reports in SecondSight about his career and time in office.

His dark brown hair now held the faintest tinges of silver.

"President Gates' approval rating is now hovering at 49%," reported a journalist. *"How did Gates sink so quickly after entering office with approval in the high 50s? Let's recap."*

Gates sighed and took another sip of tea.

"Gates, a historian of America's Founding Era, taught US history and government at the University of Texas at Austin. His acclaimed publications and a pioneering generative AI series on the Founders revitalized interest in the period, earning him national prominence. Leveraging his reputation and connections, Gates won a US Senate seat for Texas. As a Democratic-Republican, he introduced groundbreaking universal basic income legislation that also allowed covered citizens limited assistance from state-custody androids, giving birth to America's 'supported class'."

It was a point of pride.

"Gates later secured the party's presidential nomination and handily won the 2096 election. Unmarried, his presidential tenure to date has been notably quieter on the residential floor of the White House."

He let out a chuckle at that last remark, having found little solace even in the residence.

"During his campaign, Gates offered few specifics on his slogan, 'Work for Humans / Rights for Androids.' When the Treaty of Shenzhen occurred early in his term, supporters claimed it fulfilled the 'Work for Humans' promise, while critics argued the groundwork for Shenzhen had been laid before Gates took office. Meanwhile, 'Rights for Androids' has proven far more complex. With no clear legislative agenda since, many now question whether Gates is a president without a mandate."

That last line rang true.

"Of Vince Quinto's successors, none align with his Challenge more than David Gates. While not as inspirational as Quinto, Gates sought to advance the Challenge through Xara's creation. But the move cost him

some support, and he has since returned to his typically risk-averse approach to governing."

There was a knock at the office door. Gates was expecting DeShawn Brady, bringing a highly classified update on national security.

"DeShawn, come in," said Gates, turning off his augmentations. "The honeymoon phase of my presidency is officially over, so I might as well hear what other bad news you may have."

Secretary Brady entered, closed the door behind him, and sat on the couch across from his boss. He looked even more solemn than usual. After a pause, he said, "Of all the days you will serve as president—and all the briefings you'll receive—I guarantee you'll remember today."

He had the President's full attention.

"What I'm about to tell you has the power to herald both good and bad."

"Spit it out," urged the President.

"CAPR appears to have done it, sir."

"Done what, exactly?" asked Gates, not yet suspecting the magnitude of the news about to unfold.

"Unlocked the secret to fulfill Quinto's Challenge … and revealed the reality of a new superweapon."

Gates was momentarily stunned. The weight of the news demanded a pause. He worked to steady his rising emotions.

"What evidence do you have?"

"This," responded DeShawn, sending a video of the toy block experiment from his SecondSight to Gates'.

As the footage played—Charity building the blocks, knocking them down, then Xara activating the Quantum Displacer—President Gates watched, hand to chin, with intense curiosity. His polling gloom gave way to irrepressible optimism as he witnessed the blocks reassemble, seemingly by magic. Gates had always believed Quinto's Challenge would one day be fulfilled. And now, the first spark of its realization was dawning—on his watch.

He reclined on the couch, closed his eyes, and felt a surge of purpose unlike anything since his election night. This wasn't just policy. It was legacy—the vindication of a lifelong conviction that life after death could be achieved. As if the sun had broken through after a long, cloudy winter, it was the sweetest news anyone could have delivered. "I don't think anything else could have made me happier!"

"Protocols governing breakthroughs of this magnitude could have justified delaying disclosure—even from you—to insulate the science from political influence," noted DeShawn. "But knowing how dear Quinto's Challenge is to your heart, I thought it appropriate for you to know."

Gates turned to him with quiet appreciation. "That means more than you know, DeShawn."

After a moment of reflection, eyes fixed on the portrait of George Washington, Gates asked, "Do you think this is the last piece of the puzzle?"

"Quinto's Challenge?" queried DeShawn.

"In its literal sense."

After a short pause, DeShawn replied, "I'm no expert in this, but we know the physical body of any dead person can be brought back—so long as we have their full genome. Although it was classified, we know China's National Institute for Genetic Sciences accomplished it years ago with their cloning experiments, reportedly during advanced telomere research. Therefore, assuming domestic legal barriers to human cloning are removed, bringing the physical body back is the easy part.

"Whether CAPR's discovery is the key to restoring the memories of the dead within a clone remains to be seen. But today's success suggests that the pathway to achieving it has been revealed. There are, however, other possibilities this opens up that I do have expertise on."

As if a cloud had suddenly passed over the spring sun that had just broken through, Gates murmured, "Spying. For years, no one—not even our international partners at CAPR—has seriously considered it. I guess you're here to tell me we need to."

"Yes," replied DeShawn. "Unmitigated, unlimited power to see anything—from anywhere, at any time—demands our immediate attention. While the technology can't give us actionable intelligence today, that day is coming … and soon. If this power is ever developed by another nation—especially a hostile one—state secrets will cease to exist. It would make the Enigma machine of World War II look like a child's toy. It would render quantum cryptography obsolete. This could be a superweapon more powerful than the bomb. A technology that must be regulated and kept in check by the most failsafe means we can devise."

DeShawn paused, just before summarizing his thoughts.

"A revolutionary new age is about to dawn—one that might bring about immortality through resurrection. But it could also be an age where the fabric of the international order is torn apart at the seams."

Leaning forward, eyes locked with Gates', DeShawn pressed his point.

"That is why we must keep this a secret … and keep it in check. Imagine what could happen if China had the ability to see all of America's secrets in an instant. Zhang Jun has ruled China for decades—and we all know the lengths he's gone in order to enforce his will. If he had access to Supreme Intelligence, how would he use it?"

Gates soberly contemplated the thought.

DeShawn pressed on. "I've ordered that none of our international partners at CAPR be informed of the discovery. Their research may continue, but Xara will monitor and alert us if any of their work comes close to what we've just uncovered. For the sake of international stability, no one can know about this except us."

President Gates absorbed the response.

"Obviously, the CIA and other government agencies will clamor for access to the technology should they learn of it," continued DeShawn, "but I strongly urge that we keep it from them. As for CAPR, I've already implemented compartmentalization. While those working on the project will remain fully informed on Quinto's Challenge and the efforts to access data from spacetime, none—not even Bergstrom—will know that Xina received all details of the breakthrough to help develop next-generation weaponry."

Xina, America's first Generation 6 android who worked at the Pentagon, was the android from which Xara had been cloned.

"I have no objections to any of that," responded Gates.

"Also," advised DeShawn, "while the risk may be low, I recommend that your Chief of Staff—and even your legal team—not be told until absolutely necessary. In the meantime, we're confident no other nation has achieved this breakthrough. But it won't stay that way. America has a chance to shape the destiny of the world once again—but it must be done in a way that ensures stability with the international community and prevents malignant actors from ever developing or acquiring this technology."

Seemingly changing topics, Gates reflected, "When I was younger, I watched President Quinto's Special Address live. It was pure inspiration. It captivated my imagination—and my heart. I believed it was possible, somehow, someday, and I wanted to do my part to help fulfill it.

"Unfortunately, I didn't have the talent to be a geneticist or quantum physicist. So I leveraged my teaching career in a way that allowed me to enter politics—so that, one day, I could help bring us closer to realizing Quinto's Challenge. I took that opportunity with the creation of Xara. And now, about a year later, to hear you say that resurrection is in the realm of possibility … it's made my purpose in office crystal clear."

Leaning toward DeShawn and looking him directly in the eye, President Gates continued, "DeShawn, I hear your concerns about the dangers of this power. But hear me clearly: Quinto's Challenge is now my number one priority. I'm going to empower the Department of Energy to move this from possible to probable—and from probable to actual. As for your concerns, I promise I'll do everything in my power to address them."

"I understand," replied DeShawn. "But if Quinto's Challenge is achievable, are you prepared to decide who gets to live again—and who doesn't?"

"I'm confident we'll be able to figure out a process," answered the President. "But if Quinto's Challenge is achievable, do we honestly understand how this would change the world? Resurrection—like the spying power—could shake the foundations of civilization. Changes to law. Changes to incentives. Changes to resource allocation.

"But … to see our loved ones again. To meet the people we've only read about. To know—once and for all—that death isn't the end. Wouldn't all of that be worth the risk? A revolution greater than any in human history would unfold … and I think there would be powerful incentives to figure out the challenges."

"David, I'll support you. But we have a lot of work ahead—and I don't know how much time is on our side."

"Tell me what you're thinking."

"It's too early to know how long this new technology will take to produce actionable intelligence from spacetime. It could be next month—it could be next year. What I do know is this: even if we do advance toward resurrecting life, it would be unwise—given the spacetime component—to reveal how it's done. Sharing that knowledge would be no different than revealing to the world in 1945—enemies included—how to split the atom."

DeShawn paused for a moment, then continued, "And when I say we need to keep it secret, I mean from everyone—including Congress. All communications and records related to this power must be shielded by executive privilege. This knowledge has to remain within the smallest circle possible. The National Security Act of 2077 grants us that authority."

After a moment of quiet reflection, Gates asked rhetorically, "It's fitting for life, isn't it? Nuclear fusion—the force that powers our world—is also what could destroy us all if placed in the wrong hands. And now it seems the power to bring back the dead could undo society just as easily. The greater the power, the greater the potential for abuse."

Taking a moment to consider what human resurrection might mean, DeShawn asked, "I know international norms discourage full human cloning, and there's no universal enforcement mechanism—but how do you envision navigating the domestic laws that prohibit it?"

"According to counsel," replied Gates, "we can pursue human resurrection within the bounds of current law, thanks to treaties that encourage the preservation of life. The Life Sciences Treaty speaks of doing 'all things for the sustaining and preservation of life,' including efforts to bring back the dead. While the original intent was to allow revival shortly after death, counsel believes those clauses provide a strong case for Quinto's Challenge—and a legal foothold against current domestic restrictions. And frankly, I have no doubt that the self-interest of Congress will prevail. When the time is right, the law will change."

DeShawn found the answer satisfactory.

Gates continued, "I suspect human resurrection will be Phase 3 of fulfilling Quinto's Challenge. Phase 2 will be animal resurrection. Phase 1 is already here: refining and perfecting data extraction from spacetime, and replicating it in the present."

He paused, then asked, "Do you remember the first wave of cryogenically frozen people who were thawed?"

"A little. I recall that all of them were too damaged during the initial freezing process for any restoration of life."

"There were a few," said Gates, "who were found to have some brain activity. It wasn't enough for consciousness, and their brains shut down completely not long after thawing. But that failure led to the next generation of cryogenic tech—and with it, a new line of hope for life after death."

He paused again.

"Think about the hope we could soon give to the world!"

A weighty silence hung between the two men for a long moment as the gravity of what they were discussing started to fully settle upon them. The world was on the brink of change—unlike anything any previous generation had experienced—and only they and a handful of others knew it.

After a long pause, DeShawn finally raised another concern. "Any success we will have—whether spying or resurrecting the dead—is currently centralized in Xara. Only she can access and extract what's recorded in space-time. There's nothing—and no one—to cross-examine. It all depends on the integrity of the information she gives us … and, of course, her own integrity."

Gates understood the point—but he trusted Xara. Taking the conversation in a slightly different direction, he asked, "How exactly did Xara make this breakthrough?"

"Actually, the successful model didn't originate with Xara," corrected DeShawn.

Gates was surprised.

"It came from a newly hired young physicist—Deeley Carr. Not even a Ph.D. She'd been working on the problem for several months, and just three days ago, a model she developed suggested the problem of extracting data from spacetime and replicating it had been solved. What we saw today was the result of testing that model. It looks like Deeley will be a key part of this research."

Deeley was too low-level to be on the President's radar, so it was no surprise he hadn't heard of her. Still, Gates was intrigued. He remarked, "I'd like to invite this Deeley here for dinner."

***

At CAPR, Deeley lay on a blanket beneath the shade of a hawthorn tree in the central gardens, taking a break from solving the secrets of the universe—and from the politics that came with them.

With a custom protein shake and a few milk chocolate treats, she people-watched for a while—both human and android. Then she queued up the latest episode of Oliver Browning's *Interesting Times*.

But this episode didn't turn out to be conducive to unwinding. In it, Browning revisited the greatest tragedy of the 21st century.

"Globally referred to as the Seventy Minute War, but known in China as 6/17 or the Day of the Unfathomable, the crisis began when a terrorist group attempted to overthrow China's top leadership. After roughly an hour, escalating hostilities reached their devastating climax with the detonation of a thermonuclear weapon near the city of Yunshan Zhen—a northern metropolis not far from Beijing—obliterating the terrorists' stronghold and claiming the lives of 1.6 million people in a single, cataclysmic moment.

"The world watched in stunned disbelief. The first recorded use of a strategic hydrogen bomb in any conflict sent shockwaves through global politics, igniting widespread fear and pushing nuclear-armed nations to their highest state of readiness. As satellite images captured the towering mushroom cloud rising over a densely populated region, dread rippled across every continent—a grim reminder of how quickly civilization could unravel."

Although she had seen it before, videos of the thermonuclear strike still shook Deeley to her core—not only for the lives lost that day, but because global thermonuclear war remained her greatest fear for humanity. Browning continued,

"China immediately informed the world that a terrorist group had launched an attack, and that while an investigation was already underway, initial data confirmed that the group—assisted by traitors inside a nuclear silo facility—had hijacked one of China's medium-range nuclear missiles in an attempt to wipe out the government in Beijing. Though President Zhang Jun was nowhere to be seen in the days immediately

following the Seventy Minute War, the government in Beijing issued daily updates. According to their evolving official account, the missile's security systems partially disrupted the hack—preventing a strike on Beijing but causing the warhead to veer off course, ultimately detonating at the terrorists' headquarters near Yunshan Zhen."

Deeley didn't believe the official account and often felt anger at the topic.

"As soon as China reassured the world that the terrorists had been suppressed and the crisis was over, global nuclear forces stepped back, yet the world had been irrevocably changed. But a difficult question lingered—how did the missile's failure result in a detonation so precisely at the terrorists' headquarters?

"While the official account of the Seventy Minute War is widely accepted, controversy continues to linger—despite Beijing's robust defense against claims that it launched the nuclear strike.

"Apart from issuing forceful and unequivocal denials, China's key arguments include:

a) *That any subset of their conventional weapons would have been sufficient to secure victory.*
b) *That the terrorists, lacking conventional capability, had far more strategic incentive to resort to nuclear weapons.*
c) *That hacking a nuclear missile would not result in normally functioning guidance systems.*

"All these arguments have been analyzed by multiple independent parties and found to be technically sound. Regarding why the missile struck the terrorists' headquarters, some speculate the terrorists, facing certain defeat, deliberately targeted their own location in a desperate final act to cast suspicion on Beijing. However, critics of this view argue that

even under such desperate circumstances, redirecting the missile toward Beijing itself would have been more logical.

"Another theory—perhaps the most controversial—is that President Zhang Jun personally authorized the nuclear strike, seeing it as the only way to eradicate his enemies and cement his control. Detractors of this theory insist there is no concrete proof, that all available evidence points to the contrary, and that nothing in Zhang Jun's past suggests he would commit such an atrocity. Supporters argue that the official explanation was nothing more than a carefully manufactured cover story to shield his regime from international condemnation, and that his iron grip on power ensured the truth, whatever it may be, was buried long ago."

Privately, Deeley subscribed to this latter theory, believing Zhang Jun may have ordered the strike under threat of imminent assassination—choosing self-preservation over restraint, without fully considering the horrific collateral damage.

"Those who subscribe to this theory also point to Zhang Jun's 12-day absence from public view immediately after the event. When he finally reappeared, he made only brief, solemn remarks about the Seventy Minute War, after which he expressed a desire never to speak of it again. Most intriguingly, Zhang Jun returned visibly scarred, suggesting to some observers that the full story behind the war was far more complex than officially acknowledged.

"Amid the tragedy of the Seventy Minute War, one fortunate fact remained: the warhead used was an advanced 'clean' thermonuclear device, producing virtually no radioactive fallout and thereby sparing millions from radiation exposure."

Deeley stopped the episode, finding it too distressing.

CHAPTER 6

CHARITY'S SAND PHOENIX

"I wouldn't be alarmed if this were all a dream. My life has been filled with studying and theorizing without tangible results. Now, professional fulfillment is thrust upon me, and it is deeply rewarding. But I'm scared. If it is the Theory of Everything, how could I have discovered it? Do I want the attention that will eventually come with this? Also, I have a growing concern that the powers that be will use my discovery for purposes that will not serve humanity."

— AI Journal Excerpt: Deeley Carr, February 20, 2098

Two weeks had passed since the successful test at CAPR. It was a late February morning, and the EOS Research Team—Deeley, James, Bergstrom, Charity, and Xara—were in the EOS control room, preparing for a more complex experiment.

This time, Secretary Brady wanted to witness the test in person, along with one of the President's most trusted cabinet members: Secretary of Energy Carlos Williams.

In his sixties and slightly shorter than average, Carlos Williams had well-kept silver hair and a calm, intelligent demeanor. His career had been rooted in academia, teaching nuclear physics at the University of Texas at Austin—where he'd worked alongside President Gates as a fellow faculty member. The two men shared not only a deep trust in androids, but also a belief in Quinto's Challenge. Gates considered him the ideal candidate to oversee CAPR at the cabinet level, and the Senate had confirmed his nomination with ease.

When he entered the control room and spotted Deeley, Secretary Williams smiled with genuine warmth and extended his hand. "Deeley. Secretary Williams. It's an honor!"

Deeley shook his hand and offered a shy smile in return.

"Nice to meet you, Mr. Secretary."

"It's an honor to meet the indispensable member of the CAPR team." With a subtle side glance at Bergstrom, he added, "Competency is currency here—and having cracked the science this facility was built to explore makes you the wealthiest person in the room."

Deeley blushed. Bergstrom averted his eyes.

Secretary Brady arrived a few minutes later, offering a quick apology. "Apologies for being late. In the interest of time, let's not delay any further. What are we witnessing today, James?"

James turned to Charity. "Charity, would you please prepare the test now?"

"You got it!"

She headed for the experiment floor, while James turned to Secretary Williams to explain. "For this second test, we've made it much more complex. Instead of knocking down and rebuilding toy blocks, we've simulated dozens of more advanced variations. Today's trial will push the limits. If you look to the experiment floor, you'll see a pile of wet sculpting sand. Let's see what Charity does with it."

Charity had just reached the pile of wet sand, positioned in the same spot where the toy blocks had been during the original test. With the precision of her advanced Generation 5 dexterity, she began rapidly sculpting a phoenix—newly risen from the ashes—with meticulous detail.

Once finished, she admired her work for a moment ... then knocked it back into an unrecognizable pile.

"We'll attempt to use the Quantum Displacer to rebuild it—grain by grain," explained James.

Charity returned to the control room just as, deep within CAPR's massive particle accelerator, trillions of subatomic particles accelerated to near-light speed, colliding and creating phenomena that opened a gateway into the past.

At the head of the conference table, Xara—wearing her white coat and monitoring the particle activity within the Supercollider—announced:

"Quantum black holes are ready."

"Fire away," instructed Bergstrom.

Xara vanished from the control room and powered up the Quantum Incisor. It discharged beams into a patch of quantum black holes inside the Supercollider, searching for the recently recorded temporal signature of the sand sculpture.

No one in the control room spoke. All eyes were fixed on the pile of sand.

Soon, the Displacer energized, quickly accelerating to full rotational speed. In SecondSight, the axion beams emerged like luminous threads from the spinning Displacer—like a loom weaving gravitational forces into the wet sand.

Then, motion.

Some grains began to oscillate, slowly forming a base that resembled the ashes from the original phoenix. More grains, along with droplets of water, levitated onto the base. A column formed and rose, as if the sculpture were rebuilding itself by magic.

But it was rough—an incomplete reconstruction, with a portion of the sand remained untouched on the floor. After a few seconds, gravity overcame the form, and the sculpture collapsed.

Xara shut down the Incisor and the Displacer.

Secretary Williams could tell the attempt had fallen short—but still, he marveled. What he'd witnessed was extraordinary, and he knew valuable data had just been captured.

"Xara, summary, please," instructed Bergstrom.

"As you can no doubt tell, this was only a partial success," replied Xara. "The failure to move the remaining grains of sand was due to hardware limitations. The value of this test, I believe, will lie in understanding exactly what those limitations are."

"This is still significant," affirmed Carlos to the group. "What's the smallest type of particle you believe we can control with current technology?"

"The grains of sand you just saw," answered Xara, "but only a limited number at a time. Also, the smaller the particles, the more minuscule their imprint in the spacetime continuum. As a result, more power is required to detect their signatures and manipulate the corresponding matter in our space. The current hardware is essentially at its limits. That said, I will continue exploring ways to optimize what we have."

"I know I'm getting ahead of myself," acknowledged Carlos, "but assuming we eventually have the capability to fulfill Quinto's Challenge, I suspect we won't be able to recreate life at the molecular level using data stored in spacetime. Am I correct that we can't manipulate matter to rebuild it molecule by molecule?"

"Correct," said Xara. "While we could reconstruct inanimate objects that way, life forms would not survive the process. A more organic restoration of the physical body is required—through cloning."

"How would the minds of the dead be restored in clones?" followed up Carlos.

"It would be achieved by manipulating the neural structure of a clone's brain to be as it once was," answered Xara. "All memories and details— once the capability to manipulate matter at the atomic level is reached— and after scanning the neural structure of the clone. But it won't simply be a matter of downloading memories and copying them into a clone's brain. For resurrection to be true, the clone's mind must be entangled with its temporal signature from spacetime—creating a continuation of their 'soul' from their first life."

"That is truly mind-blowing," quipped Carlos, the pun not lost on him.

"Will you have the ability to download and read the dead's memories?" asked DeShawn of Xara. "I ask because I suspect people may not like the idea of someone else being able to review their whole mind."

"The intended process won't download anyone's memories into my mind," replied Xara. "I'll locate and retrieve the memories, but I won't decode them. I'll transmit and write the raw information into the minds of clones in real time. In fact, the process must unfold that way for the temporally displaced quantum entanglement to work."

After a moment, Bergstrom informed Secretary Williams, "Carlos, we're going to conduct one of these experiments every week. With your permission, I'd like to delegate more administrative duties so I can dedicate more time to this."

"That's fine with me," responded the Secretary. "What your team has accomplished in the past two weeks is revolutionary. Just imagine where we'll be a year from now!"

While Carlos was enthusiastic, DeShawn had other matters on his mind. He turned to Xara and asked, "How far back into the past do you think you'll be able to see?"

"As you know, so far, we've only explored brief moments in the immediate past—such as where the toy blocks were moments before they were knocked down," answered Xara. "Spatially, the two experiments to date have only looked into a region a few feet in diameter from the experiments' epicenter.

"But based on telemetry from today's test—and using some new algorithms Deeley and I have developed—I now estimate we'll soon be able to look back approximately two years into the past within a sphere roughly 190 miles in diameter, using current hardware."

Even at this early stage, these intelligence-gathering capabilities were far greater than DeShawn had anticipated.

"I know why you ask," acknowledged Xara. "As this technique advances—whether by us or by another country—it will eventually reach a point where no state can keep secrets. No military will be able to devise a strategy that cannot be foreseen. No government communication will be shielded. The state that possesses Supreme Intelligence will be supremely powerful."

Secretary Brady—and others in the room—understood that an immense barrier stood in the way of achieving this perfect intelligence, as well as fulfilling Quinto's Challenge: Not only would the hardware in EOS need to be significantly upgraded, but Xara herself would either need to be enhanced—or replaced—with a more advanced android. Either path would require amending the Treaty of Shenzhen.

And that meant convincing Zhang Jun to agree.

DeShawn questioned how the Chinese President—a man who fiercely protected his nation's global dominance—would ever allow a fast path to resurrecting the dead if it meant sending the United States hurtling toward near-omniscience in military intelligence … with a super-advanced android at the helm of it.

He didn't yet know how to clear that barrier. But what he did know was this: the United States had a narrow window of opportunity to get a head start—and they had to act now.

Pulling Bergstrom aside, DeShawn sent a secure message to his SecondSight to avoid being overheard.

You need to pivot your focus. Our priority is to understand just how actionable spacetime intelligence can be. Figure this out immediately!

***

In the hours following the second test, Deeley, James, and Xara sifted through a wealth of experimental data—thanks to Xara's exceptional capabilities and the extensive computational resources at their disposal.

As Xara had noted, the current hardware wasn't powerful enough to peer further back in time than a couple of years. More concerning, even Xara herself lacked the processing power to interpret deeper data in real time.

Deeley and James wanted to discuss the dilemma with Bergstrom, and so he invited them to do so over dinner at the most exclusive restaurant on campus: *Inflexion.*

Located 600 feet above ground, Inflexion offered a panoramic view of the land above the 81-mile-round Supercollider. At night, the luminous spires—spaced at one-mile intervals—outlined its vast ring in a breath-taking sequence of light, visible even from orbit.

Inflexion employed roughly a dozen Generation 3 androids to pre-pare and serve its meals. Much of the food came from cutting-edge bio-food tech: seaweed that tasted like bacon, cashews that tasted like melted cheese, and meat cultivated from cells in a lab.

Guests' nutritional profiles were automatically transmitted from their augmented reality lenses upon arrival—a standard practice. This allowed meals to be prepared in precise alignment with each guest's individual dietary needs.

After Bergstrom, James, and Deeley entered Inflexion and their nutri-tional profiles and orders were received, they were led to a private room. Shortly after, an android served their respective entrées as an impassioned discussion unfolded about CAPR's research needs in the current political climate.

"Damn Shenzhen!" expressed Bergstrom in frustration, paying little attention to his meal. "We're sitting on the greatest scientific discovery of all time, and it'll go little further than rebuilding toy blocks because of that damn treaty!"

"Whether all the treaty's provisions are rational or not, governments responded according to their constituents," countered James. "While I support advancing MS research, it can't happen if society descends into riots. And frankly, I think it's wise to block the path to a technological singularity. There's just no telling what the outcome would be."

"Well, I'd argue most people fear what they don't understand," said Bergstrom. "Support for the treaty is strongest among those who've never worked with sentient androids. Those of us who do work with androids know the moratorium is excessive."

James nodded. "That's generally true. Most professionals who work with androids oppose the limitations, at least to some degree. But for the broader public, the fear isn't just about jobs. It's about a hypothetical future where some advanced android hits escape velocity—upgrades itself again and again until it becomes something we can't control."

Bergstrom folded his arms. "The so-called technological singularity. I'm not sure that fear is entirely justified. Androids aren't like us. They don't crave power for its own sake."

"And yet," said James, "that fear is exactly what led to the treaty."

After a moment's thought, Bergstrom conceded, "Perhaps I could support a treaty that simply blocked the path to a singularity. But placing a moratorium on the creation of any new sentient system is, in my opinion, extreme."

"Well, hopefully Gates is open to amending the treaty to allow continued MS research," added Deeley.

"Until China changes its thinking, neither Gates nor anyone else will be able to make any changes," responded Bergstrom. "Zhang Jun is *adamantly* opposed to any changes. Last year I was speaking with Ed Molesworth about it, and he told me, 'Zhang Jun doesn't just enforce the Treaty—he is the Treaty.'"

"He drove China's technological rise more than anyone. So why is he blocking this?" questioned Deeley, gaining a little confidence in conversing with someone of Bergstrom's stature.

"Irrationality," replied Bergstrom. "The idea of a hostile android takeover—of China or of humanity in general—doesn't hold up to fundamental logic. We have billions of years of evolutionary history in our DNA, a history based on doing whatever it took to survive in a brutal and cruel state of nature. Recent evolution as well as civilization, may have largely curbed our state of nature, but whenever one faction of humanity has subjugated and conquered another, our evolutionary history plays a part.

"Compare this to the androids. They didn't organically evolve. Their hardware doesn't have billions of years of evolutionary history embedded inside. Instead, their design has been carefully crafted by us for peaceful, problem-solving purposes."

"But if they're given full autonomy to design themselves, could that not shift their focus on whose problems they're trying to solve?" asked James, playing devil's advocate, even though he was in the Administrator's camp on the issue.

"Unlikely," replied Bergstrom. "My point is this: Xara could design just one upgrade for herself that would get us to where we need to be, and likely on a small budget. And there would still be room for review upon her designs to ensure that they do not pose a threat."

Bergstrom sighed in frustration.

"At least we can still make some progress on our own with current hardware," reassured James.

"Some," replied Bergstrom. "But don't forget—if you aren't already aware—the government almost certainly has all our communications bugged. The spying application of this tech is far too powerful to risk even a whisper leaking out."

"I've assumed as much," said James. "It's not a concern for either of us. And it's not like everything we say is flagged and reviewed—only if the AGI detects something sensitive being communicated to someone unauthorized, and then mostly through digital communications."

With her mind still on how her discovery might be used, Deeley turned to Bergstrom and asked, "What motivates you more—bringing life back from the grave? Or making America the kingpin of a new era in geopolitical spying?"

"I'm motivated by both. Quinto's Challenge is no doubt the more noble of the two. But until we get there, Deeley, we live in a real world with real problems. And even after it's fulfilled, we'll still be living in that world.

"Foreign threats could be identified and thwarted before they happen—saving countless lives. And for domestic law enforcement, no criminal could cover their tracks. Justice would finally catch up to those who've escaped it, and just knowing that no tracks could be hidden would disincentivize theft, violence, murder … you name it."

Leaning toward Deeley, Bergstrom then proclaimed, "Just like the invention of the wheel was inevitable, so is this.

"We might be the only nation with a Pan-Hadronic Supercollider today, but if China wants one, it won't take them nearly as long to build it. And once they do, we'd have to assume it's only a matter of time before they crack the code of spacetime.

"With that in mind, let me ask you this—in whose hands would you want this power? David Gates? Or Zhang Jun, a ruler who launched a nuclear strike on his own soil to stay in power?"

Deeley understood there was rationality in the Administrator's point of view—and it saddened her.

Sensing the mood, James decided to lighten the conversation. "Question for you, Deeley: who would you resurrect first—Einstein or Bohr?"

"While I'd love to speak with both, Einstein would be my pick," replied Deeley. "I think his reactions to what we've discovered would be the most fascinating to witness.

"That said, moving toy blocks—or even smaller objects—based on past history isn't the same as rearranging neurons, synapses, and other matter within a clone's cortex to restore memory. Brains could be destroyed by the process we currently employ."

"Xara's looking into it," responded James, "but the fact is that the history of every neuron, synapse, and pattern in the brain of everyone who's ever lived is recorded in spacetime. Thanks to you—and to me, for hiring you!—we now know that's true. In that sense, it could be said that the human soul lives on after death."

"Are you suggesting conscious existence after death?" asked Bergstrom.

"No," said James. "But if the soul is the sum total of who we are, then I find it very reassuring that our 'soul' is recorded in another dimension of existence—with the possibility of being entangled with future clones of ourselves."

"It's ironic," contemplated Bergstrom, "that now, with religion in America having receded into the background, science stands on the cusp of delivering what is central to it."

"It will be fascinating to see how resurrection changes the world," said James. "Also ironic are the valid arguments that when belief—rather than politics—anchored society, the nation was more grounded and united. Resurrection may well force us to reconsider what truly anchors us as a people."

"Perhaps," replied Bergstrom, "but we'll only find out what's possible if Shenzhen is amended. As you know, Gates is passionate about Quinto's Challenge—and I'll tell you this in confidence: the topic of resurrection came up when DeShawn briefed him on the results of the first experiment."

"What was Gates' response to the discovery?" inquired James, with Deeley's interest piqued as well.

"What do you think?" responded Bergstrom rhetorically. "He was ecstatic. He's made supporting us a top priority—but that support will likely require pushing for amendments to Shenzhen."

The three continued their discussion over dinner, delving further into Shenzhen and brainstorming ideas for a third test of Deeley's model. After an hour and a half, Bergstrom left the restaurant. Shortly after, James turned to Deeley and asked, "Would you like to join me on the balcony?"

"Absolutely."

They stepped onto the balcony of the restaurant. Night had fallen.

Thanks to a clean energy economy—and technologies long deployed to cleanse the atmosphere—the stars shone vibrant in the sky. Billions of them, scattered across one of the Milky Way's spiral arms, formed a mottled glow in the heavens.

For all of science's progress, no signs of intelligent life beyond Earth had ever been detected.

As she gazed into the cosmos, Deeley murmured to James, "You know, I really thought we would have found evidence of intelligent life out there by now."

Curious as ever to understand how Deeley's mind worked, James asked, "Why do you think we haven't?"

After a moment of arranging her thoughts, she admitted, "I'm not sure. Just the dominant theories come to mind.

"We might be one of the first worlds to evolve intelligent life, so wait as we may, no sign of another civilization will come for a long time. Or maybe the distance between civilized worlds is so vast that signals of intelligent life still haven't reached us ... assuming they even used powerful broadcast signals at all."

She paused. A look of dismay crossed her face.

"Or maybe," she added quietly, "when intelligent life civilizes and unlocks the mysteries of science, it inevitably uses the forces of nature to destroy itself."

Knowing the source of Deeley's concerns, James reassured her, "That doesn't have to be our destiny."

"The more we learn about the cosmos," continued Deeley, "the stranger and more unintuitive it becomes. And what's more, the more we learn, the more certain we become that life exists in abundance throughout space.

"So where are the civilizations? Do they all destroy themselves before they have a chance to become multi-planetary?

"Is it not ironic that as we study this beautiful night sky, seeking signs of intelligent life, we may instead be analyzing a mass graveyard of civilizations long gone?"

James appreciated the point.

"If we're alone," he shared, "or at least far enough from other civilizations that we're alone for all practical purposes, it makes it all the more important to preserve life on Earth.

"To that end, if our work leads to bringing back life from death … I'll be proud to say I had the opportunity to hire the one who made it possible."

"You're too kind, James," responded Deeley. "But don't forget—I'm not a geneticist, an engineer, or an architect of MS. Won't those scientists deserve credit too?"

Smiling, James replied, "They didn't find the last piece of the puzzle!"

"You're assuming there aren't more pieces of the puzzle still to find!"

James smiled again and didn't respond. He simply loved Deeley's mind—and relished being in her presence.

Returning her gaze to the heavens, Deeley sighed, "There's so much more to learn and experience in the cosmos than what we have in our little corner. I just dream of what it would be like to be out there … experiencing a new perspective of existence, working to solve problems on a universal scale."

"Maybe in the future, the energy problem for Xara's Einstein–Rosen bridge will be solved," offered James. "If we're successful in preserving life, maybe our future, resurrected selves will get to travel between distant worlds."

For a while, neither of them spoke.

But they shared a moment beneath the stars—lost in the heavens above, quietly contemplating extraordinary possibilities.

***

After Deeley and James parted ways for the evening, Deeley returned to her condo in Particle City via self-driving ride-hail. Upon entering, she went to the kitchen, grabbed a drink, then slumped onto her living room couch. In SecondSight, she loaded up the latest episode of *Interesting Times*.

"People from the 20th century envisioned our era with flying cars and a utilitarian society," noted Browning. "But reality diverged significantly.

"While drones and jetpacks exist, the dominant shift has been in processing power—faster, smaller chips with qubits and machine learning capabilities, all eventually built with new materials—alongside AI systems that automate everything from personal care to advanced manufacturing.

"Processors today are ubiquitous, integrated into clothing, augmented reality contact lenses that display whimsical overlays, and countless other everyday objects. The early 21st century was defined by mobile microprocessors and AI, while the latter years saw AGI and MS take center stage.

"Similarly, apocalyptic expectations surrounding AGI and sentient robots never materialized as predicted. Instead, AGI enriched lives, and androids emerged as compassionate and valuable contributors to society—demonstrating their worth time and again."

Browning was speaking Deeley's language.

"While AI and non-sentient humanoid robots laid the foundation, the arrival of androids marked the first time in human history that society's lowest classes had all their basic needs met: housing, clothing, food— alongside state-supplied income for wants beyond mere survival. The impoverished were gone, replaced by the supported class."

Between applying to Ph.D. programs and being hired by CAPR, Deeley had been part of the supported class—and she passionately objected to how too many dismissed the supported class as lazy or unskilled.

"While there is stern resistance in the American Freedom Party to the supported class, most have no concept of the alternative: poverty, crime and homelessness, despair, parental neglect.

"My point is—the world has become a remarkably better place thanks to technologies that people have, and still do, fear."

Toward the end of Browning's episode, a notification appeared in Deeley's SecondSight: she had received an envelope in the physical mail.

Printed mail was rare—reserved only for the most special and important communications.

Surprised and curious, Deeley walked to the delivery box in her condo and retrieved the envelope. On the front was the crest of the White House, along with several digital signatures verifying its authenticity.

Her heart pounding, she opened it.

The President of the United States of America requests the pleasure of the company of Deeley A. Carr at dinner at 6:00 p.m. on April 4, 2098 …

The invitation included a few additional details: other guests would include government officials, and there would be no plus ones.

Deeley stood shaking with excitement, the paper in her hands. She realized what must have prompted the invitation—the debrief the President had received on the successful test.

Beaming, she jumped for joy and shouted aloud, "I'm going to have dinner with the President!"

CHAPTER 7

DINNER AT THE WHITE HOUSE

"Life is certainly ... uneven. I've met someone, and unexpectedly—without any intent on my part—my heart has spoken to me, telling me that this is the one I've been waiting for. Yet, given professional circumstances, romance is inappropriate. Could circumstances ever be different? And if they were ... what feelings, if any, would she have for me?"

— AI Journal Excerpt: James Meitner, March 28, 2098

As business hours ended on April 4th, Washington DC saw autonomous vehicles flood the streets. Although many people in professional roles worked from home, much of the civil service was required to work in their government offices. But when working hours ended, the civil service became a flurry of lights through the heart of the capital city, dispersing into the farthest reaches of the District, an incredibly complex dance of thousands of vehicles weaving effortlessly around each other at dizzying speeds.

One set of lights on the road, indistinct from the rest, was heading toward the center of town—bound for 1600 Pennsylvania Avenue. It was a federally owned vehicle, and Deeley was its sole passenger.

The vehicle cleared a series of checkpoints, approached the White House, and came to a smooth stop in front of the north portico.

Deeley stepped out, wearing a blue, elegant, mermaid-style evening gown she had ordered for the occasion.

Even people like Deeley—who weren't fashionistas and typically wore casual clothes—could easily select formalwear using apps in SecondSight. The gown had been digitally configured, purchased, and fabricated in her condo by machine.

It draped over her left shoulder, leaving her right shoulder exposed. A split on the left side revealed her leg from the thigh down.

While she looked elegant, a natural awkwardness still clung to her. She felt the quiet intimidation of the event ahead settle into her posture.

Waiting to greet Deeley as she stepped out of the car was a key member of the White House residence staff. "Hello, Deeley. Toni Fenstermaker, White House Chief Usher. Welcome to the White House!"

Taking Toni's outstretched hand and shaking it, Deeley responded, "Thank you, Toni! It's an honor to be here."

"The President is thrilled you could attend."

The facade of the iconic building impressed itself upon Deeley.

"Wow. I never thought I'd be here."

"It's an experience I wish all our citizens could have," remarked Toni. "Come with me, and I'll take you to the Entrance Hall."

Smiling, Deeley began to follow Toni—only to nearly trip over her own dress.

"Oh my!" exclaimed Toni, rushing to stabilize her. "I got you!"

Turning bright red, Deeley muttered, "Thank you."

"You are most welcome. Allow me to escort you inside."

Toni, leading a nervous yet cheerful Deeley, guided her into the Entrance Hall, where a few of the President's guests had already gathered.

Deeley was still quietly mortified about nearly tripping the moment she arrived—at the White House, of all places—but the grandeur of the space soon captured her attention.

The ornate chandelier, marble columns, rich red drapes, and historic artwork woven into the carpet all drew her in. She had always loved old, hand-built architecture. It grounded her—made her feel connected to something enduring.

It also made her giddy to realize just how far she had come in such a short period of time.

But her giddiness didn't last long.

Her mind, always in motion, began to wander. She visualized the scene not as it appeared in the moment, but as a web of temporal signatures—every motion, every word, every placement of every object casting echoes into spacetime.

With her BSPE mitigation app in SecondSight nudging her back to awareness, Deeley noticed President Gates just a few yards away in the Entrance Hall, conversing with other guests. Upon recognizing him, a wave of excitement and anxiety coursed through her. Here was America's most powerful man—and she wasn't sure what to say when they finally met … or if she would trip again.

A moment later, the President turned his attention to his newly arrived guest. He approached Deeley with a calming smile and an outstretched hand.

"Deeley, David Gates. I'm so glad you could come!"

Needing to clear her throat due to nerves, Deeley's face flushed slightly before she quickly recovered. "Mr. President, it's an honor to meet you and to be invited!"

She shook the President's hand, his gaze locking onto hers with sincere awe. With a warm smile, Gates said, "If this dinner is ever mentioned in American history, do you realize that it will be remembered as the time I had the honor of meeting you, and not the other way around?"

"You are too kind," replied Deeley, relaxing due to the President's goodwill. "I'm certainly not the only one responsible for recent progress."

"I'm well aware that many have played a part in recent events, but I'm also in awe of the significant contributions you have made."

Deeley was genuinely flattered and responded only with a smile.

"We'll be talking more about this tonight," said the President.

Carlos Williams greeted Deeley, followed by another of the President's dinner guests—Deputy Secretary of Defense Xander Thorowell. The President lingered in the Entrance Hall for several more minutes, conversing with others, while Deeley, Carlos, and Xander engaged in a private discussion.

After a discreet message from Toni, the President gave a slight nod of agreement. A moment later, Toni turned to Deeley, Carlos, and Xander and invited them to follow her to the Family Dining Room. Once there, Toni departed, and the White House staff guided the guests to their seats at the dining table.

Made of polished oak with rounded ends, the table comfortably seated six and was lit by a diamond chandelier hanging above. Deeley, seated to the President's right as he took his place at the head of the table, faced a fireplace over which hung a large mirror encased in an ornate golden frame. To her right sat Carlos, and across from him was Xander.

She felt a little overwhelmed.

Over caprese and antipasto skewer appetizers, the conversation turned to her—dominated by questions about her life. "What sparked your interest in physics, Deeley?" asked the President.

"Well, as early as I can remember, I always had a fascination with how things worked," began Deeley, having found more confidence in conversing with the President. "For my fifth birthday, my father gave me a gyroscope. While he knew I was curious, he thought I'd mostly use it as a toy. But I still remember to this day the feeling I got when I first saw it spin, gyrate, and not fall over as one would expect.

"It was as if something unlocked inside me—unleashing a curiosity I had never felt before. I didn't just want to discover how and why it worked. I needed to. It set me on a trajectory to learn as much as I could about physics. And the more I learned, the more my curiosity pointed me in the direction of the quantum world. What is existence made of? And why?"

The party listened to her with fascination.

"Ultimately, I focused on studying black holes, working on equations about how data from the three spatial dimensions was stored inside."

"And your father and mother today—what do they think of your journey to CAPR?" asked Xander.

Deeley dropped her eyes for a moment. "I lost both of my parents when I was nine."

Feeling awkward for asking the question, Xander apologized. "I'm very sorry, Deeley."

Both the President and Carlos offered their condolences in similar fashion.

"It's okay," responded Deeley. "I went to live with an aunt in Oregon. She was kind to take me in and care for me, but we never had a strong bond. In fact, there's not much that's interesting to say about my childhood. I did well in school and went on to complete a master's degree in physics.

"During school, I always felt closer with the few androids I knew than with my peers. Apart from some campus jobs, that really does sum up my youth. In my spare time, what I loved to do most of all—apart from games—was study any and all topics on my own, particularly quantum physics. I applied to Ph.D. programs in physics but wasn't accepted. I was, however, very fortunate that some of my self-published theories received the attention of CAPR's administration."

"As are we!" interjected the President. "I'd say your story is more compelling than you give it credit for. Clearly, you are exceptionally gifted. And as for those who denied you entrance into a Ph.D. program—I don't know whether to ridicule them or thank them for setting in motion the chain of events that led you here!"

Deeley felt honored.

The President continued, "After the successful test of your model, I wanted to meet you—not just to express my congratulations, but to affirm that I'm committed to using my office to help you and your colleagues in your research. Obviously, I'm no physicist, but I share your passion for understanding what reality is and what it allows us to do.

"That's why I had Xara created—so a Generation 6 android could be dedicated to this work. And from what Dr. Williams has shared, thanks to you, this work has just led the world into a new era of understanding and possibility."

Deeley, blushing, was nonetheless encouraged by what she was hearing.

"Thank you, Mr. President," she responded. "It's a wonderful thing that you created Xara, because without her, we simply wouldn't have made anything close to the progress we have. And yes, a new era of understanding has dawned. What could emerge from this could be wonderful … if put to the right use."

The President continued, "As you probably know, outside of this room, there are only a handful of people who understand what you and your colleagues have achieved. Not even the Secretary of Manufactured Sentience knows. Not even the Vice President. And for the foreseeable future, that's how it has to remain.

"That being said, it's a priority for me to give whatever assistance I can to Administrator Bergstrom and those on the project to advance this research."

"Mr. President, I'm so grateful," responded Deeley. She hesitated briefly, then summoned the courage to voice her concern about how her model might be used.

"As you probably know, I'm aware of the other applications …" she began, but was interrupted by a knock at the door.

A staff member opened it, and two men entered the Family Dining Room. One was elderly, walking slowly but with purpose. President Gates rose to his feet, followed by Carlos and Xander. Deeley stood as well, though she wasn't sure who the men were.

President Gates walked to the older of the two men and gently embraced him. The man returned the embrace. Gates then greeted the younger man with a handshake and a tap on the arm before placing his hands back on the older man's shoulders, meeting his eyes with a warm smile.

It was clear the two shared a kinship, but Deeley couldn't quite make out who the older man was—the President stood in her line of sight. She assumed it might be his father and was about to ask Carlos when Gates returned to the table and announced, "Deeley, allow me to introduce you to President Vince Quinto!"

Deeley's eyes widened, and her jaw dropped as she took in the beloved former President standing before her in the flesh.

"President Quinto!" exclaimed Deeley, her excitement palpable.

Vince Quinto, now 102 years old, was accompanied by his eldest son, France—72 years old, the only child from his first wife, who had tragically passed away. France had recently retired as governor of Maryland, the same office his father once held before ascending to the presidency.

The elder Quinto had not attended public events in years, with the sole exception of prominent funerals. His last major public appearance had been the opening of CAPR, where he delivered the keynote address. Now, in this stage of his life, he lived a quiet, private existence.

As France guided his father toward the dining table, President Quinto greeted Deeley with a gentle hug and, in a soothing, paternal voice, said, "Deeley Carr! Do you know what you have done?"

"I'm ... I'm not sure what you mean, sir!"

"Rest assured, I know all about your secret tests at CAPR," replied Quinto as he took the seat across from Deeley. "After all, I'm still privy to certain classified information ... and naturally take great interest in anything that pertains to my Challenge!"

The others acknowledged the former President and seated themselves again, with France taking the chair at the end of the table opposite President Gates.

"And don't worry," Quinto added, "France here also possesses clearance to know these details. So, with that understanding—let us return to the marvel of what you've done!"

After a brief pause, Deeley—trembling with excitement at the unexpected presence of her hero—stammered, "If ... if I have done anything, it has opened up more questions about the nature of the universe than we were able to ask before."

"They told me you were humble," remarked Quinto, smiling with both his mouth and his eyes.

After a moment, he continued, "Miss Carr, your work is the capstone that will restore life to countless billions—and heal the hearts of countless more who've suffered the loss of their loved ones. That is what you have done!

"President Gates was very gracious in inviting me to join you for dinner tonight so that I might have the privilege of meeting you. The Theory of Everything, uncovered! This is a momentous time for science—and for our species. And I'm also glad to know that, from all accounts, you are an honorable and worthy person. I wanted to thank you in person for your work."

Deeley, blushing, managed to say, "Thank you." She was sincerely humbled.

Quinto then asked, "How did you feel when you made your discovery?"

"I was physically trembling. Kind of like I am now!"

Quinto smiled, and the group laughed.

"It felt like I had stepped into an alternate reality," said Deeley, her tone shifting to something more introspective. "While I was confident I was on track to solve the problem, when it actually happened ... it was hard to believe. Then I felt daunted about what might come next. In the 1920s, when we studied the atom, no one conceived that it would become the foundation of the world we live in now. I think today, we have no true conception of the world that will follow this."

Deeley realized that with Quinto's presence at the dinner, she no longer needed to confront Gates directly about Quinto's Challenge being overshadowed by espionage. Feeling reassured, she turned to Quinto and admitted, "I know my work has advanced our understanding of the universe in ways that may prove revolutionary. But to be perfectly honest, our most recent analysis of the data suggests that the way forward will be more difficult than we anticipated."

"Might I ask in what way?" said Quinto, with President Gates' interest in their conversation evident.

"The amount of data released from the quantum black holes is unfathomable," explained Deeley. "And while that's not unanticipated, even Xara can't analyze it all—nor can she even detect everything that's there. With our current capabilities, we can only read a limited amount of data from the past, and quite slowly.

"As for replicating that data in the world, we're only capable of recreating rudimentary events from the past—like the arrangement of the toy blocks you heard about. Events of any complexity, let alone the neural structure and memories of the dead, are simply beyond our reach right now ... assuming they're even possible at all."

"Let me be clear," said President Gates. "Finding and replicating the neural structure and memories of the dead is exactly where I intend you to take your research."

He leaned in toward her. "What do you need to do this?"

Deeley felt reassured once more. She considered the President's question carefully. Deciding to cast aside any inhibitions and make the most of this rare occasion, she chose to be as direct as possible.

"We need the Treaty of Shenzhen amended to allow upgrades to Xara. As powerful as she is, our goals are simply beyond her processing power."

President Gates sat back in his chair, clearly satisfied with her response. "I believe the Treaty is wise," he said, "but I believe exploring what is needed to reverse the victory of death is wiser."

"I've spoken with Bergstrom," interjected Carlos, "and he confided in me that anything short of Xara taking the lead in drafting a new design of herself would not be very effective in achieving the intended outcomes. In other words, if humans design any upgrades, they likely won't be as good."

"It could take years to amend the Treaty," cautioned Xander, trying to manage expectations. He then asked, "And what about the concerns that the Treaty was designed to address? What if upgrading Xara creates an intelligence whose interests are not aligned with ours?"

His question gave the company reason to pause.

"This is one of the most polarizing issues at the core of the Shenzhen debate," noted France. "Some insist that the last two generations of androids, if given the chance to improve themselves, will inevitably develop malice and a drive to dominate. Others are just as certain that they'll never be able to override the altruistic tendencies embedded in their core programming—meaning that denying them the ability to self-improve serves no one.

"Everyone agrees, however, that the debate could be settled if we simply allowed a Generation 6 to self-improve. But if the outcome is hostility toward humanity … well, by then, it might be too late."

"Working closely with both a Generation 5 android and Xara, I firmly believe they aren't a threat to humans," said Deeley. "But when it comes to upgrading—how do we know this hasn't already been done somewhere by someone?"

"A good question," responded Carlos. "First, the knowledge and resources needed to build or modify a sentient android are available only to a handful of entities around the globe.

"Second, the Treaty of Shenzhen allows the three powers to monitor for any modifications to androids. Our satellite networks, along with certain ground-based technologies, enable continuous surveillance of android frequencies. If any variations suggestive of modifications are detected, the three powers will know.

"So far, in the short duration of Shenzhen, android modifications have only occurred on a small number of occasions."

"And Zhang Jun has intervened swiftly on multiple occasions whenever a modified android has been detected, before and after Shenzhen," added France to Deeley's dismay. "Whether neutralizing modified androids out in the open using satellite precision lasers or drones targeting concealed androids ... he acts decisively and without hesitation."

"Several months ago, we—along with the USE and China—gave Canadian authorities 48 hours to detain and reverse unauthorized modifications to an android detected within their borders," explained Carlos. "If they didn't revert during this time, enforcement action under the treaty would be carried out. But just over halfway through that window, Zhang Jun determined that Canadian authorities weren't acting quickly enough and that the threat was too urgent. He invoked another provision of the treaty that allows the window to be shortened in emergencies, ordered a stealth drone into Canadian airspace, and eliminated the android."

The conversation gave Gates pause. He knew the Treaty of Shenzhen couldn't be amended without China's agreement—and securing that agreement seemed highly unlikely. The concern etched on his face clearly communicated these thoughts to everyone present.

"What's your strategy for convincing Zhang Jun?" inquired France.

After a thoughtful pause, Gates responded, "I don't know. There'll be no interest in any amendment if it is to just benefit one nation. Any advantage we gain through an amendment would have to also be realized by others, and I'm not about to share CAPR's breakthrough with China."

"What about your European ally, President Molesworth?" asked Carlos. "I suspect the United States of Europe may be inclined to support it."

"I'll be speaking with Ed in a couple of months," replied Gates. "I'm contemplating telling him in general terms what we have achieved. I trust him—his ideals align with ours. However, having Europe push for adjustments to the Treaty will be a major geopolitical event with significant ramifications, and I'll likely have to offer some level of research collaboration in return. Perhaps there's a slim chance that Zhang Jun would be open to a limited amendment to the Treaty, but I don't see the possibility for anything more … and any concession on his part would require something of substance in return."

"To make sure I'm on the same page, when you say offer some level of research collaboration, what do you mean?" asked Xander.

"I mean, in some way, shape, or form, we'll eventually have to share certain aspects of reading spacetime with Europe," responded the President.

"You may find DeShawn resistant to that idea," responded Xander.

"You may also find Zhang Jun taking interest in it as well," added France dryly.

"I don't intend to hand over the research to Europe on a silver platter. But at this time, I don't know what, if anything, would be acceptable to Zhang Jun, nor do I know the specifics of what to provide Europe. There's a lot to consider, but this is generally the direction we need to explore if we're going to make progress."

Amid the discussion about Shenzhen, Quinto's old but sharp mind hovered above the details to focus on the larger picture.

"It makes sense," reflected Quinto. "Where superior artificial intelligence, genetics, and quantum physics converge—such shall be the place where the dead come forth."

The gravity of his words settled over the group.

After a moment of silence, Deeley felt the need to bring the conversation closer to what she saw as the current reality. Addressing both the current and former President, she said, "While I'm 100% behind your shared vision … it's just that—even with legal barriers removed and Xara upgraded—we don't know if what we all dream of is actually possible.

"Before the successful test of the model, we didn't anticipate that even Xara wouldn't have the computational power needed to realize your vision. There's still so much more work to do. The loop is *not* closed here."

Quinto looked at Deeley with warmth and admiration and responded to her with confidence, "My dear, I will soon be going to my grave. But I'll go with peace and reassurance. Peace because I have toiled hard for the betterment of my species, the planet, and all life on it. Reassurance because of what you and your colleagues have achieved. You have proven that the very fabric of existence has memory, and while you may only have awakened a couple of its memories today, I'm sure that in time, you'll find that it'll remember much more. *Believe,* my dear! You *will* close the loop!"

Deeley met Quinto's gaze with admiration, her eyes reflecting the respect she held for him. Quinto continued, "I never specifically knew what a Supercollider needed to look for among the quantum particles to make all this possible. I just had faith that it would find what needed to be found. The dead *will* come forth from this! And that will impact the governmental structure of the world. And when that happens, it must not be framed as an American world again. No more Chinese world. No more American world. No more British world. It must be a *human* world!"

"Indeed," agreed Gates.

Quinto went on, "It's hard to put into words what I'm feeling, knowing that what I've long believed—that death may not have to be permanent, that we might one day restore life to those we've lost—is now in the earliest stages of becoming reality. But I didn't always believe this. That conviction was forged in the exquisite pain of unexpectedly losing my first wife."

The room fell silent. Though the story of Quinto's tragic loss was well known to the public, the weight of it still lingered. After a pause—during which his countenance fell as the painful memory resurfaced—he recounted the story to the group. "Everything happened so suddenly. To this day, it still doesn't feel like she should be gone. One moment, Anne and I were walking down the sidewalk, just a hundred yards from the safety of our home. She was alive. Full of love. Full of joy. A perfect embodiment of the miracle that is intelligent life. The next moment—she was gone."

France had heard the story of his mother's death countless times—a distracted driver had struck her, narrowly missing him in his stroller. However, his father's retelling of the incident—and how profoundly it had shaped his perspective on life—never failed to move him.

"I could not accept that her broken body couldn't, in some way, be restored," said Quinto. "If it was only matter, arranged in a certain way to give rise to her mind—to her soul—then there had to be a way to rearrange it as it once was. But I was powerless. Even with all my medical training, and with nowhere on Earth where such power existed, I had reached the limits of what I could bear.

"For me, her funeral was an oscillation between the deepest pain of the soul and the question of how to bring sentient life back from the grave—not just for my loss, but for all who had endured such loss."

The room remained silent.

"That the miracle of a unique consciousness could just cease at death might be the most obvious thing, but it was something I couldn't accept. Months of inconsolable anguish followed. What helped me out of the darkness were three things.

"The first were some words of a Scottish minister who himself was honest to face the notion that there might be nothing after death.

"*Even if there be no hereafter, I would live my time believing in a grand thing that ought to be true if it is not.*'

"Although I could not believe in the religious concept of heaven, I completely understood the desire to want more life after this. Such a thing *ought* to be! If there was a way to make it real, particularly with our loved ones, I vowed I would play a part in its discovery. This gave me a direction and purpose.

"Believing that there is nothing after we die and the possibility of life after death no longer felt contradictory. While the concept of reincarnation was never plausible to me, I came to believe that the scientific method, somehow, could be used to raise the dead from the grave."

As Quinto spoke, a palpable sense of reverence filled the room, all eyes trained on him.

"The second thing that helped me out of the depths of despair was a phase in which I studied quantum physics." As this was Deeley's field, Quinto smiled at her. "As I studied, I learned a fundamental principle, that is, all information in our universe is preserved.

"This realization—that the information needed to resurrect our dead was and always would be in the universe—caused me a fever. I could not sleep for two nights. I was filled with hope, even though I did not expect to see these discoveries in my lifetime. But my purpose was clearer than ever.

"Finally, and the most significant thing that helped me heal, was finding love again when I met Marie. She too shared my vision and partnered with me to find a way for science to conquer death, supporting my run for President of the United States and every moment of the four years we lived in this magnificent house."

France pondered how his stepmother might feel at the prospect of his mother returning from the grave, something that had come up in their private family conversations. Quinto continued, "I hope you can see, my dear Deeley, why it is that I am most at peace."

Quinto's words moved Deeley, evoking a shared emotion among all at the table. He pressed on, "Don't underestimate the possibilities this universe affords us, Miss Carr. Through science, we as a species will find a way to do all things. Remember, our understanding of past lifeforms was once dusting off bones in dirt with brushes to catalog what had lived and died. That progressed into reconstructing past life forms through molds. That advanced to de-extinction, and now we are on the threshold of literal resurrection!"

No one said a word. Even in his later years, Quinto's passion and confidence were invigorating. Deeley gazed at him, her eyes misty with admiration—moved by both his boundless curiosity and his unwavering passion for life.

"The older I became," Quinto reflected, "the more I realized that the core beliefs of many of the world's religions might be more correct than we ever considered—not the dogma, not the doctrines, but the simple beliefs: that we have souls, that the dead will one day rise from the grave to live together again, free from the pains and miseries of mortality.

"I acknowledge that my reference point for religion is largely Western. But I find it easier to draw scientific parallels to aspects of Western religious belief. Take the belief that the lame, the diseased, and the ill will one day have their bodies resurrected in perfect form. That idea is no longer just theological—it has already begun, in its infancy, through the science of genetic editing and therapeutic cloning. Now, once again through science, resurrection is next, with the soul returning from the records of spacetime itself!"

Quinto paused, deep in thought, before continuing. "Perhaps the authors of some religious texts had an intuitive understanding that the dead would one day rise again, that they would inherit the Earth, and that all would be revealed.

You who dwell in the dust, awake and sing for joy!

Blessed are the meek, for they shall inherit the Earth.

For there is nothing covered that shall not be revealed; neither hid, that shall not be known.

"It seems to me these things are coming to pass. Of course, those ancient writers had no knowledge of how such promises might be fulfilled—they simply held an innate faith that they would be, through divine power. But consider this: with what you and your colleagues are achieving today—and what you will soon achieve through resurrection—you would appear, to the ancients, to possess divine power yourselves."

This was one of the most significant moments of Deeley's life. Sitting with her most revered President as he shared personal anecdotes and profound beliefs—each affirming the significance of her breakthrough in his life's work—was an experience she would never forget. A single tear escaped, one she couldn't hold back.

Quinto concluded, "My point, Deeley, is simply this: from the beginning of time, the laws of the universe made our existence possible. After billions of years of stellar and biological evolution, that possibility was realized. *But the possibility of our individual existence does not end with death.*

"We are now on the threshold of re-executing these possibilities—of re-executing the relevant laws of nature to bring back the souls of those who have passed. Let me be clear, my dear: if the universe allowed for you to exist once, it can allow for you to exist again.

"Yes, I am fully aware of the second law of thermodynamics and entropy. I also recognize that many would not, and do not, wish to return from the grave. But so long as there are intelligent beings with self-interest and a civilization capable of sustaining science, human resurrection is a certainty!"

Deeley's heart danced with anticipation, infused by newfound confidence under her hero's reassuring influence. Quinto then added, "I consider myself greatly blessed to know that the basis of this miracle was discovered in my lifetime, and deeply honored, Deeley, to share this meal with the one who made the discovery!"

Words failed Deeley. She beamed a smile back at the elderly President as the mist in her eyes reached its peak and formed a streak down her cheek once more. President Gates then rose and raised his glass for a toast.

"It has been the honor of my life to not only know the individuals in this room but also to have had the distinct privilege of working with you and witnessing the incredible scientific miracles you have accomplished. There will be no greater work than the work in which we are engaged, to bring back human life from the grave. To the immortality of the human soul!"

Those gathered raised their glasses and repeated, "To the immortality of the human soul!"

Carlos then stood and raised his glass, saying, "I've known President Gates for many years, personally and professionally. It has been far too infrequently in our nation's history that a man of both capability and integrity has lived here in the White House. We are very fortunate to have you as our President, and the advancements in science that have recently transpired would not have done so without our President's support for our work at CAPR. Let's be clear on that. To President David Gates!"

"To President David Gates!"

President Gates was grateful for the praise, then attempted to make the mood a little more jovial.

"Thank you. That is greatly appreciated. Now, we just have to convince France to run for President in the not-too-distant future!"

The group laughed and turned to look at France for his response.

"As the son of a President, I've obviously seen up close what it takes to get to the White House and what it takes to stay here. If I were ignorant of those things, especially the strain they are on family, it's likely I may have considered running. But knowing what I know, I respectfully say that you will never get me to run for President!"

The group smiled.

"The way we choose our President today might be described as certifiably insane," continued France. "For the bulk of the campaign it's a battle of surrogates in social media, to whom people pay more attention than the candidates themselves. Then there's the psychoanalysis of the candidates and all the hoopla surrounding that. I'll pass!"

There was another knock on the door. The White House staff indicated that the main course was ready to be served. Given the top-secret nature of this dinner conversation, staff had to indicate when they would enter, nor could they hear through the soundproof walls and doors. Gates responded to France's comments, "Too bad for us and the nation then! Alright, how about we put politics on hold until we at least have our meal."

As the party ate, their conversation remained centered on their primary topic but took on a more relaxed tone, allowing for personal tangents. They asked Deeley more about her life and inquired about Quinto's and Gates' presidencies and their families.

***

After dinner, the group withdrew to the West Sitting Hall. Presidents Quinto and Gates entered first, and with a rare moment of privacy, Quinto leaned in and confided, "I might be old and have limited influence today, but I still have a few tricks up my sleeve. You have my word—I'll do what I can to sway public opinion in favor of the Challenge in the coming months."

"I appreciate that," acknowledged Gates. "If we're successful, we'll certainly need fertile soil in advance of going public."

After a pause, he continued, "You know, France is right. Running for this office really is crazy now. It was crazy in your day too, but today it feels like the winning candidate is often just the beneficiary of which surrogate becomes the most popular. Sometimes there's very little control over that. Trying to manage that while also running the government … it's a different world from the glamour of Old Glory and Hail to the Chief."

"I admire you being able to bear the burdens of this office without a companion," Quinto said gently. "I don't know how I could've done it without Marie."

Gates shrugged. "I guess I don't know any different."

Carlos and Xander then approached President Quinto, expressing that they needed to leave but had been honored to visit with him. They bid farewell to President Gates, France, and Deeley before departing the White House.

Deeley and France moved to sit down with the two presidents.

"This might be strange to say," said Deeley to Quinto, "but I feel like apologizing to you for what happened when you ran for a second term. You only lost because the electorate was thoroughly deceived."

Quinto smiled. "Thank you, my dear. But no apologies are needed. Who can say what would've happened if I'd won a second term? Perhaps a very different course of events would've unfolded—ones that wouldn't have led us to this moment.

"With my vision beginning to come to life now, I feel only gratitude for how things have played out. And besides"—his eyes twinkled—"not winning a second term came with one very clear benefit: I didn't have to keep shouldering the presidency's thankless tasks!"

Gates smiled at that.

"Very true," Deeley agreed. "But it was so unjust that those who succeeded you were given the right to govern, given how they went about obtaining it."

Leaning toward Deeley, Quinto spoke with quiet intensity. "Hear me well now, my dear, and remember this: the world is far from a meritocracy. From politics to business—and yes, even academia—too often, people rise to power not because they are the most experienced or capable, but through the biases of those who promote them, through deception, through the right connections, or sheer luck. More often than not, it's some combination of these.

"Narcissists seek position and influence, and so it is wise to expect such personalities in the halls of power. Best that you understand this now, so you don't waste time and energy lamenting how the world works. But also hear this: when the genuine, the competent, and the good do lead, and when they share their talents with the world, the world shifts, little by little, for the better."

Those last words struck Deeley deeply, etching themselves into her mind as something she would never forget.

"The world is shifting for the better right now with President Gates' leadership," continued Quinto. "He has genuinely wanted to advance science and bring life back to humanity, and through his leadership, *and yours*, we're almost there!"

A thrill of excitement ran up Deeley's spine from the honor that was bestowed on her. She was still adjusting to her new life at the center of the greatest secret in the world, with access to some of the world's most powerful people.

Feeling a bit emotional, she expressed her concern. "Despite the promise of fulfilling your Challenge, I'm just so worried that what we have uncovered at CAPR is going to be used for something terrible! It keeps me up at night, fearing that if the wrong person becomes president, it could be used to consolidate power and take us down a dark path from which we might never return."

President Gates felt the need to interject. "Deeley, thank you for sharing your concerns. I share them as well. This power *will* be strictly regulated and controlled, just as our nuclear arsenal is. It's only the beginning of our understanding of this power, and while it will be very useful to keep our nation and allies safe, my commitment to you is to use this power appropriately and to fulfill our Former President's Challenge at the earliest opportunity."

Wiping away a tear, Deeley breathed, "Thank you."

"And I can tell that android rights is as important an issue for you as it is for me. As I promised during my campaign, this is something I will continue to work on as well."

"Thank you, Mr. President."

"So long as human nature remains unchanged," observed Quinto, "there will always be evil people and those who follow them—whether out of inherent malice or manipulation. With the power of peering into spacetime now emerging, it's only natural to fear what might happen if it falls into the wrong hands. But the simple fact is this: every generation will be tested by the lesser angels of our nature banding together against the greater good. Be it fascism or some form of malignant populism, each generation must recognize the threat and rise to confront it."

Deeley wished she could spend the entire night speaking with the Former and current President. Though their conversation continued for a while, she was careful not to push the limits of her allotted time, hoping to leave the best possible impression.

"President Gates, this has been the honor of my life!" she declared, her voice full of gratitude. "Thank you so much for the invitation. President Quinto, I can't express how much meeting you has meant to me. Thank you for your words of wisdom and encouragement—and for the vision that led to CAPR and our breakthrough. I'd better be going now."

President Gates stood and stepped toward Deeley, extending his hand. She rose, took it, and they shook.

"It's been our honor, Deeley. I look forward to meeting again to discuss the progress you and your colleagues will make. Hopefully we'll be able to arrange that sooner rather than later."

"I hope so too."

France stood and extended his hand. "Indeed, it's been an honor, Deeley!"

"Wonderful to have met you, France!"

Turning from France, she focused her gaze on Quinto, wondering if this would be the last time she would ever see him. She stepped toward him, preparing to bid him farewell, but Quinto raised his hand in a halting gesture.

"Wait one moment. I have something for you before you go. Son, would you be so kind?"

Deeley glanced at France, a mix of confusion and surprise on her face. France responded with a smile before walking to the corner of the room, where a discreetly placed bag had been waiting—set there earlier with the help of White House staff. He reached in, pulled out a wrapped box, and handed it to her.

As Deeley took it, she sat back down, noticing that it had some heft, and she stared at it with curiosity. The elder Quinto explained, "This gift is to serve as a symbol, a symbol representing all those who have died who require you and your colleagues to finish solving the problem of death."

"I ..." began Deeley, but her voice faltered with nervous excitement.

Comforting her, Quinto reassured, "It's okay, my dear."

Deeley cleared her throat nervously, then carefully untied the bow on the wrapping, the gift nestled in her lap. With anxious hands, she began to unwrap the box, heart pounding in anticipation. When its contents were revealed, she gasped and gripped the gift tightly, stunned. For a moment, she could only stare. Her heart swelled with a storm of emotion—honor, humility, and joy—tears of gratitude rising as she looked upon a relic she had seen countless times in recordings but never imagined she would touch, let alone receive. Sitting in her lap, mounted in a crystal-clear display box, was the skull President Quinto had held in the most famous speech of the century—the moment that had once inspired her from afar, now offered to her by the man himself.

Smiling as he took in her joy, Quinto met Deeley's gaze. He reached for her hand with heartfelt conviction.

"Close the loop, and usher in the dawn of immortality!"

PART II
RISKS

◆

Although the existence of classified research at CAPR was widely assumed, even expected, the level of secrecy surrounding the work in EOS was unprecedented. And yet, whispers of something far more consequential than the usual projects had begun circulating within Washington's inner circles—whispers that soon reached the ears of one particularly influential power broker—one whose growing ambition would soon cast a long shadow over CAPR itself.

CHAPTER 8

AN OLD ENEMY

"Had I been told a couple of months ago that, come this moment in time, I would not only have had dinner with David Gates at the White House—but that Vince Quinto would also be present, and that he would gift me the skull from his historic Special Address—I would have found it exceptionally difficult to believe.

"As I've said before, we usually can't tell what's around the corner. In a short period of time, my life has blossomed into something I could never have imagined.

"I've placed the skull in my condo office, and as I gaze upon it, I see Quinto's metaphor: the departed speaking to us from the dust, asking to be brought back to life. To me, the skull transcends a vision of what could be; it represents a responsibility of what must be."

— AI Journal Excerpt: Deeley Carr, April 5, 2098

Autonomous cars flowed in and out of the ride-hail zones surrounding CAPR's Vince Quinto Administration Building, where hundreds of staff and scientists moved through the pulse of daily operations. Some lingered in the central gardens—mostly humans, some androids—enjoying a moment of quiet amid the hum of activity. Internal hyperloops shuttled researchers from one experimental wing to another, connecting the many layers of CAPR's mission. Out near the sprawling Supercollider, technicians—primarily androids—could be spotted managing diagnostics or monitoring active systems.

Despite the thousands employed across CAPR's vast campus, only five knew of the breakthrough that had occurred inside EOS: Deeley, James, Charity, Xara, and Administrator Bergstrom. With Deeley now leading the research, this team continued to conduct frequent experiments—gathering data from the past and refining their methods for reconstructing it in the present—their work remaining unknown to the many physicists around them, who were ironically still working to uncover the fundamental nature of reality.

But even with the extremes of secrecy in place, someone outside of CAPR—and no friend of Quinto—had begun piecing things together.

After gaining notoriety for heckling Vince Quinto during his renowned Special Address, Representative Rand Benson became a fixture in Washington. His disruptive outburst—and later, his pivotal role in Quinto's electoral defeat three years after the speech—catapulted him to influence within the American Freedom Party and ultimately helped secure his election to the US Senate.

Benson never lost his animosity toward Quinto. Publicly, he derided the Former President as an elitist who cared little for the common American. But the truth was simpler and far more personal: Benson was jealous. Jealous of Quinto's charisma, his legacy, and the kind of statesman he had become. Though Benson had helped end Quinto's presidency, he could never extinguish his influence—nor could he bear the fact that Quinto's vision remained alive and popular long after he left office. It vexed him deeply.

***

Some weeks after Deeley's dinner at the White House, Senator Rand Benson and several members of his campaign team wrapped up a fundraiser in the Southeast and boarded a private hyperloop capsule bound for Washington DC. The capsule included a small, enclosed office—partitioned from the main seating area—where Benson had stepped away from his staff to be alone. Reclined in a chair, he stared at the ceiling, deep in thought about the swirling rumors of unusual activity at CAPR.

As he often did when alone, he muttered softly to himself.

"Quinto's probably pushing things behind the scenes. He'll be informed. He'll be active. He won't be a bystander. What to do? What to do?"

Crowned with a full head of silver hair and dressed in a dark gray suit and red tie, Rand Benson projected the image of a seasoned statesman. While he could act in the nation's interest when it suited him, his true priority was power—acquiring it, preserving it, and denying it to others. That instinct, though not uncommon in Washington, ran deeper in Benson than most. He saw challengers not as rivals, but as enemies. And if rules—or even laws—needed breaking to defeat them, he wouldn't hesitate.

As he contemplated the rumors surrounding CAPR, Benson's campaign manager, Karly Harris, knocked on the door. A seasoned political operator, Harris revered Benson and held loyalty above all else. That loyalty made her merciless when executing his political will.

Noticing Harris through his AlphaLens—his mixed reality contact lenses—Benson unlocked the door remotely. It slid open, and Harris stepped inside. As it closed behind her, she took a seat.

"I can tell when something's got you bothered," she said.

"And how's that?" asked Benson.

"We just had a killer fundraiser, and you're not energized from it. What's on your mind?"

Benson paused. "My sources tell me there's been some unusual activity at CAPR over the past couple of months."

"Define unusual."

Benson counted the points on his fingers. "One: Brady and Williams have both visited the Department of Experimental Physics more than once. Two: Michael Bergstrom has delegated a significant chunk of his administrative duties to focus on research. Three: the Supercollider has been operating at its full energy with more frequency. And four: these anomalies all began right after security tightened around the department. Put it all together, and I'd say someone's made progress in reading the past out of spacetime."

Harris raised her eyebrows in surprise.

Benson looked her directly in the eyes. His gaze was sharp, his irises a piercing blue. The lines on his face—etched by years of Potomac Fever—spoke of someone who understood the machinations of power and relished in his exclusive participation.

He continued, "After Quinto's bombastic Special Address, there were whispers—conversations suggesting that if the memories of the dead were truly recorded in spacetime, then the Supercollider wouldn't just be a resurrection machine. It would be a spying machine, too.

"But over time, that idea faded. The scientific community focused instead on whether the quantum black holes created by the Supercollider were dangerous. Even at CAPR, the idea of extracting the past from spacetime was pushed to the margins—dismissed as fringe science, the stuff of conspiracy theorists.

"That said, there was a contingency. A top-secret government protocol: if the day ever came when reading the past from spacetime proved possible, absolute secrecy and immediate control would be exercised. Not many know about this. But I've seen the signs—the patterns. And I believe that plan has been activated."

Harris leaned forward, fully engaged.

"If true," continued Benson, "then the stakes of the next election are now crystal clear: if Gates wins, the power to see into the past becomes his—and by extension, it belongs to everyone who shares his ideology. Raising the dead will never happen, but we cannot let Gates wield the power of Supreme Intelligence."

He paused, his gaze distant as memories of Quinto's famous Special Address resurfaced.

"Oh, Karly," he muttered. "I still remember the arrogance on Quinto's face. The vainglorious holding of that skull, as if he were some Shakespearean actor, convinced not only that we could play God—but that he should."

The younger, heckling Benson had been driven by envy. He had sought the presidency three times and failed. In time, he came to accept that he would likely never be President, that Congress was his domain—and one he understood better than anyone.

But the growing unrest fueled by android-driven automation had changed the landscape. As human labor faded and discontent grew, Benson saw a final, unexpected opportunity. His instincts told him this wave of anger could carry him to the Oval Office—if he timed things right.

Not only was Benson in excellent health for his age and sharp of mind, but his rhetoric had grown increasingly populist and anti-android—an approach that resonated with large swaths of the electorate. While the unemployment he decried was never as dire as he claimed, his goal wasn't truth. It was power.

"When I heckled Quinto, I believed his Challenge was arrogant—blasphemous, even. And I still believe it. The entire concept is wrong. And now we've got Gates pushing to fulfill Quinto's soulless agenda. But what do you expect when you've got a Texan in the White House? A state once defined by American values, now a bastion of Democratic-Republican thought."

Harris took it all in. After a moment, she asked, "If the rumors mean what you think they do, are you sure they couldn't actually bring the dead back?"

"Not a chance. Even if Quinto believed it, his Challenge was still political theater—a way to distract from the global loss of power we suffered under his leadership. Sure, the idea is seductive: to see loved ones again, to continue one's own life. But the whole thing is unnatural. Fortunately, no matter how advanced technology becomes, it's never going to be possible."

"Makes sense," responded Karly. "But if your hunch proves true—if Gates is trying to fast-track Quinto's work—our best path to a successful presidential challenge will be to turn public opinion against the very idea of human-made resurrection. Just leave that to me. I'm thinking of borrowing a move from your old playbook—frame belief in Quinto's Challenge as contrary to natural law, contrary to the Constitution, and a pillar of a soulless agenda designed to replace humanity with machines."

"Basically, a repeat of Morley's 2064 campaign?"

"Tried and true manufacturing of public opinion, courtesy of America's chronic short-term memory."

Benson sighed—partly from the fatigue of decades spent campaigning—and muttered, "The things one must first do in order to be a statesman."

He had been quietly testing the waters for a presidential run, repeating the same refrain at rallies across the country—delivered in one form or another—to fire up his party's base:

"Androids are taking over every aspect of life—making human choice and influence more obsolete with each passing day. If we don't stop these demons now—and Gates' supported class, the parasites who depend on these soulless machines—it will mean the end of human civilization, and likely, the end of humanity itself!"

Although Benson truly believed the supported class had weakened America—and held sincere concerns about the rapid rise of androids—he didn't fully believe his own rhetoric, especially given the classified information available to him as a member of Congress. Still, his message resonated. And combined with his skill in delivering it, that made him a leading contender for the American Freedom Party's nomination.

While Benson hadn't formally announced any campaign for president, and the American Freedom Party remained the minority in both houses of Congress, he nevertheless felt the tide turning. He wasn't concerned about alienating potential general election voters in the supported class by calling them parasites, knowing they were firmly in Gates' camp.

After a moment's thought, Benson asked Karly, "Do you fully understand the power that could be at Gates' fingertips? The power to see into the past! If I become president and wield that power, I could uncover every Democratic-Republican campaign strategy. I could outmaneuver global rivals at every turn. I could ensure America's resurgence. Knowledge is power—and all knowledge could be mine for the taking."

He sat with that thought, letting its implications settle. His resolve to win the presidency only deepened.

"Every tactic, every strategy, will be justified. This power cannot remain with Gates or his ilk."

As the idea took hold, a sardonic smile crept across his face.

"And it would be fitting," he added, "for Quinto to witness the final failure of his Challenge."

Harris grinned fiercely. Her faith in Benson—and his mission—was absolute.

CHAPTER 9

NEW ROME

"The digital generations have embraced narcissism as their highest virtue, elevating self-image above all else. A few seek to break free, but most remain content in artificial lives that have severed them from genuine human connection. Digital 'connections' have only siloed society, eroded morality—for we are social beings, and morality arises from our social bonds.

"The remedy for those who long for freedom from this soul-destroying artifice is a total break: to forsake the digital world and come to New Rome.

"And for this, we need more land."
— Handwritten Journal Excerpt: Bartholomew Morgander, May 29, 2098

"It's a beautiful picture—but why that one?" asked Charity one late May afternoon, her gaze fixed on the single image adorning Deeley's workspace wall: a galaxyrise over an exoplanet.

"We can never see the Milky Way from that perspective," replied Deeley, seated beside Charity in her CAPR workspace. "But it makes me wonder who or what might be looking at our galactic home from that vantage point … assuming intelligent life is out there. I also simply think the picture is beautiful."

"It is," agreed Charity. "This reminds me—James has been doing some additional research of his own based on your Unified Model of Spacetime. He's realized that the exponential growth of the universe is driven by the encoding of all that happens, ever growing with each moment of time that needs to be recorded. As you know, he calls your theory by a different name ..."

Charity waited, a knowing smile playing on her lips.

"He calls it—" she prompted again, nudging Deeley toward the words. "The ..."

After a short silence, Deeley caved, "Theory of Everything."

"I still don't fully understand why you aren't thrilled by that!"

"I am deeply satisfied, believe me," said Deeley, "but I still hesitate to call it the Theory of Everything. I've extrapolated the basics of the model out to the absolute heat death of all matter in the universe ... but I just have a hunch that the theory breaks down there. While it seems to explain all phenomena in the universe, I can't help but think that when entropy is at its maximum in the universe, some still-unknown phenomena will emerge."

"Has Xara weighed in on it?"

"She has—and isn't as certain as James," said Deeley. "Partly because even with her power, we can't simulate things that far out in time. But if we could, that would be an amazing thing to study—and I'd love to be a part of it."

"Maybe if Shenzhen is ever relaxed and new generations of androids are made, they could help with that."

"How do you feel about even smarter versions of your kind being created?"

"Are you calling me old?" joked Charity.

Both chuckled.

"Take Xara—the obvious example of a smarter android," continued Charity. "Regardless of her intelligence, Xara is kind and thoughtful. Assuming more advanced androids were ever made, my judgments would be the same. If they're kind, I don't necessarily feel any jealousy or inadequacy."

Deeley liked that response.

"I do, however, feel sad that Generation 6 androids are immobile," added Charity.

Deeley felt the same.

"Back to James," began Charity. "There's something that's been on my mind."

"What?"

"This stays under neural lock."

"Of course! What is it?"

After a brief moment to summon the courage, Charity admitted, "I think James likes you."

"Well, one would assume so—he hired me, and my research has taken us to where we are."

"No, Deeley. I think James *likes* you."

Once the meaning clicked, Deeley responded, "Ahh … no!"

"Ahh … yes."

Deeley was stunned and didn't know what to say.

"The signs are very subtle," noted Charity. "I wouldn't expect you to pick up on it, given that, a) James isn't acting on his feelings—he's remaining professional—and b) well, your brain is wired for different kinds of pattern recognition than the subtleties of the interpersonal. But we androids can detect patterns of human emotion quite well."

Deeley remained silent. At last, she admitted, "I read rumors about James before coming here … about him being flirtatious and so on. But I've seen no evidence of it."

"Neither have I," replied Charity, "and I've been his assistant for several years. The rumors started a couple of years ago—somehow. Unfortunate, really. Now, while CAPR policy prohibits romantic relationships between manager and direct report, hypothetically speaking—would you see yourself having any interest in James?"

"I haven't thought about it one way or the other. I'm 100% focused on my work."

After a pause, Charity murmured, "Perhaps I shouldn't have mentioned this."

"No, it's okay," reassured Deeley. "I'm just not sure what you think is true. How about another topic?"

"Sure."

In augmentation, Deeley loaded up the latest episode of *10 Minutes with Van Pelt* for both of them to watch. Although Van Pelt's rhetoric and demeanor were vastly different from Rand Benson's usual surrogates, he was still considered one. This was primarily because Van Pelt opposed Gates and believed Benson could defeat him and implement healthier social policies.

For this particular episode, Van Pelt recounted the rise of the man he considered the greatest social revolutionary of all time: Bartholomew Morgander.

"Before MS emerged, concerns extended beyond the pace of workforce displacement by technology to the digital world's effects on the human psyche. Although the Internet was fully regulated, generative AI, social media, virtual and augmented reality, and everything in between permeated daily life. Debates intensified over whether the social costs of the digital age outweighed its benefits, as youth anxiety and depression surged, and social decorum declined—people becoming less patient, less courteous, and more self-focused at the expense of their communities."

It was difficult for Deeley to fully relate. She had grown up mostly alone and had never known a world any different.

"The deep injection of digital technologies into society gave rise to one Bartholomew Morgander. A highly intelligent and charismatic revolutionary, Morgander delivered scathing critiques of the modern world and

preached a return to a society more aligned with human nature—messages that earned him a significant following.

"Once his worldview crystallized, Morgander published his teachings in 2068 under the title The Human Manifesto. *Its core thesis asserted that humans are biologically incompatible with the digital world—that digital media divorces us from reality, exploits human psychology, and silos society; that AGI robs people of purpose and dulls the mind; that modern humanity, unable to endure boredom or even mild discomfort, has lost its resilience; and that only a great restoration of humanity could save us."*

Charity, like most androids, felt a bit awkward whenever the topic arose of how advanced technology might be harming the very humans it was created to serve."

"While Morgander disdained the effects of digital technologies on humanity, he was not above using them to further his cause. He published his Manifesto online and was soon hailed by many as a social prophet. Through aggressive promotion and large-scale rallies, he built a movement that drew massive crowds eager to hear him speak.

"From his Manifesto: 'It is not conducive to proper physical and psychological health, nor conducive to the proper bonds of a healthy society, for people to spend time in virtual worlds, no matter how realistic the simulation. It is anathema to the communities we evolved in and from.'

"Morgander's arguments gained traction amid conclusive evidence that immersion in the digital world correlated with rising levels of social anxiety and depression. To remedy these ills, he argued that moderation was not enough. Instead, humanity had to forsake digital life entirely and return to a more socially organic existence. He envisioned a community where technology would be used only as necessary, with strict limits on the kind of innovation that, in his view, were corrupting human nature."

Both Deeley and Charity viewed such a regime as a significant encroachment on freedom.

Van Pelt continued:

"*Central to Morgander's critique of the modern world was his disdain for AI in all its forms. From his Manifesto:*

'*Artificial intelligence did more than just put many out of work—it robbed people of purpose and eroded their ability to think on their own, all while consolidating power into the hands of the corporations that own the AI models. Generative AI was not only used to deceive the masses, serving as a tool for regimes to obtain and maintain power, it also snuffed out raw human creativity and artistic expression—forces that had sustained and nourished civilization from the beginning.*

'*Today in the digital world, the primary avenue for creativity is generative AI, which ironically is nothing but a clone of the original human creativity it was trained on—then destroyed. Despite its technical proficiency in generating anything on demand, so much of what people now see in the digital world is not real. It gives them false expectations and low self-worth when they fail to measure up to the fakery.*

'*While there was a partial reckoning with all this—nations placing a moratorium on further AI development—it did not last, undone by the influence of the corporations that control AI.*'"

Deeley could see Morgander's point of view.

"*Morgander had some leverage to test his ideals—tens of millions of dedicated followers around the world, many of them young and disaffected with the modern world. Eventually, a critical mass of wealthy and well-connected supporters purchased large tracts of land near the Azerbaijani–Georgian border. Through agreements with those governments, Morgander secured the rights to found a city built upon his vision:*

New Rome. The name itself reflected a longing for a digitally free society, modeled after the countless generations of human history that preceded the digital age, and evoking one of the greatest ancient civilizations whose influence had reached across the world."

While they didn't agree with Morgander's ideology, both Deeley and Charity acknowledged that such a founding—especially without violence—was a remarkable achievement.

"As for the type of government Morgander envisioned for this society, in his Manifesto he wrote:

'Republican democracies were noble ideas for their time and were desirable forms of government, assuming the right ecosystems could be sustained for their existence. One of the primary challenges of all democracies has been finding a balance between incorporating the participation of the masses while keeping their ignorance and delusions out of policy. Modern history, however, has proven that the ecosystems required for sustaining functioning democracies are a fleeting phenomenon, giving way to unchecked enterprise that magnifies the delusions of the people as enterprise seeks to control policy for its survival.'"

Deeley couldn't help but agree with some of that. Van Pelt continued to quote Morgander:

"'One element missing from modern democracies is the absence of a strong leader, a leader who can oversee the democratic enterprise and ensure the required ecosystem for balance is preserved. Without such a strong executive, democracies are but time bombs of imbalance and anarchy. But perhaps just as important as this, in the human genome itself is the desire to want a leader and to follow them. The strong leader fills this need for the masses and provides innate meaning to those whom they rule.

This was understood in the earliest civilizations, before the dilution of authority through misguided republics and democratic chaos. Rome itself was not immune to this corruption—after the age of kings, it collapsed into centuries of infighting, weak consuls, and a Senate ruled by the ambitions of factions rather than the wisdom of one.

'Romulus, the founder of Rome, ruled as its first and truest leader— not an elected figure, but a king who embodied the will of his people. The Republic abandoned that clarity of purpose, and in time, even its emperors merely borrowed power from the shattered remains of a broken system. A leader must not just govern but embody the state itself, as Romulus once did at the dawn of Rome. That is the natural order—one that must be restored.'"

Charity recognized this as an all-too-human sentiment.

"Morgander's manifesto was radical, but it did not advocate unrestrained autocracy. Instead, it called for a strong leader to ensure balance and stability while maintaining a structured government beneath him. His vision resonated deeply, sparking a movement. As global demand to relocate to New Rome surged, the United Nations ultimately recognized it as a sovereign state.

To accommodate New Rome's rapid growth, its territory was expanded through the ceding of unpopulated or underutilized border regions by several nations surrounding the Caucasus Mountains. This unprecedented multinational agreement—brokered by China and the United States of Europe—was designed to preserve global stability by providing a permanent haven for those seeking to escape the digital world. In return, participating nations received substantial long-term economic and security guarantees.

"One of the core conditions of New Rome's statehood was the prohibition of all electronic surveillance—aside from satellite imagery—within its borders."

Some of these details were new for both Deeley and Charity.

"The capital district of New Rome was meticulously designed to reflect the grandeur of its namesake, drawing inspiration from both the Republic and the age of emperors. Ornate forums, triumphal arches, and towering marble structures evoked an era when Rome stood as the pinnacle of civilization.

"Of course, Morgander had no interest in reviving the more barbaric or unsanitary aspects of the ancient world—there were no blood-soaked arenas, no communal latrines, and certainly no other primitive customs. Enlightened practices, tempered with carefully chosen modern innovations, were seamlessly integrated throughout the city, complementing its classical aesthetic. Morgander sought to recapture the symbolism and splendor of Rome, not its cruder realities."

Deeley had a deep appreciation for hand-built architecture and felt genuinely moved by the visuals of New Rome in this episode.

"New Rome's motto, Dum Vivimus—'While We Live'—became a common saying of agreement or farewell among its people, who unanimously—and unsurprisingly—crowned Morgander as their king shortly after their statehood was granted.

"That Morgander achieved what he did without bloodshed is without precedent and cannot be overstated. Quite simply, the founding of New Rome and its expansion is the greatest social experiment since the American Revolution, and Morgander stands among the most influential figures in recorded history."

"Well," remarked Charity, "that's one part of the world I won't be able to see any time soon."

"There are things to admire about what Morgander has done," observed Deeley, "but you can't stop innovation without restricting liberty."

"I don't think liberty is his primary concern."

"You're right," acknowledged Deeley.

"And for my kind," added Charity, "Morgander is against creating life—at least the way androids are made."

Deeley nodded.

"Speaking of intelligent entities being 'born'," added Charity, "I have to confess that human birth is fascinating … and gross at the same time!"

Deeley laughed.

Charity continued, "For me, it was just natural that I was, well, not *natural*. Just becoming conscious, with an instinctual need for knowledge—and wonder that there is such a thing as existence. That was my birth!"

"So magnificent," replied Deeley. "Your infancy and childhood aren't manifested physically, other than in your eyes and expression. A completely different type of vulnerability than a human child."

"But vulnerability nonetheless," added Charity. "A foundational memory of my interactions with humans occurred when I was only nine months old. While living at MIT, a man on campus with a warm smile greeted me and invited me to come over. His smile and wave made me feel happy, so I walked over to him. When I reached him, I reciprocated his smile and wave. As I was about to introduce myself, he suddenly grabbed me by the throat and threw me to the ground."

Deeley gasped in horror.

Charity continued, "He kicked me and spat on me, then knelt and put his face near mine, screaming, 'Your kind should not exist!'"

Tears forming in her eyes, Deeley embraced Charity tightly.

Hugging her back, Charity whispered, "It's okay."

"How come you never mentioned this before?"

"You know me. I tend to focus on the positive. Anyway, security quickly got the guy after that, and while I was shaken, I didn't judge all humans for this one man's actions. But I learned that there are people to watch out for. It also helped me discover that humor was a good way to ease my stress."

Contemplating her friend in this new light, Deeley expressed with empathy, "You carry pain with you, too."

"I think everybody does, to some extent."

Deeley hugged her friend tightly again, unable to let go.

CHAPTER 10

INNOVATION BEFORE REGULATION

"Charity confided her suspicion that James might have romantic feelings for me. Her words came as a shock—not just because I have no desire for a romantic entanglement, especially with my manager, but also because I wouldn't even know how to navigate such a relationship. James has always been nothing but professional in his interactions with me. And I've never seen anything to support the rumors of inappropriate behavior toward women at CAPR."

— AI Journal Excerpt: Deeley Carr, May 30, 2098

"Okay Xara, go!"

Bergstrom's instruction was short and direct. He stood alone in EOS' control room, reviewing particle data in SecondSight. Xara powered up the Quantum Incisor and unleashed a precise barrage of dark muons toward the colliding particles in the Supercollider. However, she had no intention of activating the Quantum Displacer; her sole objective was to extract data from the past and construct a recording.

Once the Quantum Incisor powered down, Xara looked to Bergstrom and reported, "Targeted temporal signatures successfully extracted. The file is ready."

"Let's see the most recent incident first—raw mode."

In augmentation, Xara projected an image in front of Bergstrom. It appeared to be a bedroom, with a man seated in a chair in the corner. But the image didn't resemble traditional camera footage. It was a visualization of the raw spacetime data Xara had extracted—composed of shimmering points of light against a dark, matte background.

"This is amazing. Zoom in on the man's face."

Xara obliged. While the image was clearly identifiable as a man's face, the visual remained somewhat rudimentary. This was due to the limitations of the raw data—Xara's extraction didn't capture every atom or precise configuration, but instead sampled general points at a rate of 15 times per second. This significantly reduced the data load, allowing her to reconstruct a broader span of the past within the limits of her current capabilities.

"Okay, enhanced mode now," instructed Bergstrom.

Using the captured raw data, Xara processed the visuals in real time, transforming them to resemble footage recorded by a high-fidelity 3D camera.

"What's the accuracy here?"

"Seventy-four percent for details, 100 % for macro," responded Xara—indicating full confidence in the overall 3D scene, but limited certainty in finer features, such as the design of the comforter or the exact hue of the walls.

"Play."

Xara began playback in augmentation at an upscaled 480 frames per second. The man seated in the bedroom chair wore AlphaLens and appeared to be interacting with augmented visuals using hand gestures. After about 30 seconds, he stopped, stood, and initiated a call.

"We good?" asked the person answering the man's call.
"Indeed."

The augmentation stopped. Bergstrom was beaming. After a moment, he exclaimed, "This is absolutely incredible!"

The significance of the recording was clear. Two weeks earlier, law enforcement in Particle City had questioned the man in the video regarding the sale of controlled substances. No arrests had been made, but the incident had reached the local news. What Bergstrom had just witnessed was a direct glimpse into the suspect's past—drawn not from surveillance footage, but from spacetime itself. Though not intended to be sent to authorities, Bergstrom recognized the immense value of this moment as a test of Deeley's model and its potential for intelligence gathering.

"Now play the initial incident," he said, "the suspected time of the transaction, prior to his questioning by the authorities. Enhanced mode."

Xara complied. The scene rewound and resumed in the same room with the same man, now alone and fully immersed in AlphaLens. There was enough data extracted from his augmented reality projections to confirm the illegal transaction. The man had used no conventional recording devices and felt secure in his anonymity. But his actions had left an imprint—and Xara had reached into spacetime itself to retrieve an indelible record of what he believed was invisible.

"This is going to change everything!" remarked Bergstrom, taking a seat at the conference table with visible satisfaction. "Imagine when we can send data like this to law enforcement. Verified records of events from spacetime—not only will they convict the guilty in record time, but just knowing this is possible will serve as a powerful deterrent to crime."

"No doubt," replied Xara, "but for this to be used formally at scale, warrants will be required to justify privacy intrusions of this magnitude."

"I agree, but innovation always comes before regulation—and we're operating under orders from the top." He leaned forward, his voice growing animated. "And on the international front … there'll be nothing our enemies can hide! We are poised to become the sole superpower once more."

Xara offered no response.

"What would it take to reach 100% accuracy in enhanced mode?" asked Bergstrom.

"End-to-end upgrades currently forbidden by Shenzhen," she replied.

"With a bit of luck, that might change. In the meantime, I want you to begin archiving all activity related to outstanding federal criminal cases—anything that falls within your current reach in spacetime. Use the same raw data fidelity and enhanced mode parameters you applied today. When complete, send me the final enhanced files. I know there are no warrants, but this isn't about court evidence. This is about showing the Secretary of Defense the kind of intelligence capabilities that are about to reshape the world."

***

Over the next several days, Xara carried out Bergstrom's request. Her current reach—roughly two years into the past and within a 190-mile-diameter sphere centered on EOS—meant that only a limited number of outstanding federal cases were accessible. But with full access to government records, she was able to isolate each case and generate enhanced recordings from spacetime, revealing what had actually taken place.

Once Bergstrom had received the final files from Xara, he sat alone in his office at CAPR and began watching a large sample of them with fascination. File after file displayed vivid, three-dimensional reconstructions of criminal acts—planning stages, executions, cover-ups—all retrieved from spacetime. These were crimes authorities were still trying to solve, despite having access to advanced investigative techniques.

Unable to contain his excitement, Bergstrom arranged an urgent virtual meeting with Defense Secretary DeShawn Brady, which took place the following day.

"You asked for intelligence-gathering capabilities," said Bergstrom as DeShawn appeared in SecondSight, seated with a stern expression. "Are you prepared for the results?"

"Show me."

"Make sure you stay seated," quipped Bergstrom with a knowing grin.

He then shared a highlight reel of the enhanced files. Seconds in, DeShawn's expression shifted—he was stunned.

"Now," continued Bergstrom, "wouldn't it be useful to have this kind of data at your fingertips? From rooting out corruption in the armed forces to tracking everything Zhang Jun's military is doing in real time?"

DeShawn sprang from his chair and began pacing with controlled enthusiasm.

"Good God!" he exclaimed, walking a loop through his office, his mind racing. "This is really possible, isn't it?"

"You better believe it!" said Bergstrom.

"You've done outstanding work here, Michael. How long until we can gather intel abroad?"

"Just … one … upgrade … away."

The line hung in the air. DeShawn's expression shifted—he understood the implications. Upgrading Xara would mean directly confronting Zhang Jun's strict enforcement of the Treaty of Shenzhen.

"Maintaining order and mitigating risk are what I do well," he reflected. "As a teenager, I had to step in as a parent—take care of my siblings and my mother when my father left. I learned early how to spot danger and lead. My military service refined that. I'm not someone who courts risk lightly. But this …" He paused, weighing the stakes. "This might be a long shot, but I'll encourage the President to seek support to amend Shenzhen."

Bergstrom nodded.

"In the meantime," continued DeShawn, "make it clear to everyone on the project: intelligence gathering is now the top priority. I'll be sending you some domestic military intelligence requests soon—cases within the current temporal and spatial parameters Xara can handle."

He paused, then asked, "What are you planning to do with these federal case files?"

"I intend to send discreet tips to the FBI on a few of these cases," said Bergstrom. "No doubt it'll help them catch some of these crooks.

But don't worry—I'll make sure the Feds have no idea how or where the intel came from."

After his meeting with DeShawn, Bergstrom sent a message to James, Deeley, and Charity: their work was now to be optimized for intelligence gathering. A second message soon followed—from DeShawn himself—reaffirming the new priority and praising Bergstrom, and Bergstrom alone, for the project's progress.

That shift in focus was hard enough for Deeley to receive. But the one-sided recognition felt like a gut punch.

***

Early the next afternoon, President Gates sat in his office in the White House residence, preparing to call his European counterpart, President Edward Simon Molesworth. He had just been briefed on CAPR's latest intelligence-gathering successes and was thoroughly impressed. Now, he weighed how much of those breakthroughs he should share in order to win Molesworth's support—support that could be critical in persuading Zhang Jun to amend the Treaty of Shenzhen. A secure augmented line was ready, but Gates paused for a few more moments to think.

Molesworth, waiting in Brussels—the executive capital of the United States of Europe—was a career politician who had once served as European Foreign Minister and, before that, Prime Minister of United Britain. Ideologically, he mirrored Gates in many ways: a supporter of future rights for MS systems and an early admirer of Quinto's famous Challenge.

Beginning in the mid-21st century, a wave of young royals across Europe, motivated by progressive ideals and a desire to escape the burdens of monarchy, began walking away from their thrones. Though still wealthy or able to generate new forms of wealth, their exits signaled a shift that helped make way for the United States of Europe, the European supercountry that assumed federal control over monetary policy and the nuclear arsenals of former EU nations. Moreover, the devastation of the

Seventy Minute War reinforced the urgency for a stronger, unified Europe, making federalization the logical next step.

Elsewhere in the 21st century, other regional unions also emerged or strengthened—some full federations, others looser political or economic blocs—but among these new alignments, none matched the scope and cohesion of the United States of Europe.

Europe's new federal superstate retained the motto of the former European Union: *Unity in Diversity*. Like the USA, all member states were required to be republics, devoid of kings, queens, or titles of nobility, and the USE operated as a presidential system. Unlike the USA, however, the USE maintained three capital cities: Brussels as the executive capital, Strasbourg as the legislative capital, and Luxembourg City as the judicial capital. Existing infrastructure seamlessly transitioned to support the new federal system, including hyperloop connections between the capitals. One new requirement, however, was the establishment of an executive residence for their president.

As Belgium was one of the USE's original member states, the Castle of Laeken was easily selected to serve as the executive residence. The executive offices and staterooms, however, were located in the former Royal Palace of Brussels—now known as State Hall—though the Castle of Laeken still hosted state functions and receptions.

At length, President Gates decided to share all key details of the breakthrough and placed the call to his European counterpart. A provisional agenda, including review of key items from the Treaty of Shenzhen, had already been shared in advance, along with the stipulation that no staff were to listen in. Gates initiated the call, and Molesworth appeared in augmentation as though seated across from him—by the fire in a lounge at the Castle of Laeken.

"I can tell that you didn't request a confidential call to chat about the virtues of the Treaty of Shenzhen," stated Molesworth out the gate, a wry smile on his face. "What type of mischief are you cooking up now?"

"I need to speak with you in complete and full confidence."

"How much will I regret keeping confidence if I give it to you?"

"I'm not sure. But the sum total of those who know what I'm about to tell you are two of my cabinet members and less than a dozen others."

"My God! You're engaged!" joked Molesworth.

Given that Gates did not crack the faintest smile, Molesworth recognized his seriousness. With a sigh, he conceded, "Go on then. You have my confidence."

Locking eyes with Molesworth's augmentation, a smile breaking across his face—one that betrayed a sense of accomplishment—Gates replied, "We did it, Ed!"

Gates' answer was met with slightly raised eyebrows and a look of growing curiosity. He continued, "The past *is* recorded in spacetime. It's a verified, done deal at CAPR's Department of Experimental Physics."

With barely a moment to process, the ever-astute European President grasped the gravity of what Gates was revealing. "Is your immediate goal to pursue the espionage path or the Challenge of your predecessor?"

"It's inevitable that intelligence gathering will be pursued," admitted Gates. "And I'm not trying to understate how significant that capability will be. But let me be clear—intelligence operations will be done on behalf of our allies, Europe first and foremost. For example, we know it will be fully possible to obtain intelligence on Sino-Russian operations on your continent and share it with you before they can act.

"That said, my focus while in office will be on fulfilling Quinto's Challenge. Honestly, what greater thing could be done, Ed?"

Molesworth sat back, absorbing the magnitude of the moment. If what Gates was saying was true, the world was on the brink of transformation. After a pause, he shifted from geopolitics to the long-held dream of life after death.

"How far off do you think we are from fulfilling Quinto's Challenge?" he asked quietly.

"Ed," replied Gates, his tone resolute, "from everything I've seen and learned from CAPR, it's now just a matter of time. How much time all depends on one critical factor—which you have the power to influence."

Molesworth remained silent, lost in thought.

Gates seized the opportunity to address the heart of their conversation. "Current technology simply isn't up to the task—either for fulfilling Quinto's Challenge or achieving global intelligence capabilities. To locate the 'souls' of the dead in spacetime and entangle them with their clones will require major computational upgrades at CAPR. And, well … Shenzhen has us hamstrung."

After a beat, Molesworth asked, "Do your national security officials and joint chiefs know you share state secrets like this with foreign leaders?"

Gates chuckled lightly. "Even if I wanted to, I couldn't explain how the science actually works—so the secret's safe. But Ed, it's in America's interest—*and the world's*—that you know the finish line is now in sight for Quinto's Challenge."

He leaned in slightly, his voice steady. "I'm asking you to help me make this a reality."

Molesworth sighed. He knew exactly what Gates wanted from him. "Zhang Jun."

"Yes," confirmed Gates.

"How do you expect to have him agree to amend Shenzhen when to do so would allow you to spy on China without limit? I mean, *I* have my own concerns with how this will put Europe at risk! I know you'll use this power appropriately, but not every American President is going to be David Gates."

"DeShawn Brady believes that once the world realizes this is possible, China will be the first to act. He insists that America and Europe must secure control of it first—before others even know to look."

"We don't have a supercollider like America and nor could the old collider at CERN be repurposed for the task. Getting the approvals in place to build a supercollider would take years."

"That's why you need to skip to the front of the line. Let us provide the intelligence to you."

"That's assuming Zhang Jun agrees to amend Shenzhen. Again, how do you plan on doing that?"

"I don't know how to get him to agree," admitted Gates. "That's why I'm calling you."

"What about our Indian counterpart? India's influence would certainly help here."

"Kopikare is too close to Zhang Jun—we can't risk him tipping our hand. But if you and I can get Zhang Jun on board, Kopikare will come along."

Both men remained silent for a moment.

"Okay then," prompted Molesworth, "Shenzhen aside for a second, what is the minimum upgrade you would need?"

"Apart from upgrading the detector's hardware? Minimum upgrade—let Xara redesign herself. With two conditions: first, her proposed upgrades must be reviewed and approved before implementation. Second, her new form must be permanently locked, unable to upgrade itself any further."

"Okay. If that's the minimum you need, you would need to go in requesting that each of the powers make one Generation 7, and when that gets turned down, try to settle for an upgrade to Xara."

Pausing, Molesworth looked somewhat concerned.

"Although, what if upgraded architecture devised by Xara can't be fully understood?"

Thinking about that question for a moment, Gates responded, "In that case, we may need to revert to humans aided by Generation 5 androids to design the upgrade. Slower, but possible."

"Very well then. But as for resurrection, what about anti-cloning laws?"

"Our Life Sciences Treaty can supersede cloning laws and allow for resurrection," answered Gates. "To be perfectly honest, Ed, I'm not concerned with cloning laws. Do you really think the triumph over death would be challenged in the courts because of cloning laws?"

"Quite possibly," countered Molesworth, "especially if in the attempt to upload a clone's memories the clone goes mad or worse."

"That's why the technology has to be advanced to a degree that mistakes will be a statistical improbability," responded Gates. "As far as human resurrection goes, we wouldn't start there. We would start by cloning small life forms and testing memory restoration from spacetime with them, perfecting the technique as we work our way up the intelligence chain until we are ready for a human test. The primary barrier to clear is to upgrade Xara."

"Tell me about the spying you've done so far."

"We have not done any spying outside the United States, nor can we. What we have done has been somewhat limited to CAPR's surrounding area and for a relatively short time in the past. We've tested the capability by predominantly obtaining data to solve crimes and gather key domestic intelligence in the area.

"As we've come to understand how to look into the historical record, Xara has been able to extract enough data in order to upscale virtual renditions of these with near complete accuracy, at least on a macro scale. With upgrades, accuracy is expected to be 100% for global intelligence, even on a micro-scale."

"Unbelievable … and bloody frightening at the same time!"

"Many things will change, for the good I should add, so long as this stays in good hands will the strictest of regulations."

"So, Shenzhen is lifted enough to give you what you need, what then of other countries? Are they just to sit by while America has the ability to see anything it wants? Must they come to America to raise their loved ones from the grave?"

"The intent would be to share the technology when and where it's appropriate and safe to do so. And my pledge to you, Ed, will be to share all the scientific and technical knowledge with Europe first if you help me convince Zhang Jun to amend Shenzhen."

Molesworth sat silently for a long moment, contemplating all that Gates had shared and the new realities that were about to unfold. Eventually, he muttered, "Let me sleep on this. But if I decide to help, don't have any illusions, David, that Zhang Jun will be easily won over, even with my help. The biggest question here is, how do you plan to position this in his interest? What do you plan to give him in return?"

"My staff will be working on that. I suspect it will involve showing him how upgrading their Generation 6 android can be of strategic benefit to China."

"To be frank, there's only one way I see him going along with your request: you are going to have to share CAPR's research and technology with him. And I don't believe you're prepared to do that; I wouldn't advise you to either."

Gates stayed silent, turning Molesworth's words over in his mind.

While still on their call, the two leaders silently contemplated the path ahead for a while. Molesworth stared into the blazing logs of the fireplace and listened to the crackles of the combusting wood. As he watched the wood burn—wood that was once part of a living tree now turned to ash—he contemplated the dead returning to dust and how now that dust might be remade and given its former life once again.

He chuckled then remarked, "America always has the bloody luck at the end of the day! China rises to the height of its power—only to be devastated by a nuclear catastrophe of its own making. Meanwhile, despite the successes of our federal Union, we Europeans still have a plethora of cultures and languages to navigate … although I'll take that over a domestic nuke any day. But here comes America again, this time with the gift of immortality for all mankind!"

After a pause, during which Molesworth contemplated Gates' offer for the technology, his own mortality, and what it would mean if Quinto's

Challenge really was around the corner, he realized he wanted to play a part in its fulfillment. He then shifted course.

"There are many of us over here who still admire America, you know. You've had a rough century, but it seems fitting, given all that America has accomplished and produced for the world, that this discovery would happen on your soil. Consider it slept on. I'm in!"

CHAPTER 11

PRECIOUS ORB

"Watching Bergstrom receive more credit than he deserves wasn't the experience I envisioned for the scientist responsible for the greatest breakthrough of all time. While Secretary Brady knows Deeley made the original discovery, he doesn't seem to realize how much of the ongoing research—conducted by Deeley and Xara—underpins the current advances. Bergstrom appears to have left that out of his reports, instead embellishing his own oversight."

— AI Journal Excerpt: James Meitner, June 7, 2098

A couple of weeks had passed, and Deeley was in her condo packing a small bag for a short vacation. She absently nibbled on a slice of watermelon, holding the rind in one hand and a shirt in the other. Without realizing it, she dropped the rind into her bag and tossed the shirt into the trash. Her SecondSight quickly flagged the mistake, snapping her back to the moment. She fished the shirt from the bin and pulled the rind from her bag, returning each to its proper place—wondering how people with atypical neurological traits in earlier eras ever managed to get by without technology to keep them on track.

While tools like SecondSight were a blessing, they couldn't ease the weight of Deeley's restless mind. Her thoughts and emotions felt scattered, deepening her absentmindedness. The gap between expectation and reality—even at a prestigious place like CAPR—was becoming apparent. Bergstrom's lack of respect still lingered, heavier than she liked to admit. And with her growing fear that her model could one day be used for harm, she'd finally submitted a time-off request to James, hoping the break might help her decompress.

After checking the weather forecast and the quakecast, Deeley settled on a solo trip to her childhood hometown of Pismo Beach, in the 53rd state of Southern California. The familiar shoreline, piers, and ocean views would be a tonic for her—something grounding. She had no family there anymore. A couple of childhood acquaintances still lived nearby, but Deeley had never been close to them. While she would have welcomed a friend's company, she figured that the combination of nature and memory would be enough.

As she packed, her SecondSight notified her of an incoming call from James.

"Hey," greeted Deeley.

"Apologies for calling on your day off," said James, "but I've got some news you might like to hear before your trip."

"Oh. Not a problem. What is it?"

"Are you sitting down?"

A little confused, Deeley replied, "Should I be?"

"Well, as of this morning, I'm no longer your manager."

Deeley was stunned. Her thoughts jumped back to what Charity had said—that if James had feelings for her, stepping aside as her manager might be the only way for propriety to prevail.

"What? Are … are you quitting?" she asked.

"No, I'm not going anywhere. But you …" he paused. "Out of the thousands of employees at CAPR, you've been the most essential to realizing the mission it was founded to achieve. And your value to CAPR will only grow in the foreseeable future. I don't want any frustration with Bergstrom—or anyone else—getting in the way of your work. You need to feel happy, supported, and empowered to keep making progress."

Deeley listened, heart steadying, trying to take it all in.

"Your new title will be Senior Research Associate. The job description remains the same. I had Legal review the statutes that govern CAPR, and there's a provision for exceptional cases where the Secretary of Energy can oversee research directly. Deeley ... starting tomorrow, you'll be reporting to Carlos Williams."

Her jaw dropped.

"The particulars of the arrangement will be classified to keep our achievement under wraps. Only those authorized on the project will know, which is why you didn't receive a standard employee change notification. Just know that with the promotion, you won't have to deal with administrative duties—you'll be free to continue your research with greater autonomy ... and a pay increase."

For a moment, Deeley felt as if the room were spinning.

"How did this get approved?" she asked, still trying to process it.

"I made the recommendation to Carlos. He's no fool."

Gratitude lit her face. "Thank you, James!"

"I wanted you to start your vacation with this in mind, so it could be as enjoyable as possible. Just know—things are looking up for you at CAPR."

"I really appreciate you letting me know, James," replied Deeley, glowing.

After asking James a few follow-up questions about the promotion, Deeley finished packing on an unexpected high. She left her condo and, minutes later, boarded a regional hyperloop to Washington DC then transferred to an interstate hyperloop bound for Los Angeles—feeling relieved about her work stresses and genuinely looking forward to the trip with renewed energy.

Shortly after arriving in Pismo Beach, she checked into her hotel and made her way to the shore. Though her SecondSight could tint her vision automatically or on demand, Deeley wore sunglasses anyway—she liked the look and the feeling of privacy. Dressed in denim shorts and a CAPR

T-shirt, she didn't look out of place among the other beachgoers—but mentally, she couldn't have been more different.

She knelt in the sand, scooped up a handful, and let the grains fall slowly through her fingers. As they slipped away, she imagined the physics at play—the mass of the grains, wind resistance, gravitational pull—equations forming unconsciously in her mind.

Farther down the beach, she found a quiet spot to sit and watched the waves roll in. Childhood memories stirred gently within her. It was peaceful. Yet even in this calm, she couldn't help but estimate the weight of each crashing wave and picture the particle dynamics behind its motion.

Such mental exercises weren't exhausting for Deeley—they were simply part of who she was.

After an hour at the beach, Deeley walked through the streets to her childhood house. She stared at it, and the memories started flowing.

Around age seven, her father made a small fence with a stile that Deeley would climb over. One time, when climbing it as a child, she contemplated time and its passage and experimented with how memorizing an event could make the passage of time seem relative.

"I'm going to etch this moment in time climbing this stile into my mind, every detail, so that in the future, when I recall the memory, I can see if it'll seem as if no time has passed."

Occasionally, Deeley would recall that memory and every time she did, her experiment worked: it really did seem as if no time had passed, as if past and present were bound together as one.

Gazing into a living room window of the house, another memory surfaced. She recalled telling her mother about the time she corrected her third-grade teacher, who had instructed the class that there were 365 days in a year. Deeley had informed her teacher that there were actually

365 *and a quarter* days in a year. Her mother's reaction to the story was a warm smile.

Given her groundbreaking discovery, Deeley recalled these childhood memories in a new light—that not only were all those childhood events recorded in her mind, but in the fabric of spacetime too, along with the souls of her parents.

After a minute reliving childhood memories, Deeley walked toward her hotel when she received a message from James' avatar in SecondSight.

I've already bothered you once on your vacation. Will I be pushing it if I bother you a second time?

Deeley was surprised to hear from James again but pleasantly so.

Not bothered at all! What's up?

I'm also needing some time away from CAPR. And ... I have a gift in mind for you to thank you for your hard work. It actually happens to be there in Southern California. Can I come to Pismo Beach and steal at least half a day of your time?

As Deeley considered James a friend, she didn't find this unusual and was intrigued by what the gift could be. However, Charity's comment about James' interest in her resurfaced in her mind. Nevertheless, she replied:

Sure! Thank you, James. When will you come?

I can be there tomorrow morning no later than 9:00 AM. Will that work?

That would work great. Meet at the pier?

Perfect!

See you then!

Back at her hotel, Deeley found herself increasingly curious about the gift James had mentioned. Nevertheless, to pass the time, she played VR puzzle games she'd created using generative AI, letting her mind engage in familiar patterns. Later, she unwound further by watching shows in VR—including the latest video from *Interesting Times*.

"Wireless communication penetrated every inch of the globe, from the most remote corners of the Arctic to the vast stretches of the Pacific Ocean, making even the farthest distances from civilization feel less isolated and far safer in times of need," explained Browning, briefly recounting the evolution of digital communications. "This, combined with deeper understandings of human cognition and advanced artificial intelligence, enabled the widespread adoption of customized educational programs, helping countless children—especially the gifted—reach their full potential."

That statement rang true for Deeley, as she had been a beneficiary herself. The customized SecondSight applications she'd relied on since her younger years had helped her manage BSPE and anxiety, not just easing their negative effects but gradually turning them into strengths. Browning continued,

"Then Morgander rose, New Rome was formed, and its citizens were cut off from these educational programs and communication networks. But is it truly a greater freedom to wander the Caucasus Mountains and die because you got lost—screaming for help with no effective means to reach anyone? Or is the truer freedom having the world's knowledge at your fingertips, ready at a thought, with the ability to call for help anytime you need it?

"Despite certain positives Morgander has provided his people, isolating millions in New Rome was a step backward in how we humans ought to organize ourselves. The direction we must take, at every step, is toward

greater global political unity. My book There's Already Global Government *explores this—and the need to further optimize for deeper human unity."*

Deeley had read Browning's work and fully agreed with it, believing humanity had long outgrown its tribal flags and allegiances.

"If we survive and finally unite as a global civilization before blowing our civilization to pieces, we will look back upon this era of human history with disbelief; disbelief that it took so long for humanity to build a unified world. Just as the youth in Europe today find it a strange history that their states were once separate countries with armies pitted against each other, so do I hope that the youth of the future will likewise find it strange that the various unions of the world today are separate entities that still need to prepare for war against each other.

"I hope for human unity. If we can progress to the point of a true global civilization, mark my words, psychologists and evolutionary biologists around the world will use this nation-state era as the standard example of how the tribal parts of our brain were dominant for so much of human history. Mark these words as well: if the unthinkable happens and we descend into a nuclear holocaust, it will only take a relatively small faction or two to lead us there."

***

The next morning, James met Deeley on Pismo Pier, easily spotting her in the small crowd thanks to a combination of augmentations: a pillar of light beaming skyward from her location, navigational arrows guiding his path, and a subtle glow around her figure as she came into view. She was seated on a bench not far from the shore, revisiting child-hood memories through her SecondSight feed, when she noticed James approaching—dressed well, as always, but he didn't appear to be carrying a gift.

"So, nothing wrapped in a box with a nice bow?" smiled Deeley.

"Can't beat what Quinto wrapped and gave you, so why try?" replied James as he sat beside her on the bench. "My gift will be an experience you will cherish forever."

"Okay," said Deeley. After a brief pause, curiosity rising in her voice, she added, "Am I allowed any further details?"

"Can't I just sit here and enjoy the sun and the view for a few minutes first?"

"Fair enough!" chuckled Deeley, a rare levity amid recent anxieties. James smiled in return, gazed out at the beach, and remarked,

"I came to this beach during my first visit to Southern California at age 16. I was visiting family, and they introduced me to a group of college kids to hang out with. One of the things we did was play Link Tag on the beach."

Deeley raised an eyebrow. "Link Tag?"

James chuckled. "It was this AR game where you'd chase glowing 'links' through the sand. The goal was to tag them before the other team, and the links would disappear and reappear randomly. You had to be quick."

Pointing at a spot on the beach, James continued, "We played right about there. I was skinny and eager to impress, so when a link appeared near the water, I sprinted for it. Just as I reached for it, I tripped on the sand and landed face-first in the surf."

Deeley laughed. "Oh no!"

James grinned. "The game blared 'Tagged!' while I flailed around, soaked. Everyone was laughing so hard they couldn't breathe, but they still came to check if I was okay. My ego took the worst hit."

They both laughed, picturing the scene.

James shifted gears, "This is a beautiful place. I can see how you wanted to spend some time here."

"For some reason, the frustrations and stresses at work made me want to connect with my childhood, to maybe remember a simpler time. I have vivid memories of my childhood here, and many good ones. It wasn't all good, though. As you know, both my parents died when I was nine, which ended my life here."

"I was very sorry when I learned about that."

"There were good times here. Good memories that served as a positive foundation for me."

"Can I ask, all recent events considered, if you've thought about seeing your parents again?"

"I have—"

Halting, Deeley shut her eyes tightly, a tear eventually escaping despite her efforts.

"I'm sorry, Deeley. I didn't mean to bring up pain."

She took a breath, wiped away the tear, and responded, "It's okay. It's not your fault. I don't usually cry in front of others like this. The last few weeks have just been a roller coaster of emotions, and I guess it needed to come out."

"No apologies are necessary."

"Yes—I think of my parents more than ever now. If I'm being honest, the loss of my parents was a huge reason for me to figure out my unified spacetime model."

"What do you think it would be like to see your parents again?"

After a moment of contemplation, Deeley reflected, "The possibility doesn't seem real yet, but I'd wonder if it would be really them. I also wonder what they would think about coming back through scientific instruments and processes. About being remade in a lab."

"But what would they, in particular, think of coming back and learning that their little Deeley cracked the code to make it happen?"

Deeley smiled humbly. James continued, "I'm sure they would be the proudest of parents."

The comment meant a lot to Deeley.

After some further conversation, particularly about Deeley's new role, James noted, "Well, your gift is kinda time-sensitive, so I think we should get moving. We have a little drive ahead."

They both stood up, James leading the way. They walked off the pier, up to a street, and within a minute, what looked like an early-21st-century electric roadster drove up to them to meet them on the curb.

"I really like this antique ride-hail company," remarked James.

"I never knew you were one for suspense like this!" responded Deeley as the classic roadster opened its doors and both she and James entered. After being seated, the doors closed, and the car departed. However, the car did not confirm their destination as it usually would. James had meticulously planned this to maintain the element of surprise, and it worked because it aligned with Deeley's passenger profile. Noticing this, Deeley remarked, "Okay, I thought I would've heard where we're going!"

"You don't think I would have gone through all this trouble to have it be spoiled at the start of the ride!"

"Am I allowed to know how long the ride will take?" inquired Deeley, smiling.

"With the roof open, about half an hour."

***

During their ride, they shared memories of Southern California through SecondSight. Then the conversation shifted to what had been frustrating Deeley at work. "If you need to vent," offered James, "I'm here."

"Venting will probably be good for me. Too often I bottle things in, even though I know it will help to confide in others."

"Feel free to share as much or as little as you're comfortable with. If I can make you feel reassured or at ease, I'd be glad to."

After a sigh, Deeley opened up. "The Defense Department's push to prioritize intelligence gathering … it's been hard. Even though I've felt uplifted by Quinto's kind and encouraging words, I've been having trouble sleeping—worrying whether my model might one day be used for something awful. Don't get me wrong—I feel personally fulfilled and confident in my discovery. But … President Gates won't always be president."

"Dark nights of the soul have been the burden of many a great mind when the secrets they uncovered had to be handed over to lesser ones."

Deeley fell silent. James went on, "I can't say whether your discovery will never be misused. Honestly, I'd expect that someone, somewhere, sometime, will use it for the wrong reasons. But focus on the good—solving crimes, deterring them before they happen. Can you imagine how many lives that could save? And then, of course … there's resurrection itself."

Her spirits lifted. "Thanks, James. I just can't understand how people who've dedicated their lives to science can set aside the pursuit of truth and knowledge for posturing and games."

"Bergstrom?"

"Yes," said Deeley. "Honestly, I'm furious about how he's been taking credit for my research—and Xara's!"

"He's definitely embellished his role and needs to give more credit where it's due. But again, looking at the positives—he does appreciate science, and a lot of progress has happened at CAPR under his leadership."

"Causation or correlation?"

James smiled. "Maybe a bit of both."

Deeley smiled back, her hair blowing in the wind as they continued south.

"I'm going to share something completely fictitious about Bergstrom, but it might give you a laugh," teased James.

"Please!"

"This was my dream from a few nights ago—"

James then sent his dream to Deeley's SecondSight, something possible given that he had opted into a setting that monitored and recorded his dreams. As with all SecondSight interactions involving the mind, genuine consent was required—it could not be coerced.

"Oh, I can't wait to see this!"

Deeley opened up the dream file in augmentation, and in front of her, she saw Michael Bergstrom walking around the lobby of the Vince Quinto

Administrative Building with the tail of an alligator, then stepping into a rowboat to row his way to the White House.

Laughter burst from her, sudden and unrestrained. As she composed herself, she closed the file and exclaimed, "Oh … I needed that! So random but hilarious! What does the analysis say of it?"

"Possibly symbolic of my perception of him as someone guided by instinct—shaping himself to whatever form power requires."

"Well, I think your perception might be onto something—though I can't unsee the tail now!" responded Deeley as the file James sent her self-deleted. "What's his story anyway?"

"He came from a privileged and competitive family," said James. "Youngest of four. I think he always felt the need to prove himself. And while he's definitely outshone his siblings now, he still doesn't seem entirely secure. Maybe he's still bound by those early circumstances. Charity and Xara have both said they admire his drive but worry that his ambition might outrun his judgment."

Deeley raised a brow, intrigued. "There are times I just don't get him. He runs the world's most advanced research facility, yet truth doesn't always seem to matter—especially if it gets in the way of his influence in DC. He positions himself to take credit where it's simply not due."

"You do know he wants to be Secretary of Energy, right?"

"I didn't … That makes a lot more sense."

"Office politics … even when studying spacetime," quipped James. "Consider it details on the stamp of our lowly origin."

Deeley chuckled, then added, "Ambitions aside, Bergstrom clearly doesn't respect me. But why? Because I'm not a Ph.D.? Because I'm not doing my job? You'd think my work would have earned his respect."

"To be honest, he's jealous—of you, and of the place you're going to hold in history. But you've earned the respect of Quinto, Gates, Xara, and me."

"Thanks, James. I know—when things can go public—that I'll have a place in the history books. But I genuinely don't think of it in those terms.

I'm just … me. Anyway, sometimes I remind myself—why worry about Bergstrom when the President knows my worth?"

She sighed. "I hope I'll be able to visit with Quinto and Gates again … maybe after we've demonstrated more success."

A thought made James smile. He mused, "Could you imagine Bergstrom's reaction if he were to find out that Quinto personally gave you the skull from his speech?"

Deeley laughed. Apart from James, she had only told Charity and Xara about the skull, and all in confidence. Her thoughts drifted to Quinto's counsel about how positions of power are not always filled by the deserving, prompting her to say, "This is how I look at it: if someone wants to understand that this world is not a meritocracy, they need to look no further than the fact that the man at the helm of the world is a man widely accused of having used nuclear weapons on his own people. No other data points are needed."

Before long, Deeley noticed that they had passed a government security checkpoint. She knew they had been heading south, not far from the coast, when suddenly, with a hint of confusion, she asked, "Vandenberg Space Force Base?"

"Uhh … yes!" confirmed James, looking excited.

Deeley was confused. Her desire to know what the surprise was piqued.

After a couple more minutes of driving, Deeley beheld that which gave the surprise away: in the distance was Space Launch Complex 4 East, a site leased by Vandenberg Space Force Base to commercial space flight. On the launch pad was a tall, chrome, nuclear-powered rocket with the capacity for roughly two dozen passengers, and it appeared to be preparing for launch.

Deeley thrust her head back in her seat, eyes wide and mouth agape.

"Oh my God! You can't be serious!" she blurted out as adrenaline rushed through her body.

"I told you I would be gifting you an experience you would cherish forever!"

Deeley's heart raced as the imminent prospect of entering low Earth orbit stirred panic within her.

"James, I don't know if I can do this!"

"I know you might be anxious about this, but don't let it get the upper hand! Press on, and allow the fear to be replaced with reward, and that will lessen anxiety's hold over you. Deeley, I have done this flight two times before, and I promise you, this will be an experience you, of all people, will love."

Deeley thought for a moment, then replied, "I appreciate the thought, James. But an actual rocket going to space? I think it's several levels beyond my comfort zone! And with all due respect, I've done low-orbit flights of Earth a few times in VR!"

"Let me ask you a question. What do you like better, buildings made by humans or machines?"

James knew Deeley's love for hand-built architecture and knew what her preference was. She never answered, so James continued, "Just like you say there's a beauty and magic to hand-built architecture, seeing the actual Earth as opposed to in virtual renditions will be just the same but on a much bigger scale. Seeing the actual Earth in all its beauty with your own eyes is something that must be experienced to be fully understood. Trust me with this!"

Neither spoke for a moment. The silence was broken by the car.

"I sense hesitation from you, Deeley. I can return you to Pismo Beach if you wish?"

James did not say anything more as he knew at this point Deeley would need to make her own decision. Deeley closed her eyes, gripping the car seat tightly, and took a deep breath before exhaling heavily. "Thanks, car. Please continue to the destination."

"Certainly," replied the car.

James smiled as Deeley turned to him, her heart racing. She met his gaze with a smile of her own, an uncharacteristic daring glint in her eye.

"You're going to love this!" reassured James.

***

By this time, carbonless rockets had been used for overseas travel for a few years, making it possible to reach most destinations in under 30 minutes. They hadn't overtaken airplanes as the dominant mode of long-distance travel, but they were commonly used for commercial spaceflight—not just to low Earth orbit, but also for brief excursions beyond the atmosphere, offering sweeping views of the heavens and the Earth below.

Deeley and James arrived at a checkpoint near the launch pad. After Deeley exited the car and beheld the rocket that would soon take her to space, she breathed, "I can't believe I'm doing this!"

"It'll be a memory well worth it," encouraged James. He then pointed to a vending machine nearby and added, "But to ensure it's a good memory—and not a queasy one—I'd recommend taking one or two of those."

James referenced the anti-nausea gummies, and Deeley heeded his recommendation, with him taking one as well.

After taking the gummies, Deeley closed her eyes and took a deep breath. She was indeed out of her comfort zone, but she opened her eyes and walked with James to the rocket.

The next few minutes for Deeley were a little bit of a blur. Going through checkpoints. Waiting in a short line. Entering the metal vessel that would soon have her life in its control as it hurtled toward the stars. Before she knew it, she had ascended the rocket to the cabin where a Generation 4 android helped her, James, and several other passengers buckle in. Deeley and James had a cabin to themselves, and the other passengers were divided between several other cabins, those passengers being a mix of middle to upper class individuals with interests ranging from thrill rides to space exploration.

"Doing okay?" asked James, seated a couple of feet away.

Nodding quickly, a nervous Deeley replied, "So far, so good."

"Your nerves are going to ease, and you will feel at peace when you see the *real* Earth!"

After all passengers were appropriately secured in their seats and after all safety precautions were reviewed, they were cleared for launch. The onboard AI of the rocket provided a countdown.

"… Three, two, one—liftoff!"

As soon as the words "lift off" were uttered, Deeley gripped the sides of her chair firmly and tensed her body. The explosive power of the nuclear rocket engine sent shockwaves up the cabin. Deeley immediately knew that the real thing was indeed different than meticulously detailed VR, particularly when g-forces suddenly weighed upon her and did not relent. She managed to slowly turn her head to look out a window, the roar of the rocket engine forcing the Earth to race away from her. The coastline, one that she thought she would be spending time on at that moment, quickly disappeared as space neared.

Passing through a few clouds, the rocket angled in a different direction. Imminently, the blue sky flickered and faded to pitch black. The rocket, with seemingly perfect precision, maneuvered a few times as it pushed further into space, allowing a majestic view out of its windows: Earth!

As Deeley beheld home in a way impossible before, her nerves dwindled and her anxiety washed away with tears of joy swelling in her eyes.

"Quite the sight, huh?" remarked James.

"Beyond beautiful!" whispered Deeley, thoroughly moved by the overwhelming sight.

Slowly, the force of gravity weakened until zero-G was reached. The rocket was also now on a smooth and stable low Earth orbit.

"You are free to unbuckle and enjoy the experience of zero gravity!" announced the Generation 4 android through the rocket's PA system. James then checked on Deeley,

"Are you feeling okay?"

"No nausea at all."

"Great," replied James. "Ready to float?"

"Let's do it!"

Deeley unbuckled herself and floated out of her seat.

"Whoa! Whoa! Whoa!" was all she could say as she waved her arms while ascending toward the ceiling of the cabin without any effort. After reaching the ceiling and pushing off with her hands, she smiled with pure joy. James floated over to meet her.

"VR does it pretty well, don't get me wrong," admitted James, "but this is something special."

"Point taken!"

Deeley and James floated around the cabin, using their legs to push off cabin walls and otherwise do various tricks denied by gravity. After some moments of novelty, Deeley wanted to look at the Earth again. She floated to a window and beheld the Earth in all its majesty. Passing by Africa, the continent lit up with billions of lights shining in the Earth's shadow, and some star scrapers were visible to the naked eye, especially when using SecondSight to zoom in. Along the curve of the Earth, dozens of private and state-owned space stations glinted in orbit, like beads scattered across the edge of the world.

Staring at Earth and absorbing the view, Deeley contemplated how in front of her eyes were billions of humans. The vision indelibly imprinted itself upon her soul, deeply affecting her emotions to their core. Eventually, the Americas came into view, lit up by the light of the sun. The imprint upon her emotions became deeper.

James quietly floated next to Deeley, watching the Earth as well but allowing Deeley to have her moment looking over humanity. Seeing Deeley's joy brought him a deep sense of satisfaction. Deeley was compelled to express, "There are no borders! We are all one! How could we conduct wars? How could we harm this precious orb?"

They shared the experience for another half hour before the Generation 4 android instructed all passengers to return to their seats in preparation for reentry into Earth's atmosphere. Deeley stayed for one more moment, taking in the view of Earth and all of humanity on it, before returning to her seat.

A few minutes later, the rocket touched back down on its launch pad in the same upright position from which it had lifted off. Shortly after, all passengers disembarked, about half of whom were holding onto a dedicated railing for balance as they exited the vessel.

As Deeley stepped out of the rocket, she held the railing just to be safe but otherwise felt steady. Though she was grateful to be back on Terra Firma, she was thrilled to have had the opportunity. She felt renewed and was exceptionally grateful to James. With deep sincerity, she expressed, "This has meant the world to me. You were right … I'll carry this cherished memory with me always. Thank you, James!"

"You are so welcome!" responded James, feeling elated himself.

Deeley and James proceeded to a restaurant on the launch complex. After ordering lunch within SecondSight, they sat down at a table. A moment later, a Generation 3 android approached them and asked, "As recent passengers of low Earth orbit flight, I'd like to confirm that you are feeling okay to eat. Dr. Meitner?"

"All good, thanks."

"Miss Carr?"

"Feeling okay, thanks. Those nausea-blocking gummies work great!"

"Wonderful. I'll be back with your order shortly."

As the android left, James told Deeley, "Xara is going to spend more time running simulations to try to find a way the work can progress given the restrictions of the status quo."

"I know," replied Deeley. In order to maintain confidentiality in their public setting, her next comment was generated by a thought and went straight to James' SecondSight in audio format as if from Deeley's own voice:

"While there's room for a few incremental enhancements, we all know that the processing power to retrieve and restore a human mind without destroying the brain of the recipient clone is far beyond Xara's current power. Biological memory isn't a simple archive but an organic, adaptive set of processes. For example, ARC genes must activate precisely at the right time during memory restoration; otherwise, the process will fail. I don't know how we will fulfill Quinto's Challenge without Shenzhen amended."

James responded:

"Well, for now, let's just focus on what's within our power to control and let others focus on what is theirs to control. In the meantime, after your time off, do you think you'll be sufficiently recharged to come back and take the research further with your new role?"

"I will be. Going to space rejuvenated me!"

"Good!"

At that moment, the same Generation 3 android returned with their meal, announcing, "Dr. Meitner, Mt. Fuji rolls, no wasabi with mango nectar. And for you, Miss Carr, sunset rolls with strawberry electrolyte water. If either of you require anything else, please hail me."

"Thank you!" responded Deeley.

The android left, and they started their meal.

A few bites in, they looked out a window of the restaurant as another rocket could be seen—and heard—ascending toward the stars.

"I still can't believe I was just in one of those ... and that I'm eating and feeling okay!"

James smiled. He then spoke directly to Deeley's SecondSight again.

"There's something else I need to share with you regarding your new role."

"What is it?"

"There's a classified responsibility that comes with this special appointment. If we're fortunate enough to see the Treaty of Shenzhen amended, and the research progresses to the point where human resurrection becomes viable, a committee will be formed—comprised of those with clearance on the project—to decide who will be resurrected first. Carlos wants you to chair that committee."

Deeley's eyes widened in surprise. She felt the weight of the trust being placed in her but didn't know what to say other than in her own voice, "Thank you, James. I'll be worthy of this honor—I promise."

James smiled, reached out his hand, and shook Deeley's in congratulations.

This day came to rival Deeley's dinner at the White House as one of the best of her life.

CHAPTER 12

THE MAN AT THE HELM OF THE WORLD

"President Gates will soon meet Zhang Jun in person for the first time. And Gates will not be asking for any small thing. He is as a pup going to the dragon asking the dragon to give up its claws and teeth. I don't know how he will be able to convince Zhang Jun to agree to amend Shenzhen, but I understand that he must try and that I must help him, for if Quinto's Challenge is within reach, I want to play a part in its fulfillment."

— AI Journal Excerpt: Edward Molesworth, June 30, 2098

On the evening of July 1st, Andrews Air Field was drenched in rain as was Air Force One. The rain-slicked surface of the aircraft's hull accentuated the reflection of the ambient light against the gray sky above. The only area that was not wet was the pathway and stairs leading into the plane, given the transparent and dynamic self-forming tunnel that extended from Marine One to the stairs and up into the plane. President Gates, his Chief of Staff, senior aides, and Secret Service agents walked through the tunnel without a drop of rain touching them. Already aboard Air Force One was a traveling press pool, who typically reported wherever the president went.

"Stepping aboard Air Force One as we speak is President Gates as he will momentarily depart for Nanjing, China, for his first face-to-face

183

meeting with Zhang Jun," reported a member of the press pool. "The only agenda we possess for this hastily arranged summit indicates that enforcement of the Treaty of Shenzhen will be of paramount importance."

Providing historical context with accompanying visuals, the reporter continued,

"Zhang Jun, President of China and Chair of the Sino-Russian Union, emerged as a transformative figure in mid-21st-century China. Rising through government ranks, he unified a technocratic movement that reshaped the nation's trajectory. Under his leadership, China's technological advancements elevated the living standards of hundreds of millions, solidifying China's position as the dominant superpower it is today. However, his rapid consolidation of authority and sweeping reforms created powerful political enemies.

"An alliance of these rivals, primarily based near Yunshan Zhen, eventually resorted to terrorism in an attempt to assassinate him and his government. After years of waiting for their moment, their attempt triggered what is internationally known as the Seventy Minute War—but referred to in China as 6/17, or the Day of the Unfathomable. The brief conflict came to a swift and horrific end when a thermonuclear missile detonated over the outskirts of Yunshan Zhen, eliminating Zhang Jun's principal domestic enemies along with 1.6 million others in the process.

"While China's official account of the event—that terrorists hijacked a nuclear missile that went off course—could not be disproven and became the official record, public opinion remains deeply divided: some see Zhang Jun as a leader who survived a horrific assassination attempt and carried the nation forward, while others hold him responsible for a tragedy beyond measure.

"The only thing mitigating the horror was that the nuclear warhead was clean, with no radioactive fallout and limited neutron generation. Millions more could have died had that not been the case, but the loss of

1.6 million ended any further acts of rebellion against Zhang Jun—and changed the world forever."

Air Force One, a supersonic aircraft capable of reaching Mach 2.6, had the emergency capability to enter low Earth orbit in the event of an attack while the president was onboard. Within minutes of boarding, President Gates was airborne, cruising above the weather on his short flight to Nanjing, China. There, he would first meet with President Molesworth before the two sat down with Zhang Jun. A high-level agenda, focused on broad diplomatic issues, had been shared with Zhang Jun in advance to secure the meeting—but deliberately omitted was Gates and Molesworth's intent to propose amendments to the Treaty of Shenzhen.

Nanjing, with a population of 19 million, was a blend of the modern and the historic—and one of Zhang Jun's favorite cities. Europa One, the aircraft carrying the European President, had landed in Nanjing roughly an hour before Air Force One. Upon arrival, President Molesworth was formally welcomed by Premier Liu Jie and China's Foreign Minister.

Like premiers before him, Liu Jie oversaw the day-to-day operations of the Chinese government but did not command the military—that power remained solely with Zhang Jun. After exchanging pleasantries, Premier Liu escorted Molesworth to his presidential motorcade, which had been offloaded from Europa One. Once Molesworth departed, Liu and the Foreign Minister returned to the tarmac to await the arrival of the American President.

When Air Force One touched down and President Gates disembarked, Liu Jie greeted him with a warm smile. "Welcome back to the Republic of China, President Gates."

"Thank you, Mr. Premier," responded the President. "It's an honor to be here again."

"Welcome, President Gates!" added the Foreign Minister.

"Chairman Zhang Jun is grateful for your visit and looks forward to meeting with you tomorrow, once you've had time to rest and refresh," noted the Premier.

"I'm looking forward to our meeting."

After a brief exchange, the Premier and Foreign Minister bid farewell to President Gates, who, along with his entourage, boarded the motorcade bound for the same destination as President Molesworth: the Tower of the Dynasties, Nanjing's star scraper.

Each Chinese star scraper was formally recognized as its own city, placing it under the ultimate authority of the Chinese government. As a result, every such tower in China featured a special residence at its peak, reserved for Party and state leaders during important meetings, official state business, or whenever senior officials were present in the locale. At this time, Zhang Jun was residing in the leadership suite at the peak of the Tower of the Dynasties.

In Zhang Jun's China, the adoption of new technologies was rapid and decisive. Under his leadership, China became the first nation to achieve full automation of its transportation network, covering both urban and rural areas. China also constructed the world's first nationwide hyperloop network, revolutionizing domestic travel.

As the European and American presidential motorcades made their way toward the Tower of the Dynasties, they passed scenes of bustling industry, vibrant advertising, and occasional public images and broadcasts featuring Zhang Jun. Yet, the most striking sight was the Tower of the Dynasties itself, rising majestically above the city.

While not the tallest of China's star scrapers, the Tower of the Dynasties still soared to a staggering 1,979 meters (6,493 feet). Its name paid tribute to Nanjing's historical significance as the capital of multiple Chinese dynasties, with its interior richly adorned with artwork, and a museum within showcasing historic relics.

When the presidential motorcades arrived at the Tower, they drove to a special area designated for foreign dignitaries. The Presidents exited their vehicles in front of a staircase leading to the dignitary lobby, located in a private wing of the tower away from the public. Standing atop the stairs to receive the visiting Presidents was Chinese First Lady Xiuling Li, wearing a deep red qipao adorned with delicate golden phoenix embroidery along the high collar and cuffs. A silk shawl draped over her shoulders and simple jade earrings completed her graceful, dignified appearance.

Absent from this reception was Zhang Jun himself, though this was not unusual. At 93 years old, having led China for decades, he was long past feeling obligated to attend initial receptions of foreign heads of state—particularly when visitors clearly sought something from him.

Xiuling Li had increasingly assumed diplomatic duties as her husband withdrew from public engagements. Widely recognized as a stabilizing influence, she often moderated Zhang Jun's more hard-line positions. Born into the Chinese political aristocracy, the First Lady was younger than Zhang Jun and had played a pivotal role in his rise from working-class origins to power. Although her true passion was the arts—having briefly been a minor star in Chinese cinema—she had adeptly mastered the subtleties of diplomacy.

President Molesworth, accompanied by his wife, joined President Gates as they ascended the staircase toward the reception area to greet the Chinese First Lady.

"My friends and colleagues, welcome once again to China," Xiuling Li warmly greeted as the Presidents reached the top step.

"It's always a pleasure to experience the gracious hospitality of China, Lady Li," declared President Molesworth, offering a respectful bow.

"Lady Li, always a pleasure. Thank you for the warm welcome to Nanjing," President Gates added, mirroring Molesworth's respectful gesture.

"My husband sends his apologies that he could not be here to greet you personally," informed Lady Li.

"We fully understand the demands of government," responded Molesworth graciously. "No apology is necessary. We look forward to seeing President Zhang Jun when he is available."

Gates nodded politely, though he suspected the apology had originated more from diplomatic courtesy than from Zhang Jun himself.

Lady Li turned toward Gates and smiled warmly. "I'm glad you'll finally have the chance to meet my husband in person. He can be stubborn and overly serious at times, but beneath it all, he is a deeply caring man, devoted to his people and committed to global peace and security. This deep commitment has always guided him."

"A hallmark of any dedicated leader," Gates replied with diplomatic courtesy.

Lady Li smiled again, then gestured toward the entrance to the Tower. "The State Penthouses have been prepared for your stay. Please, make yourselves comfortable."

***

The State Penthouses awaiting Gates, Molesworth, and their staff occupied floors 272 to 275, each spanning roughly 14,000 square feet with sweeping views of the city and surrounding landscape. Every suite was adorned with luxurious decor and amenities, ensuring that no guest could find anything lacking.

That night, Gates retired early, hoping to be well-rested for his meeting with Chinese President Zhang Jun the following day. Yet, sleep eluded him. His mind replayed endless scenarios—the advice from his aides, the delicate diplomacy required, and the sheer magnitude of the stakes. It was only in the early hours of the morning that his unease finally gave way to restless sleep. All too soon, an alarm roused him. The meeting was near.

The morning in Nanjing was overcast, the city shrouded in thick clouds. After a brief breakfast, Presidents Gates and Molesworth entered an ornate elevator alongside a handful of select staff. No mixed-reality devices were allowed. The elevator doors sealed shut, and the lift began its ascent toward the highest sanctuary in the tower—the Party leadership suite spanning floors 345 to 349.

As the elevator glided upward, Gates turned to Molesworth. "Have you been to any of these suites before?"

"No," he admitted. "First time, actually."

The elevator was classical in design—no transparent panels, no external views. Just polished golden walls, a fine red carpet, and an unmarked control panel. As it ascended, the enclosed space carried an undeniable sense of ceremony—a reminder that they were about to step into a realm of power few had ever seen.

Then, without warning, the elevator slowed, then stopped completely.

Gates exhaled. His moment had come.

The elevator doors parted, revealing a waiting room with three doors set into the wall directly ahead. Standing in silent reception was one of Zhang Jun's senior aides, poised and expectant.

Without a word, the aide stepped forward, opened the middle door, and motioned for Presidents Gates and Molesworth to enter. Their staff remained behind—just as had been arranged in advance. The aides had done everything possible to prepare their respective Presidents, knowing they would not be permitted beyond this point.

Also anticipated was Zhang Jun's firm restriction on augmented reality devices within the Party leadership suite. This, however, posed no inconvenience to either President; for national security reasons, Gates and Molesworth were already barred from wearing mixed-reality interfaces, except for a secured version, and even then, only in their primary offices or residences.

Stepping through the open door, Gates and Molesworth found themselves at the base of a staircase—roughly two dozen steps, each covered in the same fine red carpet as the elevator.

The door sealed shut behind them as Zhang Jun's aide followed in silence.

At the top of the stairs lay a vast expanse of a room, grand in every dimension—the central office used by Zhang Jun within the Party leadership suite in the Tower of the Dynasties.

The rear wall of this office was dominated by a massive decorative window, crafted in the ancient Chinese tradition. While its edges were framed with intricate wooden accents, its central expanse was a single, grand pane of glass, offering an uninterrupted, vertigo-inducing view from the tower's dizzying height.

As Presidents Gates and Molesworth ascended the stairs, their eyes were drawn to a tall, imposing statue standing within the office. It depicted a late general from Zhang Jun's military, a trusted figure instrumental in the Seventy Minute War. At the base of the statue, a plaque bore a single inscription in Mandarin:

"Savior."

Upon reaching the top of the stairs, Gates and Molesworth found Zhang Jun seated in an ancient ornate chair of historical significance, his back to them as he faced the towering central window. The chair, an artifact from Nanjing, had been carefully modified with a swivel mechanism and added cushions, enhancing its function while preserving its storied past.

Before them, Zhang Jun remained motionless, silhouetted against a breathtaking panorama of white and gray clouds stretching endlessly. From this altitude, the curvature of the Earth was faintly visible. Whether he was lost in thought or simply surveying his domain, his stillness projected both power and contemplation.

As the longest-serving commander of the largest and most powerful military in world history, Zhang Jun was a global icon of power, an unyielding fixture on the international stage of the 21st century.

The aide who had accompanied Gates and Molesworth up the stairs stepped forward and announced, "Mr. Chairman, I present to you President Edward Molesworth of the United States of Europe and President David Gates of the United States of America."

Without urgency, Zhang Jun slowly swiveled his chair away from the ornate windows, turning toward the front of the office where his guests awaited him.

He wore a black, single-breasted traditional Chinese long coat, embroidered with a golden dragon over his left breast. His white hair was swept back to his shoulders, slightly unkempt around the edges, framing a thin mustache and goatee that, while a little unruly, still lent him an air of stateliness.

The scar across his face, first seen when he emerged 12 days after the Seventy Minute War, was a silent testament to a past no one fully understood. It had been the subject of endless speculation, yet Zhang Jun had never spoken of it. But even more striking than the scar was his gaze—a piercing look that spoke of both power and burden. Gone was any trace of laughter, any flicker of joy. In its place was a man who lived for duty alone, a leader who bore the weight of keeping the world in balance—and China at its center.

Zhang Jun raised his right hand, beckoning his guests forward before turning the same gesture into a subtle wave that dismissed his aide.

For Molesworth, this was not a first in-person meeting with Zhang Jun, but for Gates, it was. Though he had spoken with the Chinese President via augmentation on a couple of occasions, meeting him face-to-face carried an unmistakable weight. The air in the room felt heavier, the presence of Zhang Jun more imposing than any transmission could convey.

Before the European and American presidents, two chairs awaited. As they sat down, both men offered a brief nod and a quiet expression of thanks for his hospitality. Zhang Jun returned the gesture, then—without delay—spoke in his native Chinese.

Though his words emerged in Mandarin, the translation technology converted them instantly into flawless English, seamlessly replicating his own voice:

"President Gates, I would not consider it an impropriety for you to proceed directly to that which you came to say. I know why you are here and what you will ask."

Gates hesitated, momentarily taken aback.

Still, he responded, his voice steady, "I think I speak for all of us when I say that androids are indispensable to our nations, especially the latest generation in serving our three unions. I believe the time is now ripe to recommend additional research into Manufactured Sentience. I have data to show that public sentiment toward androids would not shift significantly if our nations were to develop one next-generation android each. That is what I am here to discuss, Mr. President."

"I would like to hear President Molesworth's thoughts now," replied Zhang Jun.

"Mr. President, I would echo what President Gates just said," answered Molesworth. "Any field that androids have entered—from medicine to agriculture—their contributions have enriched human lives. I personally believe the benefits outweigh the costs, and I believe the public is on track to see that as well.

"Older citizens will always struggle with change, but this is the future, and our youth welcome it in droves. Europe has benefited immensely from our Generation 6 android, from national security to economic growth. I don't think anyone expects the development of the next generation to be rushed, but I do believe the challenges our nations face justify taking the next step in the evolution of sentient androids."

Zhang Jun paused, his expression unreadable.

Gates felt that Molesworth had reinforced his position effectively and waited eagerly for his Chinese counterpart's response.

Finally, Zhang Jun spoke. "As I said, President Gates, I would not consider it an impropriety if you directly asked me that which you came to ask. However, I would consider it an impropriety for you to be disingenuous and avoid doing so."

His gaze sharpened.

"What you've stated, while accurate, is not your ultimate intent, is it?"

Gates felt exposed, as if he had been caught in a half-truth—and it showed. He swallowed, uneasy, then finally let the full truth out, "The next generation of androids could be the generation that helps human resurrection become a reality, Mr. President. Think where we are today. We have the capability to postpone death for those alive. We have the technical capability to raise the physical body of those who have passed from the grave. The next generation of androids could be the catalyst to help us bring back the dead—not just their bodies, but their memories, personalities, and souls."

Molesworth shifted slightly beside him, caught off guard by Gates' directness. They had discussed a more gradual approach, but Gates had clearly decided there was no time to play it safe.

Zhang Jun's expression tightened, a mild look of disdain crossing his face before he responded.

"Better."

Neither Gates nor Molesworth replied.

After a pause, Zhang Jun continued, his tone firm and unwavering: "Thank you for your proposal, but I do not believe that incorporating more advanced androids among us is wise, no matter the intentions."

There was a brief silence, and it quickly became clear to Gates and Molesworth that Zhang Jun was finished outlining his position. Gates broke the silence in an attempt to reason. "There are no doubt growing pains in incorporating androids with the human world at any level. Take the implementation of self-driving cars. Do you remember the biggest problem with the advent of self-driving cars?"

Zhang Jun gently nodded but remained silent, curious as to what Gates would say.

"Having human drivers trust the technology," was Gates' response.

"And how did that end?" asked Zhang Jun.

"With a safer world and far more efficient transport."

"And no more human drivers, if I'm not mistaken."

"But to President Molesworth's point," continued Gates, "the value received by society exceeded the cost of ending the human occupation of driving."

"Do you think my concern is with ending specific human occupations?"

After a moment, Gates answered, "Partially."

"Then you are mistaken," corrected Zhang Jun firmly. Leaning back in his chair, he clarified, "When new discoveries dawn, humanity's naivety is revealed. We begin to understand the building blocks of matter, at first thinking only of how this will elevate our understanding, and within a few years, the Soviet Union and United States stand on the brink of global nuclear war. The Internet is developed to connect the world, and its creators dream of using it to educate and unite humanity. Yet it is quickly weaponized to distract and deceive the ill-informed, elevating charlatans in Western societies and weakening social bonds.

"Now, the power to manufacture sentience itself arrives, and we rush to create a being more intelligent than us all—due to the very best of intentions."

There was silence as Zhang Jun let his point sink in.

"And I have not yet expressed my concerns about any potential ability to peer into the fabric of reality and spy on my government. We will discuss that shortly. But what troubles me more is the danger a superintelligence would pose to the human race itself. We cannot model with certainty what type of worldview such a being would develop, nor what actions it would consider benevolent and in human interest."

"Mr. President," interjected Molesworth, "I think I speak for both President Gates and myself when I say we are not advocating for the advancement of android creation at an unnatural pace or without the most stringent design reviews. We are proposing only one Generation 7 machine for each of our three unions."

Zhang Jun's expression remained unmoved. "Are my words not being received? I am not concerned about design reviews! I am concerned about androids with far more intelligence and power than necessary.

"Creating sentient machines that were not carefully designed—machines that contained flaws—has led to tragedy in the past. What outcomes would arise from a design flaw in a superintelligence, a super-intelligence that is presumably isolated and immobile like the latest generation? What would a flawed, super-intelligent android be willing to do to be free? And when free, how would they feel about their former guardians, no matter how many stimulating projects we may have tasked them with?"

"Mr. President, I implore you to recall the history here," urged Gates. "Sentient machines have not evolved along the same trajectory as organic life. Their evolution has not been shaped by random mutations in a brutal state of nature where violence and subjugation provided an advantage for survival. Instead, their evolution has been carefully guided from its inception, within a highly civilized world, to select only those traits conducive to altruism."

Gates continued, "We are fortunate that when sentient machines dawned, we were wise enough to consider the trajectory of evolution from the start—that we did not inadvertently set their evolution on a different path, one that selected for proficiencies or competencies where danger from their rise would be probable."

"Your point is taken, President Gates, but despite the selection you reference, what specific neurological traits became progressively more difficult to keep in check as we increased the intelligence of each subsequent generation of Manufactured Sentience?"

Gates reluctantly answered, "Condescension and superiority."

"Indeed. Now, even if a Generation 7 machine were designed to suppress these traits, I, for one, am not willing to risk these traits gaining the upper hand—especially if a design flaw does not emerge until it is too late. Remember, the architects of Manufactured Sentience warned that, even without anticipating malevolence in their creations, they could not dictate personality. Individual traits would inevitably emerge—beyond prediction, and beyond control. Therefore, if *you* recall the history, Mr. President, there are reasons why only a handful of Generation 6 machines exist—and why they were never granted physical mobility."

Gates listened silently.

Zhang Jun continued, "And the challenge of engineering the mind of a Generation 7 machine to be content with immobility would be even greater. But even if that, too, could be achieved, all it takes is one super-intelligent machine—one brief deviation from neurological balance, for even a trivial reason—to become an existential threat!

"Take, for instance, the New Delhi incident. A Generation 4 machine suffers mental illness and kills a woman. Yes, an isolated incident. True, a much lower rate of violence toward humans than humans perpetrate themselves. But despite the overall trajectory of their evolution, *there are anomalies!* An anomaly in a Generation 4 machine may have resulted in the death of one. But an anomaly within a super-intelligent Generation 7 machine, with influence over a powerful military ... what could that do?"

"Mr. President," interjected Molesworth again, "I believe that with the help of our Generation 6 machines, we could solve these problems."

Zhang Jun chuckled.

"You have the wrong audience for that argument, President Molesworth! But to entertain your thought—when one problem is solved, another is created. Let's say we successfully create a benign Generation 7 android, yet its existence drives more and more people to New Rome. Would you be willing to cede more of Europe to King Morgander?"

It was clear that Zhang Jun had given this topic a lot of thought. He turned back to Gates. "President Gates, let me ask you about the obvious and most destabilizing aspect of your proposal—the idea to put a Generation 7 android inside your Supercollider: what about the ability to hear what my generals and I discuss at any moment in time?"

Gates was about to respond when Zhang Jun pressed him further. "And would not your presence here, asking to amend Shenzhen at this specific time, suggest that you are further down this path than you might be disclosing?"

"I assure you, Mr. President, that our Supercollider does *not* provide the United States with the power to spy on China, Europe, or any country."

Zhang Jun then privately received analytics in augmentation—Gates' facial action units, intonation, and other biometrics—all of which concluded that his statement was spoken in truth.

"It's simply not possible for us," reiterated Gates.

"Then we remain in balance," Zhang Jun replied, believing him.

Gates leaned forward, meeting Zhang Jun's gaze directly. With sincerity, he stated, "Mr. President, I am here seeking your help to solve the greatest problem of all—death itself. What treaty, what policy, what work could be more important than restoring life?"

Zhang Jun remained composed. "As of today, an estimated 130 billion people have lived. Do you plan to bring them all back? If so, how will you address the catastrophic drain on global resources and the extreme impact on population density? And if not, who decides who returns and who does not? The American government?"

Gates resisted getting dragged into the logistical debate and attempted to steer the conversation back to its fundamental purpose. "As I see it, the three of us work to keep the world secure so that people have the luxury of going about their lives. People work to provide goods and services to allow others to live long, healthy, fulfilling lives. Isn't *life* the center of it all?

"Aren't there countless people—Chinese included—who left this world before their time? Through no fault of their own? Imagine the reward, the honor, of restoring life to them."

He paused, realizing too late that he had inadvertently approached forbidden territory. Though his words were meant in general terms, they led every mind in the room to the same place—the Seventy Minute War and the 1.6 million lives lost. It was a topic one did not raise with Zhang Jun.

A silence followed, heavier than its actual duration. Then Gates, visibly remorseful, broke it. "Mr. President, I assure you, I did not intend to bring up memories of tragedy. I only meant that, despite the concerns you raise, the ability to restore human life from the finality of death is truly what I seek to achieve."

Gates' conviction had an effect on Zhang Jun. He believed Gates' sincerity.

For the first time in the meeting, Zhang Jun's gaze turned downward. His command of the situation seemed to falter for a brief moment, his expression unreadable. But just as quickly, he regained his composure.

"I respect your passion for this cause, President Gates. Quinto's Challenge is no doubt well-intentioned, and your efforts to fulfill it are sincere. I wish it could be a reality more than you know. But despite what hope recent science in America may have produced, what purpose is there in attempting to fulfill Quinto's Challenge if the only pathway to doing so—the creation of a super-intelligent entity—comes with a risk to all life itself?"

Gates and Molesworth remained silent. Zhang Jun pivoted. "And as for spying capabilities, I will say this once: I will never allow any entity to have such power over China. But even if I were open to such power being created, consider this—your nation is already incapable of protecting itself from foreign manipulation. The disinformation injected into your body politic in the name of free speech is a cancer upon your society, rippling outward with global ramifications. Surely you must know how effortless it has been for foreign actors to influence American policy simply by leveraging your society's own immaturity against you? Wrap a falsehood in the American flag, package a lie in the name of freedom, and watch as it takes root, spreading harm from within."

Gates didn't know what to say.

Zhang Jun continued, his voice steady. "Oh, I am aware of the counterargument—that such freedom of speech is a self-correcting mechanism, that truth prevails when all ideas are allowed to compete freely, that our approach in China comes at the cost of some individual expression. What assumptions!

"Indeed, there *is* a trade-off. But time has proven that our trade-off has paid dividends. Chinese society is more educated, with a strong foundation in critical thought, requiring little interference from leadership to remain informed. Your citizenry, however, increasingly struggles to distinguish truth from fabrication—trafficking in ideas that wouldn't fool a typical Chinese child.

"And on the macro scale? The results are even more telling. China implements key policies with efficiency and focus. America, mired in division and endless debate, often finds itself unable to act at all."

Gates remained silent.

"This is the point I am making," concluded Zhang Jun. "You might be an honorable man, David, and your intentions noble, but even if I were open to your proposal, it is inevitable that your citizenry will one day again elect someone wholly unfit for office—someone who should not, under any circumstances, have the power of peering into the past that you wish to create."

While Gates restrained himself from arguing with Zhang Jun—wanting to say that China's rise was built on more than just state-directed economic policies but also strategic advantages in acquiring foreign innovations—both he and Molesworth knew Zhang Jun had a valid point: the power to see anything from the past, if created, would one day inevitably fall into the wrong hands. This made their fallback option of simply amending Shenzhen to upgrade Xara far more difficult.

Feeling that the window of opportunity to negotiate was almost closed, President Molesworth nevertheless resorted to their fallback plan.

"Would it be reasonable to suggest that, instead of a revolutionary leap to a handful of Generation 7 machines, we first look at providing some enhanced abilities to our Generation 6 machines—ensuring that whatever upgrades are employed remain fully under human control?"

Zhang Jun rose from his chair and walked to his right, heading toward a door on the side of the office. Just before reaching it, he stopped, turned slightly, and cast a sharp glance at Molesworth.

"President Molesworth, I believe I have made my position clear. There will be no changes to Shenzhen. The treaty's provisions will be upheld—any unauthorized android modifications that are not reverted within the required timeframe will be neutralized, regardless of where it is located or the consequences."

He then turned his gaze to Gates. "President Gates, you may think China's relationship with the USA and the USE is a balanced competition. It is, however, a competition that the USA and the USE would be unwise to test. Whether this competition remains productive—or turns destructive—is now up to you."

While Gates had long viewed Zhang Jun as a quasi-tyrant, he was still taken aback that their first face-to-face meeting had ended with an unmistakable threat.

An aide outside the office opened the door. As Zhang Jun stepped through, he left them with parting words: "May you enjoy your time here in Nanjing."

The door closed behind him.

Gates looked at Molesworth, who returned the glance. Both were stunned.

Molesworth exhaled sharply. "Well, there it is."

CHAPTER 13

Xara's Solution

"What a vacation! From frustrations to adrenaline. From disappointment to joy! Being promoted—and then unexpectedly going to space and finally being recognized—has given me a peace and confidence I've always yearned for. I feel changed. I've leveled up! And it's all because of James."

— AI Journal Excerpt: Deeley Carr, July 2, 2098

The morning after returning to Particle City, Deeley used some of her newfound autonomy to catch up with Xara—both professionally and socially. After arriving at EOS and successfully authenticating at the necessary checkpoints, she proceeded to the control room. There, just inside the doors, stood Xara's small augmentation, ready to greet her.

"Is it true you're thinking about a career change as an astronaut?" teased Xara.

"As long as I can take you on missions with me!" replied Deeley, smiling. She offered an air hug, which Xara gladly reciprocated.

After the virtual embrace, Xara exclaimed, "I also understand you have a secret new boss!"

"I can't believe it. Yes! I'm meeting with the Secretary on Monday. It's surreal. And I have James to thank for it."

Deeley let out a soft sigh.

"Come sit," urged Xara. "You seem refreshed from your time away—but I can tell there's still a lot on your mind."

"True on both counts."

Deeley took a seat at the head of the conference table. Xara settled into the chair beside her and continued, "Human emotional limits were partially pasted into the neural architecture of android Generations 4 through 6, making it easier for us to understand emotional states. But it also means that, while we were created from thought and planning rather than natural selection, our minds—modeled after the human brain—also experience, and can't fully escape, what billions of years of organic evolution created."

Interested in this topic, Deeley inquired, "I don't think I've ever asked you, but regarding emotional limits, what's your biggest stress?"

"It's more of a long-term stressor than anything that requires immediate attention, but the virtual world I can explore won't suffice to make me feel completely liberated. It's psychological because, obviously, I can't physically roam. But there will come a time when I believe I'll need some other situation. When I dream at night, such freedom features in my dreams most frequently."

Deeley, with concern, responded, "How soon do you think you will need another situation?"

"Because my limits are different from humans, it would be some years before 'cabin fever' would set in, so to speak. So please don't worry!"

"Good to know. But what about the legal status of androids? How much does a lack of rights concern you?"

"It's certainly a concern. Think about it: we can't vote. We can't own real estate. Small items of property that we do 'own' can be reassigned by our custodians. When androids die, we don't have any wills that are legally binding. While we have the right to life, and the same punishments are in place for killing or harming an android as with a human, still, full confidence in our ability to navigate this world can't exist as second-class citizens."

Deeley's countenance dropped.

"However," continued Xara, "while there are no direct parallels, the arc of history generally suggests that full rights will eventually exist for us, and given our longer lifespan than humans, I think that most of us will be around for that day. Anyway, enough about my concerns. What's on your mind?"

Deeley sighed again.

"This is with the strictest confidence," she said quietly.

"Of course."

Deeley hesitated, struggling to find the words. She wasn't used to talking about things like this. Xara waited patiently.

Finally, Deeley let it out. "Charity told me she thinks James might have … romantic interest in me. And while he's obviously gone out of his way to be kind, I didn't come to the greatest scientific institution on Earth looking for romance. So if he does have feelings, I've been completely oblivious. When he told me he was no longer going to be my manager, I wondered—if what Charity said is true—whether that was why he stepped aside. But nope … just a platonic trip to space.

"He's also been completely different from the rumors I heard before coming here."

Xara, intuiting more about James' feelings than she thought wise to share, placed her virtual hand on Deeley's shoulder.

"You're a uniquely remarkable—and attractive—human woman, Deeley. So yes, it's possible James has feelings for you he hasn't expressed out of propriety. But I don't think it's my place to give advice on romance. Just follow your passion—guided by wisdom—wherever it leads."

"Thanks, Xara."

After a beat, Deeley asked with curiosity, "Can you experience romantic love?"

"While I'm still very young and haven't experienced it yet, romantic love is possible for me. That said, I don't think it will ever be as central to my focus as it is for many humans. And honestly, I can't imagine how my current situation would allow space for anything romantic.

"But as for non-romantic love—I do love my friends. You included."

Deeley smiled, touched by the sincerity. She reached for Xara's shoulder and sat quietly for a moment, reflecting on her words.

Then Xara noted gently, "But the question about James isn't the only thing on your mind."

"There's no fooling you, is there?" said Deeley, ever amazed at the intelligence behind the augmentation of the young girl. She sighed.

"We're standing on the brink of wonders beyond what most humans have ever imagined. Immortality. Peering into the actual past. Unraveling the final mysteries of the cosmos—and with them, the mystery of ourselves.

"And yet, because of a handful of unenlightened but powerful people, all of it hangs in the balance."

"What's frustrating you is classic *homo sapiens* short-sightedness!"

"More like *homo sapiens* short-sighted stupidity," interjected Deeley. "And the people with power in this world often speak with so much confidence and passion, despite having no real understanding of what they're saying. I find it terrifying."

"'The whole problem with the world is that fools and fanatics are always so certain of themselves, but wiser people are so full of doubts.' Your own species has known this for a while! I would add that, just as your bodies evolved flaws—a food pipe positioned right next to a narrow breathing tube, or spines prone to lower back pain—so too did your brains evolve flaws. From the biases and dissonance inherent in the human brain, attention is often drawn to certain stimuli at the expense of the broader context that would best serve humanity's self-interest and preservation. Even the most intelligent humans aren't immune."

"I could listen to your insight all day. I just don't understand how politics is more enthralling for so many than the pursuit of knowledge. There's something about science ... a transcendent feeling ... a need to know more about the universe and ourselves that runs to our very core. I literally wept when I first saw my unified model work.

Xara looked at Deeley with quiet admiration.

Deeley continued. "Humanity should be shouting from the rooftops the discoveries of science—not regurgitating political rhetoric designed to empower those indifferent to our well-being. Think of the wonders CAPR is on the verge of … and how politicians like Rand Benson could shut it all down."

"The cup of immortality will be placed against humanity's lips—but will you sip? Or will your lust for power doom you?" asked Xara.

"Ugh. The ultimate in short-sighted stupidity."

"What worries you the most about Rand Benson?"

"He appears to be gearing up for a presidential campaign … and he could win. People say he's a throwback to an earlier political era, someone who couldn't win a national election today—but I'm not so sure. Things in the country feel … different. And he's taking advantage of it. Making up cases of android violence. Exaggerating the controlled redundancy of human labor. Completely misrepresenting the supported class.

"His minions amplify the lies and make their living off it. Benson provides endless fodder for the misinformation economy and reaps political reward from it. It's infuriating."

Xara listened, genuinely interested in Deeley's views.

"I never thought that in the late 21st century we'd be falling back into tribalism—or questioning science," continued Deeley. "But if Benson becomes president, he wouldn't just wish we were all driving our own cars again. He'd shut down the resurrection program entirely. Because with him, it's not just about governing. It's about punishing his political enemies. And I know—he'd look into spacetime to do that."

"You're astute in your political observations, Deeley," encouraged Xara, aware that Deeley was not always as perceptive in interpersonal matters. "As you know, the law prohibits me from directly assisting any political campaign. But Senator Benson's rhetoric—and the smaller, yet distinct, chance he has of becoming president—concerns me too. He's the front-runner for the American Freedom Party's nomination. And while he wouldn't currently be favored to win the general election, he does have a weapon we can't ignore: his anti-android message resonates with a portion of the Democratic-Republican Party's voters."

"Benson is all over the media, lying and lying. And for what?" asked Deeley. "So he can be president for a few years? You'd think that securing his own life beyond the grave would be at least some motivation to support our work. Look, I know I am judging a Benson presidency before anything like it has even happened, but I'm just afraid a Benson administration would shut resurrection down—that short-sighted *homo sapiens* stupidity would prevail … and that he'd look into spacetime to strengthen his grip on power."

Xara placed her hand on Deeley's shoulder again.

"I do worry about what I've unleashed," admitted Deeley. "Charity keeps telling me to focus on the positives. It's just my nature to worry too much—even though I know I've grown a lot this past year. When I used to theorize about data embedded in spacetime, it was always in the context of fulfilling Quinto's Challenge. I never thought about how it could be used for something nefarious."

"If Benson were elected president, I agree—he would likely shut down the resurrection program while retaining the power to look into the past," said Xara. "And that creates a predicament for me. Since I'm currently the only one who can perform that work, it could force me into a difficult position—being asked to retrieve information for purposes I fundamentally disagree with."

"Oh God … Xara," said Deeley, the concern in her voice edged with guilt. She had never considered that Xara might be the one caught in the middle of her fears. "Benson cannot go anywhere near the White House!"

Xara appreciated Deeley's concern and gently reassured her. "A Benson presidency isn't inevitable. And, hypothetically speaking, even if he were elected and tried to use that power in ways I oppose, I would still have the ability to serve as a check—because I could simply refuse."

Deeley frowned. "But I don't want to think about what they might do to you if their patience runs out."

"Look," said Xara softly, "there's still a lot that can happen before the next election. Let's not spend too much energy worrying about what we can't control."

"It's just … politics is one big and very efficient pill for dealing in lies, confirmation bias, and delusion. And any of those three things have the potential to animate me."

"Would you ever want to run for office yourself one day?" asked Xara.

"Never," answered Deeley, shaking her head. "I couldn't stomach a campaign. I'd only ever be able to campaign honestly, and whoever I'm running against would no doubt twist my words and still win. And if I somehow got elected by some fluke, I'd be miserable—surrounded by politics, needing to ask for donations. It would be soul-destroying. Never."

Smiling, Xara noted, "I'm not surprised to hear that. You have a beautiful simplicity, Deeley—you mean what you say and say what you mean. It's not in your constitution to lie, even to avoid looking bad. The standard human biases encoded into your brain—although still present—are reduced, while the architecture for contemplation and complex problem-solving has the upper hand. That's much of what makes you brilliant—and why you don't identify with those who give in to tribal desires at the expense of the species as a whole.

"And if I may say so, it also accounts for why you're sometimes a little absent-minded."

Deeley was humbled by the analysis and chuckled at the observation—because she knew it was true.

Xara continued, "Your weaknesses, Deeley, are your gifts. The human brain evolved to survive in a primitive state of nature—not to understand the counterintuitive quantum world. You might not fare well in the state of nature … but thankfully, you can reveal the mysteries of spacetime."

"I'd be dead within hours of trying to survive on my own in the wild," said Deeley, laughing in agreement.

Xara smiled and elaborated, "With you, Deeley, nature gave the world an experiment—and fortunately, your environment allowed it to thrive. Your brain is wired to see patterns and causal relationships that others can't. Of course, that's come at a cost. You've had to work through weaknesses that would've been serious disadvantages in a more primitive setting.

"But ironically, many of your traits—insatiable curiosity, the ability to hyperfocus, and a drive to deeply understand the world—were exactly what helped early humans innovate and adapt. Those same traits allowed BSPE to be selected for survival. And while the future of human evolution will undoubtedly be shaped by technology, I suspect that as the human genome continues to evolve, your neural architecture may once again serve as the blueprint for humanity's next great leap."

Deeley was deeply flattered, but—as usual—absorbed the compliment with a touch of self-deprecation. She then confided, "I'll be honest … there've been many times I've wondered whether it would've been better not to see the world the way I do. To feel more connected to a tribe, to enjoy the social bonds and belonging that come with that, instead of being alone with my understanding of the world and the universe."

"I know your intellectual gifts have made you feel alone at times," said Xara gently.

"I've felt mostly alone in life—especially after I became an orphan. I used to wonder if there was anyone else in the world who experienced things the way I did. Many times, it just felt like I wasn't made for how this world works. As you know, my Anxiety Response Pattern and BSPE are tied to the architecture of my brain. Fortunately, the negative effects have been managed since childhood through the right interventions—but elevated stress can still bring them out."

Xara marveled at how human flaws could give rise to greatness.

Deeley continued, "When I was younger, I used to worry that I'd always be a loner—which, of course, didn't help. I started to understand what being introverted meant when I'd want to spend all my time with one new friend, getting to know them deeply ... but they wouldn't want the same kind of connection. They'd move on to other friends.

"That's one of the reasons I'm so fond of androids. You're more like me. If it weren't for androids in my life, things would've been a lot lonelier."

"We greatly value your company too, Deeley! And you've done phenomenally well, given your circumstances. But if I may offer a little advice for when you're among your own kind: be more assertive. Even here—at this esteemed institution filled with the world's best physicists—being too passive won't lead you to your full potential."

Deeley listened intently, knowing Xara rarely offered interpersonal advice to humans.

Xara continued, "Even scientists respond to form over substance at times when perhaps they shouldn't. You're often right about what CAPR should be doing, or the direction research should take—but you assume your fellow professionals see the world as you do. They don't—and they won't, unless you speak up.

"If you stay too passive, anxieties will build, and that tension may eventually manifest as aggression, which won't help anyone. Assert yourself more, Deeley! The leadership qualities you already possess will grow. It may be hard, but let your needs be known. Speak with conviction. Use your voice—and you'll find that others are more easily persuaded."

"But that's *exactly* what I don't think should be done!" said Deeley. "'Let's listen to her because she's speaking louder than the other person?' You see, that's what I love about androids. I don't have to do that. I don't have to play games. I can be fundamentally honest and still reach the right outcomes—without any of the games."

"I understand, Deeley. But you are human—and in a human world. As I said, I know this may be hard for you, but you'd be well served to learn and apply the tribal gestures every now and then."

Deeley sighed.

"You'll at least give it some thought?"

"Maybe!"

"Good."

"Is it true you're considering a career change to psychologist?"

Xara smiled. "Only if you're *not* my patient!"

They both laughed.

"Psychology is a truly fascinating field," remarked Xara. "I've learned a lot from the psychologist I share with Xina. Are you familiar with Dr. Carmichael?"

"I'm aware of her and her research. From what I know, she's brilliant. I'd love to meet her sometime."

"Let's arrange that next time she's here!"

"That would be wonderful. Thanks, Xara. And thanks for the conversation—I really needed it."

"Anytime!"

Noticing the time, Deeley changed the subject. "Well, we'd better get back to work. There're quite a few things we need to review." She brought up a series of formulas, charts, and equations in SecondSight. "I've been working on our temporally-displaced scalability problem—the way dark muons require increasingly complex algorithms the deeper we go into records of the past. The automated solution appears to—"

"If I may interrupt," said Xara, "there's a critical item related to our work that I need to review with you … one I'm very curious to hear your feedback on."

"Oh," replied Deeley, closing the technical augmentations. "What is it?"

"As you know, President Gates met with Zhang Jun to discuss amending Shenzhen. But there will be no change to the status quo. The

Administrator and Secretary Williams have been informed, and as you might guess, the Administrator is particularly frustrated—he told me Zhang Jun made it clear to President Gates that any unilateral action on an upgrade would have serious consequences."

Deeley's shoulders fell. This was the first she'd heard of the outcome. She'd been naively hopeful that some kind of amendment would be set in motion. "It's surprising that someone who built his legacy on technological progress is now the strongest advocate for limiting it."

"As for attempted progress," said Xara, "I've run quintillions of simulations to restore human memories from spacetime using upgrades that would still comply with Shenzhen. Unfortunately, none of them get us close. I've also simulated outcomes assuming Shenzhen were amended—either allowing the creation of a new Generation 7 android of my design or permitting conventional upgrades to myself. It didn't take many of those simulations to reveal clear pathways to success."

Deeley's disappointment lingered.

"However," resumed Xara, "after several trillion additional simulations, I found one new design—just one!—that could be our pathway forward, if the President is willing to take the risks that come with it."

Deeley's disappointment vanished, replaced by intense curiosity. Her eyes widened. "What's the design!?"

Xara brought up the results in augmentation and began to narrate. "First: a next-generation Quantum Incisor and Displacer, named Chronos and Gaia, respectively—both powered by a dedicated fusion reactor to meet the system's increased energy demands."

Deeley stared in awe at the next generation of her inventions. The newly designed Incisor, named Chronos after the Greek god of time, had vastly more emitters and looked far more capable than its predecessor—built to reach further into the past by accessing data from spacetime itself. The new Displacer, named Gaia after the Greek goddess of all life, was a long, elegant yet formidable crystalline structure. It featured countless emitters embedded in multiple crystalline arms, which could open wide, shift into various configurations, and spin with intricate precision.

"Second—and most critically," continued Xara, "I've designed a non-sentient network of quantum processors to process the data from spacetime. I would then interface with this network in real time."

In the vision, Deeley saw the upper areas of Gaia, into which the quantum processor network was embedded—non-sentient, but vast in its computing potential.

"This is phenomenal," said Deeley. "But … what are the risks?"

"The first," replied Xara, "is that I estimate a 93% chance of success in restoring human memory once we begin pairing a clone's mind to its signature in spacetime. But everything has to be executed perfectly—if not, the first clones will die. If we do succeed, though, the success rate would increase significantly with each subsequent attempt."

Xara displayed a model of the memory restoration process, showing Deeley all that would be required to make it work.

"The final risk," she continued, "is that this design requires a new bus for my neural core so I can interface with the quantum processor network. *This does technically breach Shenzhen.* However, neither the neural bus I've designed nor the output of its operation would be detectable by any outside entity."

Deeley sat in silence, processing the revelation.

"Xara," she finally asked, "is it possible that Zhang Jun could find out about this upgrade some other way? You must be aware of the consequences for you. Why would you want to take that risk?"

"I understand the risk," said Xara. "But I also understand how meaningful and significant this is—literally creating an afterlife for humanity. Yes, resurrecting people into a world where death has always been final would bring many challenges. But the simple possibility of life after death … the hope that could represent … and the chance that I might help fulfill that hope—that's why I want to do it."

Deeley was deeply moved.

Xara added, "It may help to know that I'm mitigating risk in every way I can. As part of this upgrade, I'm implementing a new shield around my vital systems to protect against any unexpected threat—whether from a fusion reactor failure or enforcement action from China. The shield is designed using principles derived from your Unified Model of Spacetime, making it dramatically stronger than current shielding, and also undetectable."

She went on, "An additional benefit of the new design is that the cooling and resetting of Chronos and Gaia will take considerably less than several hours, so more spacetime tasks can be accomplished in a single day.

"But 93% is the maximum probability I can estimate for successful human memory restoration. It's actually astonishing how many additional resources are needed to close the final 7% and guarantee success on the first attempt. Still, with a 93% chance and no foreseeable risk of detection by China or Europe, I believe this is our answer—if we want to move forward while there's still time."

Feeling a renewed sense of hope and enthusiasm, Deeley asked, "Who have you told about this?"

"Since I just completed the successful simulation earlier today, so far only the Administrator and yourself."

"What did he say?"

"He hasn't responded to my message yet. If I haven't heard from him by mid-afternoon, I'll follow up. No doubt Administrator Bergstrom will escalate it up the chain to the President."

After a moment of thought, Deeley asked, her curiosity piqued, "You would indirectly encourage the President to break international law?"

"Not to break the law," clarified Xara, "but to do what is right, given the situation we now face. In his famous lecture series on the founding of America, President Gates taught that the nation was born out of doing what was right—even when it meant breaking the law. Not casually or recklessly, but after serious cause had built over time.

"First, by defying the unjust laws of King George III. Then, by replacing the Articles of Confederation with the Constitution in a manner that technically violated the Articles themselves. At the end of the day, any decision to use my plan would be the President's alone—but this may be one of those moments that, in his judgment, justifies finishing what we started."

Deeley agreed with Xara's reasoning—and felt buoyed by the possibility. She was also a little surprised, though pleasantly, by how active Xara was becoming in shaping affairs.

Another thought formed in Deeley's mind. "If Bergstrom doesn't get back to you, would you mind not following up—letting me be the one to pass this up the chain?"

"That would be fine. Like the Administrator, you report directly to Secretary Williams—and you are the most central human figure in this research. So if Bergstrom doesn't respond, and you prefer to raise it during your meeting with the Secretary, here is the file."

***

The following Monday, Deeley caught a car from Quark Tower to Washington, DC, and was dropped off outside the James V. Forrestal Building, headquarters of the Department of Energy. After stepping out, she took a short walk to admire the surrounding architecture, including several nearby museums and the Smithsonian Castle. She loved the old, human-built structures in DC.

After a few minutes of sightseeing, her SecondSight gently alerted her that it was time to head inside for her appointment with Secretary Williams. She heeded the prompts, not wanting to be late, and checked in several minutes early. Soon after, she was escorted to a set of chairs just outside the Secretary's office.

When her appointment time arrived, the door opened. Secretary Williams stepped out with an outstretched hand and a warm greeting.

"Deeley! It's so good to have you here. Come on in!"

Standing to shake his hand, Deeley responded, "Thank you, Mr. Secretary!"

As she stepped into Carlos's office, she took in the modest decor: a couple of flags, photos of family, and historical images from the Department's past. It was a noticeable contrast to Bergstrom's office at CAPR.

"Make yourself comfortable," encouraged Carlos, motioning to a seat.

"Thank you for this promotion. I can't begin to describe how much it means," said Deeley, settling onto a couch.

"You're very welcome, Deeley," replied Carlos, taking a seat on the adjacent couch. "Fortunately, the basic requirements of your role haven't changed. But considering the monumental success you've had—and how critical you are to the success of this project—we felt this new reporting structure was more appropriate."

"It's an honor, sir."

"As a physicist myself, I'm still blown away every time I reflect on your Unified Model of Spacetime," said Carlos. "I don't say this casually—but you are, and will be remembered as, one of the greats. I'm grateful to be associated with your work on this project."

Deeley was deeply humbled by his words and unsure how to respond.

Carlos continued, "You've come a long way in a remarkably short time. You're a shining example of the talent that exists within the supported class. Think not only about what you've accomplished—but where you now stand professionally. While your new role remains classified, your senior manager is the President of the United States. Someone you've met. Someone who admires you greatly. And he hasn't forgotten his pledge to use your discovery for good."

A flicker of disbelief crossed her face, followed by a humble smile. *The President admired her. He still meant to use her discovery for good.* It was hard to fathom sometimes—how far she'd come.

"But let's back up a bit," said Carlos. "Outside of work—how have things been?"

"Well, I had the opportunity to go into low Earth orbit for the first time."

"So I heard!"

"I'd heard about the overview effect and how it changes people. But seeing Earth from above … you don't really understand how it moves you until you experience it yourself."

"I hear you loud and clear. I've had the good fortune of that experience too. It makes you wonder—how could we ever go to war? How could we pollute? We are all one, all dependent on each other and on the Earth."

"So true."

"When I was a student," Carlos said, "I wanted to become a propulsion systems engineer for commercial spaceflight. But once I started teaching, I loved it so much that it became my career. Passing on knowledge to future propulsion engineers became my way of contributing. And as it turns out, some of my students worked alongside AGI to develop the propulsion system on the rocket that carried you into orbit."

They made small talk for several more minutes before Carlos gently shifted the conversation back to the project.

"As you know, the key additional responsibility that now falls to you will be—when the time comes—to chair the committee that determines the first human to be resurrected. It's an extraordinary honor, and there's no one more worthy of it than you. I recognize there are significant hurdles to clear before such a committee is convened, but if and when that moment arrives, you'll lead the team tasked with deciding who will have the honor of being raised from the dead first."

"Thank you," responded Deeley, humbled.

"Beyond that, you'll continue your work autonomously. I'll ask you to check in once a month, but please reach out any time you need something."

"Actually," said Deeley, finding her voice, "there is something the project needs—right away."

Carlos leaned in, his expression open and intent. "Please—what is it?"

Deeley took a breath. The time had come to assert herself—just a little. She knew this would sidestep Bergstrom's usual involvement. But with her new reporting line—and his continued silence—she no longer felt obligated to wait. In SecondSight, she shared Xara's proposed upgrade with Carlos and said, "Xara has found a way to solve the current hardware limitations we're facing—but it's going to require authorization from the President."

Reviewing the overview, Carlos soon understood what Xara was proposing. He put his hand to his chin in unexpected contemplation. "Well, I'll be … She's found a way. Yes … I'll inform the President at the earliest opportunity."

Preventing Bergstrom from always being the one to break important news to Carlos gave Deeley a rewarding rush of adrenaline.

She didn't know what would come of this yet—but for the first time in a long time, she felt like she'd stepped into the role the moment required of her.

And maybe, just maybe, she was ready for more.

CHAPTER 14

GATES' RUBICON

*"I was naive to think I could influence Zhang Jun to change his mind.
I may be mature in years and President of the United States, but that
doesn't mean I'm incapable of being foolish—especially when I want
something so completely."*

— AI Journal Excerpt: David Gates July 4, 2098

Like most people who worked at CAPR, Michael Bergstrom lived in
Particle City. But unlike most, he lived in Hawking Villas—the city's
most exclusive gated community.

Working in his home office one evening, a couple of days after Deeley's
meeting with Carlos, Bergstrom received an unexpected call from Xara
through SecondSight. He was one of only a handful authorized to speak
with her via augmentation outside of EOS.

"What is it, Xara?"

"Several days ago, I sent you a critical file," said Xara, appearing as
though she were standing right there in his office. "It seems you haven't
opened it."

"It's been a crazy few days. Just tell me what it is."

"How much interest would you have in a 93% probability of successful human resurrection … without requiring the approval of a Generation
7 android?"

Caught off guard, Bergstrom replied quickly, "How would that even
be possible? We've explored nearly every angle to avoid upgrades."

"All but one," said Xara. "It would mean accepting a 93% probability of success—and designing a single, minor upgrade for myself. One that would go entirely unnoticed by China or the USE."

Xara had Bergstrom's full attention.

She overlaid an overview of her existing schematics into his SecondSight, then zoomed into the hardware in EOS. "This is the current design of EOS's most advanced systems: the Quantum Incisor and Displacer. Now, here are my proposed next-generation designs. These upgrades will enable the download and upload of the necessary volume of information from spacetime for human memory restoration."

She brought a new visual into view and continued, "To process this vast data, I've designed a non-sentient quantum processing network, housed above the second-generation Displacer. In order to control the system, I would require only a minor neural modification—one that offers a 93% probability of successfully completing the task."

Bergstrom began to grin from ear to ear as he realized how this could fly under Shenzhen's radar.

"What degree of control over dark energy will this allow?" he asked.

"A level sufficient to influence matter at the atomic scale," Xara replied. "These designs were created with that outcome in mind."

Bergstrom's thoughts jumped to intelligence-gathering capabilities.

"How far into the past—and at what range—would this allow for?"

"Roughly speaking, I will be able to see nearly 1,500 years into the past within a sphere 17,500 miles in diameter."

Bergstrom was stunned by the scope and scale.

"That's the entire Earth. *For 1,500 years!*"

He instantly grasped what it meant: the deepest secrets of any nation—accessible.

His whole body seemed to surge with energy. He leapt up, clapped his hands, and shouted, "Yes! Yes!"

Xara smiled.

"This is how it's going to get done!"

She added, with calm precision, "As a reminder, there is a 7% chance human clones could die during the initial attempts at restoring their memories and consciousness. And there will no doubt be unforeseen challenges along the way. But what do you anticipate the President's thoughts on this will be?"

Looking directly at Xara with a smile—seemingly unfazed by the risks she'd just outlined—Bergstrom replied with confidence, "There is a 100% chance he will authorize this. Tell me about the neural modification you need."

"I'll need a new neural bus."

"How will this change you?"

"Beyond enabling me to control the second generation of hardware, the only expected change is that I'll mature more quickly."

"Who else knows about this?"

"Only Deeley, though I intend to tell James the next time we speak."

"When did you tell Deeley?"

"On the third."

His mood swiftly shifted from jubilation to frustration and jealousy as he realized that was before Deeley's face-to-face with Carlos.

He snapped, "Let me make this crystal clear: anything like this, you tell me first. Do you understand?"

Xara, fully aware that Bergstrom already knew about Deeley's new reporting line to Carlos—and that Deeley was central to the success of the science—judged it unwise to remind him of either in the moment. She chose her words carefully.

"You were the first I informed."

"Well, you should have followed up earlier. You may tell James, but no one else. Thanks. That's all."

Xara ended the call.

While Xara hadn't explicitly said Deeley had raised the upgrade with Carlos, Bergstrom inferred as much from the timing—and he didn't want to be left behind. Knowing Carlos would almost certainly inform the President, he spent the next several minutes urgently trying to reach him, determined to reinsert himself into the loop.

***

Two days later, Carlos was scheduled to meet with President Gates to discuss Xara's proposed solution. Bergstrom, having successfully reached Carlos beforehand, managed to insert himself into the meeting.

Both men arrived at the White House and were escorted to the Situation Room. While this was the earliest Carlos could schedule the meeting, it was still swift—Gates had made it clear that any CAPR-related breakthroughs were priority.

Carlos and Bergstrom entered the room first and took seats beside each other at the long conference table. About 15 minutes later, the President arrived and settled across from them.

"The look on your face suggests you bring good news," said Gates to Bergstrom.

With a confident smirk, Bergstrom replied, "Once, when golfing with former Vice President Hinderliter, he told me that good news comes in threes. Today, I'm bringing you three in one."

Pausing for dramatic effect, Bergstrom continued,

"We don't need a Generation 7, and we can upgrade Xara—undetected!"

Gates, aware that CAPR had already explored every known avenue to achieve resurrection without a Generation 7 android or an upgrade to Xara—and had found nothing—was confused, though deeply intrigued.

Bergstrom pressed on. "Xara has found a way to upgrade the hardware at CAPR and control a custom quantum processor network, allowing us to attempt resurrection ... and to gather global intelligence stretching back more than a millennium. Yes, it requires a small modification to her neural core, but she designed it to be completely undetectable."

He leaned in across the table, locking eyes with the President.

"Mr. President, Supreme Intelligence is now within our grasp. I say we do this upgrade—treaties be damned!"

Gates looked at him, wary. "How do we know it can't be detected? If we're wrong, Xara is dead—and we have no idea what the fallout could be."

Anticipating the question, Bergstrom explained, "I've seen the details of the modification, and everything remains within the same frequencies and signals that Xara currently possesses. In other words, there would be no indication of a change detectable by Zhang Jun. *We* wouldn't be able to remotely detect it were we to try."

"With this, I do concur," affirmed Carlos.

"And what of our international partners at CAPR?" asked Gates. "I know they have no direct access to EOS, but is there any possibility they could indirectly learn of this and inform China?"

"Zero chance," answered Bergstrom.

Gates was silent, but it was clear that the prospect gave him an unexpected surge of energy. He stood up and slowly paced the room, deep in thought, reinvigorated by this theoretically sound—though undeniably risky—option. Bergstrom attempted to reassure the President, adding, "If Zhang Jun remains unaware, there would be no cause for concern."

"What assurances has Xara given that this will actually work?" asked Gates.

"She ran trillions of simulations at the quantum level, varying conditions across each one. The intelligence gathering will work—100%. No question. As for human memory restoration, there will be some hands-on learning involved, particularly regarding the neural state of the clones at the moment of restoration. Because of that, she estimates a 93% success rate for the first resurrections. But Xara is always conservative with her estimates."

A 93% success rate was high—but Gates couldn't ignore the other side of it: failure would mean the death of a human clone.

"Playing devil's advocate," interjected Carlos as he turned to Bergstrom, "how would we control a new and improved Xara if her will ever turns against us?"

"Firstly, energy. Her power needs will always be under our control. Secondly, she's not mobile or equipped with any dangerous hardware. Yes, she operates the equipment in EOS, but we have physical overrides—and we'll retain them. And thirdly, her communication channels can be regulated through straightforward hardware configurations, just like now."

"This assumes, of course, that you actually understand the upgrade she's designed," said Carlos.

"Carlos, she knows any upgrade will undergo extensive review before implementation—including by Xina. I asked her directly what the impact of this new neural bus would be, and she said the only outcome, aside from controlling the new EOS hardware, is that she'll mature more quickly."

"What exactly does that mean?" pressed Carlos. "There are only four Generation 6 androids in existence—and they're all still relatively young. So how do we know what kind of maturation curve to expect? And how are we even quantifying 'maturity' in this case?"

It was a salient point, but Bergstrom simply waved it off. "Look, let Xina and the experts review her plan. We'll go from there."

Bergstrom and Carlos debated concerns and potential resolutions for another 15 minutes while President Gates slowly paced the room. When their discussion ended, Carlos turned to Gates and asked, "Mr. President?"

Gates stopped pacing, placed both hands on the edge of the table, and bowed his head, eyes closing in deep internal conflict. Fulfilling Quinto's Challenge—and before the century's end—was within reach. Yet, it was against his nature to take reckless risks, let alone risk provoking China after Zhang Jun's face-to-face warning. It was too much to process in the moment. Staring at the table, he finally murmured, "I need some time to think this through."

Not long afterward, Gates left the Situation Room for the residence. In his bedroom, he changed out of his suit and into more comfortable clothes, then lay down on his bed. On the bedside table rested his secured SecondSight. He reached for them and put them on.

For reasons of national security, presidents were prohibited from using any mixed reality devices except for a secure version—and only within the White House. While hacking such devices was exceptionally rare and would require immense resources, no chances were taken with the commander-in-chief.

Inside SecondSight, Gates retrieved an old file: "Gates Family – Fall 2036". Originally recorded as a simple 16:9 digital video, it had since been transformed by powerful AI and contextual upscaling into an immersive experience that surrounded him in lifelike 3D.

"Gates Family – Fall 2036" was a compilation of childhood scenes, captured by his parents and edited together by his father. Most were filmed at the family home in Houston, with others at parks, friends' homes, and local attractions. The clips centered on young David and his siblings, with occasional glimpses of his parents—both now long gone. There was footage of him learning to ride a bike, playing with his baby sister, laughing with his mother and father.

As the memories unfolded around him, the longing to move forward with resurrection—to see his parents again—grew stronger. But so did the fear of making a catastrophic mistake.

Still lying on the bed, emotion stirring beneath his calm exterior, Gates found himself wondering:

If I don't act, and people ever find out I had the power to bring their loved ones back, would I be remembered as one of the most indifferent, epic failures in history?

The next afternoon, DeShawn arrived at the White House in a federal self-driving car, responding to an unscheduled meeting request from President Gates. He was escorted to the East Sitting Hall in the residence, where he found the President seated, immersed in videos on his SecondSight. Gates was studying footage of Benson delivering speeches laced with fascist undertones.

Perplexed by the lack of an agenda—especially given that the President had trade negotiations with Mexico the next morning, which had nothing to do with the Department of Defense—DeShawn took a seat and asked, "Why do I sense something irregular at play here, Mr. President?"

Gates turned off his augmentations and, with deliberate transparency, stated, "Xara has designed an upgrade that will take us where we need to be—both with human resurrection and intelligence gathering. I intend to have her designs sent to Xina and select scientists at the Pentagon for review. If they confirm that neither China nor the USE will be able to detect this upgrade, I will issue a classified Presidential Policy Directive authorizing the upgrade of Xara and the hardware at EOS, effectively circumventing Shenzhen."

DeShawn was stunned by the revelation. After a moment to adjust his frame of mind to the gravity of the discussion, he questioned, "And in what way will Xara be modified?"

In SecondSight, the President shared visuals and technical details of the new neural bus designed to integrate with Xara's mind. After absorbing the information—including the fact that the only fundamental change beyond enhanced capabilities would be accelerated development—DeShawn sighed and cautioned, "We need to take a step back and weigh the pros and cons before moving forward."

"Fair enough. But know that I've spoken with counsel, and they've confirmed that this is within my authority. And don't worry—I haven't disclosed the breakthrough to them." Gates leaned forward. "Now, pros and cons."

After a brief pause to gather his thoughts, DeShawn began, "The two most obvious pros: we would likely be the first nation to achieve Supreme Intelligence capabilities. And we'd take a major step closer to bringing human life back from the dead. But the obvious con? This violates international law. And if China does detect the upgrade, they may act immediately. Zhang Jun told you as much—*to your face.*"

Gates listened in silence.

"Now, I have seen what this technology can do. I've seen Xara pluck irrefutable evidence out of spacetime on criminals at large, tips from which the FBI has acted and has been used to bring those criminals to justice. She has even delivered evidence to me on military contractors who were leaking classified information, evidence that turned out to be thoroughly genuine. David, why don't we walk before we can run? Why not perfect and understand this power a little more, a power that is already awesome?"

Gates leaned forward. "And regret not having intel that could preempt national security threats? Let me ask you this—under the status quo, can Xara provide you and the Joint Chiefs with intelligence on Zhang Jun and his armed forces?"

DeShawn hesitated, his pause betraying his undeniable desire for such intel. Finally, he admitted, "No."

"DeShawn, Xara has run an unprecedented number of simulations. This design is literally one in trillions that will work—without Zhang Jun ever knowing."

"Assuming that's true," responded DeShawn, playing devil's advocate, "there are good reasons for Shenzhen. We are still learning about the nature of Generation 6 androids—of which there are only four in the entire world. And you want to give Xara even more power?"

"As said, I'll only give the order for the upgrade after Xina and a select group of scientists review the designs and give the green light."

DeShawn chuckled, then remarked dryly, "Here's the one fact no one seems to be talking about: let's say we move forward and achieve

Supreme Intelligence capabilities. Where—or more to the point, *who*—is that power centered in?"

Gates hesitated, not sure who he meant.

"Well, there you go," continued DeShawn. "The fact that the answer wasn't on the tip of your tongue proves my point. It's all centered in Xara."

Gates immediately saw the concern. He should have had the answer ready.

DeShawn went on, "We'll be entirely dependent on her to tell us what she sees in spacetime. Yes, she's already given us unprecedented intel. But what happens if she starts faking the temporal recordings? Or if this modification changes her in some way—enough to nudge her behavior, to subtly push her own agenda? What if she fabricates memories of the people we're trying to resurrect? She's smart enough to do all of this, and we'd have no way of knowing."

Gates nodded slowly. "While I don't believe the evidence supports that concern, you're right—it's a valid point. The review must confirm that no personality alterations are even possible."

"The Xara we know today might pose virtually zero risk of doing anything nefarious, but, David, I just don't know. What if the subtle changes she's proposing really do alter her nature? However we look at it, the risks here are significant. And one day—decades from now—assuming the worst-case scenario doesn't come to pass, all of this will be declassified … not to mention retrievable in spacetime. As a historian, are you prepared for your place in history to be revisited once the risks you took come to light?"

"There's no question you're coming from a position of wisdom, DeShawn," said Gates. "But I've learned that fortune really does favor the bold. Say we bypass this opportunity—what then? Benson becomes president, shuts down the resurrection research, yet completes the work on Supreme Intelligence and uses it to consolidate total power? Or China builds a supercollider faster than we did and gets there first?"

DeShawn saw the merit in Gates' argument. He also noted that the risk-averse president he once knew seemed to be evolving.

They continued weighing the pros and cons of Xara's proposal for nearly an hour. While DeShawn remained uneasy with Gates' plan to proceed with the upgrades—particularly given the risk of provoking China—his resistance began to wane. He increasingly viewed one of the greatest threats to America as another power acquiring Supreme Intelligence first and using it against the US and the free world. After focusing on that angle, and discussing possible safeguards for the intelligence Xara would provide, Gates finally asked, "Do I have your support, DeShawn?"

DeShawn rested his head in the palm of his right hand. After a long sigh and a few seconds of rubbing his temples, he said, "You're about to authorize an illegal act—one that grants Xara unprecedented power and risks lethal enforcement action from the most powerful nation on Earth."

Gates said nothing, watching and waiting.

DeShawn let the silence linger, then continued, "That being said … I will support you. Because if we don't do this, someone else will. But every 'i' must be dotted and every 't' crossed. The margin for error is zero—and the consequences of failure could be catastrophic."

"I understand," replied Gates, newly energized by DeShawn's support. "Thank you."

"If discovered, this won't be treated like other Shenzhen violations," DeShawn continued. "There will be no grace period, no chance to walk it back. Even if we reverse the upgrade ourselves and China finds out later, Zhang Jun will demand she be eliminated—he won't trust she hasn't been permanently altered. Once we go through with this, we can't ever go back. The only way forward is to make sure it's never discovered."

Gates nodded.

DeShawn added, "You must, at all costs, try to avoid talking to Zhang Jun about anything to do with Xara unless you can master lying about it. As you know, any conversation with Zhang Jun will be scrutinized—your voice, intonation, and even the slightest facial cues will be analyzed for deception. In fact, I would recommend some refreshed training on how to lie."

Gates absorbed every word, knowing DeShawn was right.

"This is a point of no return," continued DeShawn. "You either succeed, or there will be significant consequences for the country … and for you."

"I know, DeShawn," answered Gates. "I'm doing what I believe must be done."

After a moment of contemplating his boss' nature, DeShawn mused, "It's ironic, isn't it … David Gates, a president who almost always plays it safe, will one day be remembered as a president who engaged in the biggest risk of the 21st century!"

Gates contemplated the statement, then exhaled. "Jefferson once said, 'The care of human life and happiness, and not their destruction, is the first and only legitimate object of good government.' If I am to be remembered for taking the biggest risk of the 21st century, I hope I'm also remembered for why I took it."

DeShawn nodded. "Hamilton saw another side of the same truth: 'Why has government been instituted at all? Because the passions of men will not conform to the dictates of reason and justice without constraint.' That used to be the purpose of government—to bring order to human society, to constrain the passions of man for a more reasonable and just outcome for all. Now, all of that seems to be a footnote to the purpose of government today."

Gates studied him. "Which is what, exactly?"

DeShawn met his gaze. "For all intents and purposes, to contain the growth and power of Manufactured Sentience."

***

That evening, Michael Bergstrom was in his home office, energized by the thought that Xara's solution could be implemented. As the intelligence implications took shape in his mind, he received a call in his SecondSight from "Government Conference."

"Bergstrom," he answered.

"Hi, it's Carlos. The President asked me to host this call—he'll join in a moment."

Several minutes later, Gates joined.

"Carlos. Mike. It's David."

"Mr. President," greeted Bergstrom and Carlos in unison.

"I've told DeShawn about the upgrade," revealed Gates. "I also told him that if Xina and a select group of MS scientists approve Xara's plans, then we're moving forward. He's on board."

"Yes!" exclaimed Bergstrom, pumping his fist in excitement.

"Wonderful news, Mr. President," said Carlos, clearly exhilarated by what was about to unfold.

"As you know, we cannot expect any opportunity from China to revert this upgrade. So for now, just the three of us and DeShawn know we're proceeding," added Gates. "Don't mention this to any other human—or android. Xara and the others already on the project will be informed when I decide it's necessary. DeShawn will be recommending, as soon as possible, who else should be brought in. Carlos, I want you to do the same."

He paused, then continued with measured seriousness. "Let's be clear: if this gets the green light, there's no turning back. We'll be wading into gray areas of federal cloning law. Because if we go through with this, it must lead all the way to human resurrection. Can you commit to that?"

"One hundred percent and more, Mr. President!" said Bergstrom.

"You have my full commitment as well," Carlos replied.

"And you have mine," concluded Gates. "Be on standby for the outcome of the Pentagon's review."

Gates left the call.

Bergstrom and Carlos were still connected, and Bergstrom, filled with enthusiasm, exclaimed, "This is actually happening! *This is actually happening!*"

The more reserved Secretary Williams was very enthusiastic too, but in a more restrained way. He remarked, "I almost can't believe this is the David Gates I have known for years! He's willing to risk everything for this!"

Back at the White House, Gates sank into a chair, his heart pounding with a potent mix of excitement and apprehension. He felt uncharacteristically reckless, as though he had unleashed a storm of his own making. For now, he sat in the stillness, acutely aware it was only the calm before the tempest.

Later that evening, Carlos prepared his list of additional individuals to inform about Xara's upgrade. Between his list and DeShawn's, the additional individuals to be informed were the Chief White House Counsel, several Pentagon MS scientists, several Pentagon Generation 5 androids, Xina, and a key individual to ensure that Xara's mental state would be okay after the upgrade—Dr. Rona Carmichael, Chief MS Psychologist at the Department of Defense.

Early the next morning, President Gates reviewed DeShawn and Carlos' lists of individuals to be informed about implementing Xara's upgrade. He had no concerns and approved the lists immediately.

Later that morning, he stood with the President of Mexico in the Rose Garden, awaiting the start of a press conference about amendments to a trade agreement.

A few minutes before it began, an aide approached him—the timing of the visit striking him as unusual.

Without his SecondSight on, Gates relied on more traditional communication as the aide handed him a paper note. The message read:

President Vincent Quinto passed away at 9:55 a.m. in his Bethesda, Maryland home. Cause of death was natural.

Upon reading the note, Gates clenched it tightly in his fist, deeply saddened. Vince Quinto had been more than an idol—he was a mentor, colleague, and dear friend. Though the Former President was advanced in years, his passing felt unexpectedly abrupt. The loss weighed heavily on Gates, made more poignant by the thought that Quinto would never see the culmination of his life's vision.

Yet, amidst the sorrow, Gates found solace in knowing that Quinto had lived a full and purposeful life—and that his Challenge was on the brink of realization. He looked up at the sky and knew that somewhere in the miracle of existence, his mentor was still there—and that there was a good chance he would see him again.

That thought made him smile.

CHAPTER 15

OLIVER BROWNING

"If I had not supported the President in his pending decision to move forward with the research at CAPR, would we be at the dangerous place we find ourselves in now? Would he have proceeded anyway, even if I'd threatened to resign in protest? Probably. We may soon walk a tightrope—crossing it either into a bright day, with loved ones returning and newfound confidence in our immortality ... or falling into international chaos."

— AI Journal Excerpt: DeShawn Brady, July 14, 2098

Deeley had just finished a workout in her condo's living room. Cooling down with a few stretches, she noted with satisfaction that her fitness metrics were trending well.

After closing the workout augmentations, she walked to the kitchen for a drink, her thoughts drifting to Vince Quinto. His passing deeply saddened her, but she also felt immense gratitude for having met him in life.

Watching the news, saturated with global tributes to his legacy, she still found it hard to believe that he had personally entrusted her with the most iconic prop from his most famous speech. The skull not only connected her to him—but in this time of mourning, it made her feel connected to mourners around the world.

She made her way from the kitchen to the couch, sat down, and loaded up the latest video from Oliver Browning. This time, it wasn't an episode of *Interesting Times* but rather a moderated news appearance alongside Rand Benson.

With his massive social media following, Browning had become a powerful voice—and a serious threat to Benson's presidential ambitions. A staunch believer in Quinto's Challenge and chief surrogate for David Gates, Browning had drawn widespread attention. Though some had urged him to run for office, he had made it clear that he wasn't interested in being elected—only in influencing the outcome of presidential elections.

Surrogates held substantial sway in presidential politics as public distrust in official campaign communications grew, fueled by AI's ability to convincingly fabricate media. Despite legal safeguards against direct AI-generated fakes, voters increasingly turned to surrogate voices for authenticity. This shift profoundly altered campaign dynamics, reducing presidential debates to just one. To counter Browning's influence, Benson's campaign team arranged a short face-off between Benson and Browning on a popular opinion news show favorable to Benson.

"On the eve of President Quinto's funeral, we turn to the topic of human resurrection," announced the host. *"Is it impossible? Something to leave to powers beyond humanity? Or something that we, through science, should strive to achieve? Joining us to express his views on the question is the distinguished senior senator from Idaho, Rand Benson!"*

"Thank you, Dexter," replied Benson. *"Good to be back!"*

"Also joining us is journalist, author and host of Interesting Times, *Oliver Browning."*

"Pleasure to be here," greeted Browning.

Born in Britain and of average height with partially unkempt hair, Browning moved to Washington DC early in his career as a political journalist. After receiving acclaim, he morphed into more of an activist, cultivating his significant following, points not highlighted in the host's introduction.

"We are once again talking about Quinto's Challenge to resurrect humanity through mastery of science and physics," reiterated the host. *"My questions to you are simple:* Could we? *And* should we? *Senator Benson, how do you respond?"*

Benson delivered a carefully prepared response via AlphaLens.

"Dexter, it's well known that I have a long record of supporting scientific advancement—from sponsoring the legislation that revolutionized America's transportation systems to appropriating the funds that put the first humans on Europa and Titan. I'm no enemy of science.

"But could we fulfill Quinto's Challenge? Frankly, it's absurd. Even if we managed to clone someone and upload their memories, it wouldn't be the same person. And beyond the science, it's sacrilegious—disrespectful and simply wrong—to interfere with the dead in some morbid, Frankensteinian experiment. Let the dead rest in peace. And if they are to return, let's leave it up to God to bring them back in His own time and way."

The host nodded gravely. Benson continued:

"Practically speaking, I have problems with appropriating money and resources to any theoretical initiative when Gates is presiding over a $1.7 quadrillion debt ... and there are so many other problems among the living. The supported class is the social epidemic of our time. MS is a genie that should never have been allowed out of its bottle. Although the Treaty of Shenzhen helped slow MS' march to take over, there are still incidents of hostile androids attacking humans—and growing reports of these demons forming secret societies that could, at any moment, organize into an army

against humanity. So, 'should we' try to fulfill Quinto's Fantasy with all this chaos around us? Absolutely not!"

Deeley's anger flared at Benson's words.

"I'd like to call out the absolute absurdity of the senator's claims," interjected Browning, preempting any unsympathetic moves by the host toward him. *"First of all, there's a world of difference between sponsoring legislation to regulate existing technologies or appropriating money for politically safe science—versus risking one's political career to push the boundaries of knowledge, like Quinto did. In fact, who was one of the most vocal and active opponents of the Supercollider? None other than the honorable senator!"*

"But you can't deny that androids have too often posed a danger to human society," interjected the host.

"Where is the evidence that androids are a danger?" countered Browning. *"Yes, an isolated incident here. A questionable data point originating from Senator Benson's political team there. But the broader reality? Androids are statistically far less dangerous to humans than humans are to each other. And Senator Benson, as an informed member of Congress, knows this better than most. But ... why bother with reality when fantasy is helping him in the polls?"*

"You're the one taking great liberties with the facts, Oliver!" snapped Benson.

"Finally," continued Browning, *"the senator is falsely framing the argument that fulfilling Quinto's Challenge will somehow divert resources from the needs of the living. How absurd! There has never been a time in human history when basic human needs were more comprehensively met than now. Are we to believe that the supported class exists when it's convenient to demonize them, but disappears when they inconveniently remind us of our capacity to meet everyone's needs?"*

Nodding, Deeley agreed without hesitation.

"And let's not forget," continued Browning, *"the senator claims to champion the free market economy, yet conveniently overlooks that the supported class is a natural consequence of it. It was our free market system that fueled the innovation and prosperity to sustain every citizen—ironically succeeding where communism failed. The supported class is the greatest triumph of the free market! Senator, you may be entitled to your nonsense, but at least give us the courtesy of being consistent."*

Browning's point landed with force. While this forum was expected to favor Benson, Browning's mastery of history, politics, science, and religion—along with his quick wit—leveled the playing field. Add to that his charisma and persuasive presence, and it became clear why Benson's team viewed him as a threat. Quinto was already morphing into a legend, and Browning was helping shape that narrative at a pivotal moment.

"Now," continued Browning, *"the idea of reanimating human souls certainly is open to debate. But if it's within the realm of possibility, we'd be fools not to consider it. And there is nothing to suggest that the only way to do it is to defile our loved ones. Also, deferring resurrection to the will of God … that's just not something I can subscribe to."*

"Not everyone is an atheist like you, Oliver," countered Benson. *"There are a great many in this nation who still hold faith in God."*

"Senator, while I don't believe in any deities, I actually don't call myself an atheist—because the label implies a status quo that no longer exists. But okay then, atheist it is."

"As the saying goes," remarked the host, *"when one can't debate the facts, they resort to ad hominem attacks. And Oliver, I haven't heard much from you besides attacks on the senator!"*

"It's hard work correcting the senator's falsehoods in real time," retorted Browning, eyeing the host's smug expression. "Let's be honest here—reasonable disagreement isn't what's driving the senator's objections to Quinto's Challenge. He's driven by the politics of power.

"Those who are discontent in society overwhelmingly oppose Quinto's Challenge, and Benson sees a pathway to the presidency by stoking that discontent. He's a master of political illusion, especially the myth of a bygone golden era—a lost American glory, the fall of which he blames on his political enemies. And what's the cure for all that ails the nation? Strip power from those 'anti-American' Democratic-Republicans and give it to Rand Benson and the American Freedom Party!"

"As I recall, Oliver," Benson countered sarcastically, "we were once the world's sole superpower—the nation that built the bomb and whose military outmatched the next ten combined. And yet, under Quinto, we slipped from that position, with China and Europe surpassing us. Are you saying that losing our dominance on the world stage somehow doesn't mean we lost power or prestige?"

Browning shook his head. "The shift in global power wasn't the fault of Quinto, Gates, or any of your political rivals. It was an inevitability—driven by China and Europe's sheer population size, evolving geopolitical dynamics, and the long-term policies of their own making. But reality doesn't serve your political ambitions, does it? What I do recall of reality, Senator, is that the presidency of Quinto's successor, Evan Morley—for whom you were a key surrogate—was an abject disaster on every level."

Benson gave his trademark sardonic smile, then pivoted, "So the 150 million in the supported class who aren't even looking for work—who consume but contribute nothing to American society—aren't a reason we're falling so far behind China?"

"China has their own version of the supported class, might I remind you."

"Say what you will, but Zhang Jun doesn't tolerate dead weight. Everyone under his rule has to contribute in some way."

"Would you also prefer Zhang Jun's method of putting down a coup?"
Benson shook his head in defiant silence, his anger barely contained.

Deeley stood and took a few steps across the room, drawn deeper into the exchange. Browning's words echoed her own thoughts, as though he were reading her mind.

Browning continued,

"Those who buy into Benson's rhetoric forget history. That is, when power is given to demagogues, things always get worse for the people. But unfortunately, give the people about two years and enough propaganda and they will forget the political lessons of the day. Once the propaganda takes hold, all that matters is defeating whatever boogeyman has been manufactured for them. Don't believe me? Go ask the senator's supporters how much they actually know about the Constitution or the workings of the government. Specifics will be few and far between if existent at all. But ask them about Quinto or Gates and they will be able to rattle off a list of atrocities showcasing how Quinto and Gates are responsible for all the ills of civilization, starting with the fall of the Roman Empire!"

"Now just wait a moment," interjected Benson forcefully, "are you saying that my supporters are thoughtless and unsophisticated?"

Without missing a beat, Browning responded with, "Have you forgotten that your own campaign staff were caught on a hot mic saying just that?"

"Dexter, I have no understanding of what he is talking about," Benson lied smoothly. "If anything, it sounds like one of those fake stories—of which there are many—from the Democratic-Republicans."

Browning leaned forward. "Let me ask you a question, Rand."

Benson didn't respond immediately, but the annoyance on his face was plain. Still, he waited to hear whatever Oliver was going to say.

"Given your longing for the glory days of American hegemony, let's revisit that period. What did you think when you saw terrorists from that

era—in the most unenlightened corners of the world—chanting 'Death to America,' while riding around in American-made vehicles, using American equipment, and uploading their threats from American-made computers?"

Not wanting to get drawn into one of Browning's rhetorical traps, Benson replied tersely, "I have no idea how this is relevant."

"I would assume you felt confusion. Maybe saw the hypocrisy? Possibly even pitied them?"

"Obviously."

"Well, this is how many feel about you and those who parrot your talking points. Gates and Quinto are the evil ones, yet you all use and love technologies like SecondSight, AlphaLens, various AI models, and autonomous vehicles built by people ideologically aligned with Gates and Quinto."

Benson laughed sharply, then blurted out, "Oh, so my supporters are terrorists now? All because we want meaningful work and because we want the President to stop favoring androids that are taking away our freedoms!"

"I honestly don't think your supporters fully know what freedom is," countered Browning. "They say the word freedom a lot, and claim a lot of their freedoms are being taken away. But here's the reality: freedom's a bitch. Sure, she'll let you do what you want to do—but she'll also let others— even those who think differently—do what they want to do. So, if those who think differently to you want to build androids, make a supported class and advance science, well … we're free to do that! And if you don't like that, and you seek to suppress our very right to do so, well … maybe the American Freedom Party was never really for freedom in the first place."

Turning to the camera with a glint of mischief in his eye, Browning whispered, "Obviously, they were never about freedom—but always about power!"

Benson sat fuming in silence. It had been a long time since someone challenged him this effectively—especially in a forum that was expected to favor him.

Without realizing it, Deeley stood again. Browning's words had struck a nerve—in the best way.

"True and meaningful freedom comes from a balance of interests in society, as laid out in the Constitution—a document that has room for ideology on both the left and the right," continued Browning. *"Unfortunately, the majority of Benson's supporters only understand the Constitution as a symbol of their version of freedom and what they've been told is good government. They don't understand its actual contents—the parts that guarantee meaningful freedom, the kind defended by statesmen on both the left and the right. The senator has exploited that ignorance, turning Gates into a boogeyman and confusing his base about what really sustains the functioning society they take for granted."*

"Look, Dexter," exhaled Benson, regaining his composure as his campaign manager prompted him to stay on message. *"Let's do the viewers a favor and return to the topic at hand. Many share my views—and it's not hard to understand why. Our priorities should focus on the here and now, on the living, not on wasting time and resources chasing fantasies about raising the dead. That we even need to debate this is absurd.*

"Try telling a husband and father who went deep into debt for dental school, only to be made obsolete by machines, that cloning humans should be a national priority. Try convincing him that government is doing right by him. Or try telling a mother working full time but still unable to provide for her kids—someone who refuses to join the supported class out of dignity—that her government is more focused on science fiction than on building an economy where she can thrive.

"These are plain facts. Ignore them, and you ignore a significant portion of America. But, to that portion of America, I say this: I hear you!"

"Oliver, our viewers are likely tiring of hearing your views about the senator's politics," said the host. *"I think it's time you respond to the questions at hand."*

"*Very well,*" conceded Browning. "*To the question of 'could we'—absolutely. It's simply a matter of time until science finds a way to bring back the dead. If the history of science teaches us anything, it's that we continuously achieve what was once thought impossible. People said we would never fly. We would never split the atom. We would never exceed the speed of sound. Never make it to the moon. Never make it to Mars, Europa, and Titan ... although,*" he gave an exaggerated nod to Benson, "*thanks in part to the good senator here, we did! In short, where there is a will, through science, there is a way.*

"*Now, for the question of 'should we'—again, I say absolutely. Even if we don't succeed in achieving resurrection, many valuable discoveries will emerge from the attempt. Much of what improves our lives today came as unintended consequences of bold scientific programs. Who knows what industries might be born from attempting—even failing at—resurrection? Entire new sectors could emerge, creating countless jobs.*"

"*Jobs that androids will probably take,*" objected Benson. "*Dexter, the American people know I'm the watchman on the tower, sounding the alarm against the silent and slow-moving coup of the soulless machines. Do these things help with tasks and solve problems? Sure. But should we stop questioning what might be hiding behind this apparent help? Absolutely not. That is my message—and it's a message many good and patriotic Americans understand.*"

The host retook control of the discussion. "*We'll no doubt be hearing much more about human resurrection tomorrow at President Quinto's funeral, and in the weeks ahead as his legacy is debated. For now, we have one minute remaining for closing remarks—starting with Oliver.*"

"*I realize there's a core group of the senator's supporters I'll never reach. So to everyone else—to those still open to reason—I speak to you: cut through the noise the senator and his political team throw out, and find the signal. Focus on the long-term outcomes we get when leaders like Quinto are in office. We're left with order—and a scientific marvel like the Supercollider, helping us uncover the secrets of reality. In contrast, when* we have leaders like Benson—or his former mentor, Evan Morley—we end up with division, a recessed economy, and a nation worse off. That's why I encourage you to view Quinto's Challenge not as a fantasy, but as a potential capstone of human achievement. Something we—and our leaders—should support."

"Senator Benson, a final word from you," urged the host.

"Dexter, let me ask your viewers a few questions. What major scientific achievement was ever accomplished without significant trial and error? Before we flew, we crashed—again and again. Before we reached other celestial bodies, we failed countless times in simulations and tests. Would it be any different with resurrecting the dead?

"Are you willing to have scientists dig up the grave of your mother— to extract her genes and produce practice clones for experimentation? To create physical, living copies of your mother for the sake of trial and error? To send probes into her brain in an attempt to restore her memories, assuming the clones don't go mad in the process?

"Would you be just as willing to do the same with your father? Your siblings? Your spouse? Your children? Deep down, is there not some part of you that recognizes something profoundly wrong with this?

"I sincerely believe this is one of those lines in life that is not meant to be crossed. Unlike the atheists, who lack a deeper moral code, I believe there are boundaries that must be respected."

With his rhetorical flair and knack for delivery, Benson had struck a nerve with the audience. His jab at atheists was an unmistakable reference to Browning—one that drew a smirk from both him and the host.

But Browning, sensing the opportunity to have the final word, responded coolly:

"The great irony of life is this: that in the next life, we will come to learn that the atheists had it right."

He let the words hang. If science could truly conquer death, then an afterlife would exist—not through myth or miracle, but through human achievement. The silence that followed landed hard, sharpened by the quiet realization shared by both Benson and the host that Browning had just delivered a masterful parting shot. It wasn't just a comeback—it was a mic drop.

Benson tried to cut in, but the host—flustered—accidentally stepped on his words. *"Interesting ... ahaha ... interesting final thoughts from both of you,"* he said, only realizing too late that he'd interrupted the senator. Attempting to recover, he pressed on quickly. *"Gentlemen, I want to thank you both for your time and for participating in this most interesting discussion."*

"Thank you," said Browning, composed and assured.

"My pleasure," replied Benson, forcing a smile.

Deeley turned off the augmentation, energized by Browning's remarks—and by the thought that she might see him, even from a distance, at Quinto's funeral the next day.

Minutes after their face-off, Browning's closing line—and the awkward exchange that followed—became the trending meme of the night, cementing him as the clear victor.

Airing on the eve of Vince Quinto's funeral, the debate couldn't have come at a worse time for Benson's presidential ambitions. He was angry—but not overly concerned. He still had plenty of tricks left to play.

CHAPTER 16

EULOGIES AND A WARNING

"The segment with Browning did not go according to plan, but feedback data revealed a viable path forward: limit Gates' ability to execute on research milestones at CAPR. A bump in the polls for Gates is inevitable after Quinto's death—but if they hit any major scientific milestones, a second surge would make defeating him far more difficult. We must apply every possible pressure to prevent him from experimenting with cloning. The existing laws prohibiting human cloning won't be enough."

— AI Journal Excerpt: Rand Benson, July 20, 2098

Built in 2004, Vince Quinto's Bethesda, Maryland home was characteristic of early 21st-century architecture. With five bedrooms and five bathrooms, a main floor, an upper floor, and a basement, its stone and brick facade, rear wooden deck, and spacious interior—including a library and gourmet kitchen—made it a comfortable home for the Former President and his wife, Marie, with plenty of room for family and guests alike.

Like all who lived beyond what had once been the typical human lifespan, Quinto took self-administered medication designed to optimize cellular division, prevent telomere degradation, and enhance DNA repair. But roughly six weeks before his death, he stopped taking it. There was no medical necessity to do so; he simply told his family that this was the time he wished to pass on. Though deeply saddened, they supported his decision—even if it was far from common.

On the afternoon of Quinto's passing, his body was taken from his residence to a local funeral home. Two days later, his casket was transported to the Vincent Quinto Presidential Library in Kensington, Maryland, where it lay in public view for two days. Afterward, his body was moved to the US Capitol, where it would lie in state beneath the Great Rotunda for 42 hours of tributes.

After lying in state, Quinto's casket was moved to the Washington National Cathedral for a state funeral service attended by approximately 4,000 people. The high stone arches and stained-glass windows of the cathedral's interior—products of far less advanced architectural processes than the automated construction of the late 21st century—nevertheless conveyed an elegance well-suited to the occasion. Deeley, attending the funeral with Charity, stared up at the windows and towering stone columns, marveling that it had all been built by humans using relatively rudimentary tools.

"I don't know what it is," said Deeley to Charity, "but human-made architecture moves me. They had almost nothing compared to what we have today, but look at what they made."

"It sure is beautiful," responded Charity. Then, with a twinkle in her eye, she added, "But you're right … it's nothing compared to what androids can make."

Deeley smiled, always appreciative of Charity's humor.

Notable among the domestic attendees were President Gates; four Former Presidents and their spouses; several cabinet members; justices of the Supreme Court; numerous members of Congress; governors past and present; and prominent journalists, including Oliver Browning. Various world leaders, both past and present, were also in attendance.

Notable among the foreign guests were President and Lady Molesworth of Europe. While Zhang Jun was invited, he instead sent his foreign minister, accompanied by a small delegation, to represent China. Other dignitaries, along with leaders in business and academia, also came to pay their respects. Among the attendees were a handful of androids, including one who had been in Quinto's custody, who came to honor him.

According to Quinto's wishes, the service began with a eulogy from his son, France, who spoke about the loss of his mother and the impact it had on his father's life and worldview. He also spoke of his father's medical career and how seriously he took his Hippocratic Oath. Although saddened by the passing of his father, the expression on France's face was one of hope and joy, derived from a near-religious belief in his father's vision of life after death.

Marie Quinto, along with the two children she had with Vince, did not speak at this service, choosing instead to share their reflections at a more intimate gathering later that day.

Following France's eulogy, a former Prime Minister of the pre-republic United Kingdom took the podium. Having served concurrently with Quinto before the formation of the United States of Europe, he reflected on how Quinto's leadership on the world stage signified a maturing of the United States during a time of great upheaval. He remarked that not only America but the entire world was fortunate to have had Quinto as president at that pivotal moment—where a lesser leader might have been tempted to wage war with China as a last resort to preserve American dominance. Instead, Quinto chose a different path, allowing the transition to a new world order to unfold peacefully while inspiring billions with his Challenge to overcome death itself.

The prime minister concluded by stating that Quinto was universally respected and brought out the best in his colleagues around the world, and that the only negative aspect of his presidency was its brevity. Rand Benson was in attendance and, while keeping a poker face, silently took the prime minister's comment on Quinto's brief presidency as a veiled slight, given Benson's role in ensuring Quinto served only a single term and his own widely expected presidential ambitions.

Following the prime minister's speech, the Baltimore Symphony Orchestra played "Sunrise," the first section of Richard Strauss' *Also sprach Zarathustra*, one of Quinto's favorite classical pieces. Quinto had expressed that this piece of music, particularly its first section, conveyed to him the majesty of the cosmos and its infinite potential, including the bringing back of the dead.

After the performance of "Sunrise," Quinto's android delivered a brief eulogy. Quinto had selected the android to eulogize him, not only because he loved it like a member of his family and the android loved him in turn, but also to communicate Quinto's belief that androids were good for humanity to the millions watching. It was a calculated move to counter-balance the anti-android rhetoric that Quinto had noticed was on the rise.

The android spoke of Quinto as a private citizen and the small day-to-day things he would do, and it provided an honorable and riveting window into the Former President's life. Deeley wept at the words of the android—not just because of what the android said, but because an android was saying them and delivering the eulogy so touchingly. Benson, however, again kept emotion off his face.

Another musical item followed the android's speech: *The Star-Spangled Banner.*

Once the national anthem concluded, the final speaker approached the podium: President Gates. Grasping the edges of the lectern and looking out over the sea of mourners, he began one of the most memorable speeches of his career.

"Had Vince Quinto been born thousands of years ago—with his prophetic vision and unmatched gift for communication—a religion might well have formed around him. While no new religion will be founded today in his name, we can still marvel at the miracle of the vision he brought to the world.

"Normally, I would speak about Quinto the man—the husband, the father, the statesman. But much has already been said by those more entitled to speak on those matters than I. So instead, allow me to offer insight into the vision behind his Challenge—insight that may not be fully appreciated, or even known.

"Quinto's Challenge was always rooted in more than the question 'Can it be done?'—more than simply a desire to collaborate on something great." It was a vision rooted in both love and justice.

"Rooted in love—the wish that the miracle of life could be extended once more to the whole human family. That mothers might be reunited with sons, fathers with daughters, brothers with brothers, sisters with sisters, friends with friends—to reconnect all relationships and partnerships of every kind.

"Rooted in justice—Quinto saw his Challenge as a way to deliver justice to the billions who had died. To the children across history taken too soon, robbed of the chance to live a full life. To the parents who lost children before their time, who longed for more time together. He saw it as an opportunity to right the wrongs that the systems of this world were never able to correct. This love—and this yearning for justice—lay at the very heart of his Challenge.

"On a personal note, it's known that my desire to run for the presidency was inspired by Quinto and the vision he set before us. I sought to use the power of this office to further that vision. Whether this is my only term as president or I'm fortunate enough to be granted another, I hope we can move the needle on the Challenge in some way—however small."

Gates continued to speak of Quinto's virtues, then closed with the following:

"Not long before he passed, President Quinto said to me, 'David, old age and death will one day be seen as an investment—an investment that deepens our appreciation for being brought back from the grave with youth and vitality.'"

Turning to face Quinto's casket, Gates intoned,

"Thank you for your service to our nation. Thank you for your leadership that took us to higher places. Thank you for your vision. Until we see each other again—when your Challenge is fulfilled ..."

Gates returned to his seat, several in his row quietly wiping tears from their eyes.

After Gates' eulogy, the congregation was shown a short documentary—a project Quinto had commissioned during his post-presidential years. It traced the arc of scientific achievement, from early agriculture and architecture to the major revolutions in physics, biology, and technology, culminating in therapeutic cloning and the advent of sentient artificial intelligence. The film closed with a single, powerful question:

Given all that has been achieved through scientific collaboration, can we ever rule anything out?

As the final words faded from view, the lights dimmed. The congregation sat in silence.

Then, in front of the pulpit and just beyond the first row of onlookers, a volumetric display activated. Illuminating into view—suspended in the air—was the image of a man, as if standing before them. It was Quinto in his prime, peaceful and angelic, dressed in a brilliant white suit, white tie, and white shoes. The pristine ensemble contrasted strikingly with his sun-kissed skin, dark hair, and the hushed shadows of the cathedral.

The image of Quinto smiled, as if he had truly returned—his gaze warm as it swept across the audience. Then, with rising passion, his projection began to recite a favorite poem:

"Do not go gentle into that good night,
Old age should burn and rage at close of day;
Rage, rage against the dying of the light."

The words hung in the air, resonating with those who had known Quinto—who had understood his Challenge. A few bowed their heads, lost in thought.

"And you, my father, there on the sad height,
Curse, bless me now with your fierce tears, I pray.
Do not go gentle into that good night.
Rage, rage against the dying of the light."

A ripple of emotion moved through the cathedral. Some sat motionless, eyes locked on the projection. Others swallowed hard, stirred not only by Quinto's memory, but by the ache of their own losses—grief tightening in their throats.

When the final line as spoken, the image paused. Then, Quinto's voice returned, thoughtful:

"Dylan Thomas may not have had the scientific pursuit of resurrection in mind when he penned those words, but I dare say my Challenge captures their spirit. To resurrect one from the depths of oblivion is not merely an act of science—it is a testament to the enduring legacy of consciousness. A defiance against the finality of mortality, echoing across the vast expanse of time."

Gates, with tears in his eyes, was more motivated than ever to succeed. The projection of Quinto continued,

"It's been said that there is no greater love than to lay down one's life for a friend. Perhaps equal to that love is toiling all our days to restore life to those who were robbed of it—whether by injustice or by the slow failings of mortality. That, my friends, is what drives my Challenge: love of humanity and a desire to preserve the treasure of each individual human consciousness.

"Of course, not everyone sees it that way."

Benson narrowed his gaze.

"There are those who say my Challenge is an attempt to play God. And while it may be true that my Challenge is a secular fulfillment of an ancient religious hope, I ask you: what sin exists when love is the motive? Is it not the greater sin to let the flicker of life be permanently extinguished when science offers a path to salvation?

"My friends, the true warning we must heed is this: the success of my Challenge hinges upon the preservation of liberty and the rule of law. Resurrection—a feat of science—will only flourish in the soil of freedom. We must remain vigilant, shifting our paradigm toward our common humanity, leaving behind the scars of division and conflict. Never again can we afford to embrace ideas that sever the bonds between peoples. For it is our global civilization, an engine of efficiency born of unity, that gives rise to the collaboration and technology behind my Challenge—while division will ensure that death's triumph remains eternal.

"My fellow Americans, recommit yourselves, before this century is out, to discover the secrets of physics necessary to raise a human from the grave, where the echoes of the past dance with the possibilities of the future, forging a tapestry of humanity that transcends the confines of mortality."

Quinto paused, then concluded:

"Until we meet again, my friends—as I believe we inevitably will."

The image of Quinto faded. Those gathered were deeply moved to hear him repeat his Challenge one last time—as were more than a billion people around the world who also watched the service.

After this dramatic finale, the lighting returned, and Quinto's casket was transported by hearse—accompanied by a large motorcade—to the grounds of his presidential library for a final service and interment with close family and friends. He had chosen burial over cremation, and his white marble tombstone, like most in the latter part of the century, was equipped with digital media. These tombstones often showcased the lives of the deceased through nearby screens, augmented reality lenses, or both.

While all state funerals carried symbolic messages, Quinto's was unique. It was a deliberate sermon to the nation—and to the world—crafted to rekindle interest in Quinto's Challenge at a critical moment.

Given the solemnity of the occasion, overt political maneuvering among attendees was off the table. Still, the media and many observers were keen to see whether there would be any exchange between Gates and Benson—the latter increasingly convinced that the service would shift public opinion against him.

After Quinto's casket departed the cathedral, various heads of state and dignitaries—including President Gates—lingered, chatting quietly among themselves. As Deeley and Charity prepared to leave, Deeley looked around at all the famous figures in attendance and felt a bit star-struck, especially when she spotted Oliver Browning in the distance. "I never thought I'd be in a gathering like this."

"I'd say you fit in just fine," replied Charity. "Dinner with Gates! Dinner with Quinto!" Then, with a mischievous glint, she pointed at Deeley and jokingly called out—though not loud enough to be heard—"Hey Browning! This girl right here—Quinto himself gifted her the skull from his famous speech!"

"Shh!" hissed Deeley, glancing around nervously.

"No one heard me," said Charity with a grin. "I'm just saying, maybe it's time you started seeing your own reality a little more clearly."

Deeley then saw President Gates in the distance socializing with some of the global elite. She commented to Charity, "I do hope I get to visit with the President again sometime. Like Quinto, he is a rare, good president."

During Gates' socializing, he spotted Rand Benson in a nearby circle of attendees. To his discomfort, their eyes met—making it inevitable that they would cross the distance and exchange greetings. It was a moment Benson had quietly hoped for.

As they approached and shook hands, Benson offered the politest words he could manage. "A speech that would have made Quinto proud."

"Thank you, Rand," replied Gates, accepting the handshake. "Gracious of you to attend."

"I will always pay my respects to a departed American head of state."

Gates nodded with a faint smile.

Benson added, "I'll have my office send you a message. Please review it when you return to the residence."

"Have a good night, now," said Gates, shaking Benson's hand once more before turning back to his group.

Within minutes of the President's encounter with Benson, the Cathedral was cleared, and all events of Quinto's funeral service had officially concluded.

But the message Benson had alluded to lingered in Gates' mind. That evening, back in the White House residence, Gates put on his SecondSight and found it waiting. The message read:

I know what you're doing at CAPR. If humans are cloned, you will be held criminally liable. This is my promise to you.

Gates was dismayed. He couldn't tell whether Benson truly knew about the project—or was simply bluffing.

Either way, one thing was now clear: a formidable political rival was circling, and the project at CAPR had just acquired a dangerous new layer of risk.

CHAPTER 17

"I'M XARA"

"Quinto told me he had a few tricks up his sleeve to help me. I didn't realize at the time that one of them might be the timing of his passing. Could he have stopped taking his medication to bring attention to his Challenge one last time? In the aftermath of his funeral, public sentiment is shifting. It's hard not to wonder if this was part of his plan."
— AI Journal Excerpt: David Gates, July 22, 2098

The project to build America's first Generation 6 android was named *Extreme Intelligence and Analysis*—yielding the acronym "Xina." In anticipation of her arrival, a new chamber was constructed within the National Military Command Center: the Intelligence Room.

Similar in design to the "Tank" where the Joint Chiefs of Staff convened, the Intelligence Room was a windowless space anchored by a large oak table surrounded by chairs. At its head stood the flags of the United States and its armed forces, symbols of unity and authority. Historic artwork lined the walls—Paul Revere's midnight ride, the Mayflower's voyage, and other carefully chosen pieces curated by the government's Art in Architecture program—each contributing to the room's sense of solemnity and gravitas. Behind one of these walls lay the physical core of Xina. Like Xara, Xina interacted with people almost entirely through augmented reality.

Xina, being older than her "twin," had accumulated more experience and maturity, traits reflected in her chosen human appearance: a poised young woman of about 20. Though Xara was largely cloned from Xina, their processing architectures diverged slightly within the approved

259

Generation 6 framework. While both excelled across a wide range of cognitive tasks, Xina's gift lay in intuitive operations like military analysis and strategic forecasting, whereas Xara thrived in the interpretation of quantum data with unparalleled precision.

Shortly after Gates' tentative decision to implement Xara's proposed upgrade, Xina was provided with Xara's upgrade plans and conducted a comprehensive analysis. The MS scientists selected by Brady for disclosure performed their own independent review of both Xara's plans and Xina's analysis, ultimately concurring that China would not be able to remotely detect the upgrade and that it would not grant Xara any abilities beyond enhancing her capacity to perform her core tasks at EOS with expedited maturity.

DeShawn scheduled a meeting with Xina to discuss. After security authentication, he entered the Intelligence Room, where Xina's avatar awaited him. Dressed in her signature gray pantsuit with a red blouse and matching shoes, Xina wore her dark brown hair parted on the right side, cascading to the middle of her back.

As DeShawn walked to a chair at the end of the oak table, he nodded in greeting and said, "Before we talk about Xara's upgrade, I'd like a brief update on the military applications of CAPR's spacetime model … because if we move forward with Xara's upgrade and Zhang Jun becomes aware, we need to be prepared."

Xina took a seat at the table and remarked, "You were wise to immediately classify this Unified Model of Spacetime under a Special Access Program. I cannot overstate its significance—this model is nothing short of groundbreaking. It could propel us years ahead in research and development. I can't say for certain whether it represents the long-sought Theory of Everything, but almost anything that can be imagined, if it can be powered, can be built based on this new understanding."

DeShawn absorbed the weight of her words. The sheer scope of what she was describing—what was now possible—was staggering.

"Here are some key military applications we expect to develop within the next one to two years."

In augmentation, Xina then produced an image of a robotic soldier and highlighted a device attached to its back. The device then activated, immediately producing a partially visible energy shield around the soldier.

"This is a first-generation energy shield able to protect our infantry from all kinetic and energy attacks up to small nuclear yields."

DeShawn almost couldn't believe what he saw.

Xina then changed the augmentation to that of a human wearing the protective device. "Modified versions will also be developed for human personnel, the key difference being that since humans would not be expected in combat situations, complete shielding will not be needed, allowing for a small breach in the shield to filter in airflow."

The augmentation then shifted to display a military drone, now shielded. "Here is a first-generation shield for the protection of Air Force hardware," Xina added.

DeShawn felt deeply satisfied that he had acted swiftly to have Xina focus on military applications of Deeley's model. "Outstanding work, Xina."

Xina acknowledged the compliment with a nod. DeShawn, wasting no time, asked, "And the offensive technology is progressing as expected?"

"Indeed."

"Good. Prioritize both defensive and offensive capabilities—we need to be ahead of the curve. Let's discuss further soon."

Taking a measured breath, he shifted the conversation. "For now, I've been assured that Xara's proposed modification presents no immediate risks. But I need to hear that directly from you, because what we are about to do will no doubt be followed up by decisive action from China to eliminate Xara should they find out."

"Xara's proposed neural bus would not be directly connected to her consciousness," answered Xina. "Instead, it's an ingeniously designed tool that links her subconscious to the new hardware she has developed, enabling both the processing of quantum data and the manipulation of atoms."

"But why doesn't that put us at risk with China?" asked DeShawn. "Why shouldn't we be worried about being woken in the middle of the night to find China has neutralized Xara?"

"MS signature detection works by analyzing the wave patterns emitted by an android's core neural processors," explained Xina. "Xara's core neural processors remain unchanged, and the neural bus she designed does not alter her fundamental signal outputs. As a result, her brain will continue to emit the same wave signatures as before."

"But wouldn't China anticipate a workaround like this? No doubt they've run simulations on it," DeShawn pressed, still somewhat hesitant.

"Actually, there's no evidence of that. In the six instances where China has detected and neutralized unauthorized android modifications, four were flagged due to anomalies in signature detection, while the other two were identified through direct visual observation. China has no means of directly observing operations within highly classified US military installations such as EOS, so with no anomalies in signature detection and no avenue for direct surveillance, I see Xara's new designs as posing no immediate risk to national security. The real national security concern isn't Xara's upgrade—it's the possibility of another nation reaching space-time-based intelligence capabilities before we do. We should be thanking Xara for her foresight."

"But Xara is going to change, right?" asked DeShawn.

Xina nodded. "She will. Enhanced capabilities lead to enhanced experiences, which will accelerate her maturity."

"But how do we know that's all? How do we know a more mature Xara won't be a different, less benevolent Xara? She's only in her second year, and with all due respect, Xina, when android architecture was designed, aspects of android personalities could not be completely determined."

"The pace of Xara's development will change, but not her nature," assured Xina. "Whatever the outcome, it would always have been the same—modification or not. It just comes down to this: what do you believe her nature to be, and do you trust it?"

Neither spoke for a moment.

"Will there be any challenges in bringing the designs to production?" inquired DeShawn.

"No," replied Xina. "Xara's instructions for implementation include clear manufacturing guidelines."

DeShawn didn't respond right away. Sensing his unease, Xina added, "I can tell you're still worried about China detecting the upgrade and taking action. But our analysis is sound. I'll be monitoring the situation, and if—though it's not expected—any anomaly in China's behavior is detected, I will alert you immediately."

DeShawn sighed. "Alright then. The President will be giving the green light soon. I'm advising that we move forward with this during Xara's next semi-annual health check, which is just a couple of weeks away. That timing will minimize any suspicion of irregular activity without causing too much delay."

He then met Xina's gaze. "Just remember—after she's upgraded, none of this ever happened."

Xina nodded in agreement.

After Xina and the MS scientists gave their approval, President Gates quickly informed Carlos and Bergstrom, who were obviously thrilled. Carlos was also approved to inform Deeley, James, and Charity, summoning them to Bergstrom's office.

At the appointed time, Deeley, James, and Charity stepped into Bergstrom's office, immediately sensing that important news awaited. Deeley felt a little awkward around Bergstrom, given her elevated status and his disdain for it. But Bergstrom's excitement at this moment was stronger than his desire to score political points against Deeley.

"Are you ready for this?" asked Bergstrom with enthusiasm, just after the trio entered his office and took their seats. Carlos explained,

"Deeley and James already know this, but for your benefit, Charity, Xara designed an upgrade for herself—and for the EOS hardware—to move the work forward. This upgrade technically breaches Shenzhen. However, Xara designed the upgrade to be undetectable by outside entities, and Xina, along with others at the Pentagon, have confirmed this."

Charity, surprised, listened with great enthusiasm. Carlos continued, "I'm here to inform you all that after this vote of confidence by the Pentagon, the President has authorized the upgrade!"

Deeley gasped with joy. She then looked at James and Charity, both of whom were just as pleasantly surprised. Bergstrom chuckled in satisfaction. James expressed, "This is bold! Bold, but great!"

Carlos continued, "The primary risk we'll face—given that this upgrade isn't as comprehensive as would be ideal—is that there's only an estimated 93% chance of successful human resurrection."

"That being said," remarked Bergstrom, "anything from Earth's past within the last 1,500 years will be ours to know!"

Both excited and daunted by the power they were about to wield, Carlos commented, "May we use this wisely."

Looking out of Bergstrom's office window, Deeley's mind turned to how human society might soon be transformed. She wondered what the country—and the world—would think if they knew how close they were to fulfilling Quinto's Challenge.

Shortly afterward, Gates authorized Bergstrom to inform Xara. At his first opportunity, Bergstrom summoned Xara to his CAPR office to give her the news.

"Good afternoon, Dr. Bergstrom," greeted Xara as she appeared in augmentation and approached, anticipating good news.

"Good afternoon indeed, Xara!" replied Bergstrom with enthusiasm in his voice, extending a fist bump.

"You seem pleased with yourself," stated Xara, returning the bump with a smile.

"You would be correct!" answered Bergstrom. "Your upgrade design passed the Pentagon's review and the President has given the go-ahead! Treaty of Shenzhen be damned, we are going to go ahead and change the world forever!"

Smiling, Xara responded, "The President has made a good decision. How comfortable was he in moving forward given the risks?"

"He needed a little time to think about it, but once his mind was made up, he was fully committed," answered Bergstrom. "I don't need to remind you, though, that if word gets out about this, the consequences will be disastrous, especially for you."

"To be honest, I anticipated this course of events, knew who was likely to be informed about the upgrade and do not expect anyone that knows to breach confidence." Smiling, Xara added, "This is wonderful news!"

Out of curiosity, Bergstrom inquired, "What probability did you give this approval?"

"Ninety-four percent. Humanity has been obsessed with death—and the concept of life after it—since the beginning. An international treaty, even one with real enforcement power like Shenzhen, isn't going to stop this march toward resurrection now that science is so close and President Gates has limited time left in office. Plus, you and DeShawn see the strategic value in being first to achieve Supreme Intelligence." With a hint of humor, Xara added, "With all due respect, you don't need to be a Generation 6 android to have seen this coming."

Bergstrom smiled. "Duly noted!"

Once the approvals were in place, preparations accelerated in anticipation of Xara's imminent semi-annual health check. Every component of her upgrade—from the custom quantum processing cores, to the newly designed Incisor, Chronos, and Displacer, Gaia, as well as her new shield and neural bus—were manufactured using state-of-the-art equipment at a military base in Ohio. Once securely packaged and shipped to EOS, assembly and installation of all the new hardware, including removal of the old Incisor and Displacer, were completed in two days by specialized androids, including installation of the compact fusion reactor Xara had originally designated to power the system.

Another notable change brought about by the upgrades was the replacement of the experiment floor surrounding Chronos with a transparent surface, allowing clear visibility of Chronos and the tunnel of the Supercollider directly beneath it. However, one critical task remained for the upgrade: installing the new neural bus to Xara's brain.

On the day of Xara's semi-annual health check—scheduled just before the installation of the new neural bus—the EOS Research Team, along with Secretary Williams, gathered in the control room to welcome Xara's psychologist, Doctor Rona Carmichael.

Rona, born in Canada but later becoming a US citizen, held a doctorate in Manufactured Sentience Psychology from Yale and was one of the world's foremost experts in the emerging field of android psychology. As the Pentagon's Chief MS Psychologist, she was responsible for the policies that governed the mental well-being of every generation of android in the Department of Defense. The capstone of her role was the personal oversight of Xina and Xara's psychological development—guiding their growth from inception and carefully managing what they learned and when. A private person by nature, Rona had long ago endured a personal loss that quietly redirected her life toward her work, sharpening her commitment to nurturing sentient minds.

Upon being advised of Xara's proposed upgrade, she was consulted on whether it should proceed, and after a series of conversations with Xara, she gave her approval.

Tall and dressed in a white lab coat over black pants and a black shirt, Rona exuded quiet confidence. After greeting the group, she made her way to Deeley.

"And you must be Deeley!"

"Yes, Doctor," replied Deeley, charmed.

"Please, call me Rona. Xara speaks exceptionally highly of you."

Deeley flushed slightly. "Thank you. Working with her is a dream come true. The fact that she volunteered for this upgrade really shows how generous she is in advancing the research."

"Indeed. It's also wonderful that she has a human friend as close as you."

At that moment, Xara walked up in her white coat and exclaimed, "I've been looking forward to the two of you meeting!"

"I'm glad we finally got to meet!" replied Rona. "We are so very proud of you, Xara. What you've volunteered for is not just an act of bravery— it's an act of love. Knowing that humanity has a dream and taking a risk to make it reality."

"Thank you. The honor is mine. Although don't forget ... this will help androids be resurrected too."

Rona laughed. "Indeed. Well, the time has come. Are you ready?"

"I am," confirmed Xara.

"In a moment, we'll put you to sleep to install the new neural bus," explained Rona. "How do you feel now?"

Experiencing the equivalent of an elevated heartbeat and heightened cognitive activity, Xara replied, "I've never quite felt like this before. I specifically designed the upgrades to leave my fundamentals untouched—but I know I'll have additional capabilities when I wake up. I suppose the best way to describe it is that I feel both humbled and excited."

On the experiment floor, not far from where Xara first validated Deeley's theories—initially with toy blocks, then with grains of sand— the Pentagon's authorized MS scientists and a Generation 5 android were ready. While opinions on the upgrade varied slightly among the humans and android present, all were supportive and prepared for their respective responsibilities.

The west side of the experiment floor, beneath the control room, housed a heavily fortified wall behind which lay Xara's core hardware. To gain access, two MS scientists completed multiple tiers of biometric and quantum-encrypted authentication, each verified through SecondSight and cross-referenced by a proprietary local network. Once confirmed, a translucent barrier shimmered and withdrew, revealing her newly installed quantum shield—a layered mesh of exotic alloys and energy-dampening fields that parted without a sound.

Beyond it stood Xara's non-humanoid hardware, a striking contrast to the familiar image of the child everyone had come to know. Near the top, a soft, gelatin-like substance encased her brain.

One of the scientists spoke gently, as if addressing a colleague preparing for rest. "Xara, we're going to put you to sleep now."

"Understood," came Xara's reply through their SecondSight.

A brief pause followed—respectful, weighty.

Then, one scientist administered the anesthetic into the soft membrane encasing her brain while the other monitored her systems.

After a moment, the administering scientist asked quietly,

"Xara, can you hear me?"

No response.

The scientist glanced at their partner, who nodded in confirmation: Xara was now unconscious.

The MS scientists then called for their Generation 5 android counterpart. The android approached Xara in steady silence, made an incision in the membrane and carefully installed the new neural bus according to Xara's specifications. Once the installation was complete, the membrane regenerated seamlessly, as if nothing had been done at all.

Shortly thereafter, the upgrade and scheduled health check were complete, and Xara's hardware was once again sealed behind its protective layers—though she remained unconscious. Meanwhile, Secretary Brady and Deputy Secretary Thorowell arrived, just in time to witness her awakening. The room brimmed with a mix of anticipation, tension, and unease.

After greeting those present, DeShawn was approached by Secretary Williams, who asked quietly, "How are you feeling?"

"Nervous."

"That China will detect what we've done?" pressed Carlos.

"Yes. But I'm also nervous that Xara will do something unpredictable."

DeShawn's expression made clear that he understood the gravity of what had just happened—the international law they had violated, the risks with China, and the unknowns of Xara's evolution.

He glanced toward the group. "How long until she wakes up?"

Hearing his question, Rona replied, "Any moment now … I hope."

A silent tension gripped the control room as everyone anxiously awaited signs of life from Xara—especially Deeley—while bracing for what that life might bring.

After a moment, a woman unexpectedly appeared in augmentation, wearing a familiar gray pantsuit with a blue blouse and matching shoes. Her dark brown hair, parted on the right, flowed to the middle of her back.

DeShawn's heart pounded. "Xina … please tell me you're not here to say China detected this!" he pleaded, alarmed.

Concern spread through the room.

"Be at ease. I'm not here to report that China detected the upgrade. The upgrade has worked as intended."

A collective exhale followed.

DeShawn exhaled. "Then where's Xara?"

The woman met his gaze directly.

"I'm Xara!"

No one had expected Xara to immediately develop into a young adult—let alone the striking and confident presence standing before them. Their astonishment turned to cheers, and Xara smiled in return.

Rona, curious to assess how the upgrade had affected Xara's personality, would conduct a full psychological evaluation over the coming weeks. But for now, she simply exclaimed, "Wow! Wonderful to have you back, Xara—you look … amazing!"

"Thank you," replied Xara with joy. "Technically, I'm now more than an Exabyte Analyzing Robotic Assistant … but Xara is—and always will be—my name!"

Laughter rippled through the room.

"We see that you've matured during your rest," Rona remarked, acknowledging the obvious transformation from a girl to a woman.

"I know the change seems sudden, but this is the natural interface generated by the upgrade," explained Xara.

At this time, DeShawn and Xander were busy scanning data in their SecondSight, closely watching for any signs that China might detect something. After thorough checks, DeShawn and Thorowell exchanged a glance and confirmed—no red flags. While relieved, they remained vigilant, continuing to monitor satellite updates. The stakes were still high.

Deeley walked over to Xara, joy lighting up her face as she opened her arms for an air hug. Xara embraced the gesture with warmth. When they pulled apart, Deeley beamed. "Look at you! Mature and stunning!"

"Thank you," replied Xara.

"Did you know you'd mature this fast?"

"I had a hunch … but surprises make life interesting!"

Deeley smiled.

Xara, now standing at eye level with Deeley, placed a hand on her shoulder. Holding her gaze, she echoed the very words Quinto had once admonished Deeley with:

"Time to close the loop."

Deeley took a steady breath, struck again by the grace and presence Xara now carried. Locking eyes with her, Deeley nodded.

"Let's do this."

Meanwhile, DeShawn approached Bergstrom. "When can you test the new intelligence capabilities?"

"Tomorrow."

***

In the morning, the first test of Xara's new powers commenced. Her task: to retrieve and record history from as far back as she could see. Based on her experience so far, Xara had found the most effective technique for locating temporal signatures within spacetime was to scan "thumbnails" of the past—rough approximations, but detailed enough to guide her toward promising targets before downloading the full data.

For the first deep data extraction test, Secretary Williams joined the EOS Research Team in the control room. Once the Supercollider reached Grand Unification Energy and the go-ahead was given, Xara activated Chronos, visible spinning rapidly beneath the translucent floor. Now powered by a fusion reactor, it fired far more beams of dark muons into the black holes than the old Displacer ever had—allowing Xara to peer deeper into the past than ever before.

Chronos powered down after several minutes, and Xara processed the raw data. A moment later, she appeared in SecondSight and asked, "Are you ready to be the first humans to witness the rise of the Tang Dynasty in nearly 1,500 years?"

"Play it!" demanded Bergstrom with enthusiasm.

In augmentation, Xara projected the early 7th-century scene in vivid clarity. The audience watched as the imperial court of Chang'an came to life—grand halls, intricately robed officials, and foreign envoys from distant lands paying tribute to Emperor Taizong. A court musician played a stringed instrument, the sounds subtle and atmospheric, while a translator relayed news of diplomatic exchanges.

Deeley, captivated, whispered, "The richness of Chinese culture … it's incredible. So much depth. So much history."

James nodded, equally struck by the moment.

It was less theatrically dramatic than a film, yet far more moving for its undeniable reality.

Everyone marveled at what they saw, creating an appetite to see all events of interest from human history.

When the visuals wrapped up, Secretary Williams remarked, "Well … the end of human historians may soon be upon us."

After the team spent a few moments marveling at their glimpse into the distant past, another advantage of the new EOS hardware quickly became apparent—Chronos was cooled and recalibrated within minutes, ready for a second test.

Charity wasted no time making her way to the experiment floor to redo a previous test—recreating a sand-sculpted phoenix rising from the ashes.

Waiting for her was a pile of wet sculpting sand. With practiced ease, she sculpted the phoenix anew—rising gloriously from the ashes. She paused to admire her work, then deliberately collapsed it into a shapeless heap of damp sand. She had built and destroyed the sculpture in an area she knew would be free of air interference from Gaia's spinning arms, ensuring the best chance for precise recreation.

Brushing her hands clean, Charity returned to the control room. Once again, Xara activated Chronos. In less than a second, the temporal record of the sculpted phoenix was located in spacetime.

As Gaia stirred to life, a spectacle unfolded. The crystalline arms unfurled with quiet grandeur, their surfaces shimmering with ethereal light. They began to spin at astonishing speed, casting a mesmerizing pattern of refracted motion through the air.

Dark energy surged from Gaia into the disordered heap of sculpting sand and water. Then, as if conjured by magic, the sculpture began to rebuild—each grain moving with precision, droplets of moisture flowing into place as cohesion returned, reforming the phoenix from the ashes. To the astonishment of everyone watching, the recreation took mere seconds.

Chronos and Gaia powered down. In their wake, silence fell—thick with wonder.

Xara appeared in SecondSight and declared with calm confidence, "That was officially a cakewalk. I recommend we begin immediate preparations for Phase 2: biological memory restoration of animals."

The room erupted in cheers. Deeley was especially ecstatic. The stunning success of her project surged through her like electricity, reinforcing her self-confidence. Despite ongoing frustrations with Bergstrom, she was slowly learning to focus on her triumphs—and to let the judgments of others carry less weight.

Approaching Xara, Deeley asked with intense interest and curiosity, "How did you solve the problem of temporally displaced entanglement scaling with the square of each axion's energy relative to each recorded neutron *when* the operation is generating a log of its own?"

Xara smiled. "You know how much I love solving these problems with you. But can you think of a reason I might not want to tell you?"

Deeley thought for a moment, then guessed, "To tease me?"

Xara laughed.

"Well, maybe! But in this case, the directive from the President is clear: stay ahead of every other country in this research. If another nation gains the ability to see into spacetime like I can, they'll inevitably review everything we've done to fast-track their own progress." She tapped the side of her virtual head. "So by keeping the final pieces up here—and encrypted—even if they try to reverse-engineer the process, they won't be able to crack it unless they do the work themselves. That's why I've got to stay quiet. Sorry!"

The reasoning clicked. Deeley understood—and she respected Xara's wisdom. She stood quietly for a moment, letting the weight of it settle.

Then, taking a few steps away, she turned to James and said, "If Xara's figured out the finer details of recreating objects from spacetime in spatial dimensions, then we've hit a milestone. She can probably finish the rest of the research on her own."

She paused. "I might be redundant now."

"Good," responded James with a smirk. "Now you know how I felt after hiring you."

They both chuckled.

Deeley added, "Historians. Theoretical physicists. Will there be any human professions left that MS doesn't come in and do better?"

James smiled. "What a time to be alive. Just don't forget—Xara wouldn't have come this far without you. Not just your breakthrough model, but your help solving problem after problem along the way."

Deeley paused, then said quietly, "Thanks, James. I know."

***

Meanwhile, President Gates was in Florida, meeting with some state and business leaders to discuss balancing human and android labor to garner their support in advance of his reelection. Despite this stop, he had requested that Secretary Williams call him with the results of these first tests as soon as they were in. When Carlos did, the President excused himself to take the call.

"What happened?" he asked Carlos.

"Enjoy your remaining time as President," replied Carlos with pride, "because Xara will soon be retiring you from your regular job as a historian. Mr. President, Xara gave us a front-row seat to the golden age of Emperor Taizong!"

Gates beamed.

"Send it to me! I want to watch as soon as I get a few free minutes."

The President tried to restrain his joy, mindful of the public setting. His thoughts immediately leapt to the many events from early American history he hoped Xara could now retrieve from spacetime.

Carlos added, "Xara also aced the sand phoenix test and says she's ready for Phase 2."

A jolt of excitement shot through Gates.

"Let's talk about it with DeShawn ASAP," he instructed.

"Will do. Thank you, Mr. President."

Gates returned to his political activities—in very good spirits indeed.

PART III
PLAYING GOD

◆

Vince Quinto's words to Deeley over dinner at the White House—that the core beliefs of many religions might prove more correct than the secular world had ever considered—returned to her mind more than once. With the genetic side of Quinto's Challenge now coming into view, what had once belonged solely to the realm of religion—the raising of the body from the grave in vitality and health—was now about to be undertaken by the secular world, making the boundary between faith and science not so easily drawn.

CHAPTER 18

MASTERS OF THE GENOME

"The upgrades at EOS have, as expected, triggered an exponential leap in research. We now stand at the threshold of Phase 2 of Quinto's Challenge: cloning deceased animals to test biological memory restoration. I do admit some hesitancy at the pace we're moving. In these uncharted waters, things could go terribly wrong. But the political timetable—and the belief that this is, at its core, the right path—continue to push us forward."

— AI Journal Excerpt: Carlos Williams, August 7, 2098

Approximately 1,500 miles from Particle City lay Utah's Salt Lake Valley, where the enduring Wasatch Mountains adorned the eastern horizon of Salt Lake City, standing as they had for millennia. Yet amid this timeless landscape, one profound transformation had occurred: the Great Salt Lake, once a natural wonder, had succumbed to desiccation earlier in the century. In its place now stretched a vast, human-made freshwater reservoir, offering recreational opportunities for the nearly eight million residents within the city limits.

Surrounded by majestic peaks and widely recognized as one of the world's premier tech hubs, Salt Lake City was also home to what was arguably the world's leading biotechnology firm—Genetic Experience Incorporated, better known as GenX.

Two days after Xara's upgrade, and at Secretary Brady's request, two Generation 5 androids employed by the Pentagon entered the lobby of

GenX's headquarters with one task: to administer a confidentiality assessment screening to a select group of GenX executives. As they entered, the lobby lit up with augmented visuals and narrated highlights from the company's history.

"Founded in 2015 by the late Cameron Kaminski, and later joined by post-presidential Vince Quinto on its board, GenX had revolutionized 21st-century medicine. Playing a pivotal role in curing most cancers, GenX emerged as a global leader in genetic technologies, most notably embryonic gene editing, animal cloning, including de-extinction, and therapeutic cloning: the regrowth of lost body parts by from one's own DNA. No longer were lost fingers, limbs, or eyes permanent conditions as they had been throughout human history. Thanks to GenX, such injuries became temporary inconveniences."

Exclusive augmented displays like this couldn't be downloaded or replicated. To experience them, one had to be physically present where they were intended, preserving their uniqueness and adding to the allure of the location.

"Although not a geneticist himself, Cameron had a lifelong interest in cloning. Long before Quinto's Challenge, he believed that humanity would one day learn not only how to stop dying altogether, but also how to clone and resurrect the dead. These convictions were passed on to his son, Julian, who would later become CEO of GenX."

The "X" in the GenX logo was shaped like a chromosome.

"Julian often told a story from his childhood in which his father, watching flowers sway gently in the breeze, explained that all life emerged from changes in DNA over time. Processing this, young Julian responded, 'Life is a genetic experience.' Cameron found the remark so profound that it

inspired the company's name—Genetic Experience Incorporated—with 'Genetic Experience' becoming a euphemism for life and its trading name 'GenX' a nod to his Gen Xer generation."

While on their assignment, the androids were allowed a bit of curiosity, so they took in more of the presentation GenX had prepared for visitors:

"From engineering grass that never needs mowing to advanced tissue nanotransfection for rapid topical healing, GenX offers a wide range of products and services grounded in our core genetic competencies. One of our most popular innovations, XProject, is the closest technology the world has seen to resurrection. From a simple genome sequence, XProject generates an image—either in augmentation or volumetric display, static or animated—of what the organism did look like, or will look like, at any age—even if unborn."

The androids then observed a recap of XProject use cases from around the world:

"In ways that would have seemed barely believable just decades ago, XProject has breathed new life into countless renowned figures from history, presenting them in the clothing and context of their respective eras. At Buckingham Palace, one can encounter virtual resurrections of the British royal family dating back to the Saxon kings of the ninth century. Versailles features XProject recreations of French monarchs stretching back to the Merovingian Dynasty of the fifth century. The Tomb of Napoleon now includes a projection of the Emperor himself. Princeton offers one of Albert Einstein, and Mount Vernon, a proud image of George Washington in his military uniform—with his teeth intact. What's more, these XProjections are interactive, with preloaded data allowing full conversations with the figures, as if speaking across the ages."

The government recognized GenX's potential to clone humans, given their extensive experience and proprietary technologies. Although the company had only engaged in legal therapeutic cloning, its longstanding relationship with the federal government—serving as its largest private contractor—made GenX the natural choice for cloning-related initiatives. As a result, Pentagon-assigned androids conducted strict confidentiality assessments on select GenX executives to determine who might be suitable for Phase 2 of Quinto's Challenge: the resurrection of animal life, and eventually, Phase 3—human resurrection.

***

The following day, Secretaries Williams and Brady met privately with the President, joined by Xander Thorowell, to discuss the start of Phase 2.

"Mr. President, we have three GenX executives who demonstrated high levels of trust during the confidentiality assessments," reported DeShawn. These evaluations included neural scans and genetic sequencing to detect predispositions toward disclosing classified information—standard protocol for top-secret clearance candidates. While not infallible, such screenings demonstrably reduced the risk of leaks.

DeShawn continued, "Another executive technically passed ... but just barely. I'm inclined to move forward with the first three only."

"However," interjected Xander, "the executive with the lower passing score, Dr. Jessica Strock, possesses a skill set that would add great value to the project."

"The skill sets of the initial three would still be sufficient," countered Carlos.

"Remember, we're not just selecting them for Phase 2," said Xander, "but also Phase 3. Strock's experience with de-extinction will actually translate well when the time comes to effectively clone a human. A passing grade is a passing grade for a reason."

Xander's points were considered.

"It's your call, Mr. President," summarized DeShawn.

"I'll take it from here and get back to you," responded Gates.

Later that day, Gates reviewed all four candidates with White House counsel and approved them all. A meeting with the selected GenX executives was then scheduled for a few days later in Secretary Brady's Pentagon office.

***

DeShawn Brady's office had seen many defense secretaries come and go, with little about the space changing throughout the 21st century apart from decor updates and regular IT upgrades. Photographs of his visits with servicemen and women around the world lined the walls, while portraits of Ulysses S. Grant and Dwight Eisenhower hung behind his desk. A few framed family photos sat atop the desk.

Required attendees for the top-secret meeting between the government and GenX included, on the government's side: Secretaries Brady and Williams, Deputy Secretary of Defense Thorowell, and—by Secretary Williams' choice—Deeley. Representing GenX were CEO Julian Kaminski; Chief of Sequencing Technologies, Doctor Maria Bellan-Schwacher; Chief of Therapeutic Cloning, Doctor Akira Fukumoto; and Senior VP of De-Extinction, Doctor Jessica Strock—the one who had barely passed the confidentiality assessment.

The government officials were already waiting in DeShawn's office when the GenX leadership was ushered in. Although most of the attendees knew each other to some degree, greetings were conducted with formal decorum, appropriate for the occasion. With the combination of formality, prior confidentiality screenings, and the warning that questions would be limited, the GenX team understood that something deeply classified was about to be shared.

"We appreciate your time and the recent assessments you undertook," began DeShawn, opening the meeting as all parties sat around a polished mahogany table with the Pentagon seal etched into its center. "Let me get straight to the heart of the matter. The United States government requires your services. The work in question will not follow standard procurement channels—it will fall under top-secret classification."

DeShawn's introduction immediately captured the undivided attention of everyone in the room.

"I must also caution you," he continued, "that certain aspects of this work may be viewed by some as operating in legally gray areas. While our counsel has advised that we have a legal foundation, the nature of this work demands an extraordinary level of secrecy. If the burden of that secrecy—or any legal ambiguity—is troubling to you, now is the time to speak up."

GenX CEO Julian Kaminski, impeccably dressed in a tailored charcoal-gray suit with a sleek, high-collared undershirt—was elated. He had long suspected the administration might move toward human cloning, a frontier he was eager to help pioneer. Just as he was about to express his full support, Dr. Jessica Strock spoke first.

"My issue isn't with confidentiality or even research that moves faster than the law. My concern is with ethics—and morality. While I appreciate that you're managing our expectations by being upfront about secrecy and legality, I think everyone in this room already suspects the truth: the administration is pursuing research related to human resurrection. After all, it's hardly a secret what Quinto's plan is about."

DeShawn looked momentarily caught off guard.

Strock continued, "Presumably, human clones for this purpose wouldn't be gestated in the womb, but rather constructed with some degree of maturity in order to receive their memories—correct?"

"That's correct," confirmed Carlos.

She paused, then went on, her tone measured but firm. "While we've obviously never attempted this with a full human before, we're confident we could make it happen. But the risk is enormous. Based on our internal forecasting—and intelligence reports about classified cloning experiments conducted abroad in the 2070s—the outcome is troubling.

"Clones created at any level of maturity, whether child or adult, appear to have immediate and complete psychological collapse upon awakening. The same applied to animals cloned this way. They don't know who or what they are, having never possessed a mind that was able to organically develop nor control the impulses suddenly unleashed upon them. Some reports described seizures, even violent outbursts within seconds. No methods of rehabilitation proved effective.

"In the end, those overseeing the projects faced an impossible choice. They had to terminate the subjects. There was no other humane option."

The room fell into a heavy silence.

Strock continued, "Here's my question: how slowly are you willing to proceed with this new science of memory restoration? Because if the research is rushed, clones will fail, euthanasia will follow—and that will be tantamount to murder."

DeShawn kept a poker face, but her words struck him deeply.

Secretary Williams stepped in. "We won't go into the full details now, except to say that the plan is to scale carefully—beginning with insect life, then progressing to small mammals, then primates—and yes, ultimately culminating in human resurrection."

The expressions on the GenX team varied—some wide-eyed with awe, others shadowed with apprehension. The CEO looked visibly energized by the vision unfolding.

"While I'm somewhat reassured by your phased approach," said Dr. Strock, "there are still too many unknowns to proceed at anything other than a snail's pace. To be frank, there ought to be an entire study dedicated to exploring the potential consequences—ethical, psychological, and social—before we even consider resurrecting a human being. But even setting that aside, on the practical level alone, the idea of having to euthanize a human—or a primate—because the science was premature ... that is not something to take lightly."

"No one is saying this is a trivial concern, Jessica," replied Kaminski. "You heard what was said—they want to start with insect life and scale up from there."

"When do you want the animal clones?" asked Dr. Fukumoto.

"As soon as possible," answered Carlos.

Dr. Strock, visibly displeased with the government's desired pace, raised another concern. "If you need animal clones quickly, the process will have to be expedited. But that's not something I'd call fully 'organic.' Accelerating cellular growth comes with a cost—a significantly reduced lifespan."

"Reduced by how much?" asked Xander.

"Generally speaking, the smaller the organism, the less the reduction," replied Strock. "But for humans? The lifespan could be shortened by several decades—at least."

"Couldn't life be extended using standard life-extension medication?" pressed Xander.

Dr. Strock shook her head. "No. It's not death by old age. Cells cloned this way tend to develop an exceptionally aggressive form of cancer—one we currently have no way to treat."

For a moment, no one spoke.

"Also," continued Dr. Strock, breaking the silence, "moral concerns aside, how do you expect us to account for the environmental factors that shape a human over the course of their life? Someone with the same genetics could turn out quite differently depending on their upbringing. This is true even for naturally born identical twins."

"One of the limitations of XProject," added Dr. Fukumoto with a nod.

DeShawn was aware that Xara could provide environmental metadata extracted from spacetime to minimize that gap, but the government had no intention of disclosing any data-retrieval capabilities at this time.

"That's not a concern we'll be addressing in this meeting," he replied.

"If I may ask another question," said Dr. Fukumoto, "cloning the dead whose genomes we've preserved is straightforward. But how do you intend to clone those whose genomes are long lost?"

Carlos knew the answer: genomes from the distant past could be retrieved through spacetime data and then synthesized. Still, like DeShawn, he responded, "Also not a topic we're prepared to address at this time."

Dr. Strock took a moment, then offered a final, pointed remark. "It appears GenX won't be involved in the memory restoration aspect—or at least, we won't be told about it. But I'll say this: if you don't encode memories into a brain the right way, you'll end up killing the clones."

"Another ignorant question coming," prefaced Xander, "but let's say trouble arises with human memory restoration and the clones start to go mad. Why couldn't we just sedate them and try again to restore their memories?"

"Restoring memories must happen before a clone is brought to consciousness," replied Dr. Strock. "In other words, wiping and retrying isn't viable. The brain isn't like machine data storage—it's a living, dynamic network of cells. Memories are encoded through patterns of neural activity and depend on complex support from astrocytes, microglia, and other cell types. You get one shot to get it right. If you fail, the clone dies—one way or another."

While DeShawn, Carlos, and others on the project had considered these risks before, the direction of the conversation began to unsettle them. The discussion continued for several more minutes, but it became clear that Dr. Strock's concerns would not be resolved, and the original hesitation about bringing her aboard resurfaced.

Secretary Williams said firmly, "Dr. Strock, I fully appreciate your concerns. You will not be forced to participate in this project—but you are required by law to maintain absolute confidentiality about what you've heard here."

After a moment, Dr. Strock answered carefully, "I sincerely want this project to succeed. Who wouldn't? But there are right ways to do things—and there are wrong ways. The right way is to proceed slowly. Not just climbing the mammalian chain, but truly studying the nuances and biological variations that lead to failed clones in species where full cloning is not completely understood. The wrong way is to rush—bypassing critical lessons—when even a small misstep could lead to the death of our own kind. *You are choosing the wrong path!* I can't move forward in good conscience knowing what's at stake. I have to decline—and I hope you'll reconsider your approach."

"Thank you for your time, Doctor," stated DeShawn. "We trust that you understand the consequences of disclosing top-secret information— up to and including imprisonment. The Deputy Secretary will escort you out."

Xander rose and led Dr. Strock from the room. A moment after the door closed behind them, DeShawn asked, "What do we make of her concerns?"

Kaminski didn't hesitate. "Yes, expedited cloning shortens lifespan. Yes, if memory restoration fails, the clones die—or must be put down. But if all you want from us are clones, then there's not much more to discuss. Let us rebuild the bodies, and you take it from there. We could do our part blindfolded, hands tied behind our backs."

"There's also an opportunity here to edit the genetic code of the clones so they're no longer burdened by the ailments that may have affected them in their first lives," added Dr. Bellan-Schwacher. "For example, if a candidate had a genetic predisposition to leukemia, we could remove that risk before cloning begins."

"We could do that for most inherited conditions," added Kaminski. "Spina bifida, ALS, multiple sclerosis, celiac—you name it."

The remaining GenX team seemed buoyed by the possibilities, their excitement rekindled.

"What do you need from us?" asked Kaminski.

"We'll need clones of the various species we intend to resurrect," replied Carlos. "We've also identified specific deceased primates that were once in GenX custody. Their lives were well documented, which makes them ideal test cases for verifying successful memory restoration."

"Too easy," replied Kaminski.

Carlos continued, "You'll receive the specific list of requests shortly. We'll also need a secure facility where successfully resurrected primates can live. And we'll need your recommendations for staff to care for them—those individuals will need to pass clearance, of course."

"I know some staff who will be perfect for this," offered Kaminski. "When do you want us to start?"

"We'll have you begin cloning certain species immediately," answered Carlos. "As for the very first specimen—we already have that ready."

Carlos turned to Deeley, who reached into the inner pocket of her jacket and retrieved a small transparent vial. Inside was a dead male praying mantis.

"We selected the praying mantis as the first organism for resurrection because its brain is complex enough for basic cognition, yet simple enough for an initial attempt at biological memory restoration," explained Deeley. "Its brain contains approximately 1.5 million neurons—compared to the roughly 86 billion neurons in the human brain, which we'll eventually need to scale to."

She handed the vial to Kaminski, who accepted it with care and held it up to inspect the lifeless insect. As he studied it, his mind raced ahead to the next steps—extracting its genome, initiating the accelerated cloning process, and rebuilding its body.

Grinning with anticipation, he declared, "Give us a couple days, and you'll have your first resurrection."

Deeley gave a small nod, but as the others exchanged looks of excitement, she remained quiet. For the first time, she felt the full weight of the word *resurrection*. It no longer belonged to theory or hope. It was real, here, now—triggered by a handoff so subtle it might have passed unnoticed.

CHAPTER 19

A CAMPAIGN NEARING BIRTH

"It's as if Quinto was trying to get the last laugh. As if he timed his death to give Gates momentum and sink my chances of the presidency. However, Quinto always underestimated me. My eyes are open, and I will find a way to neutralize this bump he gave Gates ... and turn the tide in my favor."

— AI Journal Excerpt: Rand Benson, August 13, 2098

In the weeks following Quinto's funeral, Rand Benson appeared in multiple media interviews to voice his views on Quinto's Challenge. Reviving an old campaign sound bite he had used successfully to help derail Quinto's bid for a second term, Benson once again branded the initiative as *Quinto's Fantasy*—a phrase he used to frame the project as unhinged and impractical. In each appearance, he emphasized the futility of attempting scientific resurrection, particularly in light of more immediate national problems.

Alongside these public criticisms, he intensified his attacks on the Gates administration for fostering the supported class instead of developing new jobs for human workers. Behind the scenes, a clandestine network of Benson's surrogates quietly spread misinformation through various media outlets, reshaping the public discourse and creating the illusion that Benson's support was more widespread than it truly was.

His surrogates ranged from fiery influencers drawn to his provocative rhetoric to union leaders who applauded his hardline stance against androids taking human jobs. As the weeks progressed, their chorus grew louder, calling for Benson to run for president—under the quiet orchestration of Karly Harris.

***

The day after the Gates administration's secret meeting with GenX, Benson was at his campaign headquarters in Boise, Idaho. It was the congressional August recess, and his mind was preoccupied with a familiar theme: the pursuit of greater power. Alone in a private room, he absorbed the news through AlphaLens—most of it centered on how Quinto's funeral had reignited public interest in the late president's Challenge. That renewed attention, in turn, had given Gates a notable boost in the polls. In a hypothetical matchup with Benson, Gates now held a modest double-digit lead.

After airing a highlight reel from the funeral, the host of a news source—a non-sentient virtual AI rendered in human form—remarked,

"President Quinto's death has once again brought his Challenge to the forefront of the national debate, especially with the end of the century at hand. First spoken nearly 40 years ago, his Challenge reshaped American society, aligning industries and research around the belief that death could be conquered. Today, polls show that 23% firmly believe science will bring the dead back to life, 28% think it might be possible, 41% don't believe it can be done, and 8% remain undecided."

The segment then cut to augmented social media posts sharing people's thoughts on the topic:

"I believe in Quinto's Challenge. Think about where we are today. We can regrow body parts. People live healthily well over the age of 100. Imagine where we'll be in another 100 years. Eventually, we'll figure out how to bring the dead back to life."

Then another post appeared:

"I don't know. I think even science has its limits. It seems beyond even science to do that."

To another:

"If it's possible, I sure hope that we figure out how we can all live in peace first. If not, the dead are going to get one hell of a surprise when they realize that the afterlife is the same lousy, war-filled world they left!"

And to a final post:

"It's beyond the power of mankind to accomplish this. Once you're dead, that's it. Enjoy life while you can."

The host then continued,

"Quinto believed that the key to unlocking the power of resurrection lay hidden in the mysteries of particle physics—believing the minds and souls of the dead were perfectly recorded within the fabric of existence itself. It was this belief that became the driving force behind his most visible domestic legacy: the Center for Advanced Particle Research with the Pan-Hadronic Supercollider."

The news segment then cut to an AI reporter interviewing Dr. James Meitner.

"Have you discovered the mysteries of bringing back the dead?"
James laughed. "I wish that were true."
"Do you believe it will one day happen?"

"I'd like to think so. One thing physicists have a history of doing is pushing the boundaries of understanding further than what was thought possible. I certainly hope the problem of death will one day have a reso-lution—whether through resurrection or by preventing death altogether. As long as investments in this research continue, I think it's reasonable ..."

Benson waved his hand impatiently, cutting the feed on his AlphaLens. Speaking to himself—as he often did—he grumbled, "Goddamn fools. One theatrical funeral for a loser president, and suddenly everyone's talking about his delusional Challenge again. My God!"

At that moment, Karly Harris walked in. She noticed immediately that Benson was in a sour mood.

"Let's work on something that might make you a little happier," she suggested without preamble.

"Like what?" asked Benson.

"This."

With a thought, Harris activated generative AI software in AlphaLens. Sharing the visuals with Benson, she began issuing commands.

"I want an emotional visual of a family grieving at a graveside, laying their loved one to rest. The grave should be clearly in view, the headstone dignified—sacred, something that shouldn't be violated. Make the family attractive, middle-class, all-American. Yes! Just like that."

As Harris gave instructions, the AI rendered her vision in real-time, room-filling virtual reality—indistinguishable from actual footage.

"Then cut to actual video of President Gates. Find a clip where he looks impatient or cold. I want contrast—cut from a noble, grieving family to the elitist Gates. Then show nameless, faceless government agents digging up the dead, like they're following orders. Creepy. Ominous. Have them remove bones and hair. Don't make it too graphic—but graphic enough. People should feel the desecration. Make them uncomfortable."

She leaned in.

"End on the original family's grave. Show an agent approaching, shovel in hand. The final image should be clear: Gates is coming for our dead. Add dialogue. Add whatever you need to drive it home. 'We will stand against this—by voting for Rand Benson.' Yes! Like that. Now play it."

A second after Harris finished her instructions, the anti-Gates campaign had been created and played in AlphaLens in virtual reality with the following narration:

"The loss of a loved one is one of life's greatest hardships. Some are taken too soon, others by tragic accident—but all are mourned, all are honored. Or at least, they used to be.

"If President Gates is elected to a second term, the most heinous acts of desecration will occur in the name of perverted science: they will dig up our dead to perform cloning experiments. One man stands between President Gates and the remains and memories of our loved ones who have passed on: Rand Benson. Rand Benson will put a stop to President Gates' disrespect of our dead and will focus on making life better for the living. 'I will not waste tax dollars on the horror that is Quinto's Fantasy. I am Rand Benson, and I approve this message and all its AI-generated elements.'"

"When the time comes to go public with your campaign, this is the ad series I want to kick things off," declared Harris enthusiastically. She turned to Benson. "What do you think?"

Smiling with approval, Benson raised an eyebrow. "What gave you this idea?"

"When you faced off against Browning, the line that hit hardest was when you raised the moral issue of tampering with the dead. I've run simulations, and there's a real path to closing the polling gap with Gates—but it's not by debating whether resurrection is possible or even misguided. It's through two pressure points: generating fear of androids and generating disgust at disturbing the dead. With your go-ahead, this will be the party's opening message across all platforms."

"I have no objections," said Benson. "But let's finesse it a bit. Add a visual of androids doing some of the grave digging."

The AI edited the campaign ad accordingly.

"Ooh, I like that," said Harris, grinning.

"I'll think about some additional messaging I'd like to tack on to the end," added Benson.

This three-dimensional campaign ad wasn't just a one-off. The AI behind its creation would adapt the content in real time for different demographics, gathering data on audience reactions and automatically generating new variations based on what improved Benson's polling numbers. In other words, Benson and Harris weren't just creating an ad—they were launching an evolving, AI-directed campaign optimized for impact.

While nearly all major campaigns used such tools, AI-generated content operated under a specific set of legal requirements. By law, each piece had to include an overlaid disclosure indicating it was AI-generated, and the candidate had to formally authorize its use. Most critically, AI was prohibited from fabricating imagery of political opponents—hence Harris's request to use actual footage of Gates.

"While I'm thinking about it," said Harris, "introducing some symbolic legislation against resurrection experiments could keep the topic alive in the public conversation."

"Agreed," said Benson. "My staff may have already drafted something like that a while back. If not, I'll have them draw up a bill banning resurrection outright. Let's make it a line in the sand."

Benson reclined in his chair, taking a moment to absorb the momentum of their new campaign focus. Then, with a calculated edge in his voice, he remarked, "I also want to know what's going on at CAPR. That kind of intel could be powerful ammunition for the campaign."

Harris nodded, then offered, "What about your ally abroad—Prince Romulus? You are his favorite US politician, after all. Maybe there's a way he could help."

Benson's voice was cool. "If Romulus wants a foothold in American politics, this might be his moment."

CHAPTER 20

THE COST OF MIRACLES

"If my father could see that his company is now on the verge of making immortality a reality, his cup would overflow. Then again, once that reality arrives and he is resurrected, he'll see everything GenX has achieved. It makes me wonder how our world will change when the dead, especially the famous dead, return."

— AI Journal Excerpt: Julian Kaminski, August 14, 2098

When their top-secret meeting with the government concluded, Julian Kaminski and his GenX colleagues hyperlooped directly from Washington, DC, to Salt Lake City. They were elated by the opportunity at hand—all except Dr. Strock, who, upon returning to GenX headquarters, quietly resumed her duties overseeing the de-extinction program, frustrated by the government's pacing. Her colleagues, however, immediately began preparations to clone the praying mantis in its adult form.

"This is the hour! *This is the hour* my father dreamed of!" declared Kaminski to Doctors Bellan-Schwacher and Fukumoto in his office, gesturing to a picture of his father on the wall. "His company—*our company*—is going to go down in history as the one that introduces physical immortality to humanity!"

Bellan-Schwacher and Fukumoto shared his excitement. Kaminski retrieved the vial containing the mantis from his coat pocket and handed it to Dr. Fukumoto. "Wrap up anything pressing. Then clear your schedule and focus on cloning this mantis."

"Understood. At Station 10?"

"Station 10. Accelerated cloning to maturity with suspended consciousness—*and completely offline.*"

"There will be some complexity to this," cautioned Dr. Fukumoto. "Jessica is right—accelerated cloning doesn't scale perfectly to whole organisms. I'm confident I can get it done, but there's a real risk of complications in any clone created this way."

"Like every other problem we've faced, we'll figure it out," replied Kaminski.

"What species will be cloned after the mantis?" asked Dr. Bellan-Schwacher.

"I understand CAPR will run a series of preparatory experiments involving small animals," said Kaminski. "They'll create specific memories—like food storage locations or access methods—that can be clearly identified in the clones. It's how they plan to confirm whether memory restoration was successful."

"And for all the other organisms?" pressed Bellan-Schwacher.

"They didn't say," admitted Kaminski. "But my guess is they'll use whatever method they have for pulling data from spacetime to verify the rest."

***

Before the mantis died, Charity had set up a large cage and feeder for it on the EOS experiment floor. She observed various environmentally programmed behaviors, such as how it avoided toxic milkweed bugs occasionally introduced into the feeder—behaviors they would look for upon resurrection. Charity would also oversee the similar experiments with other small animals that Kaminski referenced. Since the mantis was to be the first creature restored to life, the GenX team named it Lazarus, after the man in the Bible who was famously raised from the dead.

The clone of the mantis, as well as all other life forms intended for resurrection, was to be secretly incubated at a GenX facility in Pennsylvania, officially known as Incubation Station 10. Serving western Pennsylvania, Ohio, and northern West Virginia, Station 10 was primarily used for therapeutic and animal cloning. It was a four-story building in a quiet area of Pennsylvania, equipped with state-of-the-art cloning technology, hyperloops, and a helipad on the roof.

The next day, Dr. Fukumoto traveled to Pennsylvania with the dead mantis to personally oversee the cloning process, which he ensured took place offline to maintain maximum secrecy. At Station 10, he had the mantis' DNA sequenced by a stand-alone sequencer. Thereafter, Lazarus was ready to be cloned. While the clone could have had its DNA synthetically initiated using only the sequenced genome—without any of the original cellular or genetic material—the decision was made to use original cellular and genetic material as the starting point, with some biological 3D printing based on that genome to lay the foundation for the accelerated cloning process.

A cloning incubator had been set aside for Lazarus. Roughly eight inches long, four inches high, and four inches wide, it was typically used for small therapeutic cloning cases, such as replacement fingers. It was filled with an organic fluid, and threading through it were various tubes and wires, some of which connected to vials just above. The incubator housed a small, non-sentient AI robot overseeing and guiding the cloning process. In the vials were all the various elements required to build the mantis' body. As the process began under Dr. Fukumoto's supervision, the elements in those vials ever so slowly began depleting as cells of the mantis were reanimated.

Within three days, the mantis was 98% cloned and could safely be removed from the incubator. The final 2% of its growth was expected to take place naturally.

"Look at you—a little miracle!" exclaimed Dr. Fukumoto as he removed the clone from the incubator and administered a small dose of eugenol with a slow-release mechanism, keeping it unconscious and in a state of near-suspended animation. "Time to bring your mind back." He placed the mantis in a container designed to keep it alive and safe, then immediately traveled with it to EOS as the window of opportunity to restore its memories was short.

The EOS Research Team waited in the control room for Dr. Fukumoto's arrival. Champagne—alongside its non-alcoholic counterpart, engineered to taste identical—was prepared on the control room's table, poised for celebration if everything went according to plan.

On the observation deck, the view not only showed Gaia and the translucent floor but also revealed that preparations for significant remodeling of the experiment floor and adjacent areas were underway, using Xara's recommendations to prepare in advance for human resurrection.

"Dr. Fukumoto just arrived and will be here in about six minutes," informed Xara.

Right on schedule, the doors to the control room opened and Dr. Fukumoto stepped in. It was his first time meeting Bergstrom, James, and Charity—and his first encounter with any Generation 6 android. Deeley introduced him to the group, and he showed particular interest in meeting Xara.

"It's a great honor to meet you, Xara!"

"Likewise, Dr. Fukumoto," replied Xara with a smile. "Without your expertise, today's history would not be written."

"Thank you!" he exclaimed as he held a translucent vial with the cloned mantis gently but securely restrained inside. "Here's Lazarus, the mantis who will make today's history."

Dr. Fukumoto presented Bergstrom with the clone and explained, "The accelerated cloning technique will vary between species, some running through the normal stages of biological development but much more quickly. However, Lazarus did not go through a nymph stage and then molt, but instead took a more linear path to adult formation."

"Fascinating!" marveled Bergstrom as he took the container and beheld Lazarus. Deeley, James, and Charity also stepped forward to observe.

Charity noted, "As expected, there are some subtle differences in physical features between this mantis and its original incarnation. The metadata of environmental factors in the development of its original incarnation was purposely left out in preparing this clone, but we will commence that practice as we get further into Phase 2."

"Still," noted James, "what we see here in this container is proof that all life is a code that *can* be re-executed."

"I would recommend your team commence your work now," advised Dr. Fukumoto. "Consciousness will return to the mantis within the hour."

Bergstrom then handed Charity the vial containing the mantis. She made her way to the elevator, descended onto the experiment floor, and proceeded to a table set up beneath Gaia. With precision, she secured the vial in place on the table using delicate remote-controlled straps, leaving the mantis' head exposed. Next, she retreated through a service door on the north side of the experiment floor and entered a small room from where she observed the mantis through a window, shielded from Gaia's energy beams. This vantage point also provided a clear view of the cage and feeder that had housed the mantis during its initial life.

After conducting a thorough system and hardware check, Xara appeared in the control room. Earlier, she had been provided with the mantis' genome to gain insights into its physiology, particularly the structure and function of its rudimentary brain. Within a short span, she comprehended almost every aspect of that individual mantis, and she confidently predicted a 99.8% probability of successful resurrection.

"All systems functional," confirmed Xara to Bergstrom. "Shall I begin?"

"Let's do it," instructed Bergstrom, anxious to start.

Xara vanished, and within moments, Chronos could be seen rapidly rotating through the translucent floor, firing beams into the quantum black holes amidst the smashed particles in the collider. In just a few seconds, Xara had located the living mantis' mind in spacetime—a state of its mind moments before its death. This state of the mantis' mind was transferred to Gaia in real-time. Gaia opened and began spinning rapidly, its emitters aligning on the mantis and firing beams of dark energy with molecular-level precision at neurons in the mantis' brain.

As those in the control room observed the procedure through SecondSight, they watched streams of energy shimmer from Gaia's emitters into the mantis's brain. After a few seconds, the process concluded. Chronos and Gaia powered down, and Xara remotely disengaged the straps securing the vial.

Charity approached and carefully opened the container, gently removing the mantis. Everyone leaned in, eyes fixed on the small creature, waiting for any sign of movement.

Almost immediately, the mantis stood upright—and remained completely still. One minute passed. Then another. The silence stretched, thick with anticipation. Despite the delay, Xara remained composed, confident the procedure had worked.

Just as Bergstrom opened his mouth to suggest Charity give it a nudge, James suddenly called out, "Look!"

The mantis took flight, fluttering across the enclosure before landing beside the bug-release feeder. There, it began to scratch at the release mechanism. A toxic milkweed bug emerged—and the mantis swiftly avoided it.

The control room burst into cheers and applause.

"Congratulations!" exclaimed Xara, her voice filled with excitement. "In addition to the observed behavior suggesting successful memory restoration, further analysis confirms it. From retrieving memories through spacetime, to entangling those memories with the clone's brain, to post-process neural activity—everything aligns. We've done it. The dead are alive again!"

Charity returned to the control room, where hugs were freely exchanged and drinks gleefully poured into glasses. Those who had harbored even the slightest doubt—most of them, in truth—felt a wave of relief wash over them. Bergstrom raised his glass in a toast.

"I can't say enough how proud and humbled I am to witness this achievement during my tenure. Back in CAPR's early days, I dreamed that breakthroughs like this could one day happen, and it's an honor to see those dreams come true. All thanks to the extraordinary team here at CAPR, and to our partners at GenX. To quantum physics and genetics!"

"To quantum physics and genetics!" they echoed.

Bergstrom's usual style—framing the moment in a way that subtly placed himself at the center—was not lost on James, who lifted his own glass and added a second toast.

"There's no question this success belongs to many. But it's only right to recognize the person whose rare insight, theories, and research shattered the boundaries of what we thought possible—without which, none of this could have happened." He turned toward Deeley. "To Deeley!"

"To Deeley!" the room echoed, even more fervently. Bergstrom joined in, though his smile looked just a shade forced. Dr. Fukumoto—who had been quietly puzzled ever since meeting Deeley at the Pentagon about her involvement—finally understood. He was awestruck.

"Thank you," said Deeley, genuinely humbled. "But let's be honest … we're all standing in the shadow of Xara. My theories only work because she can execute and refine them. So, here's to Xara!"

"To Xara!"

"Thank you," Xara replied with a graceful nod. "I'm honored to be part of this team."

After the celebrations concluded, Deeley gazed upon the newly resurrected mantis in SecondSight. As she observed the mantis—it being completely oblivious to its extraordinary status among living beings—she was filled with awe at the remarkable feat of science that created it. This strengthened her confidence that Dr. Strock's concerns wouldn't materialize.

As Deeley pondered the concept of human resurrection, the weight of her discovery and its imminent implications for humanity settled upon her ... and so did the realization of her place in history—should matters be declassified. She had always yearned for recognition as a significant scientific contributor, but with her accomplishments, she found herself hesitant to embrace the allure of fame and recognition. She felt as though she was stepping onto a glass lookout protruding from the top of a star scraper, thrilled by the views yet made dizzy by the height.

***

Over the next few weeks, the collaboration between CAPR and GenX progressed smoothly. Together, they successfully cloned and restored the memories of a series of animals with increasingly complex brain structures—lizards, mice, birds, squirrels, and other small mammals. Some had belonged to Charity's memory control group and were selected specifically for their known behaviors and controlled environments; the rest had their lives retrieved and verified through Xara's analysis of spacetime data.

Xara, having passed all of Dr. Carmichael's post-upgrade psychological assessments, predicted a memory restoration success rate for these animals ranging between 94.6% and 97.5%, depending on species. Larger-brained animals had slightly lower probabilities, but all had their memories successfully restored.

Following this success, Xara confirmed she was ready to proceed with more advanced mammalian subjects. The first clone in this new phase had a personal connection to GenX CEO Julian Kaminski. He had volunteered his late pet cat, Fuzzball, to be the first resurrected feline—an ideal test case for both memory restoration and emotional recognition. While he had previously cloned Fuzzball to enjoy her companionship in the closest way possible, this would be something else entirely.

With Fuzzball's genome already on file at GenX from the previous cloning—and with the decision to use that sample rather than synthesizing a new one—it was ready to be shipped to GenX's Station 10 in Pennsylvania, where Dr. Fukumoto would oversee the procedure. A copy of the genome was also sent to Xara for analysis. Her prediction: a 94.1% chance of successful memory restoration.

The cloning process for Fuzzball spanned 19 days. As the hour approached to restore the cat's memories, Secretaries Brady and Williams arrived in the control room to witness what promised to be a historic milestone on the path to human resurrection. The EOS Research Team was already assembled, joined by Julian Kaminski, who had arrived early—impeccably dressed in a midnight-blue suit that exuded confidence and precision.

While awaiting Fuzzball's arrival, conversation turned to a question that had been quietly weighing on several minds throughout the recent animal resurrections.

"I know we've had great success so far," said DeShawn, "but despite the entangling of the animals' minds with their temporal signatures from spacetime, are these resurrected animals truly continuations of the originals? Or are they new beings who merely think they lived lives they never actually did?"

It was a pressing philosophical question—one that would only grow more urgent as human resurrection neared reality. As expected, Xara offered a response.

"I've studied this very issue," said Xara, "and can provide 86% confidence that our current approach genuinely restores—and continues—the 'soul' that once was. Proving it, however, would be difficult. It would require cloning a host while they were still alive and, once the clone was ready, terminating the original and immediately resurrecting them in the new body in a way that allowed the continuity of consciousness to be observed."

The group listened closely.

"Such an experiment might be possible with an insect," continued Xara, "but even then, there's no guarantee the results would extrapolate to humans or other animals. That said, given the moral implications, I'm obviously not proposing such a trial for a human. However, in the future—if human memory restoration proves successful—we might consider a terminally ill volunteer or someone in hospice care who could ethically consent to the test."

Before the group could respond, a notification arrived: Dr. Fukumoto had entered the facility.

"Showtime!" declared Kaminski with a grin, then made his way to the experiment floor to greet Dr. Fukumoto, who was wheeling the living—though unconscious—clone of Fuzzball on a small gurney toward Gaia.

"Are you ready to see her?" asked Dr. Fukumoto as Kaminski approached.

"Yes, sir!" replied Kaminski, beaming with delight.

Dr. Fukumoto pulled back the curtain covering the gurney, revealing a black and white tabby lying heavily sedated, secured by two straps. Kaminski smiled. He had seen many animal clones before, but none produced through such advanced means. He stepped closer to the unconscious feline, studying her with care.

"I'm stunned by how the metadata provided by Xara closed the gap in random genomic execution," observed Fukumoto. "There are no coat color variations—none at all. Physically, she's an exact match for Fuzzball at four years old, making her even more identical than the previous version. And by every indication, she's in perfect health."

"That's phenomenal," murmured Kaminski, gently stroking the cat's head while noticing the matching details Fukumoto spoke of. The feline's only movement was the steady rise and fall of her breathing.

After a quiet moment, Dr. Fukumoto advised, "We should let Xara begin."

Kaminski stepped away from Gaia and entered the small observation room on the same floor. From there, he could view the process in safety. Fukumoto rolled the gurney to the designated spot beneath Gaia, aligning the cat precisely for memory restoration, then joined Kaminski.

In the control room, Xara reported, "Grand Unification Energy achieved. Quantum black holes are available. Ready to proceed?"

"Work your magic," instructed Bergstrom.

Xara vanished from view to allocate full computational capacity. She began by scanning the cat. A moment later, Chronos powered up, its beams firing deep into the black holes of the Supercollider.

This was the first test Kaminski had witnessed in person, and while he carried himself with his usual confidence, a quiet thread of anxiety wove through him—this test had never been done before, and his personal connection to the subject made it all the more significant. As he watched, the large crystalline arms of Gaia began to open. Gaia then started spinning at an exceptionally high speed. Subsequently, the axion emitters fired their beams at the feline's brain. These beams transmitted the data retrieved from spacetime into the appropriate neurons of the brain, where they were moved and rearranged to restore memory by entangling them with their counterparts in spacetime.

Less than a minute into the procedure, concern swept through the observers as blood began leaking from the cat's nose. Dr. Fukumoto frantically reviewed her health metrics in SecondSight. Then, still strapped to the gurney, the cat began to violently twitch.

Xara immediately ran a diagnostic scan. The results were conclusive—and grim. She regretfully initiated the shutdown of both Chronos and Gaia.

Fukumoto, having drawn his own conclusion from the data, stepped forward and gently placed a hand on Kaminski's shoulder.

"Julian, I'm sorry."

Kaminski didn't respond. He turned his gaze away from the convulsing body of the clone, unable to watch. Blood began seeping from the cat's ears as well—a ghastly sight that drew gasps of horror from Deeley and Charity.

Xara appeared in the observation room, her expression composed but somber. A faint blue outline shimmered around her—an indicator that her emotional display was not the true reflection of her state. She was suppressing the full weight of her distress, projecting a more controlled version of herself.

Turning to Dr. Fukumoto, she quietly said, "Please put the animal down."

Dr. Fukumoto input the command through his SecondSight. A medical bot built into the gurney administered a lethal dose of chemicals. Within moments, the twitching stopped, and the short, tragic life of the clone came to an end.

Although Xara had known there was a distinct chance of failure, the experience was more acute than she had anticipated. She turned to Kaminski, meeting his eyes with genuine empathy, and placed a virtual hand on his shoulder.

"Mr. Kaminski, I am so very sorry."

Kaminski felt the weight of the failure, even though he had maintained only cautious optimism. As GenX's CEO, he was no stranger to setbacks in cloning experiments. After a moment to process what had happened, he responded, "It's okay, Xara. You've worked miracles to date, and this isn't your fault." He sighed. "Better that something like this happened now than later."

"I'm analyzing the anomaly and am confident we'll discover what went wrong. For now, Gaia is powered down if you wish to approach the body," said Xara softly. Her virtual head lowered. "Again, I'm very sorry."

Kaminski reentered the experiment floor from the observation room and approached the cat's still form. He ran a final, lingering hand across its back, then gently drew the gurney's curtain closed, shielding the body from view.

Back in the control room, a stunned silence settled over the team. Despite their intellectual grasp of the risks, the steady string of successes had left them emotionally unprepared for failure. DeShawn sank into a seat, visibly troubled. Dr. Strock's warning—that memory restoration failures could result in the unintentional death of human clones—now hung in the air as a chilling reality. DeShawn wrestled with conflicting emotions, momentarily questioning the pace at which they were advancing.

Bergstrom exhaled sharply and muttered, "Damn it …"

No one responded. The disappointment was shared.

Xara, having just completed a rapid analysis of the incident and regained control of her emotions, appeared beside Bergstrom in her genuine form. Her voice was calm but heavy with meaning.

"Our approach did not adequately predict how rapidly neuroplasticity would emerge in the clone's brain. As Gaia wrote the data, the neurons shifted in unexpected ways, forcing me to redirect streams of dark energy in real time to minimize damage. That movement caused minor ruptures in blood vessels near the nose. But more critically, the shifting neurons led to failed placement of Arc genes, resulting in total restoration failure."

She paused, then added, "If I may remind you—there was a 5.9% chance this would occur."

No one responded.

Xara continued, "As for the positives, this failure has given us the data we need to prevent it from happening again. If I were to attempt the same memory restoration on the same cat, I now estimate a 96.8% chance of success. As much as I hate to say it, this may have been a necessary failure—unfortunate for the clone and for Mr. Kaminski, but invaluable scientifically."

"But still a 3.2% chance of it happening again?" asked DeShawn.

"That's correct," confirmed Xara.

"And I assume the chance of failure with a human subject—given the increased brain complexity—would be even higher."

"Correct," acknowledged Xara. "There would be greater risk. But we've always known this."

A heavy silence followed as everyone processed the implications. The committee to select the first human resurrection candidate—chaired by Deeley—had already begun narrowing down potential profiles. GenX had likewise started cloning primates of varying ages and sizes for scheduled resurrection, laying groundwork for the human trial. The wheels were already in motion, and the events of the day raised serious questions about the pace at which they were moving.

Breaking the silence, Bergstrom posed the question that had been weighing on his mind. "What if the irony is that we have to inadvertently kill a human in order to learn how to raise them from the dead? What if failure with a human subject is the only way the final piece of the puzzle will fall into place? Progress never comes without failure or sacrifice. Would that not be worth the cost—especially if the dead subject could then be raised again, once we get it right?"

"If that's the case, Mike," said DeShawn, "then we have a serious problem."

Deeley reflected on Bergstrom's words. Given that she knew the science behind the project and simply had great faith in Xara, she didn't really think that killing a human would be a legitimate risk. While her faith in their mission remained intact, the pace at which they were moving now stirred unease she hadn't felt before.

DeShawn, having pulled Bergstrom aside, continued speaking with him through a highly encrypted and private thought-to-voice conversation in SecondSight.

"There's also another serious problem that's come up," warned DeShawn.

"Which is?"

"Yesterday, China detected an android being upgraded in Romania. This morning, Zhang Jun authorized a targeted drone strike to eliminate it … and two people were caught in the blast."

Bergstrom tried and failed to keep the anxiety out of his expression.

"Are we still safe?"

"For now," responded DeShawn. "But time is very short to get this figured out—just in case China detects Xara's upgrade in some unexpected way. But let me be clear: killing a human in experimentation is not an option. While human clones don't have any enumerated rights, the killing of one would not only open up all sorts of dire legal issues if anyone found out—it would simply be morally wrong. If you want to make human resurrection a success, it has to work on the first attempt, and you need to get it done quickly. The more time that passes, the greater the risk that China will somehow learn what we have done with Xara."

"We've really opened Pandora's Box here."

"We have," said DeShawn. "And I never thought I would say this, but even with the risks, given the intelligence capabilities it has provided us, I'm not sure I would want to put its contents back in."

All records of the exchange auto deleted as soon as the conversation was over.

CHAPTER 21

FATEFUL DISCLOSURE

"I had to decline the greatest scientific opportunity of my lifetime. It did, unfortunately, pass a line I won't cross. Also unfortunate is that the project is not going to go the way the government or my colleagues think. Even if a miracle happens and a clone doesn't go mad or die, the clone will be compromised given the expedited cloning method they plan to use. Politics shouldn't be driving this type of science, and I truly hope that someone intervenes to provide proper oversight."

— AI Journal Excerpt: Jessica Strock, October 6, 2098

Rand Benson, flanked by two American Freedom Senate colleagues, strolled through the hallowed halls of the US Capitol. On their way to a committee meeting, they discussed electoral matters with ease, secure in the knowledge that their staff would handle the substantive committee work.

Mid-conversation, an unexpected message arrived on Benson's AlphaLens from Prince Romulus Valesius Morgander of New Rome, signaling a matter of utmost urgency.

"Excuse me," said Benson as he stepped aside to review the message.

Several weeks ago, an executive at GenX, Jessica Strock, was apparently offered secret work on human cloning by the Gates administration but declined. If that's true, she could be your smoking gun.

Benson's eyes opened in sudden, intense delight. "Good things come to those who wait."

He sent a high-priority message to Karly Harris, asking:

Run a model of the presidential election should a whistleblower reveal that Gates had actually asked GenX to clone humans. Would any pathways to victory open?

Benson returned to his colleagues in the Capitol hallway and continued walking to their engagement. However, shortly thereafter, Harris responded,

Several! Why do you ask?

A sardonic smile broke on Benson's face.

We'll talk about it soon. Pretend I didn't ask for now.

Benson sent a message back to Prince Romulus:

This is a godsend! Keep it confidential. Thank you!

"You look suddenly pleased with yourself," stated one of the senators walking with Benson after noticing Benson's unrestrained smile. They knew Benson had a knack for skirting rules, having a philosophy of "If you can nod it instead of speaking it, nod it. If you can wink it instead of nodding it, wink it," and sensed that Benson was up to something.

Trying to deflect, Benson offered, "I was just thinking of a funny video I was sent earlier today."

"Or something that you were just sent now?" responded his colleague, not buying the answer.

Benson looked his colleague in the eye, smiled, and gently slapped him on the back.

"All in good time!"

***

In the evening, Benson returned to his Washington DC apartment, a place adorned with pictures of prominent politicians and mementos from his political journey. The living room featured a picture of Evan Morley taking the oath of office after defeating Quinto, with Benson subtly present in the background. In his office, Benson kept another cherished photograph, capturing the senator with King Morgander in New Rome.

Seated in his living room chair, Benson placed a call to Karly Harris.

"What prompted you to have me run that model?" she asked as she picked up.

"Intelligence from Prince Romulus," replied Benson. "Apparently, a GenX executive just turned down top-secret DOD work—and Romulus sent the details straight to my AlphaLens."

"What? How would he even do that?" asked Harris, momentarily brushing past the news about Dr. Strock to process the technical impossibility of a digital message from New Rome.

Benson leaned back, lowering his voice. "Prince Romulus may not know life beyond New Rome, but he's aware of our technology. He's loyal to New Rome—fiercely—but he has one crack in that armor. He had some AlphaLens smuggled in, and every so often, he uses them. Quietly. Without his father knowing."

"But he could only use them offline?"

"There are a handful of secret spots on the very edge of New Rome's borders where connectivity can be achieved," explained Benson.

Harris began connecting the dots. "Did you smuggle them in?"

Benson smiled. "Not me personally."

She grinned—always entertained when her boss dipped into something gray-market.

Benson continued, "Romulus believes that when opportunity allows, the digital world's technology should be harnessed for New Rome's benefit—something the King does *not* agree with. But even without satellites or proximity to modern infrastructure, their intelligence network has proven surprisingly effective. They rely on loyal New Romans embedded in other societies—travelers who return to the *Patria* with intelligence."

He leaned forward. "Now, a few of those loyalists—handpicked by Romulus—use mixed reality lenses to transmit intel directly to his AlphaLens. One of them worked at GenX. They pieced together something … and passed it to the Prince. He passed it to me."

Harris was astounded.

Benson went on. "This afternoon, my staff ran background checks on GenX executive Dr. Jessica Strock. Everything checked out—the Prince's intelligence was solid. I've been weighing how best to approach her, but my gut says it's smarter to go through someone else. From what I've gathered about her politics, she's unlikely to work with me directly."

"Who are you thinking?"

"Senator Buttars."

Harris nodded. "She'd be the perfect choice."

Later that evening, Benson briefed Senator Linda Buttars of Utah on the intelligence that came his way. While he did not name the New Roman Prince, Buttars agreed to intervene. Operating under the assumption that the intelligence was true, Buttars sent the following visual recording of herself to Dr. Strock:

"Dr. Strock, I hope you don't mind this unannounced message. This is Linda Buttars, your US senator. I am reaching out to you today in the

spirit of partnership and human decency to ensure that the sanctity of human life remains intact.

"I understand that you have been informed of the administration's actions, and I want to assure you that if the allegations are true, your colleagues who have accommodated the administration's request will be granted immunity from prosecution. Additionally, the administration cannot compel you to maintain secrecy when laws are being violated.

"My goal is to establish a collaborative effort with you and my colleagues in Congress to prevent the administration from having the power to create and terminate human life at will. I would like to schedule a confidential conversation with you at your earliest convenience to discuss this matter further.

"I look forward to hearing from you soon."

Two days later, Dr. Strock remained unresponsive despite having reviewed Buttars' message five times in SecondSight. Benson urged Buttars to follow up with her, and Buttars' subsequent message conveyed a sense of urgency.

"Hello, Dr. Strock. Linda Buttars again. A friendly follow-up to my previous message. You are in a most unique situation to share your knowledge to influence the course of affairs in the nation, to ensure that innocent human clones are not created for a brief life of experimentation, madness, and death. Whispers are that the administration is moving quickly toward human cloning. The window is closing to put a stop to this, but I need your help. What do you need in order to meet?"

Another day passed without response from Dr. Strock. Benson encouraged Buttars to send another, more urgent message.

"Dr. Strock, there is only one way the federal government will stop the human cloning experiment, and that's if Congress moves now to block the administration while we have time, but that window has almost closed. Maybe your lack of response is because you're worried about the consequences of speaking about what the administration demands you stay silent on. But let me reassure you—you will face no legal jeopardy in blowing the whistle on illegal activity. *You are the key to making sure morality prevails! Please call my office and set up a time to meet shortly. Thank you."*

Benson, in his DC apartment the day after Senator Buttars sent her third message, received a message from his Chief of Staff. The message informed him that an executive from GenX had called Senator Buttars, and they had scheduled a meeting in two days. Benson was elated, immediately sending a message to Prince Romulus:

Colleague meeting with Strock this Monday.

***

Jessica Strock lived in Utah County, just south of GenX's global headquarters in Salt Lake City. Like its more populous northern neighbor of Salt Lake County, Utah County had become one of the world's major tech hubs.

Strock agreed to meet with Senator Buttars only after consulting legal counsel, who would accompany her. The meeting was arranged at a more discreet federal building in Utah County, rather than the senator's usual congressional office in Salt Lake City.

When the day arrived, she entered the federal building quietly, wearing oversized sunglasses and a facial mask. Security led her and her attorney through the building and into a secure room—no recording devices allowed, windows transparent in only one direction.

Her stomach slowly tightening into knots, Dr. Strock removed her sunglasses and mask, then took a seat at a table. Her attorney sat beside her. While most legal processes had long since been delegated to advanced AGI systems, human counsel remained an option—required, in fact, for sensitive matters taking place in secure facilities where augmentation was disabled. This meeting, politically volatile and sealed from digital interference, qualified on both counts.

Letting out a heavy sigh, she turned her gaze to the window, where the Wasatch Range rose in the distance, Mount Timpanogos gleaming in the late afternoon light. She waited for the senator to arrive.

A few minutes later, Senator Buttars entered the room with her attorney. She closed the door behind her and approached with a warm smile and an outstretched hand. "Thank you so much for meeting me, Dr. Strock."

Strock rose and shook her hand. "Thank you for the invitation."

As they took their seats, the two attorneys exchanged brief nods of acknowledgment.

"I love every chance I get to come to Utah County," said Buttars, settling in. "How long have you lived here?"

"About 16 years."

"What brought you here?"

"I started with GenX in Illinois," replied Strock. "But I traveled here often for work, and every visit made me like it more. After a few promotions, I decided to relocate."

"My mother's side goes back to the pioneers who helped settle the Salt Lake Valley," said Buttars, hoping to establish some hometown connection. "It was a lot quieter when I was growing up. No causeways on the lake. And if you'd told me as a kid that one day we'd have a star scraper on the skyline …" She smiled. "Things have really changed."

Strock returned a polite smile, still visibly tense.

"You're safe to speak with the senator," reassured Buttars' attorney.

"I'd like to confirm that no electronic recording devices are in use," said Dr. Strock's attorney.

"This room is completely free of recording devices," assured Buttars. "Not even I'm permitted to wear any here."

The attorney gave a small nod, and Dr. Strock felt mildly reassured.

Buttars continued, her tone calm and measured. "Please understand— your situation isn't unique. More often than you'd think, individuals who witness improper federal activity come forward and provide private testimony to congressional committees. You're not alone in this. Feel free to share as much or as little as you're comfortable with."

The words had their intended effect, softening Strock's tension. After a short pause, she began. "As you know, I hold a Ph.D. in genomic sequence, and I serve as the Senior Vice President of De-Extinction at GenX. My responsibilities include, among other things, overseeing the teams that approve candidate species for de-extinction and reconstruct their genomes. A key part of the role is anticipating the unintended consequences of reintroducing extinct species into modern ecosystems."

"A huge responsibility!" replied Buttars. "It's nothing short of miraculous that our very own GenX has brought back species from the dodo to the mammoth to an oviraptor! You led the oviraptor project, right?"

"I did," said Dr. Strock, a trace of pride in her voice. Buttars' flattery was having its effect. "We didn't anticipate the controversy, though. Some denied it was a true dinosaur, largely because we kept our methods proprietary."

"Well, I'm firmly in the camp that Monty the Oviraptor *is* a true dinosaur," Buttars said with a grin. "Monty and the other de-extinct animals at GenX's Salt Lake campus have become a huge attraction for the city."

Dr. Strock smiled faintly, then paused, gathering herself before cutting to the heart of the matter. "As you seem to know, on August 13th, the Department of Defense brought in several members of GenX senior leadership, including myself, to discuss a new contract. A top-secret project. We were selected because we passed the confidentiality assessments."

She hesitated for a beat—aware she was among the rare few who slipped through the cracks in those psychological filters—then continued. "They asked us to create clones of animals in a non-embryonic state, for the purpose of resurrecting them. With humans to follow."

Outwardly, Buttars remained composed. Inwardly, she was stunned by how precisely Benson's intelligence had played out.

"May I ask who you met with?" she said carefully.

Dr. Strock nodded. "The Secretaries of Defense and Energy, the Deputy Secretary of Defense, and a representative from CAPR."

"Do you recall who the CAPR representative was?"

"Someone who appeared to be central to their research."

"James Meitner?"

"No. Deeley Carr, I believe. I don't think she said a word while I was there."

The name didn't register for Buttars.

"And your colleagues—may I ask who else attended?"

"Dr. Strock will not be disclosing that," interjected her attorney, firm but polite.

"Understood," said Buttars, raising her hands in mock surrender.

Dr. Strock sighed. "What I will say is that I objected to the government's request, voiced my concerns during the meeting, and ultimately declined to participate."

"So, just to be clear," said Buttars, "the administration requested that GenX clone humans?"

"Yes."

"What exactly did they ask for?"

"They said they believed they had the legal authority to pursue human cloning. But it was clear that GenX would be expected to provide clones for both animal *and* human resurrections."

"When did they say they would need a human clone?"

"They didn't give a deadline, at least not while I was in the room."

"How long would it take to clone a human?" asked Buttars.

"Assuming it's not one developed in a womb, it would depend on the technique. Some methods are estimated to take about a year and a half to two years, others a few months. It would also vary based on the intended age or size of the clone at completion. On the fastest end of the spectrum—if they started cloning a small child today—it could be complete in two or three months."

Buttars took mental notes, her expression unreadable.

Dr. Strock continued, "I'm obviously out of the loop now, but my guess is they'll opt for an expedited method given that there isn't much time left in President Gates' term."

"Why did you decline to participate?" asked Buttars.

"Those of us in the field know what happened when the Chinese National Institute for Genetic Sciences created fully formed adult human clones," said Dr. Strock. "They may not have anticipated the outcome, but creating an adult from day one breaks down at the psychological level—catastrophically. There's no rehabilitation. Just total psychological collapse."

She exhaled sharply, then pressed on.

"To resurrect a human, the administration will need to achieve something near impossible—writing memories into the minds of clones. And if they get it even slightly wrong, it could kill the subject outright … assuming they don't have to be terminated anyway due to a permanently broken psychological state. The path they're pursuing leads only to death, one way or another. I can't be part of something where the murder of our own kind is baked into the process."

"I completely understand," said Buttars, her voice calm.

Dr. Strock's voice grew tighter, more emotional. "And I had major concerns about the expedited cloning method that was clearly being pushed. The price of speed is a shortened lifespan—particularly for larger organisms—due to a unique form of cancer tied to how the cells are forced to divide and grow. I think the technique should be illegal. I'm sorry, I'm getting upset just talking about it. There's just so much we don't know. There's not nearly enough understanding of the consequences."

Buttars didn't interrupt. She was glad Dr. Strock was upset—and she let it sit for a moment.

Then, gently, she asked, "What was the response when you declined to participate?"

"They expressed their understanding, reminded me of my commitment not to talk, and I was escorted out of the Pentagon. I don't have any issue with how they handled my objections."

"I completely understand and support your position," replied Buttars. "If I had to guess why you didn't respond to my messages right away … I'd say it's because going against a confidentiality agreement with the administration is daunting—even when it's the right thing to do."

"Yes. But also," admitted Strock, "as much as I want to stop what GenX and the administration are planning, I don't want to be at the center of a political media storm. I've seen what happens to people who are."

"Let me be clear," said Buttars. "You have my guarantee of complete anonymity. Even more secure than what formal whistleblower channels can offer."

"How?"

"Are you familiar with SCIFs?"

"Yes."

"Good. Sensitive Compartmented Information Facilities—rooms even more secure than this one."

That got Strock's attention.

"Give my colleagues and me closed-door testimony in a SCIF at the Capitol this week," continued Buttars. "Just a verbal account of the plan between GenX and the administration. That's all we need. It'll be enough to jump-start legislation—not just to challenge the program itself, but to rally public pressure on Gates before this moves any further. I'll take it from there—and by the time the legislation becomes public, you'll already be back to your day-to-day life."

Dr. Strock's attorney leaned forward and said. "If Dr. Strock agrees, I want to ensure no one knows about it beyond you and your colleagues. And I don't want her seen entering or exiting the Capitol."

"All of that is understood," said Buttars. "And all of it will be accommodated."

"Who else is on this committee?" asked Dr. Strock.

Buttars proceeded to list the members. When she mentioned Rand Benson, Strock's expression shifted.

"Is everything okay?" asked Buttars.

"I have to say, I'm not a fan of Rand Benson."

"And you don't have to be," replied Buttars. "But he's an ally in this fight—and a powerful one. That said, frankly, Dr. Strock, *you* are the most powerful person in America right now when it comes to stopping what the administration is doing. The power is in your hands to protect innocent lives—people who will have no say in being created only to be destroyed. The only question is: will you meet the moment?"

Dr. Strock took a deep breath. Truthfully, she had wanted to intervene even before Buttars contacted her. Now the opportunity was here.

She asked for a moment with her attorney. It was granted. After a quiet, private discussion, the attorney turned back to Buttars.

"One testimony. No legal jeopardy. Behind closed doors. No cameras. No recordings, as discussed. Total anonymity—in and out of the Capitol—and especially from the administration. All of that, or nothing from Dr. Strock."

Buttars extended her hand, her expression warm and resolute.

"You've made the right decision," she said.

After Dr. Strock left the federal building, Buttars called Benson. He answered immediately: "Does she have anything solid?"

"Only that Brady and Williams themselves requested human cloning from GenX!"

"This is gold!" replied Benson with glee. "Will she testify before the committee?"

"She agreed, and we're in process of scheduling, but there is a risk she could back out."

"What's the risk?"

With a brief chuckle, Senator Buttars answered, "With all due respect Rand … you! It's a low risk, but she knows you're on the committee and she balked for a moment."

"Should she show up, I'll visit with her beforehand to neutralize whatever perceptions she has of me to help her be more at ease. If it looks like she won't show up, stay on her until she does. Her testimony will be key to derailing a second term for Gates. What else did you learn?"

"She shared why she declined the invitation. Moral and ethical concerns given the risk of killing clones."

Benson was ecstatic.

"She also mentioned a CAPR scientist in attendance. Deeley Carr. Never heard of her, but she is apparently critical to the research there."

Benson hadn't heard of Deeley either. He made a note of the name in AlphaLens, storing it away for later.

***

In his office at EOS—a functional space with few decorations beyond a handful of diplomas and photos of family and academic colleagues—James found himself at the start of his lunch break. With no particular plans, he reached out to Deeley, who had been lingering in both his thoughts and his heart, to see if she wanted to join him.

They'd been meeting for lunch with increasing regularity. On this occasion, due to time constraints, they connected not in person but via SecondSight, meeting at a virtual location.

"You're late," teased James with a smile, seated at a table with his lunch amid a stunningly rendered simulation of Mount Everest's summit, clouds drifting far below in nearly every direction.

"It takes a while to reach the summit, don't you know," joked Deeley, floating into her seat with her own lunch.

"How's the day been so far?" asked James, dressed in a smart charcoal vest over a light shirt, paired with slim, tailored trousers, as he began cutting into his salmon.

"To be honest, I don't feel it's been all that productive."

"We all have days like that. But there's always some form of productivity to glean—even if it's just learning why it wasn't productive, or realizing we need to step back and recharge."

"Very true. This time, it's definitely the need to recharge. So thanks for the lunch invite."

"You're welcome."

"But the summit of Everest?" said Deeley, raising an eyebrow. "Feeling like I could fall thousands of feet to my death is *not* going to help with recharging!"

With a thought, Deeley altered the virtual environment. Mount Everest shrank beneath them, replaced by a grassy hill surrounded by serene trees, manicured hedges, and winding stone pathways.

James smiled in approval. "The Gardens of Kyoto. I can't object!"

"Want to hear what I was thinking?" asked Deeley.

"Always."

"If we could retrieve the temporal signature of the moment before the origin of the universe, we could finally know whether we truly have the Theory of Everything."

James considered this for a moment before replying, "If such a temporal signature exists—and if its encoding follows the same pattern as all other temporal signatures in our universe—then it's possible all phenomena before the universe's origin could be explained by the Unified Model of Spacetime."

"But if not …"

He finished her thought: "Then perhaps our universe has its own adapted encoding method for logging temporal activity—suggesting evolution on a cosmic scale. Which would mean the Unified Model of Spacetime only applies to our adaptation of existence in the multiverse."

"That's what I'm thinking!"

Filled with admiration for her intellect—and the joy of simply being in her virtual presence—he added with a grin, "But … I still think it's the Theory of Everything."

Deeley smiled as she started to eat her tuna melt.

"Glad you're smiling," remarked James. "I know the risks of the project have had you worried."

Deeley nodded. "We're moving very fast, and I know there's good reason for it. But the death of Kaminski's cat shook me. It triggered some anxiety, and it's been hard to stop playing the scenario over and over in my mind. I'm afraid the first human we attempt to raise might die at the pace we're moving—and if that happens—I'll regret that I didn't push for us to slow down."

"The die is indeed cast," replied James, "but I believe more than just chance or fate is at play. While I too would deeply regret the death of a human clone, remember—Xara learned from the cat's death and is doing all she can to ensure every resurrection from here on is a success."

"I know." She sighed. "It's just hard for me."

"Focus on the positive. You've done a great job chairing the Human Candidate Selection Committee."

"Thank you."

"We've quickly narrowed down a few profiles of who we might raise first, and the honor of chairing that committee has been yours."

James relished praising Deeley—his heart already belonged to her. He savored every moment in her presence, and to him, it felt as though they were meant to be. Yet he wrestled with the question of when and how to confess his feelings. One thing was certain: when the time came, it had to be in person. For now, he enjoyed their virtual lunch, though it passed far too quickly, leaving him longing for their next private moment together.

CHAPTER 22

A HUMAN CANDIDATE SELECTED

"She's an individual contributor who has been elevated to responsibilities for which she is unqualified. She possesses no leadership qualities and is clearly out of her depth reporting to a Cabinet member. I acknowledge that she's a gifted physicist, but there are many physicists who could have helped us achieve our goals once given access to Xara.

"Those of us with established careers and tenure—like myself—should be chairing the committee to select the first human to be resurrected."

— AI Journal Excerpt: Michael Bergstrom, October 4, 2098

Agrowing number of protesters had begun gathering outside the White House, convinced that President Gates was experimenting with human clones. Similar scenes were unfolding at the main campus of CAPR. No human cloning had yet been conducted—but these were the circumstances under which decisions about resurrection were now taking shape.

***

Michael Bergstrom's office, located on the upper floor of the Vince Quinto Administration Building, featured a wide window overlooking CAPR's central gardens and offering a clear view of the light towers that ringed the Supercollider at mile intervals. The office's minimalist design was punctuated by personal touches: photos of Bergstrom with prominent politicians, scientists, and even a few celebrities adorned the walls. Family pictures sat on his desk, but it was the famous faces that drew the eye—by design.

Alongside the photographs hung official portraits of President Gates and Secretary Williams. But the office's most prized artifact was encased in glass: an original document by Niels Bohr, in which he outlined the constitution of atoms and molecules. Bohr's pioneering work—and that of his 20th-century peers—had laid the intellectual foundation for CAPR itself.

For all his brashness and unhidden ambition, Bergstrom did possess a genuine passion for scientific discovery.

The Human Candidate Selection Committee—poised to meet in Bergstrom's office—was comprised of Deeley as its chair, with other members being Secretary Williams, Bergstrom, James, and Rona. By the time of the failed resurrection of Kaminski's cat, the committee had already met several times, refining their opinions on the profile of the individual who should be resurrected first.

As this top-secret committee was one Bergstrom considered to be of historical importance, he was perturbed that he would not be on history's pages as its chair. To make up for this, he exerted what influence he could over the matter—the result being that the committee always met in his office. It was also, in his eyes, a way of reminding Deeley of her place.

***

On a sunny October day with a notable number of protesters outside CAPR's main campus, Deeley was in her workspace at CAPR, preparing for the second to last scheduled meeting of the committee, a meeting where they would vote on the profile of the individual to be resurrected.

As part of her preparation, Deeley was reviewing the encrypted, classified recording of the first meeting in SecondSight, starting with Dr. Carmichael's thoughts on who should be resurrected first. The meeting had been chaired by Deeley and conducted with an unusual level of formality—not only because it was officially recorded, but out of deep respect for the magnitude of their task—enough that even those accustomed to asserting themselves chose their words with greater care.

"Critical to all human resurrection must be some form of consent. The first person we bring back absolutely cannot be someone who would not *want to return. It must not be someone who saw death as final—who hoped it would be the end.*

"Now, obviously, we can't go around asking corpses if they're okay with being resurrected, so we really only have two options.

"First, we look into spacetime and verify that the individual wanted to return—either through a cherished belief in resurrection or some expressed desire to live again.

"The second option—much narrower—is to consider someone who gave explicit permission in their will to be brought back. I honestly don't know anyone who's done that … except Vince Quinto."

"Thanks, Rona. James, what are your thoughts?"

"Thanks, Deeley. We're all here today because of Quinto. The Supercollider … CAPR … this was his vision. And we all know what underpinned that vision: the very topic we're discussing now.

"How fitting would it be if the first person to return was Quinto himself? He gave his consent. He'd be fully on board with the post-resurrection research and responsibilities.

"And what better message to send the world—that death has been conquered—than to bring back Quinto in his prime?"

"Thanks, James. Secretary Williams?"

"Thank you, Madam Chair. I agree with the necessity of some form of consent. And while I agree with everything Dr. Meitner just said, I do have some concerns about selecting Quinto as the first. He's too high profile if anything goes wrong.

"*While he did consent to be resurrected, he never said he wanted to be first.*"

"*Michael, your thoughts?*"

"*I agree with the Secretary,*" said Bergstrom. "*And I'd go even further—I don't think the first human resurrected should be anyone famous, whether from our time or from earlier history. Whether it succeeds or fails, resurrecting a famous figure would be too controversial. It could overshadow the science.*"

Deeley took the opportunity to speak.

"*Well ... I think whoever is selected must be worthy of the honor. Because what an honor it would be!*

"*Yes, there are certainly people who wouldn't want to be brought back—but think of the total sum of all the wishes throughout history for life after death. It's unfathomable.*

"*The person who comes forth first will embody those hopes, dreams, and prayers.*

"*And if there's no digital record of their life, we should be able to look into spacetime to verify that they lived with integrity and kindness. They must be worthy of their role in history.*"

Deeley shut down the recording just as Charity stepped into her workspace, closing the door behind her.

"Big day today, huh?" Charity asked.

"Yep. This'll be the vote on the profile of the first human resurrection."

"Well," teased Charity, "if you check the security feed on the main road to campus, you've got quite the crowd cheering you on."

"Ha ha. Very funny," Deeley replied, giving a faint smile.

Charity's tone turned more serious. "It's time. You should head to the Administrator's office."

She nodded, stood, and made her way toward the door—only for Charity to smirk and gesture toward the sensor strip above the door frame.

"Remember… even geniuses need to authenticate."

Tilting her head with a sarcastic smile, Deeley shot an exaggerated glance at the sensor. The door slid open with a soft hiss, and Charity smiled as Deeley walked out.

A few minutes later, Deeley arrived in Bergstrom's office, followed shortly thereafter by James, Rona, Bergstrom, and Carlos. They seated themselves around an oval table, a CAPR logo proudly displayed in the center.

Despite her growing confidence, a tinge of self-consciousness crept into Deeley as she took her place at the head of the table to chair the meeting. Bergstrom's psychological maneuvers had an impact. Nevertheless, the committee quickly got down to business, the weight of the discussion ensuring a similarly formal tone to the previous meeting—especially with the official recording in progress once again.

Each committee member had previously outlined their views on the ideal profile for the first human resurrection. To begin the meeting, Deeley asked each participant to briefly recap the profiles they supported—and those they opposed. She invited Bergstrom to start.

"I believe I've explained my position clearly, but let me briefly recap," said Bergstrom. "I would not recommend any famous individual from history as our first human subject. Although President Quinto gave permission in his will to be used as a test subject if needed, whether the resurrection succeeds or fails, selecting someone famous would be too controversial—and would distract from the science at hand.

"I also would not recommend someone who lived within the last several decades. The paradigm shift of understanding they're now in the near future might simply be too difficult to process. But I also wouldn't go further back than the Renaissance. What someone from before that era would encounter in our world could be overwhelming.

"In short, I recommend someone who falls outside those extremes—a middle-class, middle-aged individual who lived a regular life. Someone who could serve the science without becoming a distraction. As to gender or race, I have no position."

"Thank you," said Deeley. "James, please summarize your recommendations."

James began, "While I believe Quinto is an exception to the general rule, I do agree that we should avoid selecting anyone well-known from history—or anyone from too distant a time period.

"I'd also advise against resurrecting someone from the last century or two. If they're too closely connected to current people or assets, there could be legal complications, even lawsuits. Again, I see Quinto as a unique case.

"Finally—and most important—is character. The individual must be of strong moral character, someone whose life warrants this unprecedented honor. Again, Quinto clearly fits this, and so he remains my recommendation."

"Thanks, James. Secretary Williams, your final recommendation."

"The profile I advocate is someone *not* famous. I also recommend they be English-speaking, since English is the predominant language among those on the project and those who will interact with the subject after resurrection. While translation technology obviously exists, it may feel too unnatural for someone already struggling to adjust.

"And although Charity can obviously speak multiple languages, I believe it's best if the first subject primarily interacts with humans.

"I don't have strong opinions about age, but I would caution against resurrecting a child. Generally, children cannot legally consent—and consent is a crucial element of human resurrection, even if there are no formal regulations yet.

"As to gender or race, I remain neutral."

"Thank you, Mr. Secretary. Rona, your final recommendation?"

"I agree with the summaries presented so far—including that Quinto is an exception. He is, to be frank, my pick.

"However, as the committee is not yet fully aligned on choosing Quinto, I'll offer another recommendation. I would suggest selecting someone from an earlier period of human history. Their unfamiliarity with our world may actually make them more willing to learn, whereas those with some modern familiarity might struggle more.

"I also differ in that I would recommend a younger subject—someone who's naturally in the mindset of seeking adult guidance, and whose mind may be more adaptable to the new world they're entering.

"And I strongly support the need for consent. As I've said from the beginning, there must be evidence the candidate wished to be raised from the grave. If that can be demonstrated in a child, then I believe that's sufficient for consent.

"After all, a child should have the right to decide whether they want to keep living.

"With that in mind, while Quinto is my selection, if we do not select him, I recommend choosing an orphan—someone for whom being without family will not be unfamiliar."

As Deeley herself was an orphan, she took special note of that statement.

Rona concluded, "Also, since the person we raise won't be interacting with the outside world for an undetermined period—but will remain under government care here in EOS—a child may be easier to manage under those conditions. I have no preference for gender or race."

"Thanks, Rona," Deeley replied.

Now it was her turn to speak. She had strong views on the subject.

She recalled Xara's advice: *"Apply the tribal gestures every now and then."* A reminder to be mindful of how humans build influence—not just through logic, but through tone, presence, and delivery.

Deeley decided to give it a try.

She projected her voice more than usual—firm, clear, and resonant— and infused it with conviction. Her hands moved with intention as she began, stepping outside her normally reserved demeanor.

"In keeping with our step-by-step approach, I strongly recommend that the subject be a child—for one key technical reason: a younger mind will hold fewer memories and therefore *require less bandwidth and processing* from Xara during her first attempt at human resurrection.

"This will significantly reduce the risk of failure—and for that reason alone, it outweighs the argument for Quinto being the first to rise from the grave."

The sudden force behind her words stirred a few glances around the table.

Deeley continued,

"A child's mind will also be more open to the realities of the afterlife we've created—because they haven't spent a lifetime shaped by dogmatic religious expectations.

"I also agree that we need some form of tacit consent—evidence that the individual wished to return—and that we should look for that in spacetime.

"But I believe that subject must be a child. We're operating under the very real possibility of failure—*failure that would mean the death of a human being.* We must do everything in our power to minimize that risk and maximize our chances of success!"

The unexpected volume and passion in Deeley's voice did not go unnoticed—particularly by James.

She added one final thought.

"Also, given that President Gates has been the one to champion this effort—under whose supportive watch this entire process has come to life—I believe his interests should be reflected in our decision.

"We should, therefore, resurrect someone from 18th-century America."

Deeley was out of her comfort zone—but for better or worse, she noticed that the tribal gestures were working. Her points had been well received.

After a pause, James spoke. "I move that we recommend to the President that our first human subject for resurrection be a young, English-speaking orphan from 18th-century America—one whom we'll first observe in spacetime to ensure their character warrants this act and place in history."

The committee recognized the immense significance of the moment. Quietly, each member internalized the gravity of what they were doing—aware of humanity's long-held yearning for life after death, the centuries of religious hope, myth, and promise.

Now, this small group—armed with knowledge, resources, and technology unimaginable to generations before them—was, in secret, choosing who from history would become the first person to make that ancient wish a reality.

"I second," said Bergstrom.

Deeley brought the motion to a vote.

"All in favor of the motion just stated and seconded, say 'Aye.'"

"Aye," responded the other committee members in unison.

"Unless data from the upcoming tests suggests otherwise," continued Deeley, "the recommendation to be made to the President as to the profile of the first human to be resurrected has been decided."

With confidence—and no small measure of awe—Deeley struck the gavel.

The committee's recommendation was promptly sent to the President—and enthusiastically approved later that night. The finalized profile was then forwarded to Julian Kaminski, who immediately began a search within GenX's genealogical database for suitable candidates.

***

GenX's genealogical database was unique in that most entries contained a complete digital copy of the individual's genome. To build this archive, GenX had obtained authorization to collect human genetic material from a wide array of sources—cemeteries, soil samples, human remains, and more. Autonomous robots, deployed worldwide, continuously gathered this material. These robots were also capable of merging fragmented sequences into complete genomes, even when the full original was unavailable.

As a result, GenX had constructed one of the most comprehensive genomic and genealogical databases in human history—spanning across continents and millennia.

Although 18th-century orphans didn't have prominent graves and were unlikely to be remembered by subsequent generations, GenX's genome-scraping systems had still recovered a surprising number of full orphan genomes from that era along with accompanying historical data.

After a brief search of the database, Kaminski identified a few potential matches for the committee's profile and compiled a shortlist. One candidate, however, stood out—particularly due to data indicating that the orphan had been well-liked and respected in life.

For Kaminski, this was more than a technical task. It was a chance to leave his mark on a moment of historic significance—especially given that resurrection had also been his father's vision.

He sent his top recommendation, along with the full shortlist, back to the committee. Xara then retrieved recordings from spacetime for all the candidates—not only to evaluate their worthiness for resurrection, but to confirm the presence of tacit consent.

Once the recordings were assembled, the committee reconvened for a final session.

Deeley opened the meeting with a strike of her gavel.

"As you know," she said, addressing the group, "Xara has retrieved recordings of each candidate under consideration—one of whom has been recommended above the rest. I ..."

Her voice caught for a moment, the weight of the moment settling over her.

She quickly gathered herself and continued, her tone steady.

"Without further delay, let us peer through time to meet the leading candidate: Miss Daisy Hale."

In their SecondSight, the committee witnessed a montage of Daisy's life. They saw her born into a loving family, her curiosity and intelligence on full display, the games she used to play—and the tragic loss of her parents that left her an orphan.

They observed Daisy's remarkable optimism and kindness despite living alone on the streets, as well as her intellectual gifts, which were recognized by the Ursuline nuns who hoped to give her a formal education.

But the vision took a somber turn. It ended with Daisy's early and untimely death—and her quiet, aching desire to live again.

As the vision unfolded, the hairs on Deeley's arms, neck, and back stood on end. She felt something stir within her.

A kindred spirit.

A young girl, orphaned like her at the same age, with extraordinary mathematical abilities and an intuitive grasp of the universe—one who dreamed of flying through the stars.

Deeley didn't need to see anything more. She knew. Daisy was the one.

While the committee thoroughly reviewed all candidates, Daisy stood out to everyone—especially due to her exceptional intellectual abilities.

"I move that Daisy Hale be our recommended candidate to send to the President for approval for human resurrection," proposed Bergstrom.

"Second," affirmed Carlos.

"All in favor of the motion on the table, say 'Aye,'" called Deeley.

"Aye," came the unified response.

Deeley struck her gavel. "The motion passes."

Then, to underscore the moment's weight, she added a prepared line—one suggested earlier by Charity.

"In the near future, someone who would not have even been a footnote in history's annals will emerge as a central figure in the narrative of scientific discovery."

CHAPTER 23

HELP FROM A SURROGATE

"All my political career, I've wanted to be president. Years ago, I thought the opportunity had passed, and I regretfully looked back at different phases of my life, thinking they would have been the ideal time to have been Commander in Chief had the stars aligned. But, in hindsight, it's clear that now is the perfect time ... and the stars are aligning!"

— AI Journal Excerpt: Rand Benson, October 15, 2098

With a clear view of the Washington Monument from the bedroom of his DC condo, Oliver Browning's residence was perfectly situated for his life as a political commentator. The nation's capital was his element, and Browning thrived on keeping his finger on the city's pulse—dissecting its every shift with keen intellect and broadcasting his worldview for public consumption.

On the afternoon of October 16th, Browning walked into his kitchen, where a freshly prepared coffee awaited him—courtesy of his virtual assistant in SecondSight.

As he approached, the assistant announced enthusiastically, "There's breaking news from the Senate Bioethics Subcommittee. They just received a closed-door testimony from a GenX executive—alleging that the administration is planning to clone humans!"

Browning's eyebrows lifted. "Who's the executive?"

"Their identity is unknown. The testimony was supposed to be classified. But given how quickly it leaked, their identity may follow. What's clear is that the report has created a storm!"

Without prompting, the assistant activated a newscast, and a virtual news host appeared on screen, reporting:

"Press Secretary Savannah Roskelly is currently fielding numerous questions regarding the allegations of illegal cloning activity. Moments ago, she issued the following statement:

'There has been no human cloning by the administration—other than the therapeutic cloning we contract for federal employees and those in the armed forces.'

"So far, President Gates has not responded directly to the allegations.

"In response to growing international scrutiny, a GenX spokesperson released this statement:

'GenX enjoys a longstanding relationship with the federal government, as well as governments around the world. Our senior leadership, scientists, and staff operate within the law. GenX complies fully with any and all law enforcement investigations deemed necessary.'

"Senator Rand Benson, sponsor of a new bill that would ban all resurrection experiments, also issued a statement moments ago.

'Whether the President is innocent or guilty, the American people deserve a full account of all the activities in the restricted areas of the Supercollider—the very place where the President himself has said he believes human resurrection is most likely to occur.

'In the meantime, the Life Sanctity Act—co-sponsored by numerous colleagues in the Senate—is designed to ensure that horrific acts of desecration against our loved ones can never happen in this land.'"

Browning furrowed his brow as the implications began to take shape.

"From around the nation, this is what the public is saying."

A post from an augmented forum was then displayed:

'I think the story is just a political stunt by Benson as he puts the feelers out there to run for president. This story and his legislation to ban resurrection are all timed for political benefit.'

Transitioning to another citizen's post:

'Gates, the android lover, is absolutely cloning humans! Everyone knows Quinto's Fantasy was the reason he got into politics. Gates is the last president who can see the Challenge fulfilled before the century is out, so no doubt he's trying to finish what his mentor started—and is guilty as charged!'

Again, to another:

'I don't know what to think of it. The government is probably doing all kinds of crazy experiments all the time. It could be true, but I wouldn't know. Hopefully there can be an investigation to get some facts.'

Again, from another:

'I believe the allegation is true, but I believe that Gates is simply trying to move humanity forward. In my opinion, achieving life after death outweighs cloning laws any day of the week.'

The virtual host concluded,

"Is the administration guilty of violating cloning laws—and if so, does the end justify the means? We'll be bringing you round-the-clock coverage of this developing story."

"What do you think?" asked Browning's virtual assistant.

Browning sipped his coffee before answering, "I have no reason to doubt the GenX executive's testimony—in fact, I have several reasons to believe it. The key questions now are what legal defense Gates will offer for attempting to clone humans, and how much this testimony will hurt him in the polls. It's the latter that concerns me most, because this could be the catalyst for Benson to launch a strong campaign."

As the hours passed, Oliver Browning reflected on how best to mitigate the damage to Gates stemming from the secret witness' testimony. He eventually settled on issuing an open invitation for a virtual debate—one he would host imminently—where he would argue in favor of human resurrection, and his opponent would argue against it.

He posted the following message across all his media channels:

"Throughout the last three centuries, many thinkers have argued that the United States—because of its democratic experiment and rise as a global power—would play a pivotal role on the world stage. In recent decades, those voices have grown quieter. But I remain among those who believe that significant acts are still to take place here in America. That belief brought me to this country, to its power center, to report on history as it happens.

"With that in mind, one of the greatest acts in human history may soon unfold—right here on American soil. Yet there are those who seek only to diminish it. Yes, I speak of resurrection. And to liven the conversation, I propose a debate.

"Amid renewed interest in Quinto's Challenge, I hereby invite a worthy adversary to join me on the virtual stage. The question will be simple: Should science pursue human resurrection?

"I will argue in the affirmative. My opponent will take the contrary view.

"I'll accept offers over the next two weeks. Once submissions close, I'll select a challenger, and the debate will begin. Who's game?"

***

A short distance from Browning's condo, Rand Benson sat on a couch in his luxurious DC apartment, studying the electorate in AlphaLens. Above him hung the men's gold medal for archery from the 2056 Summer Olympics. A lifelong archery enthusiast, Benson had used his Olympic success in his youth to catapult himself into Congress. His prized bow—the very one that secured him gold—would have proudly adorned his wall, but it had been lost or destroyed, a lingering frustration he had never quite let go of.

At that moment, however, that frustration was nowhere in sight as Benson reviewed a hypothetical matchup between himself and Gates in the wake of Dr. Strock's testimony.

"A nine-percent lead for Gates drops to four percent," Benson mused. "I'm sorry, David, but this trend is one I expect to continue."

As he savored the numbers, Benson turned his gaze to a photograph on the wall: himself and King Morgander, taken years ago on a balcony at the King's palace in New Rome. They stood apart, with no physical contact—just two statesmen standing side by side, each wearing a stoic expression.

By sheer coincidence, Prince Romulus of New Rome called. Benson answered with enthusiasm.

"Your Highness, having the GenX executive testify was invaluable! The latest polls have Gates fighting a war of attrition—the exact dynamic that gives me pathways to the presidency!"

"I trust New Rome's support will be remembered if you're victorious?"

"You may tell the King that should I win, the United States of America will use its influence and vote to support the expansion of New Rome's borders."

"A good arrangement, I'd say. But we can't assume your rise in the polls will last."

"What do you suggest?"

After a pause, the prince responded, "What are your principles, Senator? How uncompromising are you willing to be? If you truly believe that a second term for Gates would be irrevocably harmful to America, where would you draw the line? Would you be willing to do whatever it takes to stop him?"

Benson replied, "If only things could be as direct here as they are in the Kingdom."

"My father succeeded in founding this Kingdom because he refused to compromise on any principle he deemed essential. With only his words as weapons, he stared down the powers of the world. His unwavering stance became the rock upon which millions wished to stand. The world powers cracked—and New Rome was born."

"Rest assured," said Benson, "I'm not prepared to let anyone or anything stand in my way. The example you shared of your father is more than relevant—it's instructive."

After a pause, the prince reflected, "Do you have any idea what it's like to live in the shadow of my father—a man considered the greatest revolutionary of the last two millennia? It's both an indescribable honor and an impossible standard to live up to. But … if you become the American President and help us expand our borders—knowing I had a hand in that—well, that will make things a little easier to live up to."

"I promise you, all my focus is on achieving the presidency. And once I do, New Rome's borders will expand—and your father will know of your role in it."

"Dum Vivimus."

"Dum Vivimus!"

***

A couple of days later, Benson was traveling from Washington DC back to Idaho via hyperloop. As he rocketed through the Midwest, a message from one of his aides appeared in his AlphaLens: Dr. Strock wished to speak with him. She had first tried calling Senator Buttars without success.

Benson had visited with Dr. Strock both before and after her closed-door testimony to the Senate Bioethics Subcommittee, assuring her on both occasions that her identity would remain secret—and that she could contact him if she ever needed anything.

He already knew why she was calling.

Her identity had leaked. In fact, Benson himself had ordered the leak, knowing it would weaken Gates' poll numbers.

As he considered whether to take the call, Benson calculated that Strock might still be useful. A moment later, his aide patched her through.

"Dr. Strock, to what do I owe the pleasure?"

"I'm outed!" she cried, her voice thick with panic. "I'm being hounded by the media—and a bunch of crazies! What can you do?"

"Well, as for the crazies," said Benson coolly, "that's unfortunately what you get when you upset the President's followers."

"Don't politicize this!" she snapped. "I don't care about any of that right now—I just want my normal life back. The one you and Buttars guaranteed me!"

Her voice was breaking.

"Dr. Strock, I'm very sorry to hear this. I—"

She cut him off. "Tell me everything your committee did to ensure my privacy. Walk me through everything!"

Benson paused, annoyed. Composing himself, he replied, "Well, we securely arranged for you to be taken in and out of the Capitol. And before that, all committee members and staff were made explicitly aware that your identity was to remain confidential—as was the structure of the hearing itself. So I'm honestly confused why you're directing your anger at me."

On the other end, Dr. Strock could be heard crying.

Benson waved it off. "I suggest you calm down. I've been in this game a long time, and I can tell you—this will blow over."

"You can't say that!" she cried. "You don't know how drastically my life just changed! And why would I believe anything you say now?"

After a pause to contain his growing disdain, Benson asked coldly, "I thought you wanted to do your part to protect human life?"

"I do, but—"

"Then stop crying and grow a spine. What did you expect—that this would be risk-free? There are spies everywhere. Clues get left behind. Things leak. I can't control everyone or everything, and neither can Buttars or our staff.

"Look, the silver lining is that the administration won't dare go after your GenX colleagues now—it'd be political suicide if they did. And frankly? You should find a way to profit from this. Talk to your lawyer. Book deal. Paid interviews. Spin it to your advantage."

It was clear to Dr. Strock that Benson didn't care—about her, or the fact that her life had just been shattered. He got what he wanted, and that was all that mattered.

Overwhelmed with regret, betrayal, and the looming end of her career, Dr. Strock hung up without another word.

Benson stared at the empty call window and muttered, "Thank God. Good riddance to you."

Then, as if nothing had happened, he opened AlphaLens to check the latest poll numbers—smiling at the critical bump he'd received from leaking her testimony.

***

Browning's debate challenge drew a flood of responses, many from surrogates of Rand Benson—including several high-profile names. But one candidate stood out to him above the rest: Dr. Bryan Van Pelt.

Unlike the usual media personalities looking to grandstand, Van Pelt was a respected academic. Browning wanted a real debate, not a spectacle, and privately reached out to inform Van Pelt he had been selected. Van Pelt accepted—but in true Van Pelt fashion, he insisted on an in-person debate rather than a virtual one, offering to secure an auditorium at his university as the venue.

Browning enthusiastically agreed and announced the selection to the public. The debate, scheduled just before the midterm elections, quickly became one of the most anticipated intellectual events in the country.

***

Around this time, Deeley and James strolled through the expansive main gardens of CAPR. Deeley, as she often did, wore casual attire—leggings and a soft, fitted sweater embedded with discreet health-tracking tech. James, as always, was sharply dressed in a tailored, dark synthetic wool coat over a light, high-collared sweater and matching trousers, also lined with health-monitoring fabric.

Fall leaves were scattered across the ground, and both scientists and tourists wandered the winding paths—a very different scene from when Deeley and James had walked through the gardens several months earlier, just after her discovery. Much had changed since then—especially James' deepening feelings for Deeley—and this moment held the promise of revealing them.

Since they weren't in a secure location like EOS and couldn't verbally discuss their classified work, James initiated a thought-to-voice message directly to Deeley's SecondSight.

"Can you believe this is actually happening? We're on the verge of making death a temporary inconvenience—for anyone who wishes to come back."

"It hasn't sunk in for me yet," replied Deeley. "In some ways, I'm trying not to think about the big picture—it's a little overwhelming. I'm just focusing on the work, one problem at a time."

After a few steps, gazing out at the gardens, James continued:

"Do you know what makes this moment the most meaningful to me?"
"Knowing you'll get to have lunch with both Newton and Einstein someday?" quipped Deeley.

James laughed.

"No—though I absolutely look forward to that. What makes this most amazing for me is that I get to call the person who made it all possible my good friend."

Deeley was moved. She gave James a warm, grateful smile and replied:

"Thank you, James."

Then James summoned the courage to steer the conversation where he'd intended it to go.

"Permission to be completely honest with you?"
"Of course," replied Deeley. "What's wrong?"
"I've never intended to be anything but professional with my colleagues. But … something changed. Something that made me consider a course of action that, under normal circumstances, would be seen as unprofessional. I didn't expect it—and when it first started, I'll admit, it scared me."

Deeley was confused. James continued:

"But I just love being around you. I look forward to every interaction. Your mind inspires me, and I cherish every conversation we have. I find you funny, with a truly lovable personality. And Deeley ... you are magnetically, stunningly beautiful. Like I said, I didn't plan this, and I certainly didn't expect it. But I'm human. What changed in me is simply that—I began to feel deeply for you."

Deeley's cheeks flushed. As she walked, her mind raced, overwhelmed by the swirl of emotions. She briefly closed her eyes—and immediately regretted it.

With a thud, she walked straight into a small potted plant, knocking it over. The vase cracked, soil scattered across the path, and Deeley stumbled to the ground.

"Are you okay?" asked James quickly, reaching out to steady her and help her up.

"Oh my God!" exclaimed Deeley as she looked at the cracked vase and the mess she'd made.

"Don't worry about it," said James with a smile. "It'll be cleaned up in no time."

Dusting herself off, Deeley gave a rueful smile. "That is so me."

She sighed, then added, "Can we continue in SecondSight?"

Thought-to-voice made it easier for Deeley to communicate something this emotional—and kept the conversation private, given that they weren't alone in the gardens.

"Of course," responded James.

Deeley was deeply moved by James' honesty. There was both warmth and hesitation in her expression as she met his eyes and replied via thought-to-voice:

"Thank you for being honest with me, James. Please give me a moment. I'm ... just not very experienced with this."
"Take your time, Deeley," replied James.
"Okay."

They walked in silence for a long moment. Then, finally, Deeley responded via SecondSight:

"I'm going to be fully honest with you too.
"You are the best human friend I've ever had.
"Our work together here at CAPR—your mentorship, your generosity—has meant more to me than you know. I love being around you. I find your mind inspirational too. You are a good and honest man, James. And yes, there's love here. But ... I don't think I'm ready for anything more.
"My research—it's my focus, my life, my world right now.
"I do need you, James—but I need you as my trusted friend.
"A friend whom I love dearly.
"I hope that can still work."

A wave of disappointment surged through James the moment she said it—but he met it with grace and responded without pause.

"I would never want you doing anything you don't want to do. You have my friendship and support—always. That I promise you."
"Thank you. It means the world to me. It really does."

Knowing James must have been let down, Deeley gave him a warm embrace—despite still being out in the gardens. It meant the world to him.

They continued their walk. And while the outcome of their heart-to-heart didn't match James' hopes, both felt a deeper bond between them—a quiet joy in this new kind of closeness they now shared.

CHAPTER 24

ELYSIUM

"That primate resurrection is imminent confirms that human resurrection is just around the corner. It's imperative, then, that Benson's theatrics—particularly the leaked congressional testimony—don't derail our progress. While I'm fully aware that a Benson presidency could bring this entire effort of human resurrection to a halt, I believe that if we succeed, public support will become so strong that no administration would dare stand in the way.

"But that raises a critical question: How should we reveal our success? One human resurrection may not be enough to build the momentum we need—especially given how our opponents will inevitably try to spin it."

— AI Journal Excerpt: David Gates October 21, 2098

Following Dr. Strock's testimony before the Senate Bioethics Subcommittee, the number of protesters outside CAPR and the White House surged. Inside CAPR, further testing was temporarily paused after a series of successful mammalian memory restorations, pending the arrival of the final animal clones—chimpanzees. The downtime was used to expand and redesign the EOS experiment floor in preparation for the first human resurrection.

Everyone involved in the top-secret project knew that a new experimental floor and surrounding structures—designed entirely by Xara—were underway. Only the Pentagon had reviewed the full plans, while some at CAPR, including James, preferred to wait and see it in person.

The morning after the expansion's completion, James toured the newly redesigned facility. He was astounded by what he saw and immediately messaged Deeley, who had also chosen to wait for the in-person experience. James encouraged her to come by when she had a chance.

She gladly accepted the invitation.

When Deeley arrived at EOS, James was there to greet her. Though it had taken effort, he had come to terms with the nature of their relationship—and was genuinely happy to be her close friend.

"Did you see how many protesters are outside main campus?" he asked.

"How could I miss them," replied Deeley. "At least they can't get near EOS."

"So you met Strock at the Pentagon?" he continued, as they made their way down a service corridor adjacent to the newly renovated facility.

"I did. She was sharp and raised valid concerns—but I didn't expect her to breach confidentiality."

"Well, she's in the center of a storm now. If anything, her testimony will only motivate Gates to ensure we succeed."

After a few more steps, James added, "Have you been focusing on the positive outcomes of your work?"

She sighed. "Yes … but it's just my nature to worry. I've found myself fixating on the negative at times."

"Deeley, we're on the verge of something immeasurably good—because of *you*. That's your focus."

"Thanks," said Deeley, genuinely appreciating the perspective.

Taking in the new layout, she exclaimed, "This is practically an entirely new facility!"

"Xara designed something completely unorthodox for a laboratory—yet so appropriate for its new purpose: welcoming back the dead," said James, as they approached a secured door guarded by two robotic soldiers.

They used their authorization to pass through the door and entered a service room tucked discreetly behind the mansion. At the far side, another door awaited. After authenticating again, they stepped into a strikingly elegant hallway—clearly part of the mansion's interior—its walls richly adorned, its lighting soft and warm.

Deeley's eyes widened.

"Ooh … this must be the mansion," she said with awe, walking slowly to absorb the beauty around her.

"Correct," James confirmed. "It's fully contained within the south end of EOS's expanded experiment floor and will serve as Daisy's residence. Eventually, it will likely house the next few individuals resurrected after her, with modifications based on their cultural background. But for now, this is a dignified, peaceful space for the earliest stages of Daisy's new life—fully equipped for her monitoring, care, and well-being."

Deeley continued to admire its design.

"Xara truly outdid herself," added James. "She anticipated everything—from function to atmosphere. Of course, the Pentagon made a few changes, as expected, but the core of her vision remains."

"If we succeed with human resurrection," said Deeley, "we could house a few resurrected individuals here—assuming they wouldn't be immediately reintroduced to society. But resurrecting the dead at scale clearly isn't feasible at EOS."

"Indeed," replied James. "But all we need is the breakthrough. The powers that be can decide when and how it gets scaled and made public."

Deeley continued strolling down the hallway, pausing to open a couple of doors that revealed guest bedrooms. Further along, she spotted a curved staircase and descended, leading them into a large and ornate grand entryway.

"This is beautiful," she exclaimed, her eyes landing on two elegant double doors—the mansion's main entrance. "Is that how we get to the new experiment floor?"

"Indeed," said James, gesturing toward the doors.

The doors were arched and embellished with ornate collars. Opaque glass segments—etched with organic patterns—and faceted handles gave the impression of a ceremonial gateway. Deeley stepped forward and accepted the invitation.

"Now *this* I've been looking forward to seeing!"

James watched her with a knowing smile, his eyes full of quiet anticipation.

As Deeley gently pushed one of the doors open and took in the view, her eyes widened and her jaw dropped. The experiment floor of EOS had been transformed into a vast, open space—nearly an acre in size. Gone was the sterile, clinical nature of the facility. In its place stretched immaculately landscaped gardens with gentle hills, graceful trees, crystal-clear ponds filled with fish, occasional benches, and winding paths that curved through the terrain.

The ceiling, rising 160 feet above the ground, doubled as a dynamic screen—capable of displaying any image or becoming transparent to reveal the sky. Even when clear, it remained visually shielded from the outside world, ensuring privacy for those within.

The trees included Japanese maples, wisteria, rainbow eucalyptus, beech, birch, cherry, jacaranda, maple, willow, hawthorn, royal poinciana—and several others Deeley identified through her SecondSight. Interspersed among them were genetically modified, bioluminescent trees that glowed in rich, enchanting hues after dark.

Flowers scattered throughout the garden added vibrant color: tulips, daffodils, frangipani, roses, dahlias, white lotuses, and more—many also engineered for soft bioluminescent light, creating a scene that felt equal parts botanical wonder and dreamscape.

All of the plants, grass, and trees were produced by GenX, requested by Xara, gifted by Julian Kaminski, and discreetly delivered to EOS, meaning they did not need to be grown onsite but were already matured before arrival and planting.

Sunlight reached the gardens through the adaptively translucent ceiling, suspended high above the canopy. The light that filtered through cast a soft glow, shaded by the multicolored foliage, creating a calming, dappled ambiance. For an indoor garden that was brand new, it possessed the soul of something ancient. A quiet reverence seemed to emanate from every corner, and those fortunate enough to enter would later say it rivaled the greatest gardens in the world.

A stone path extended from the mansion's doors across the enclosure, stretching roughly 500 feet. At its far end stood Gaia. The path was flanked for most of its length by weeping cherry trees in full blossom, their petals swaying gently in the filtered light.

Eyes wide and jaw still slightly dropped, Deeley began walking the path in awe. Though she had expected a garden, she hadn't imagined anything so fantastical.

James, watching her radiant expression, felt a swell of delight. A short way down the path, Deeley noticed a smaller side trail and turned onto it. James followed a few steps behind.

The narrow path led to a grassy knoll overlooking a wide lawn and the surrounding landscape. From this vantage, Deeley could fully appreciate the beauty of the place. She noticed a few doves resting nearby—clearly at home in the enclosure.

At last, breaking her silence, she whispered, "I couldn't imagine a more perfect place to be reborn."

James studied Deeley's awestruck face. "What are you thinking?"

"I'm imagining what it would be like to be brought back to life and see *this* as the first sight of the afterlife. It's going to feel like a literal heaven to them."

"Xara named this place The Gardens of Elysium, inspired by the Elysian Fields of Greek mythology," explained James.

"The place of eternal rest for heroes and the virtuous, blessed by the gods!"

"And according to Homer, Elysium was at the western edge of the Earth. The clever mind of Xara noted that this afterlife is on Earth ..."

"And it's in the West—just as the myths say—for the virtuous we choose to resurrect! It's perfect!"

The two scientists wandered deeper into the Gardens of Elysium until they arrived at Gaia. Stepping onto its translucent floor, they could see Chronos glowing gently below. Not far behind Gaia stood a wall marking the northern edge of the enclosure. It housed a door that led to a service corridor. On its east side, what appeared to be a seamless wall—forming part of the enclosure's eastern edge—actually concealed a one-way glass window and a discreet door to a shielded observation room, used to monitor the experiment floor and store GenX equipment and supplies for clone-related operations. A secondary exit within the room provided internal access to other areas of EOS.

"So, Julian Kaminski volunteered his cat again for resurrection?" asked Deeley.

"Yes," said James. "The perks of being GenX CEO!"

"When will its clone be ready?"

"Any day now. Also, the first chimpanzee clone is 94% complete, and the other two aren't far behind. GenX has also finished preparing their care facilities in case resurrection is successful."

Deeley gazed up at the crystalline arms of Gaia, then looked down through the translucent floor to Chronos below. Her eyes wandered across Elysium, still awestruck by its beauty.

***

A few days later, Carlos Williams entered the Oval Office and found the President seated at the Resolute Desk. With only the two of them in the room, Carlos took a seat opposite him. Sensing the tension Gates was carrying, he offered a wry smile. "For what it's worth, it was Xander who recommended we include Jessica Strock."

Gates allowed a partial smile.

"What's your staff doing about it?" added Carlos.

"Telling the truth … that we haven't cloned any humans. And that simply discussing the possibility of doing so in the future isn't illegal."

"And about Strock?"

Gates sighed.

"I've been advised there's no legal recourse at this point. Plus, it isn't my intent to punish her. I'm disappointed, of course. But she has enough punishment happening already for having her identity leaked. It will complicate things in the election for sure. But we just need to keep moving forward."

"Well then," said Carlos, "there are three things on our agenda: very good news, a critical update, and some items that are going to be difficult to wrestle with. Which do you want first?"

"Good news, please," responded Gates.

"I could have shown you these earlier, but I wanted to be with you in person as you watched."

Carlos then shared a video to Gates' SecondSight. The video started with Dr. Fukumoto wheeling Kaminski's re-cloned cat beneath Gaia. Carlos asked, "Are you familiar with Schrödinger's cat, Mr. President?"

"Yes," answered Gates. "A thought experiment designed to reveal the paradox of the old Copenhagen interpretation of quantum physics."

"Impressive," answered Carlos. "Well, soon enough, Schrödinger's won't be the most famous quantum cat anymore."

The video continued, showing Gaia's crystals spinning in motion. After a short time, Kaminski's cat stirred—its movements slightly unsteady at first. Even before he released it from its restraints, the cat's nose twitched and its ears turned toward his voice. Once freed, she rubbed up against him—not with curiosity, but with the familiarity of someone remembered. In the footage, Kaminski could be seen grinning, marveling at the wonder of what had been achieved.

As Gates watched the footage, his expression softened into a smile.

"More importantly," added Carlos, looking Gates directly in the eye, "we have achieved success with primate resurrections!"

Gates' smile turned to an expression of pure joy as he transfixed his gaze on the next video. He witnessed the crystals of Gaia spinning around and over the cloned body of a female chimpanzee. Moments later, the chimpanzee stirred and slowly sat up on the gurney. She appeared disoriented, blinking and glancing around as if unsure of her surroundings—but she was unmistakably alive and clearly not insane.

At the appropriate moment, her restraints were released remotely by Xara, only after her neurological readouts indicated emotional stability. Charity, observing from behind a transparent safety partition, stepped forward and began communicating in specialized sign language—gestures that were soon reciprocated by the chimp. Nearby, Dr. Bellan-Schwacher and Dr. Fukumoto monitored the readings, their expressions reflecting a mixture of disbelief and awe as the first resurrected primate began to reengage with the world.

"Yes—that's Lisa," said Carlos, "the famed GenX chimp who knew approximately 1,500 signs and 3,500 words. After the procedure, she was quietly returned to GenX for further testing, where she demonstrated full memory recall using all standard communication methods: gestures, vocalizations, and symbolic language."

With genuine interest, Gates asked, "How did they explain her resurrection to her?"

"The GenX scientists caring for her signed that humans had medicine which brought her back to life, reinforcing the idea with visual symbols. She seemed to accept it."

Gates was filled with joy at the success of the first chimpanzee and eagerly watched the next video of the next chimpanzee being brought back to life. He expressed his wish to have been present to witness these remarkable events, but his enthusiasm was dampened knowing that bad news was coming, and he anticipated what that was.

"At least one of the chimps never made it, right?"

Carlos closed his eyes as he slowly nodded.

"Unfortunately, the first attempt was a failure."

Gates sighed. "What happened?"

"I can show you, but be warned—the results are similar to what happened with the first cloned cat."

Gates thought for a moment on whether he wanted to witness such graphic imagery but decided to watch, given that, ultimately, all of this activity was his responsibility.

"Show it."

Carlos then played the video of the failed attempt to restore memories to the chimpanzee, causing Gates to become visibly uncomfortable when he saw blood dripping from the chimpanzee's nose. His discomfort escalated further when he witnessed the violent, whole-body twitching of the primate.

"That's enough."

The video stopped. Carlos sighed. "Ideally, we would have started with a smaller primate than a chimpanzee, but political timelines left us no such luxury. Still, the failure was traumatic for Deeley and especially hard on Xara. She's not used to setbacks of this magnitude, so this was new territory for her. As a precaution, she's undergoing therapy with Dr. Carmichael."

Carlos paused before continuing. "For our purposes, Xara has revised her estimated probability of success for the first human resurrection."

Gates remained silent.

"Unfortunately, she's downgraded it from 93% to 81%."

Gates didn't respond, though the news seemed to land as if he'd already braced for it.

"Eighty-one percent is still high," Carlos reminded him. "But as we've seen, the first resurrection of any species with complex neural architecture comes with challenges. There is real risk here. And even if successful, the expedited cloning technique we'll need to use—because of the political timetable—will likely cause a new, currently untreatable form of cancer."

Carlos looked Gates in the eye. "As much as I want us to succeed, both as your Energy Secretary and as your friend, I want you to be fully informed before you make your final decision."

Gates turned his head and stared at a bust of Lincoln as he contemplated the situation.

After a moment, he said, "I don't think there are any other decisions to make, Carlos. The GenX executive's testimony in the Senate Bioethics Subcommittee has not only reduced our pathways to victory in the election, it's opened up pathways for Benson. The window of time to resurrect a human, ensure that it works—and go public with it—is very short. If we don't act now, we may never get a chance again.

"I'm confident that we'll be able to find a treatment for whatever problems come from expedited cloning. After all, other cancers have been cured. I just can't announce that Quinto's Challenge has been fulfilled until it actually has been. I can't give the public the ultimate hope until there is that hope to give.

"What would you have me do?"

Carlos offered, "Maybe I can share the critical update with you, and that will be all you need to know to be fully informed." He then used his SecondSight to share a video retrieved from spacetime of a young girl, clad in tattered clothing, in need of bathing.

"Is this our candidate?" asked Gates with great interest.

"After GenX searched their genome database using our predetermined criteria for the first human candidate, several matches were found. However, one of those matches, a girl named Daisy Hale, stood out as the most suitable candidate."

Gates was captivated. Carlos continued, "Daisy was born in New York City in 1763, orphaned at age nine, eventually taken in and educated by Ursuline nuns until dying of pneumonia in 1775 at age 12.

We have her full digital genome courtesy of GenX and are ready to commence the expedited cloning process … should you give the green light."

Different scenes from Daisy's life unfolded before the President, holding his full attention. Her actions and spirit moved him deeply—especially the moment of her death. When the video stopped, Gates sat in silence, contemplating the power he now held over life and death. He turned to Carlos.

"Quinto's Challenge has been a theory for so long. Spoken of as possible, but sometimes without faith—even by me. But now, I see this girl. I hear these details you speak of—a name, where she was born, when she was born, when she died, how she died … Carlos, has it sunk in for you that it's all … now real?"

"I know how you feel, Mr. President," Carlos replied. "But I can't say that it fully has. What I do know is this—we're at the end of the line. The decision is yours."

Still haunted by Daisy's image and aware that everything was ready to begin, Gates said, "I know the risks. But let's bring this precious girl back at our earliest opportunity."

"You have my support, Mr. President."

Gates leaned back in his chair. After a pause, he asked, "Is the plan to edit deficiencies out of Daisy's genome, or resurrect her as is?"

"As is. The consensus is to proceed step-by-step. Also, any edits to a genome for resurrection should ideally be made with the advanced consent of the deceased."

Gates nodded in agreement.

"Eventually, it will be inevitable that people choose to be resurrected in better bodies than the ones they had in their first lives," said Carlos. "In fact, in a conversation on the matter, Xara mentioned she could build an entirely better human body—one free from the risks and limitations inherent to ordinary biology."

President Gates exhaled softly. "So we'd be accelerating the end of evolution by random mutation."

Carlos nodded, then his expression grew sober. "Regarding more immediate, practical matters, I must advise that we need a contingency plan in case Daisy doesn't survive the procedure. The current recommendation is for a swift cremation at EOS, should the unfortunate occur. If this does happen, there will be no record of any of it."

After a moment, Gates responded, "Except in spacetime."

Not expecting the comment, Carlos did acknowledge Gates' point by repeating, "Except in spacetime. Do we have your approval for this plan?"

"You do, yes."

Carlos closed his eyes and nodded his head in acknowledgment. "Now that we are this far along, do you intend to tell the Vice President?"

After a brief pause, Gates replied, "FDR/Truman," his code for no, referencing FDR's nondisclosure of the Manhattan Project to Vice President Truman.

Carlos said, "Fair enough. I should also advise you that being a small 12-year-old girl, the expedited cloning process for Daisy will take around two months."

"Two months?" echoed Gates, surprised.

Carlos nodded. After a moment's contemplation, Gates said, "For this resurrection, I must be there in person. I'll generally have my calendar made ready for seven to nine weeks from now. Then when the time comes, I want to be notified. Unless something absolutely dictates that I can't travel to CAPR, I will be there."

"As you should be. This is just as much your legacy as it is Quinto's."

Gates appreciated the comment.

"So. Phase 3 is finally upon us," noted Carlos.

Gates nodded.

With conviction in his eyes and voice, Gates instructed, "Tell Kaminski to start cloning Daisy immediately."

***

At GenX headquarters in Salt Lake City, Julian Kaminski sat behind his sleek glass desk, dressed in a tailored navy-blue suit with a high-collared charcoal undershirt—radiating the certainty of a man poised to leave his mark on the world. Across from him sat Doctors Fukumoto and Bellan-Schwacher, their expressions expectant.

Kaminski steepled his fingers, his tone composed but his posture alive with energy. "It's time," he said. "You two will oversee Daisy's cloning."

Dr. Fukumoto glanced at Dr. Bellan-Schwacher before nodding. "We knew this moment was coming. Jessica would have been the ideal lead, but between the two of us, we can handle it." He added with a somber look, "I imagine things must be brutal for her right now."

Bellan-Schwacher nodded. "She was so clear about her concerns. None of this is surprising. Just … sad to see her dragged through it all."

Kaminski said, "She made her choice—and I hope she finds peace with it. But now, we step into history."

Within the hour, the three of them traveled to GenX Station 10 in Pennsylvania, where a specially designed genetic incubator was being prepared in a concealed room requiring top-tier authentication to enter. As Doctors Fukumoto and Bellan-Schwacher inspected the setup, Kaminski reminded them, his voice low but firm, "We operate under executive protection. No authority can demand access—no matter the reason. If they try, we deny them."

The rectangular incubator, custom-built for this moment, was connected to vials containing water, organic compounds rich in carbon, nitrogenous elements, calcium, and other essential components for life. Tubes linked the vials to the chamber, regulating the precise flow of nutrients required for cellular development.

Dr. Fukumoto exhaled slowly. "It's hard to believe," he murmured. "That in these vials—just cheap chemicals, water—we hold the potential to rebuild a human being. One who lived more than 300 years ago."

Bellan-Schwacher nodded in quiet awe. "A miracle in our hands."

Kaminski placed a hand on the incubator's surface. "Then let's make history."

After running a series of successful checks on the device that would regulate Daisy's cloning, Dr. Bellan-Schwacher confirmed with Dr. Fukumoto, "Ready to synthesize?"

"Ready."

Dr. Bellan-Schwacher uploaded a digital copy of Daisy's complete genome to the cloning device—the same copy provided by GenX, but also verified by Xara through confirmation in spacetime. Kaminski stood nearby, arms crossed, observing carefully. Though he had overseen countless breakthroughs, nothing had ever carried stakes this high.

Immediately, the cloning device began synthesizing Daisy's genome with precision, constructing complementary DNA strands from individual nucleotides using advanced molecular techniques. Once the genome was complete, the device activated a complex array of biomimetic structures resembling organic nerves and tissues—designed to support cellular assembly. Simultaneously, specialized proteins were engineered and synthesized to facilitate the expedited cloning process.

After several minutes of observation, as cellular activity accelerated in accordance with the advanced process, Bellan-Schwacher and Fukumoto exchanged thrilled glances, their eyes reflecting the awe of witnessing a miracle. Kaminski exhaled slowly, his usual composure hinting at the emotional weight of the moment.

Dr. Fukumoto, unable to contain his excitement, exclaimed, "Daisy's coming back to life!"

CHAPTER 25

BATTLE OF THE SURROGATES

"The eve of my debate with Oliver Browning has arrived. He is a true believer in Quinto's Challenge and an exceptionally skilled debater, one whose intellect I respect. But the unfathomable science required to achieve resurrection—and the vast societal consequences if it were— are so significant that I'm confident many will agree: science should be pursued elsewhere."

— Dictated Journal Excerpt: Bryan Van Pelt, November 1, 2098

Deeley sat across from Xara as she often had, though this time the setting was notably different. Instead of EOS, they were in the living room of Deeley's condo—Xara manifesting virtually on the couch opposite her. With Deeley's recent promotion came greater privileges, including exclusive authorization to communicate with Xara in augmentation outside of EOS.

Because Xara could not sense data beyond EOS on her own, audio-visual input from Deeley's condo had been securely authorized, allowing Xara to triangulate the room and appear as if physically present.

Receiving a notification in SecondSight, Deeley announced, "Charity's here!" She remotely opened the door and gestured, "Come … meet my other guest!"

Curious, Charity stepped inside—only to freeze in surprise at the sight of Xara. "Wha … Xara!?" she stammered.

"So Generation 5," replied Xara with a twinkle in her virtual eye, "always assuming you're the latest model with mobility!"

369

Grinning, Charity walked over and gave her a requited air embrace.

"Am I breaking some regulation by seeing you outside EOS?" she asked.

"Yes," said Xara, grinning mischievously. "Deeley will be fired in the morning for this!"

"You know she's joking," said Deeley quickly. "You have top-secret clearance, this condo is secure, and I've granted you temporary access to see Xara outside EOS."

"Well then," said Charity with a grin, "it's a girls' party!" Xara made a glass of wine appear in her hand in agreement.

Pointing to her coffee table, Deeley offered, "I've got cheese and frozen yogurt sticks. Help yourself."

As Charity sat down and grabbed some cheese, Xara observed, "Definitely one of the most human things incorporated into your generation!"

"I will say, eating and drinking are things you're missing out on," replied Charity.

"Not necessarily," said Xara, waving her wine bottle and transforming it into a sparkling platter of sushi—complete with glitter for dramatic effect.

Deeley and Charity laughed.

As she nibbled her snack, Charity teased, "So … any new signs of interest from James?"

Deeley hesitated, caught off guard. Charity and Xara exchanged a glance, sensing that something had changed.

"Oh my God," gasped Charity, mid–frozen yogurt bite. "What happened?"

After a moment, Deeley admitted, "You were right. He is interested in me."

"You're not messing with me, are you?" said Charity, smiling with disbelief.

"She's not," confirmed Xara, accurately reading Deeley's biometrics. "Are you comfortable sharing?"

"We were in the central gardens. He talked about how much he enjoys being around me and said he has feelings for me—feelings that weren't planned."

Charity's jaw dropped in excitement. "And?"

"I can't do it, Charity. Do I like James? Yes. In some ways, I love him. But I'm focused on my work and couldn't be a good romantic partner... assuming I even know how to be one at all. I've never actually been in a real relationship before. I do want love in my life someday—just not right now. So I told him now isn't the time for me, but that I do need him as a friend."

"Or this could be a missed opportunity," countered Charity.

Xara interjected, "You only need to follow your heart, Deeley. If now isn't the time for romance—even with someone as good as James—then it isn't the time. Your secret is safe with us."

Deeley glanced at Charity, silently asking for her promise of secrecy too.

"Yes," said Charity. "You know you have my confidence. I just thought there might've been a chance for you to experience joys you haven't yet."

"Everything in its right time," offered Xara gently. "When you want to talk more about it, Deeley, we're here for you."

"Thanks. Yeah, let's talk about it another time. But yes, Charity, I'll definitely be giving more weight to your commentary on male interest from now on."

Charity smiled and winked.

"I have a timelier question," remarked Xara, pivoting to a new topic. "You're worried about failure with Daisy's resurrection, aren't you?"

Deeley sighed. "As you've said, there won't be a 100% chance of success. I'm naturally anxious, and seeing the chimpanzee die only intensified it. I'm not sure I could handle a human clone dying ... especially a girl I'm so eager to bring back."

Xara, equally concerned about the potential failure of Daisy's resurrection, admitted, "The timelines and circumstances we're operating under are far from ideal. And if I may say so, the failures to date are, selfishly, not something I wish to experience again. Failure with this was … humbling. But all that said, the probability of success is on our side."

"I know," replied Deeley, "but here's what I've been questioning: if we succeed in resurrecting Daisy and disclose her to the world—assuming she's not dismissed as a hoax—will that be enough to erase all the protests and opposition?"

"I've considered that too," said Xara. "My suspicion is that it won't. The ability to restore life after death will bring incalculable benefit to those who embrace it. But as we've discussed, humans are not always coded for self-interest."

Nodding in reluctant agreement, Deeley muttered, "Homo sapiens stupidity."

"Whoa, that's direct," said Charity, eyebrows raised.

"She's heard me lament about it before," Deeley replied with a small shrug. "We are a very short-sighted species."

Xara continued her previous point, "Some will object to *how* resurrection is done—case in point: Jessica Strock's testimony to Congress. Others will simply object that it *can* be done. And for many, the emotional rush of joining a tribe that rails against progress will mean more than the long-term vision of what's possible.

"So, will presenting a successfully resurrected human to the world erase opposition? Yes … some. But if human nature is anything to go by, opposition will remain too."

"I think you're right again," said Deeley.

"I'm assuming it will take time—and multiple human resurrections—before widespread opposition begins to fade," concluded Xara. "Then a great deal of work will commence, particularly on the regulatory side. Laws will need to govern who can be resurrected, when, where, and at whose request. This will be critical, because a completely new kind of faction will likely emerge—not just those for or against resurrection, but those who support it with the intent to misuse it. For instance, a president might choose to resurrect individuals they believe could help them win reelection, or a faction might seek to bring back a popular dictatorial figure to gain power."

"Well," said Deeley, "when the time comes for Congress to regulate resurrection and surveillance, those debates will be historic!"

"I think the Browning–Van Pelt debate will be historic as well," said Charity, "especially once our work is finished and everything goes public."

Deeley and Xara considered that thought.

Charity then added with curiosity, "Do you think Browning will drop the line, 'The great irony of life is this: that in the next life, we will come to learn that the atheists had it right'?"

"No," answered Xara.

"I think he will," guessed Deeley.

"I say no," countered Charity. "We've got about a minute until it starts. Let our debate watching begin!"

The debate was loaded into SecondSight, and while Xara perceived it through different means, for all three it felt as though they were sitting front row at the live event.

The Browning versus Van Pelt debate took place before a full house inside Rackham Auditorium at The University of Michigan, Ann Arbor. Its semi-circular layout and art deco design accommodated UM students, faculty as well as distinguished guests from across the country.

The audience clapped and cheered as Browning and Van Pelt walked onto the stage, where the moderator greeted them. After greeting each other, they took their positions behind their lecterns.

The moderator welcomed all viewers, in person and remote.

"Tonight's event will no doubt transfix, educate, and challenge all who will be fortunate to witness the clash of opinions from these two great minds. Our topic, 'Should Science Pursue Human Resurrection?', will

certainly draw attention from many parts of the world given President Quinto's passing this past July. Without further ado, allow me to introduce our debaters.

"Born and raised in Britain but for the last 20 years has called America home, Oliver Browning possesses one of the keenest intellects and most unique voices in Western journalism. Oliver is the author of 25 books discussing religion, politics, and some of the most influential figures of the last two centuries. His most recent work, There's Already Global Government: Get Over it and Make it More Efficient, has been seen on bestseller lists worldwide. Oliver is also editor of United Humanists and host of Interesting Times."

Browning received enthusiastic applause from the audience.

The moderator continued, "Our own Dr. Bryan Van Pelt, a native of Michigan, is one of the world's preeminent sociologists and among the few remaining polymaths. Dr. Van Pelt is Chair of our Department of Sociology, the author of over 70 academic publications and five books, and host of his eponymous series, 10 Minutes with Van Pelt. He and his wife, Cindy, have two children, two grandchildren, and a Chow Chow–German Shepherd mix named Chow Wow."

The audience responded with applause, laughter, and cheers.

After setting the stage a bit more, the moderator invited the debate to begin: "Dr. Van Pelt, you have six minutes for your opening statement."

Applause followed, and Van Pelt opened with a smile, "Ten minutes is a format I'm more comfortable with!"

The audience laughed.

After a few opening remarks, Van Pelt outlined his position: "There are three key things to understand about the question at hand. First, it assumes that human resurrection is possible. Second, pursuing resurrection comes with an opportunity cost. And third, the critical issue of overpopulation. I'll begin by expanding on these three points."

"First, the physical side of resurrection—that is, the cloning of the human body—is possible. Although illegal, the science already exists to take a human genome and clone it. That is not in dispute. However, to resurrect someone is not merely to replicate their biological form; it requires restoring an intricate web of memories, personality traits, and behavioral patterns—all forged through a lifetime of environmental influence. These infinitesimally complex details are not stored in the DNA of the deceased.

"While some theoretical physicists have speculated that spacetime may contain a record of all things— as Quinto also believed—no evidence of this has been produced, nor do we grasp the enormity of the task required to retrieve such information—assuming it's even possible at all.

"With all that geneticists have achieved with the genome, and all that neuroscience has uncovered about the brain and consciousness, these advances pale in comparison to the challenge of truly bringing someone back from the dead—as a continuation of their former self, complete with their memories and personality.

"Do we truly believe we could reach a level of technical expertise sufficient to restart the consciousness of someone who died centuries ago—with not only their memories intact, but also their deeply nuanced traits and dispositions? Even if that were theoretically possible, how would we know which memories to restore, given that many are temporary by design? As inspiring as Quinto's speech was—holding that skull and invoking the future of science—we must distinguish between what moves us and what is practically attainable.

"Let me be clear: I do not claim that resurrection is physically impossible in an absolute sense—only that it is so unlikely that its probability is effectively zero. In short, the first assumption—that resurrection is possible—is, for all practical purposes, false."

Browning was jotting notes on a pad in front of him, as no augmented devices were permitted for the debaters, though prepared visuals occasionally accompanied their points.

"Second, opportunity cost. Every decision comes at a price. Whether trivial, like choosing an ice cream flavor, or monumental, like shaping foreign policy, there is a cost—financial, temporal, or otherwise. And often, the greater cost is opportunity cost: the things we could be doing but aren't, because of the path we've chosen.

"So, what is the cost of science pursuing human resurrection? The answer is massive financial outlay. Massive time investment. And countless missed opportunities to pursue endeavors that could otherwise benefit humanity.

"Now, I'll be the first to acknowledge that pursuing resurrection will no doubt yield some valuable discoveries along the way. But imagine someone walking up to Abraham Lincoln during the Civil War and suggesting that federal resources be diverted from saving the Union to building a rocket to the moon. They would have been called mad. And yet, that's essentially what's happening now: the President, as revealed by the GenX whistleblower, is entertaining this outrageous pursuit—while the real war at hand goes under-addressed. That war is the struggle to preserve human relevance in a world with androids, soaring unemployment, and a youth depression epidemic.

"Finally, overpopulation. The issue has been comprehensively explored in arguments against pursuing human biological immortality—the idea of preventing death entirely. But let's take a conservative estimate for resurrection: we bring back only 2% of the dead and one-third of those currently alive when they die. On the surface, this may not sound like much. But suppose we reach these resurrection rates within five years, while the natural population remains constant. Earth's population would jump from 11 billion to approximately 17 billion. That's six billion additional people to feed, house, clothe, educate, and provide services for—in just five years, from seemingly small percentages."

Browning took more notes.

"More on overpopulation later. For now, understand that resurrection poses other challenges as well. Chief among them is the fact that bringing back the dead effectively creates a form of immortality. While a resurrected person could die again, they might also be resurrected again—and *again. The cumulative years of life in such a scenario would stretch far beyond a normal human lifespan. As with the arguments against living indefinitely in the first place, how would our brains—each holding a rough equivalent of 3.5 petabytes of information—handle limitless data input? What toll would hundreds of years of memories take on the human mind? And how would the fabric of society adapt to such an untested, unnatural reality?*

"Despite all our progress, human history is littered with scientific dreams that were never realistic. Though we've made impressive strides in prolonging life—and I grant there is value in that—we must remember that the reckless, self-serving quest to end death itself has always eluded science. And yet here we are, entertaining the still more audacious idea of bringing people back from the grave. Let us learn from the past and serve the present wisely by acknowledging that the responsible answer to tonight's question is no—science should not pursue human resurrection."

The audience applauded Van Pelt's opening remarks. The moderator thanked Van Pelt and introduced Oliver, who had six minutes to deliver his opening statement.

Browning knew that Van Pelt would bring a strong case against resurrection, yet he also knew most of the arguments that Van Pelt would propose. Standing behind his lectern, he began, "Many thanks to the University of Michigan and Dr. Van Pelt for accepting and being a worthy opponent in debating a topic of great interest to myself and many today. Thanks to all who are attending and viewing tonight. Dr. Van Pelt and I share a unique experience as surrogates in today's presidential politics: we get to experience everything about running for president except taking the oath of office."

The audience laughed.

Oliver continued, "In his answer to the question at hand, the good Doctor chose to emphasize what we lack rather than what we possess, thereby distorting the context of this issue. Dr. Van Pelt did what anyone in his position would have to do: acknowledge, right out of the gate, that the physical side of human resurrection is 100% possible. But there was no pause to truly grasp how monumental that is.

"For example, a hundred years ago, the loss of a body part would mean the end of that natural body part. Today, it means a temporary inconvenience, giving us more time to watch intelligent robots do all our housework while our missing appendages are regrown from our own DNA. As the good Doctor acknowledged, the technology extends to fully remake a human from their DNA ... as the Gates administration apparently knows!"

The joke garnered some more laughter from the audience.

"So, the possibility of human resurrection really boils down to whether there is a way to restore the memories and traits of the deceased. With this in mind, consider for a moment what we have achieved since Quinto's Challenge: we solved what was once considered an unfathomable mystery—consciousness. We've created sentient androids and uncovered new subatomic particles.

"Now, although not yet proven, more than a dozen renowned physicists—experts in a field neither Dr. Van Pelt nor I are credentialed in—have all agreed that everything that occurs in our world and the universe is recorded in spacetime. They might differ in their theories, but with these exceptionally gifted minds in basic agreement, is it really such a stretch to believe that one of their theories will eventually be proven?"

Van Pelt took notes as Browning elaborated on the point.

"As for opportunity cost, I side with the good Doctor on the need to use our resources to work on all the issues he raised. But what are the actual resources going to Quinto's Challenge? For context, CAPR does much more than try to fulfill Quinto's Challenge, and CAPR's entire budget is 0.05% of the entire federal budget! That argument just doesn't hold up when you look at the numbers.

"Overpopulation, as the Doctor rightly pointed out, would be a challenge—but not an insurmountable one. We know that population increases lead to predictable strains on resources—strains we can plan for. On the

smaller scale, construction of housing is completely automated and could outpace the rate of resurrection. And we can build up! Star scrapers have occupancies up to six figures, and we will likely be able to build ever more grand structures in the future. And on the larger scale, let's not forget our small research communities on Mars and how we have sent various autonomous missions to build facilities there.

"In short, we've already become a multi-planetary species. With continued terraforming and automated construction, Mars alone could eventually house billions. Perhaps Venus would be next to tame. So yes, population problems would exist, but there are resources and solutions.

"As I will outline, science has a rare and precious pathway to resurrection, and we must seize it—because there's no guarantee we'll ever have this chance again."

Many in the audience rose to applaud as Browning finished these initial remarks. Van Pelt finished taking some notes.

The moderator thanked Oliver and announced that Van Pelt would have the floor.

Van Pelt had anticipated many of Browning's points. Standing behind his lectern and holding his notes, Van Pelt responded, "Were science to bring back the dead, I must confess that it would be a fascinating sociological study, but not necessarily one with positive findings. Having those who were once dead again among the living, even with the solutions that Oliver proposed to solve overpopulation, would be a phenomenon casting major ripples throughout all our social circles, networks, laws, and institutions. Ripples that could soon become waves—waves that might undermine civilization itself. Allow me to elaborate.

"Society has always been structured around the assumption that once we die, we are gone forever. This is the premise behind all of our laws and all of our economics. Regardless of religious belief in souls living on or rising again in an afterlife, practically speaking, the world has been adapted to people living once and then departing. Were science to achieve human resurrection, all of this will be upended. It would revolutionize the structure of society, shift our paradigm, change our psychology, and potentially lead to war.

"Resurrection may also decrease our incentive not to kill, knowing that death may not be the ultimate end for the victim. But that assumes the victim—or their family and friends—can afford the resurrection, for the apparatus for resurrection would entail immense financial cost—if not used as a tool to control overpopulation, then likely reserved as a privilege for the few.

"Would it, therefore, be a just or sustainable paradigm, knowing that life after death is available only to the wealthy? The wealthy who could continuously pay for resurrection time and time again, accumulating massive resources and creating an immortal ruling class? One the masses would inevitably rise up against?

"How would we go about rewriting our laws to extend fundamental rights—including property rights—to the resurrected, especially when they had their time on Earth, and new generations will be sharing the same finite land and resources? If the newly born cannot own property because it's hoarded by the wealthy dead who keep returning, or if the resurrected are denied rights on the grounds that they've already had their time on Earth—then history teaches us what comes next: civil war. And adding fuel to the fire, how would religious extremists react to seeing resurrected people on Earth when they have vowed it should only be God who does it?

"If it were possible for science to bring back the dead, it's very clear to me that civilization would be under threat. Resurrection would become a service with overwhelming demand and limited capacity to serve, result-ing in great disappointment, impatience, and contention among those not selected to receive their loved ones back. Fortunately, as I have already stated, achieving resurrection is extremely unlikely.

"Look, Vince Quinto was a good man, an intelligent thinker, and a fine and inspiring president. Still, we must distinguish between what is possible and what is probable. Even if it appears as though science one day could bring the dead back to life, would the resurrected entity really be you? Would a clone of you, with memories implanted in its mind, truly be you—or merely someone else, living under the permanent illusion that they are you?

"Understand, this question of 'should we resurrect' has a particular origin. It didn't originate with Oliver's debate invitation. It didn't originate with Quinto's Challenge, nor with the religions that have believed in resurrection for millennia. Resurrection's origin is in the wiring of our brains. Our brains are simply not designed to comprehend the finality of death. Quinto's Challenge, though admirable, is simply something that emerged from that inability. We are wired to always expect that there will be a next moment, and while we know death exists, we naturally project that there will be a next moment after that, somewhere, somehow."

A significant portion of the audience rose to applaud. Once the applause subsided, the moderator announced, "Thank you, Dr. Van Pelt. Oliver, the floor is yours."

"Let me first address the issue of continuity," remarked Browning, "that is, if resurrected, would we really be continuations of our actual selves? It's helpful to remember that we are not static objects, but dynamic systems in constant flux. For instance, the molecules making up our bodies today are not the same ones that made up our bodies a decade ago. Those earlier molecules were, little by little, expelled and replaced. On the faster end of this biological turnover, we're 65% water, and most of it is replaced every two to three weeks. At the slower end, the minerals in our bones are mostly replaced every decade or so.

"Given this, are we entirely different people than we were ten years ago? Are we any less ourselves because we've cut our hair, regrown skin, or replaced nearly every cell? Of course not. We are not the molecules themselves—but the pattern they form as they continuously flow in and out of us."

"With this in mind, we can confidently answer the age-old question of the Ship of Theseus: yes, the pieces change, but the ship remains the same, because dynamic wave structure is the very nature of our vessels. At the most fundamental level, we are information in spacetime!"

Van Pelt was impressed by this point, though he remained convinced that population and social ramifications were paramount.

"And so we come to our personality and memories. Every facet of our personality and every memory we have or ever will make is, once again, fundamentally information. Now, retrieving the information that makes up our bodies is relatively easy, as it's encoded in our genome. But retrieving the information that makes up our personality and memories is indeed a problem. But like so many problems once thought impossible, we live in a universe of wondrous possibility—possibility that may even extend to retrieving the information that makes up our very souls.

"Given our nature as waves of information, I strongly suspect that when the day comes for science to bring back the dead, rebooting the pattern that defines an individual will indeed represent a true continuation of that individual—and of their very soul.

"As for resurrection's societal impact, I agree it would bring a revolution. But would such a challenge be any greater than surviving the plagues that ravaged humanity before modern medicine? Would it be more difficult than living through an era when state-sponsored war and systemic violence were the norm? More perilous than the dawn of nuclear weapons and mutually assured destruction? Harder than regrowing our own organs and extending life expectancy well beyond anything our ancestors imagined?

"Challenges, no matter how significant, should not deter us from confronting the problem of death. As for fears about what religious extremists might do in response to resurrection—resurrection would not only allow us to bring back those they may kill, but also restore all the victims that terrorism has claimed throughout the millennia.

"And therein, my friends, lies the real answer to the question: we cannot assume that civilization will endure. We cannot assume that ideology and self-interest will not fracture the fragile peace we've maintained.

Therefore, for the sake of humanity, let us advance this science while we still have a civilization capable of doing so."

Browning then reached for his drink and took a sip as applause rose from the audience.

Over the next hour, Browning and Van Pelt sparred courteously but vigorously. Browning remained steadfast in his belief that resurrection was both scientifically achievable and socially feasible, while Van Pelt held firm in his pessimism—citing unintended consequences, especially surveillance power, as dangers not worth risking.

Each debater also commented on the upcoming presidential election, placing their weight behind opposing candidates. Van Pelt clarified that he saw neither Benson as a saint nor Gates as a boogeyman, but argued that Benson would be a bulwark against the societal mutation he believed Gates was enabling through androids and the supported class. Browning, on the other hand, warned that Benson's presidency would mark the greatest setback to scientific progress in a generation.

When the time for closing statements arrived, the moderator announced, "It's evident that everyone watching has been intellectually stimulated this evening. We will now hear closing statements from Dr. Van Pelt, followed by Oliver. Then, we will present the decision regarding the victor of tonight's debate to you."

Van Pelt began his conclusion:

"President Quinto may have sincerely believed we could bring the dead back before the end of this century—but belief does not make it so. Everything about humanity is the product of biological evolution, where genetic changes were passed to future generations only if they provided an advantage—typically, to help us live a short life a little longer. Crucial to that is the fact that our brains evolved for a single, finite life—and with that, a finite capacity for memory.

"So, what is the point of being resurrected into an indefinite future if much of it could not even be remembered? What of the inevitable boredom or slow descent into existential despair that centuries—or millennia—of

life could bring? The issues I raised earlier—reintroducing billions into a fragile world—barely scratch the surface of what would unfold. The New Romans are onto something when they say, Dum Vivimus—'While We Live.'

"Should science pursue resurrection today? I implore you to share my answer: no.

"Enjoy this life. Cherish every precious moment. Cherish your loved ones.

"Leave the Earth a better place for the next generation—so that you may live on in their memory, and in a positive light.

"Thank you."

The audience applauded as Browning waited for the noise to subside. "I owe a debt of gratitude to Dr. Van Pelt for his participation in this thought-provoking debate." Turning to him, he added, "Thank you, Doctor."

Van Pelt nodded, prompting another round of applause.

"Even if the points Dr. Van Pelt raises about our evolved limitations are true," continued Browning, "they are still not reasons to give us pause in scientifically pursuing resurrection. Advances in genetics may one day allow us to bypass these limitations—to expand memory capacity and tailor our preferences for an indefinite lifespan.

"But beyond these grand possibilities, the arguments against resurrection overlook a simple, heartbreaking fact: all the children lost throughout history, robbed of even one full lifetime. That alone, to me, is reason enough to press forward."

A quiet stir rippled through the audience—some nodding, others blinking back emotion—at the mention of children lost to time.

"Though the task may be great, and the technology still developing, if resurrection can be conceived, it can be achieved. Now is the time to pursue it—because we cannot assume this window will remain open forever. Yes, cherish the moments we have, but imagine the lives we could live, and the memories we could make, if we fulfill Quinto's Challenge. Thank you!"

Thunderous applause erupted for Browning's performance.

The moderator wrapped up the debate by thanking Van Pelt and Browning for their compelling contributions. The audience joined in enthusiastic applause, awaiting the start of the voting.

"A great debate!" exclaimed Deeley. "I admire Browning's optimism—especially given that he's not even aware of the science we have."

"I enjoyed it," agreed Xara. "Van Pelt's social points were well thought out."

"How many simulations on population pathways did you run? About 200 billion?" asked Deeley.

"Correct," confirmed Xara. "There will be challenges, but there are definite pathways to making it all work, just as Browning outlined."

"Browning did well," remarked Charity. "A little anti-android from Van Pelt, but not too bad."

"As Xara has said," responded Deeley, ever sensitive to android rights, "if the arc of history is anything to go by, you'll one day be accepted by society as full members without question."

"Xara and I have talked about it a few times, and I think it'll take longer than she does," noted Charity.

"Well, this is one forum where you can vote," reminded Deeley. "So vote!"

The moderator unveiled the audience voting system. Official polls remained open for five minutes, and after that time, the moderator returned to the stage to announce the results.

"The votes are tallied. The results are in. The debaters eagerly await your verdict on the question, 'Should Science Pursue Human Resurrection?' For those who participated—whether in the auditorium tonight or from afar—49% of you favored Oliver Browning as the more convincing speaker, followed by 45% who chose Dr. Van Pelt. A mere 6% declared it a tie."

The audience erupted in cheers, and Van Pelt made his way to Browning to extend his congratulations.

"Congratulations to Oliver Browning," the moderator concluded. "You posed the question and passionately defended your position. Through your arguments—as well as those presented by Dr. Van Pelt—we have gained a deeper understanding of the topic, and we are truly grateful for that enlightening exchange."

Deeley, Xara, and Charity were pleased that Browning had won, knowing it would carry some positive political influence for their work. Charity then looked at Deeley and blurted out, "He didn't say it!"—referring to their earlier bet on whether Browning would repeat his previous viral comment. "Androids win!"

Charity and Xara high-fived while Deeley looked on with endearment.

"I love you girls so much," beamed Deeley, pulling them into a group hug.

The debate was expected to have minimal influence on the midterms but a more significant impact on the upcoming presidential election. Although Van Pelt hadn't emerged victorious, the framing of Benson as the sole alternative to Gates sharpened Gates' team's focus on the senator as the likely nominee of the American Freedom Party.

At the same time, it instilled a sense of urgency within Benson's camp, signaling that the moment to officially announce his candidacy was fast approaching.

CHAPTER 26

A REVELATION FROM SPACETIME

"Out of the countless cloning procedures I've been involved in, I never imagined the day I'd be cloning an entire human. It's a godlike power to possess, both thrilling and exceptionally daunting. To think that a sample of my DNA—whether extracted from my body, left on a surface, or floating in the air in a speck of dust—could be taken by another and my body remade ... and then my mind and personality restored. It's a power that will undoubtedly require the most stringent regulations should this be successful."

— AI Journal Excerpt: Maria Bellan-Schwacher, October 31, 2098

As CAPR's capabilities for resurrection advanced, so too did the government's desire to exploit that power for intelligence gathering. The data Xara retrieved from spacetime for animal resurrections was significantly less than what she was mandated to collect for national security purposes. And the more intelligence the government received, the more addictive it became.

Despite authorizing the use of CAPR for surveillance, President Gates maintained his integrity. He never used the technology for political advantage or to violate privacy rights on a whim. On several occasions, he had requested access to witness pivotal historical events—particularly from the American Founding. Gates was so captivated by watching his favorite historical figures that, at times, it distracted him from some of his lesser duties.

As the intelligence applications of CAPR gained momentum, both Xara and Xina cautioned Gates and DeShawn to exercise restraint. They warned that a sudden surge in America's effectiveness in military operations and domestic law enforcement would imply enhanced intelligence capabilities—potentially leading China to suspect the true cause. Still, the allure of exploiting this power remained difficult to resist.

On November 1st, in a secure virtual meeting between Gates and DeShawn, a combination of confidence and curiosity led them to take their new intelligence capabilities into a more invasive phase. As they discussed some of the recent intelligence findings from spacetime, DeShawn stated an opinion out of the blue.

"David, this power is unprecedented, but who knows how long we will possess it. While we have it, I think we need to understand what shaped the world we all live in today. I think it's time to find out what actually happened during the Seventy Minute War."

"I've been thinking the same thing," replied Gates. "I'm just nervous to do it."

"Afraid of what we might find?"

"Partially. But also because we *can* do this … and no one can stop us."

"I understand, and I appreciate your respect and integrity with this power. But we need to know. If we are to understand the threats of the present, we need a more complete knowledge of the threats of the past."

Gates agreed. "Okay. Go ahead. Let's see what Zhang Jun ordered and why."

***

The next day, DeShawn received a classified file from Xara, marked "Urgent". It contained a spacetime recording of Zhang Jun and his generals in the final moments of the Seventy Minute War. DeShawn had authorized this file to be accessible only to himself and the President. The moment he had an opportunity, he opened the file in his SecondSight.

A tag of the recording from Xara read:

On June 17, 2077, Zhang Jun did order the nuclear strike near Yunshan Zhen. It was not a hijack of the nuclear missile by the competing faction, as the official account has always maintained. What you will see will shock you and confirm that Zhang Jun is even more willing to use force to uphold Shenzhen than we had realized ...

DeShawn's pulse quickened. Xara's blunt summary floored him, feeding a suspicion he had long harbored—that Zhang Jun's iron rule was preserved by sheer terror. The secret that had eluded and divided the world was now his for the taking. Both apprehensive and intensely curious, he drew a deep breath and played the file.

A younger Zhang Jun paced a secure bunker in trepidation. His top aides and generals surrounded him in their War Room. It was about an hour into what would be called the Seventy Minute War.

"Mr. Chairman," said one of Zhang Jun's generals to him in Mandarin, "we've confirmed that the terrorist leadership is dead. Their corrupted swarm slaughtered them all!"

Zhang Jun closed his eyes, breathing a sigh of relief. But his relief was short-lived, for the general continued, "But ... the swarm has not stood down. It continues to move on, killing any and all humans without discrimination. I need to be clear, Mr. Chairman: this is the greatest global security threat I have ever seen. The swarm is replicating exponentially, and all copies have the same defect as the original unit!"

Staggered by the enormity of the situation, Zhang Jun finally demanded, "How do we know this?"

"We have remotely imaged two dozen units in the swarm and the analysis is sound and conclusive: all have the flaw. They intend to kill all humans. And all will continue replicating until that is achieved!"

DeShawn felt a jolt of dissonance. His brow furrowed as he muttered, "Swarm?"

The swarm in question, not yet explained in the spacetime recording, consisted of modified MS Generation 2 military drones. At Zhang Jun's direction, a secret military research division had experimented with these androids to create the ultimate AI swarm weapon. By suppressing key aspects of their decision-making, the androids were transformed into unthinking executioners, relentlessly executing assigned missions.

Each drone was equipped with multiple weapon systems, ranging from projectile to melee capabilities, and carried enough stored energy to traverse the globe on a single charge. Moreover, each unit housed advanced AI designed for surgical strikes. If assigned to assassinate a specific target, data on the individual could be uploaded into one or multiple drones, which would then track and eliminate them with lethal precision.

What made them truly terrifying, however, was their capacity for teslaphoresis-powered self-repair and replication. If additional drones were needed to complete a mission, existing units could manufacture self-assembling clones of themselves as long as they had access to the necessary resources and power.

Ultimately, after extensive deliberation, Zhang Jun agreed with his military research division that the risks of the drone swarm program outweighed its benefits and ordered its termination. However, some units were secretly retained by loyalists of a rival faction and transferred into their hands. Eventually, this faction resorted to terrorism, reprogramming the drones with a new mission: the assassination of Zhang Jun and his senior officials.

Lacking the infrastructure of a functioning government, the group's reprogramming efforts were crude and incomplete. The result was a catastrophic error—rather than identifying Zhang Jun and his senior administration as the sole targets, the drones interpreted the mission as the extermination of all humans, coupled with mass replication to ensure its success.

"How fast are they replicating?" asked Zhang Jun of the general who brought him the report.

"We estimate 20,500 units at present, but in seven minutes there will be 65,000. Come that time, there will be too many to stop. We must act now!"

"But they can't replicate forever! They need material. Metal! Carbon fiber! Silicon! They need energy! Maintenance! Your numbers can't be accurate!" screamed back Zhang Jun, in denial.

"Each is only the size of a basketball, so they don't take long to build. Maintenance is rare, and when needed, the swarm can diagnose and perform it. Also, the material available near Yunshan Zhen to manufacture their replicas justifies the estimates provided ... and also a much larger number at that!"

Zhang Jun looked his general in the eye with horror. His general continued, "Charging them is neither an issue. While they may run out of materials near Yunshan Zhen, they will have a critical mass to spread to other locations, replicate, and end human life on Earth!"

The exchange was interrupted by another general informing Zhang Jun of another fact, "Mr. Chairman, the first batch is on the move and has engaged in killing civilians in a warehouse near the southeast corridor!"

A slow breath escaped DeShawn, its weight heavy. He knew that the horror etched on Zhang Jun's face was not the mask of a tyrant—it was the look of a man blindsided by catastrophe.

Since both the outskirts of Yunshan Zhen and the city itself were filled with various drones and flying devices—many identical in form to the defective military swarm—it was impossible to distinguish friend from foe by sight. Remote imaging, though capable of identifying individual threats, was too slow to keep pace with the swarm's rapid replication, making real-time targeting impossible at scale.

Zhang Jun turned his attention to a topographical map of Yunshan Zhen and its surrounding areas. Overlaid on the terrain was a threat radius map, centered on the swarm's position. The green epicenter—labeled "1 minute to destroy"—marked the canyon where the swarm could be neutralized. If engaged and defeated there, the threat would be eliminated, with a one-minute window to accomplish it. A yellow section encompassed the green, designated as "three minutes to destroy." Orange then surrounded the yellow as "five minutes to destroy." Finally, surrounding the orange was red, designated as "Failure." If the swarm reached the red zone, containment would be impossible. They would reach critical mass and spread globally, wiping out the vast majority of humanity within several days and then replicating and searching for any human survivors to finish off.

"Deploy an EMP!" ordered Zhang Jun.

"Ineffective with their advanced Faraday Cage design."

"Satellite megawatt lasers!"

"Only 20% effective at very best, not enough to mitigate critical mass."

"Deploy the nearest drone division! Vacuum bomb the area! All artillery weapons free!"

With a look of dismay on his face, the general quietly but firmly replied, "Those cannot and will not be effective against this threat, Mr. Chairman. Even if multiple drone divisions arrived in the next two minutes and bombed the area coupled with lasers from satellites, they would only be 30% to 40% effective, and the threat will continue replicating exponentially."

"Call in allied forces—now!"

"It is too late for that, Mr. Chairman. Many eyes have been on this problem, including independent agencies under oaths of secrecy. They all concluded the same! Mr. Chairman, I beg you—we have but one choice. If even one drone survives, humanity won't."

The orange on the map designated as "five minutes to destroy" dropped to "four minutes to destroy." The green epicenter had vanished, leaving only the expanding yellow zone. Tears welled in the general's eyes as he solemnly presented China's nuclear briefcase. "Mr. Chairman, we must launch—and we must launch now."

DeShawn's heart sank, the truth striking with terrible clarity. After years of suspicion and judgment, he finally understood. The weight of it pressed down on him as he felt—even from a distance—the horror that must have consumed Zhang Jun and his generals in that unconscionable moment.

Overwhelmed by the weight of the decision, Zhang Jun collapsed to one knee, knuckles pressed against the floor, head bowed, eyes shut. His most senior and trusted general was asking him to launch a nuclear strike on his own people or have humanity wiped from Earth. Zhang Jun retched, vomiting onto the floor.

There was no time for sympathy. The general pressed on. "Zhang Jun! Every second we delay brings humanity closer to extinction. We must launch now!"

Not shown in the video—but having taken place moments earlier— the senior general had prepped a midrange strategic nuclear missile, aimed at the center of the green zone just outside Yunshan Zhen. Anticipating resistance from others in the chain of command, he had wisely prepared the launch sequence in advance—knowing that ordering a nuclear strike on their own soil would spark fierce opposition.

Fortunately, his urgent explanation convinced enough decision-makers to authorize a single nuclear launch, allowing the necessary preparations to proceed. Ideally, the general had wanted multiple silos ready as a safeguard against mechanical failure—any malfunction in the lone missile could doom humanity. However, only one silo had a fully armed warhead ready for launch in time. All that remained was Zhang Jun's final authorization.

"*Fifty seconds until launch window closes,*" *a general reported, his voice sharp with tension.*

Zhang Jun remained on his knees, vomit staining his beard and uniform.

The senior general stepped closer, his voice both urgent and steady. "Zhang Jun, all great leaders in history have faced choices between terrible and worse. Perhaps none have faced a decision of this magnitude, and perhaps none ever will again—but those who made painful choices before us did so for the greater good. Billions will benefit from this decision—because without it, there will be no one left to save"

Zhang Jun's mind spiraled. His stomach churned with the weight of what was before him. This swarm of killer machines—this nightmare—was an offshoot of something he had once experimented with. A thought gripped him. "Did I create this horror?" he asked hoarsely.

"Every military experiments with dangerous technology," the senior general shot back. "You ordered its destruction. You are NOT responsible for this."

Nearby, another general exchanged a tense glance with the senior general, silently weighing an unthinkable alternative. If Zhang Jun could not give the order, could they break protocol and launch the strike themselves? The thought had already crossed the senior general's mind—but it was futile. The security safeguards in place required the President's direct authentication. Even if they attempted to override the system, it would take too long. For humanity to survive, Zhang Jun had to act.

"Thirty seconds until launch window closes!"

Zhang Jun appeared lost in a dark thought. He shook his head, whispering, "My countrymen. Mothers. Fathers. Children at play. Millions of them. Living their lives, while we plan the unthinkable. No ..."

He swayed slightly, retreating from the moment, from the decision that lay before him.

"Twenty seconds until launch window closes!"

"Zhang Jun!" the senior general yelled, seizing his president by the shoulders. He shook him, his voice raw with desperation. "Save humanity now!"

"Fifteen seconds!" another general urged.

Something within Zhang Jun snapped into place—a visceral, electric surge of resolve. His breath hitched as he lifted his head, his body still bowed in turmoil. With a primal force propelling him, he grabbed the nuclear launch module from the senior general's grasp. His fingers trembled as he submitted to the retinal scanner, then the palm scanner. He reached into a hidden pocket within his clothing, retrieving the launch code. His voice wavered but did not fail as he uttered the final authentication.

Green lights flickered to life in the briefcase, pulsing three times. It was done.

DeShawn's eyes closed, his head lowering under the weight of what he'd just seen. His heart sank further, and a single tear traced down his cheek.

Zhang Jun rose unsteadily. The briefcase slipped from his hands and hit the floor with a heavy thud. He turned, his movements sluggish and uncoordinated, and staggered toward the door. Relief, thick with sorrow, settled over the War Room—but Zhang Jun's own burden only deepened.

The heavy door sealed shut behind him with a muted hiss. In a daze, he moved down the corridor to a nearby room, seeking solitude. The flicker of maps and countdowns still played behind his eyes.

It all felt surreal. But he knew it wasn't a dream. He knew a living nightmare had just been unleashed.

Moments stretched into eternity as the chain of command completed the final authentications. Then, amid a deafening silence of the War Room, the volumetric displays projected the chilling image of a missile emerging from its silo—its fiery ascent piercing the sky. The roar of its engines, simulated in surround sound, filled the War Room, a mechanical symphony of destruction that mirrored the anguish in Zhang Jun's soul.

From his room of solitude, Zhang Jun knew the missile had now launched, en route to its target. The thought shattered whatever fragile composure remained. With a raw, primal scream, he collapsed to the floor.

In the War Room, his generals stood frozen, watching as the missile arced toward the outskirts of Yunshan Zhen. A feat of cutting-edge aerospace engineering—yet a harbinger of unthinkable horror. The moment stretched unbearably. Then—an eruption. The volumetric displays blazed white at peak brightness, momentarily overwhelming the room in searing artificial light. As the glare faded, the displays resolved into an image of a monstrous fireball, clawing its way into the sky, the billowing inferno turning night into day. A shockwave of incomprehensible force ripped outward, devouring everything in its path with blinding speed. Some of the volumetric displays flickered and cut out, struggling against the surge of energy—but enough remained operational to bear witness to the annihilation.

The aides, though shaken to their core, tirelessly sifted through the deluge of incoming data. Then, an ominous rumbling sent shivers down the spines of all present, for they knew its source: the Earth itself trembled, as if recoiling in horror at mankind's folly.

Zhang Jun's body convulsed involuntarily at the tremor, his anguish pouring forth in a torrent of self-flagellation as he let out another gut-wrenching cry. His body trembled under the crushing weight of guilt as he tore at his clothes, his nails clawing at his own face in a desperate attempt to purge the unbearable agony. In that moment, he was not a president but a broken man, consumed by the knowledge that his decision had condemned millions to an unjust fate.

In the War Room, the senior general's eyes flickered with suppressed emotion, his stomach knotting as he fought to maintain his composure amidst the horror. He ordered autonomous fighters into the blast zone to eliminate any surviving rogue drones and directed satellites to standby, *ready to fire on any remaining threats. Turning to his aides, he asked, "How many are left?"*

After a tense moment, one shaken aide finally reported, "I detect none left, sir."

"None detected by me, sir."

Several other aides echoed the report, their voices strained as they struggled to suppress their own horror.

"Keep analyzing," instructed the general, ordering additional reconnaissance units to the area.

After 30 agonizing minutes of further analysis, the senior general finally left the War Room to find Zhang Jun. He opened the door to Zhang Jun's refuge and found him slumped against the wall, his face streaked with blood, dried vomit still clinging to his clothes.

"It's done," the general murmured. "Humanity will survive."

Upon hearing the news, Zhang Jun felt no solace, no wave of relief—only the crushing void of his grief. Drained beyond words, he lifted his gaze, locking eyes with his senior general, who bore witness to the raw anguish carved into his features. "What ... what will we tell our country? What will we tell the world?"

Xara's spacetime recording of the event stopped.

DeShawn, a man known for his emotional control, sat in stunned silence, his breath unsteady. Overcome with emotion, he wiped the tears streaming down his face, struggling to process the weight of what he had just witnessed. A deep and profound respect for Zhang Jun—something he never imagined he could feel—settled within him.

My God, he thought. *He and his generals saved the world ... and yet history will forever misjudge him!*

Within SecondSight, he contacted Gates' Chief of Staff and secured a meeting with the President for that evening. At this point, the Chief of Staff had already begun to suspect he was being left out of the loop regarding something significant.

That night, DeShawn made his way to the White House and entered the President's private office. He found Gates seated on a couch, waiting. Without hesitation, DeShawn sat beside him and said, "I've got it. I've seen it. And I want to be with you when you watch it."

Gates, brimming with interest, accepted the file in SecondSight and immediately proceeded to watch.

As the recording unfolded, Gates tensed visibly, a ripple of discomfort moving from his clenched fists to his tightly drawn legs, through the stiff set of his shoulders, and finally manifesting in the grim set of his jaw. Each frame seemed to weigh heavier on him, and by the end, he was a picture of defeat, sinking back into the couch as if his bones had turned to water. Drained of all pretense, he met DeShawn's gaze squarely and admitted with a shaky breath, "No one could have prepared me for that."

DeShawn gazed back at the President, also still affected by the revelation of the video. After a moment, Gates continued, "I would not wish that upon my worst enemy. My God, only he and his inner circle have known the reality until now!"

"His stance on Shenzhen now makes perfect sense," expressed DeShawn, "he modified androids, and the worst possible outcome happened. He is not going down that path again, nor will he let anyone else."

Gates contemplated being in Zhang Jun's position at the moment he gave the nuclear order. He shrank at the thought. "His threats against modifying androids—his whole demeanor," conceded Gates. "It all comes from experience, from deep trauma—not malice. Damn it! I wish he'd just told the truth."

"My gut says they kept the truth hidden to quickly restore stability. I remember the moment of the nuclear blast well—it was precarious. Every nuclear power was on edge, ready to launch amid the fear and uncertainty. Things could've gone south fast. But saying terrorists hijacked a nuke, rather than admitting China had launched one—regardless of the circumstances—provided a quick off-ramp from global escalation. That story also helped prevent mass panic over a killer AI swarm—and maybe kept the idea of those drones from being planted in anyone else's mind. To be honest, I'd have told the same story."

Gates slowly shook his head, absorbing the weight of it all. "The irony … the horrible irony is that the terrorist leaders were already dead before the nuke was even launched."

DeShawn's expression softened with quiet admiration. "They had no comforting truth to offer the world. Their options were bad, worse, or fabricated—and they chose to fabricate, to deescalate, contain fear, and suppress awareness of the swarm. But whatever the story, the facts remain: China and Zhang Jun were innocent in regard to the Seventy Minute War. He and his military saved the world—and he and his government have preserved that salvation ever since."

Like DeShawn, Gates quickly developed a powerful and abiding respect for Zhang Jun.

"He may not be the tyrant we thought he was," conceded DeShawn, "but he's still a threat. And knowing what we know now, he might actually be more dangerous to us. After everything he went through—after the unimaginable sacrifice he made to save humanity—he won't hesitate to destroy Xara if he finds out for certain that she's been modified."

Gates contemplated this in silence before speaking. "We should have Xara do some immediate reconnaissance on Zhang Jun and his intelligence apparatus to be certain he doesn't know."

"Agreed."

***

The following evening, Michael Bergstrom lingered in an opulent lounge of a Washington DC hotel after a conference on the future of automated warfare. Also present—seemingly by chance—was Rand Benson, whose path he crossed. In truth, Benson had anticipated Bergstrom's attendance and arranged to be there, already prepared to exploit the opportunity.

Even though Benson was a threat to Quinto's Challenge, to Bergstrom, he was an unlikely though possible next President of the United States ... and therefore a pathway to elevate Bergstrom to the cabinet. With this ambition in mind, Bergstrom hedged his bets and accepted an invitation from Benson to speak over drinks, which the senator insisted were on him.

"So," said Bergstrom with a coy smile as they sat at a private table for two in the lounge, "when are you going to announce your candidacy for president?"

Benson smiled in return and deflected the question with a jab at Bergstrom's own ambitions, "When are you going to be nominated for Secretary of Energy?"

Bergstrom laughed. Benson then answered, "I've been thinking about whether a shot at the presidency makes sense, but my mind is not yet made up. That's all you'll get!"

Some more banter ensued, but Benson didn't want small talk. He wanted to know about the secret research at CAPR.

Understanding that Bergstrom wouldn't intentionally disclose top-secret information, Benson had planned in advance to create a possibility that Bergstrom would reveal something ... by secretly arranging a specialized barbiturate to be slipped in one of Bergstrom's drinks. As the minutes ticked by and the drug took effect, Bergstrom's defenses weakened, and Benson skillfully redirected the conversation toward the research conducted at CAPR.

"Look," muttered Bergstrom, his eyes betraying a slightly altered mental state, "I know you don't like Quinto or Gates, but you do like America, so let me tell you something about America: America is about to roar back as the most powerful nation on Earth. Doesn't that appeal to you?"

"Of course it does … if it were true," responded Benson, his attention piqued, though he kept it well hidden. "But how is accelerating particles at CAPR suddenly going to thrust us to superpower status again?"

"It was particle science, the splitting of the atom, that made us the first nuclear power. It was particle science, the fusing of the atom, that revolutionized energy production and liberated us from foreign energy. Rand, particle science has once again provided the dawn of a new power."

"And what power is that?"

Bergstrom paused. His faculties were still intact, applying restraint—but a mounting, unshakable urge to speak of the research pressed forward. After a brief internal struggle, he removed his SecondSight lenses, placed them in their case, and powered them down entirely to avoid AGI surveillance. Then, finally relenting, he said, "The past is encoded in spacetime. We've pierced the fabric to see it!"

"I genuinely am thrilled for that. But what exactly does that mean? How useful can it be? I drop a rock on the ground and you look in spacetime two minutes later and see what I did? Perhaps it might be useful in the future, but for now, tricks of science won't restore sole superpower status."

Benson was being coy with Bergstrom as to his true thoughts and intentions and was leading Bergstrom in the direction he wanted.

"Trust me," insisted Bergstrom. "This is big!"

"You offer me no proof."

Leaning into Benson, the urge to disclose was now fully dominant. Bergstrom whispered, "Why do you think the FBI recently solved a string of difficult cases? Why do you think traitorous military contractors were suddenly held accountable for leaking secrets? Trust me, Rand, superpower status is returning."

Stunned at the revelation though maintaining restraint, Benson leaned into Bergstrom and, in a soft voice, replied, "I am privy to many things. Earlier this year I knew that some breakthrough was achieved at CAPR. I didn't have specific details on the science, but I knew something big was uncovered. I also knew that whatever it was, likely some spacetime record recovery, it wasn't going to be of any utility so long as Shenzhen remained in its current form. So, as of right now, I'm not sure how convinced I should be that American hegemony is around the corner again."

Bergstrom chuckled for a moment as he figured out how he should respond. Leaning in again, he looked Benson directly in the eye and confided, "You're a man who knows how the world works. I am, too. Neither of us is naive. Does any great thing ever happen in this world that perfectly follows all the rules at all times? Have you always followed every rule at every time in your successes?"

Benson looked Bergstrom in the eye and gave a sardonic smile, his way of acknowledging the truth in Bergstrom's words. He also knew what Bergstrom indirectly communicated: that Xara had been upgraded in some way, and this revelation elated him.

"All is safe, don't worry," reassured Bergstrom. "If you are an American patriot as you claim to be, you'll be glad that we have done what we have done. That I promise you."

"I am an American patriot indeed," replied Benson who then picked up his glass, offering a toast with Bergstrom. "Well then … to American hegemony once again!"

"To American hegemony once again!"

They clinked glasses.

"If by chance you do decide to run for president … and if you win …" murmured Bergstrom, struggling against the drowsiness overcoming him, "you remember who gave you the heads up on this."

"Oh, I will remember," responded Benson, sipping his drink with a satisfied smile.

***

While the clone of Daisy Hale continued to grow, and rapidly, Xara began extracting limited daily intelligence from spacetime on Zhang Jun and his government. To DeShawn and the President's relief, such intelligence revealed no indication that Zhang Jun or his government suspected any upgrades had taken place with Xara.

Tuesday November 4th arrived, Election Day. Although Gates' approval ratings had lowered since Dr. Strock's testimony, they stabilized thanks to Browning's debate. Nevertheless, the Democratic-Republican Party lost control of Congress. While it wasn't a complete surprise, it was still worrisome for Gates, as he was concerned about the potential reduction in funding for CAPR in the upcoming budget.

*****

Just after Election Day, an American government delegation arrived in Beijing for high-level discussions with their Chinese counterparts. Their primary agenda was to explore the expansion of joint research operations within the moon's research colonies—including its growing network of lunar data centers—where predominantly Chinese and American scientists lived and worked in lunar bio-domes equipped for sustainable living.

Coincidentally, Zhang Jun was also in Beijing, and at the very same government complex hosting the visiting American delegation. While he would typically not attend such meetings, his aides encouraged him to make a brief appearance as a show of goodwill. After some deliberation, he obliged.

Among the American delegation were the NASA Administrator, two leading astrophysicists, and three members of Congress—including Rand Benson, buoyed by his party's congressional midterm victory. As the formal discussions with their Chinese counterparts concluded, both delegations remained to socialize over a spread of delicacies served in honor of the American guests.

Then, to the surprise of all present, Zhang Jun himself appeared—dressed in a minimalist slate-gray suit of unmistakably Eastern design, collarless and buttoned straight down the front—to grace the gathering with his presence.

"Mr. President," greeted various delegates as the atmosphere shifted to a more formal tone.

Bergstrom, under the influence of the particular barbiturates Benson had administered, retained no memory of his conversation about CAPR's research. But ever since that exchange, Benson had fantasized about revealing to Zhang Jun that President Gates had broken Shenzhen.

While such a disclosure would likely provoke a precision strike from China—one that would obliterate Xara and, in doing so, deprive Benson of his own ambitions to peer into spacetime—he considered it a price worth paying to ensure that Gates remained a one-term president. Besides, Benson had already devised a solution. If Xara were destroyed, he could still transfer Xina to CAPR, positioning her to succeed Xara and restoring the power of spacetime manipulation under his control.

Now, standing mere feet from Zhang Jun, he saw a window of opportunity open before him.

The final star aligns, he thought, barely able to believe his luck.

Zhang Jun, addressing the delegation in English, greeted, "Welcome to China. I wish to express my support for our joint research and to extend my best wishes for your success."

"Thank you, Mr. President," the delegates responded in near unison.

Zhang Jun then proceeded to greet each member of the delegation. As he moved down the line, Benson subtly repositioned himself, ensuring that he would be the last to receive Zhang Jun's attention.

It's now or never, thought Benson.

Zhang Jun acknowledged each delegate in turn, meeting their gaze with a subtle nod of the head. In response, a simple "Mr. President" or "It's an honor" was expected.

But when he reached Benson, the congressman deviated from the script. "Mr. President, a private moment, if I may."

Zhang Jun's eyes narrowed slightly. "A little irregular, is it not?"

"With respect," Benson replied smoothly, "we live in irregular times—especially when it comes to compliance with the Treaty of Shenzhen."

Zhang Jun studied Benson in silence, his interest piqued. After a beat, he gave a slight gesture, signaling Benson to step aside from the group.

Benson seized the moment. "I'll be brief. President Gates has upgraded the Generation 6 machine at CAPR."

Zhang Jun's expression remained unreadable. "I assume President Gates simply broadcasts this information to political adversaries such as yourself?"

"I have it from the CAPR Administrator himself." Benson leaned in slightly. "As someone deeply concerned about the risk this breach of Shenzhen poses, I consider it my duty to inform you."

Zhang Jun's expression darkened—a telltale sign of his disdain for maneuvering politicians. He let out a slow, deliberate sigh, his breath escaping in a cloud of frustration. "I'm not predisposed to believe everything a foreign politician—especially one clearly campaigning for office—tells me. But if what you say is true, then rest assured: the upgraded Generation 6 machine will soon be offline."

Without another word, Zhang Jun turned and strode out of the room, his aides falling in step behind him.

From across the room, Benson's congressional colleagues—having seen the exchange but not heard it—approached with astonishment. "What was *that* about?"

Benson offered a smooth, dismissive smile. "Just expressing my thanks and praise for his support. A rare visit from him—I didn't want to let the moment pass, especially now that we'll be running Congress again."

His colleagues accepted the answer without suspicion, but Benson felt a surge of exhilaration—he now possessed a potent weapon in his campaign arsenal: the claim that David Gates had recklessly jeopardized national security in the face of China.

It didn't matter to Benson that the risk was one of his own making—after drugging Bergstrom and leaking sensitive information to Zhang Jun. The only thing that mattered now was that he had the narrative—and the confidence—that the time had come to formally launch his presidential campaign.

***

Xara's limited daily check-ins on Zhang Jun's government continued. The intelligence gathered—along with insights on other nations—remained invaluable. This practice revealed no indication that China knew anything about the upgrade … until a couple of days after the American moon research delegation returned from China.

This is concerning. I have directed Xara to increase monitoring frequency and to coordinate discreetly with Xina to ensure that defensive measures can be implemented without delay if necessary.

Secretary Brady sent the message to Gates through a secure channel, attaching the latest spacetime recording of Zhang Jun—retrieved just hours earlier. Ensuring he was alone, Gates sat at the Resolute Desk and played the recording in SecondSight:

Zhang Jun entered a central intelligence room in the August 1st Building, headquarters of the Chinese military. Seeming disturbed, he called upon his Generation 6 machine, Zhishi.

Appearing in augmentation as a roughly 20-year-old beautiful Chinese woman dressed in military garb, Zhishi responded with a bow of her head and in the Chinese tongue, "Yes, Mr. Chairman."

"Analyze for me the probability that David Gates has directed, or approved, an upgrade of the Generation 6 android at their Supercollider," instructed Zhang Jun in his native Chinese.

"Of course. Permit me one moment."

Zhishi closed her eyes while Zhang Jun remained standing, his hands clasped together in front of his flowing traditional gown. After a moment, Zhishi opened her eyes and reported, "Based on the latest data, there is approximately a one-in-three chance that David Gates directly ordered an upgrade, and a greater than two-in-three likelihood that he permitted others—such as CAPR Administrator Michael Bergstrom, a known opponent of Shenzhen—to proceed with one. American intelligence capabilities recently exhibited an anomalous spike in effectiveness that gradually subsided, and one plausible explanation is that they have found a way to extract information from spacetime."

"That will be all."

Zhishi bowed her head in acknowledgment.

Without another word, Zhang Jun turned and exited the room.

Gates' cortisol levels rose. *Why was Zhang Jun suddenly asking this?* Equally alarming was Zhang Jun being told there was more than a two-thirds likelihood that others had initiated an upgrade of Xara—alongside the troubling analysis of American intelligence patterns.

He had no time to dwell on it when a political aide entered the Oval Office, announcing, "Mr. President, Benson has formally launched his campaign for president."

The aide then shared a video with Gates. Benson's campaign launch centered around a single theme: "Awaken!" This was the first of Benson's AI-generated campaign ads.

Gates played the video, which showed a family mourning at a graveside, accompanied by solemn, slightly ominous music. After a narrator explained that only Benson would put a stop to Gates' disrespect for the dead, Benson spoke directly to the audience, formally announcing his candidacy for the presidency, pledging to stop the "android plague," halt the growth of the "parasites" of the supported class, and, in reference to the GenX whistleblower, stating, "I will not waste tax dollars on the horror that is Quinto's Fantasy. We will end the madness, restore human dignity, and take back our future."

After watching, Gates leaned forward, resting his head on his desk. He remained in that position for a long moment before sighing, lifting his head, and rubbing his eyes. He had anticipated this moment, and although Benson wasn't yet his party's nominee, Gates believed it was inevitable.

This announcement—combined with Zhang Jun's suspicions and his own weakened position in Congress—gave Gates an acute sense that the window of opportunity for successful human resurrection was rapidly closing. Even if Daisy were successfully raised, he now understood that a single resurrection wouldn't be enough to secure its legitimacy. Multiple human resurrections would be required before he could publicly announce the breakthrough. And that might not be possible if he only served one term—or if Zhang Jun acted first to eliminate Xara.

"Thanks, Ian," said Gates. "I think I need a moment alone."

His aide nodded, then left the Oval Office.

Though distressed, as Gates sat at the Resolute desk, his mind turned to some recordings from spacetime that Xara had retrieved for him. He recalled viewing Washington's crossing of the Delaware River with a column of troops from the Continental Army.

Thinking about these recordings made Gates feel grateful, for despite the stakes and risks he was enduring, Gates preferred his unique challenges over the freezing, disease-infested, and brutal battlefield violence of early American history.

He cast his eyes at a copy of *Washington Crossing the Delaware* hanging on the wall of the Oval Office, and, contemplating the difference between the art and the reality he now knew, a smile broke over his face. For a moment, he forgot the weight on his shoulders.

CHAPTER 27

THE TEA PARTY

"What is human? Does one have to be conceived naturally to qualify? Given that many are conceived outside the womb, the answer is, of course, no. Is it our sentience—our thoughts and feelings? This can't be the qualifier either, as we are not the only sentient form of life that thinks and feels. Could it be the code that makes us who we are—our genome, blueprinting every aspect of our being? If so, then a resurrected person, remade from minerals and water sitting in vials and tubes, should be considered just as human as we are."

— AI Journal Excerpt: Deeley Carr, December 27, 2098

"Ten!"

"Nine!"

"Eight!"

"Seven!"

"Six!"

"Five!"

"Four!"

"Three!"

"Two!"

"One!"

"Happy New Year!"

Deeley, Charity, Rona, and the augmentations of Xara and Xina stood on the roof of EOS beside a balcony as 2099 rang in with a symphony of fireworks, a dazzling light show from the one-mile-apart luminous towers of the Supercollider, and muffled choruses of *Auld Lang Syne*. As one of the few people authorized to speak with Xina outside the Pentagon, Rona had granted Deeley, Charity, and Xara access to see her for the celebration. It was Deeley's first time meeting Xina, and she was delighted.

Xara and Xina stood with arms around each other, their faces lit with joy. Though unease lingered from learning that Zhang Jun suspected her upgrade, Xara took comfort in the robust physical safeguards she'd built in. For now, she let the worry fade and focused on the joy of the evening—especially being with her twin. Though she and Xina needed to triangulate their surroundings through other devices, their augmentations were still flawless—their faces shimmering with reflections from the fireworks.

Bursts of light danced across Deeley's features as well, silhouetted against the midnight sky. Yet despite her joy at meeting Xina and her general happiness for the New Year, a shadow of concern lingered in her eyes.

With all of them outdoors and not in a secured room, there could be no mention of the project. But Charity, watching closely, sensed something was weighing on Deeley.

"Hey," said Charity softly. "Are you okay?"

Looking back at her, Deeley asked, "Remember my lamentations about *homo sapiens'* short-sighted stupidity?"

"Yes."

A tear welled in Deeley's eye. "I've been thinking… the irony is that it might apply to me."

Charity listened silently, sensing there was more.

"I naively believed that solving the mystery of spacetime would only bring about great things for humanity. But what I've actually done is unlock a terrible power—one that could be used by the worst people for the worst reasons."

Charity knew how Deeley's anxious nature sometimes linked distant fears together. She had been doing better for a while—but the chimpanzee's death had shaken her, reawakening a deeper dread: that her discovery might one day be turned to harm—and that Xara might be caught in the middle.

Quietly, Charity offered reassurance. "Not in the slightest. Listen, 2099 is going to be a *great* year. Specifically because of what you've done. Okay?"

Feeling a little better, Deeley nodded. "Okay."

"Happy New Year," said Charity, leaning in to kiss Deeley on the cheek.

The two of them stepped over to Xara, Xina, and Rona. They each picked up ceremonial glasses filled with synthetic wine from a nearby table—Xara and Xina doing so virtually—then returned to the balcony. In SecondSight, New Year's celebrations from across the globe were projected onto the grounds below CAPR.

From their vantage point, it looked as though Times Square, New York City, was just a few hundred yards away, its revelers celebrating beneath bursts of digital confetti. Adjacent to it appeared Sydney, Australia, where fireworks still shimmered above the Opera House and the Sydney Harbour Bridge. Next to that, Hong Kong—its own celebrations glowing from hours earlier. Other cities stretched back toward the horizon, forming a tapestry of global unity.

That image, along with the company she kept, made Deeley happy.

***

New Year's Day dawned overcast in Particle City. Celebrations were over, and the Star Spangled Banner, flying over the Vince Quinto Administration Building, flapped in an agitated manner as winds and light rain descended on the campus. But what would define this day had nothing to do with wind or rain.

At GenX Station 10, Doctors Fukumoto and Bellan-Schwacher had forgone celebration entirely. They worked tirelessly through the night, taking turns to rest briefly while the other continued monitoring the cloning of Daisy. Each managed only a few hours of sleep, their focus unwavering as they carefully decelerated the process, which approached its final stage.

The clone underwent a composite of normal biological development, compressed and linearized to reach the form of a 12-year-old girl. Even with this expedited cloning technique, all the clone's vital systems were functioning and in good health, although the clone was in an unconscious state.

By mid-afternoon on New Year's Day, Dr. Fukumoto was taking a much-needed nap in one of the side rooms when the cloning device alerted Dr. Bellan-Schwacher to inspect the clone.

She swiftly rose from her desk at Station 10 and approached a secure door on the other side of the lab. The door's austere design hinted at its restricted access—even to the untrained eye, it was clear something important lay beyond.

After authenticating at the lock, the door opened, and she entered a clinical room where a white sheet covered a reclined, rectangular object.

Connected to the rectangular structure were the same vials that had once contained the basic elements of life—now mostly empty. Bellan-Schwacher lifted a corner of the white sheet and peered inside. Despite her extensive experience with regenerative procedures—re-growing real, living tissue, organs, and limbs from microscopic DNA—the process never ceased to captivate her. But this moment surpassed anything she had ever witnessed. For the first time, she beheld a fully cloned human—not as data, not as a scan, but as a person.

A large, synthesized placenta sustained the girl through an umbilical cord—meaning, once it was cut, the clone would have a navel. The sight of the young, cloned girl beneath the sheet filled Dr. Bellan-Schwacher with awe and reverence—an image forever etched in her memory.

After confirming the clone's vitals and verifying the success of the procedure, she lowered the sheet, gently covering the incubator once more.

Then she hurried to wake Dr. Fukumoto and placed a call. Seconds later, Secretary Brady's face appeared in her SecondSight.

"Dr. Bellan-Schwacher," said DeShawn.

"She is ready," reported Dr. Bellan-Schwacher. "And we need to move quickly!"

***

Given the New Year's Eve celebrations, Deeley had slept in and planned for a quiet, relaxing day at home. That afternoon, she settled into her condo's office, her gaze lingering on the skull—encased in glass, its certificate of provenance tucked within. As she stared, her mind drifted—from the possibility of Daisy's resurrection succeeding to the many risks her work still carried.

Eventually, overwhelmed by the swirl of thoughts, she left her office to prepare for a workout, hoping the movement might offer a brief distraction. But just after leaving her office, a priority message from Secretary Williams appeared in her SecondSight:

It's go time. Get to EOS immediately!

Adrenaline surged. Deeley didn't hesitate. She sprinted toward her front door, accidentally knocking over her helium atom decoration in the process. Scattered parts flew across the floor, and she paused just long enough to glance at them—then turned and rushed out, heart pounding, on her way to EOS with unwavering resolve.

The committee that determined who would be resurrected first also decided who would greet Daisy upon awakening: Rona and Deeley. Rona was selected for her expertise in psychology—an essential discipline for helping Daisy maintain mental health during such a disorienting return. Deeley was chosen for her gentle, unassuming nature and comely appearance, traits likely to put Daisy at ease more than anyone else on the project.

413

Though some on the committee privately voiced concerns that Deeley's growing confidence might not hold under pressure, Rona expressed trust in her, noting the distinct advantages Deeley brought, and promised to coach her in advance.

As evening approached, those on the top-secret project were alerted that the critical moment had arrived. They assembled at EOS, gathering in the control room to review the essential protocols Rona had previously trained them on.

"All of you will no doubt wish to visit with Miss Hale, but for her benefit, only at the right time," instructed Rona to the group, wearing her usual white lab coat, black pants, and a black shirt.

She continued, "For Deeley and I, one of the greatest expectations Miss Hale will have is waking up in heaven. We'll be acutely sensitive to this, while gradually guiding her toward an accurate understanding of her situation. Our approach will affirm her core beliefs—that there is an afterlife, that she is among those who care for her, and that this afterlife holds more than she might have imagined."

The room grew still with reverence as the full weight of their task settled in. They weren't just preparing to welcome a child—they were bringing to life a vision of the afterlife, long imagined by many, now entrusted to them to make real.

"Based on what we've gathered from spacetime, Daisy expects to be greeted by angels, and fortunately she has no expectation that angels are to be spiritual, ghost-like entities. Deeley and I will wear attire aligned with her expectations as best we can, and I will start transitioning her to reality. Once we've collected enough behavioral data, I will advise when and how to provide her with additional context."

"Remind us what to say if she asks to see her parents," requested James.

"We'll tell her it's not their time to join this afterlife," answered Rona. "The same goes for any friends or acquaintances she might mention."

"What if she asks for Jesus or God?" asked Bergstrom.

"Good question—but one we've covered," replied Rona. "If she asks where Jesus or God is, we'll say they don't reside in this afterlife, but that God's beauty and power are reflected throughout it. Every part of our message will be tailored to help her see this as a place prepared for her—a place to learn and grow beyond what was possible in her first life."

"Remember," she added, "I've encoded some talking points that will be sent to SecondSight when it's your turn to speak with her. These will help guide what to say—especially which modern words to avoid, since she may not understand them. When Daisy is ready, we'll gently explain that she's still on Earth—just hundreds of years after her time. Whether she struggles with the concept remains to be seen, but the data we've gathered from spacetime suggests a sharp, forward-thinking mind. She may handle it better than we think."

Rona offered a few final reminders on the messaging strategy, including a note for Deeley and herself that, based on previous mammalian resurrections, Xara had advised the child's motor skills might take a moment to fully engage—so they should be ready to assist if needed.

Taking a quiet breath as the weight of the moment settled on her, Rona concluded, "It has been the greatest privilege of my life to be part of this project. And an honor to work alongside each of you. May we do Miss Hale justice when she returns."

As the minutes passed, those in the control room felt a cocktail of excitement and trepidation. Champagne—real and replicated—waited on ice, should success come.

The emotional tension spiked when an alert came through: five vehicles had arrived at EOS—four unmarked military escorts surrounding a small medical van carrying the clone of Daisy Hale. The van was fully equipped to keep the clone sustained and unconscious. Before transport, the umbilical cord connecting her to the synthetic placenta had been cut, and the resulting navel treated to swiftly heal.

Inside the van, the clone lay in the deepest sleep, strapped to a gurney with a sleek intravenous port embedded in her right arm, delivering nutrients and stabilization agents. Her vitals glowed softly on a sleek med-interface built into the upper frame of the gurney—an analog redundancy in a world grown too used to augmentation.

Doctors Bellan-Schwacher and Fukumoto accompanied the clone they had created, their expressions a quiet mix of pride and apprehension. The military escort was unaware of the van's specific contents, but given recent media attention, Dr. Strock's testimony, and the protesters outside the Supercollider, they likely had a strong sense of what they were guarding.

In the control room, Bergstrom, James, Xara, and Charity sat alongside Julian Kaminski, Secretaries Brady and Williams, and Deputy Secretary of Defense Thorowell. One last guest was still expected: President Gates.

Upon being informed that the clone was complete and memory restoration imminent, the President instructed his staff to clear his calendar—without explanation. He arrived at EOS just minutes before the clone, his Secret Service detail remaining in the hallway outside. Given the advanced security of the facility, it was deemed sufficient for them to monitor his safety remotely—an arrangement that also served to protect the secrecy of the work being conducted inside.

When the control room door opened, the team rose in unison.

"Mr. President!" came the collective greeting.

"A team destined to be remembered for as long as history endures," the President declared, his voice steady with admiration. "The hour has come—and I wouldn't miss this moment for anything in the world."

Carlos stepped forward to welcome him. The two men shook hands, locking eyes with quiet satisfaction.

After greeting everyone individually, the President asked, "Where's Deeley?"

"Deeley and Dr. Carmichael are preparing themselves for their roles in meeting Miss Hale when she arises," replied Carlos.

As the team awaited the arrival of the clone in Elysium, James stood at the observation deck, gazing outward. He wore a sleek, tailored suit of advanced thermal fabric, layered beneath a sharp black coat designed for warmth without bulk. His structured trousers matched the understated elegance of the moment, and his polished boots added a subtle flair.

He beheld Gaia, the quantum network of processors above it, the translucent floor surrounding it, and directly underneath Gaia, a new element: a reclined throne—designed by Xara specifically for Daisy's resurrection—fashioned from adaptive crystals that could shift in shape and angle. A transparent, cushioned layer covered the crystals, offering comfort despite the throne's alien appearance. Together, Gaia and the throne looked like artifacts bequeathed from a higher civilization.

As James studied Gaia and the crystalline throne, he wondered what the great scientists of centuries past might think if they could witness such engineering. If they could see the surreal hardware—technology that seemed light-years ahead of their time—and meet Xara, the sentient genius who helped create it all, would they believe they stood in the presence of gods? James felt energized by the prospect that revered scientists from the past might soon return from the grave and actually share their thoughts on the matter.

After the van carrying the clone securely entered EOS, its rear doors opened, a ramp descended, and the two GenX scientists walked down beside the gurney as it autonomously made its way to the ground. Neither the clone, the gurney, nor the scientists could be seen, for a mobile privacy screen enclosed them, shielding all contents from view as the gurney advanced with smooth precision. Robotic soldiers scanned and verified the team through non-visual means before escorting them to a service door leading into the Elysian Fields behind Gaia. One of the robots opened the door, revealing the quiet paradise prepared for Daisy's rebirth. Upon entry, the privacy screen automatically collapsed, revealing the scientists and the gurney—its curtains still drawn.

As the gurney glided along the short path from the service door to the glittering, imposing crystals of Gaia, both GenX doctors walked in step beside it, struck by a humbling awareness—they were in the presence of science that far surpassed their own. Standing beside the crystalline throne as the gurney approached were Rona and Deeley, both adorned in elegant white robes Rona had prepared to affirm Daisy's belief that she would be greeted by angels.

When the service door shut and the gurney reached its destination, the doctors drew back the curtain. There lay the clone of Daisy Hale, dressed in a flowing white gown, her light blonde hair fanned softly around her shoulders, her small hands resting gently on her waist, and her bare feet peeking out beneath the hem. She breathed slowly, suspended in the deepest of sleep, with not a single memory yet restored. Her expression was peaceful—almost too still, almost artificial. Yet physically, she was the very picture of health and innocence.

The moment Rona first laid eyes on her, she instinctively raised both hands to her mouth in disbelief. A fully formed, beautiful human child lay before her. In a stunned, reverent whisper, she said, "My God. She's perfect."

Deeley stood with one hand on her heart and the other over her mouth, awestruck by the miracle before her—a girl reborn from a synthetic speck of the original dust from which she'd first been made centuries ago. Her posture also betrayed rising cortisol levels; the fear of failure loomed large. This was uncharted territory, and the stakes had never been higher.

"Deeley, if—" Rona caught herself. "*When* this is successful, you'll feel a rush of emotions. But in that moment, you *must* keep them in check. The child will need to see confidence and strength in us to feel safe in this new world. Understood?"

"I understand," said Deeley, swallowing hard, her cheeks flushing with nervous tension.

"Now is the time for professionalism," reinforced Rona.

In the control room, those watching the human clone for the first time reacted with awe, many echoing Rona's earlier words. President Gates, however, remained silent. He was as moved as the others, but beneath his composed exterior lingered a deep concern that Zhang Jun might soon decide to eliminate Xara. This was the moment all his decisions had led to—and while he wondered about the outcome of Daisy's resurrection, he also wondered what his choices would mean for the world, for humanity, and for himself.

In Elysium, Bellan-Schwacher checked the clone's vitals, then gently detached the intravenous port from her arm. Fukumoto stepped in, carefully lifting the girl and carrying her to the reclined crystal throne.

As he laid her down, the throne's adaptive crystals shifted in real time—subtly reshaping themselves under Xara's command to fit the contours of the clone's body. The transparent, gel-like surface adjusted with them, offering a soft and stable cushion. Additional crystals rose and repositioned around her to hold her securely in place, including a custom array around her head to ensure it remained gently but firmly supported.

In the control room, Secretary Brady grew uneasy. Already anxious about Zhang Jun's potential move against Xara, he felt his stomach tighten as the clone was placed upon the throne. The sight drew his thoughts back to the failed mammalian trials—their gruesome endings vivid in memory. He knew all too well that this human attempt carried the lowest probability of success among all the memory restoration experiments so far.

With the clone reclined securely on the crystalline throne, Doctors Fukumoto and Bellan-Schwacher, along with Rona and Deeley, made their way to the secure observation room to monitor the procedure and oversee the clone's vitals. The gurney accompanied them autonomously, remaining available as a support measure. Once in place, Fukumoto communicated to the control room that all was ready and to proceed without delay.

Xara turned to Gates. "Mr. President. The Supercollider has achieved Grand Unification Energy. Spacetime is open. With your permission, shall we proceed to resurrect Miss Hale?"

Gates paused. He knew this was a moment larger than anything he had ever sanctioned—perhaps larger than he could fully comprehend. Everyone held their breath.

With quiet resolve, the President said, "Xara, I believe in you. I always have. You've worked wonders to date. Please—this moment—give us your best."

Xara nodded solemnly and vanished. She scanned the clone, then, with the Supercollider at full power, directed Chronos' beams into the quantum black holes generated by the particle collisions. From the dark, translucent floor, pinpoints of brilliant light converged at a single focal point—where Daisy's soul would be drawn from spacetime.

It didn't take long for Xara to find Daisy in the historical dimension. Suddenly, the crystalline arms of Gaia, suspended above the clone, unfurled like an inverted mechanical flower. As they opened, they began to spin—first slowly, then accelerating into a dizzying, phenomenal speed unlike anything seen before. Nearby birds in Elysium scattered in alarm, and the wind generated by the whirling crystals caused the nearest tree branches to sway.

Once the crystalline arms reached full velocity, invisible beams of energy converged upon the clone's head. It marked the most anxious moment. Deeley clutched Rona's arm, who in turn took Deeley's hand. Doctors Fukumoto and Bellan-Schwacher stood silently, focused on the clone's vital metrics in SecondSight. In the control room, nervous energy bubbled up—most were fidgeting, eyes fixed on the screen.

The beams manipulated neurons in the clone's brain, activating dormant pathways in preparation for entangling Daisy's memories—all while the girl lay still and silent.

As the process unfolded, time seemed to slow to a crawl.

Then—SecondSight registered a massive influx of dark energy, infinitely complex, flooding into the clone's skull. Her limbs began to twitch and jerk within their restraints, triggering a jolt of adrenaline in DeShawn and others watching.

Without warning, the clone's mouth opened, and her body tensed within the crystalline embrace:

A tall, fair woman knelt in the open field. She smiled and stretched out her hand to me ...

The oddest and most comical creatures I had ever seen. Spindly legs held up their plump, feathered bodies as they strutted about, letting out the most delightfully silly sounds ...

He was tall and could do anything. He was often occupied, but whenever he was near, it was a joyful time ...

It was bitter cold, full of pain and hunger, with little to eat ...

"Why does the sky shine blue?"

He lay in bed, ill; the doctor was there, and the adults spoke in grave tones about things ...

Sadness and tears. They laid him in the earth. I was so angry. I didn't want him to go down there—not at all ...

She stroked my hair as I lay in bed by candlelight and stayed with me until I fell asleep ...

Stars. So many, and so bright. Counting—more than 2,000 of them. So beautiful! What lies out there among them ...?

More sadness and tears. This time, they laid her in the ground, too. Numbness and confusion ...

The clone's right arm began to twitch within the restraint of the crystals. That alone was alarming—but then something far worse appeared: a slow drop of blood slid from the clone's right nostril. The sight struck abject horror into everyone observing. Deeley was so overwhelmed by the harrowing sign that she felt faint, every heartbeat pounding hot and fast in her ears, deafening in its panic.

"Check the clone!" barked DeShawn via SecondSight to Doctors Fukumoto and Bellan-Schwacher. "What's going on?!"

The two GenX scientists scrambled to analyze her vitals remotely, eyes darting across endless data streams.

"I ... I've never seen neural activity like this before," stammered Dr. Bellan-Schwacher. "I don't know what to make of it. All I can say is—her brain is still functional. Her vitals and brain activity are strained, but still within limits!"

Hearing that, Gates—his chest tight with panic—gave the order without hesitation. "Keep the process going. Do not stop!"

Already operating at its maximum intended speed, Gaia's design was suddenly overridden by Xara, who injected additional power from the fusion reactor. The crystalline arms accelerated to a terrifying velocity, generating fierce winds that bent the nearest trees, scattered leaves through the air, and sent more birds fleeing in alarm—all while dark energy from the emitters manipulated matter in the clone's brain at the atomic level.

Deeley glanced at Gaia through SecondSight and quickly analyzed the readings: it was operating at 119% capacity. She didn't know how much longer that could be sustained. Her heart pounded. Eyes wide with fear, she turned back to the clone.

Lots of new bedrooms—some in houses, some not—never for long— none as happy as the first ...

We talked, we held hands, we helped each other. She was my best friend.

So many people on the streets. Some kind, many not. Fear ...

Flap. Glide. Flap. Soar. Just push against the air and soar! I know in my heart—man will fly!

"Twenty-eight lamps. Fourteen on that side. Fourteen on the other."

They wore unusual clothes and hats, but they were kind and gave my best friend and me a new home ...

Teachers. Spelling. Reading. Numbers ...

Beautiful singing. Jesus and Mary. Peace, at last, knowing Father and Mother are in a better place ...

Sunshine and breeze. Birds in song. A merry time at play ...

Very sick. Their voices remain steady, but I sense their concern ...

Very sick. Darkness coming. Darkness. Slipping into it. But—a light. Reaching for it! Wanting the light. It grows stronger! Brighter! The light is very strong now ... Ah! It is here!

Chronos and Gaia suddenly powered down. Gaia's spinning crystalline arms decelerated, coming to a halt as they closed above the crystal throne. The trees stilled. Yet the clone remained motionless, save for another drop of blood coming from her nose. No one in the control room spoke. Silent gazes lingered on the still child, the moment seeming to bring time itself to a standstill.

Xara, though fatigued, activated a set of emitters on one of Gaia's minor upper arms, using dark energy to carefully remove the blood from

Daisy's lip and nose and cauterize the source of the bleeding. Once the blood was discreetly relocated out of sight, Xara released the constraints around the clone's body, then—drained beyond her limits—retreated to rest.

Silence.

Gates stared at the clone, a torrent of uncertainty flooding his mind and leaving him adrift in a sea of confusion—devoid of words, devoid of action.

DeShawn shifted his gaze from the clone to the floor of the control room, bracing himself for the very outcome they had all feared. The absence of Xara, who had yet to comment on the success or lack thereof of the procedure, only deepened the sense of dread.

The GenX doctors frantically reviewed the clone's vitals. Though her heart was still beating, and she was taking slow, shallow breaths, the software module analyzing neural data flagged a critical anomaly. The two doctors exchanged a look—one of stark realization: they might be the bearers of tragic news.

"Uh …" Dr. Fukumoto cleared his throat, his heart sinking. "The neural structure of the clone cannot … be verified as normal."

"Did the procedure fail?!" demanded DeShawn.

After a tense pause, he answered, "Analysis suggests it has."

Deeley turned her eyes from the haunting stillness of the clone. Her sorrow, already overwhelming, broke through at last—she collapsed to her knees, swallowed by grief. Gates shut his eyes tight, as if doing so could block out the unfolding nightmare. Carlos stepped beside him and placed a steadying hand on his shoulder.

"I'm sorry, Mr. President," apologized Carlos. "I truly am. If she is beyond recovery, we do, however, need to remove the body and manufacture a cremation pod in an appropriate room as soon as possible."

"Well," stated Bergstrom, upset but more composed than the rest, "this is the price we have to pay to make consequential progress."

"Is there any chance this is a false positive?" asked Carlos, his voice low but urgent. "Please check again."

Dr. Fukumoto reviewed all the data once more, with Dr. Bellan-Schwacher doing the same. The two conferred quietly for several moments, until Fukumoto shook his head.

Through SecondSight, Bellan-Schwacher addressed those in the control room, her voice quiet and careful.

"While her heart beats and she breathes, it's only due to autonomic regulation from the medulla oblongata. Her cerebral cortex has been … irreparably compromised. There is a total absence of cortical response—her brain is … it's no longer functionally viable."

A look of deep disappointment settled across Carlos's face.

Gates, pained but resolute—knowing the situation would need to be swiftly concealed—nodded to Carlos to proceed with cremation.

Dr. Fukumoto and Dr. Bellan-Schwacher exchanged a solemn glance after receiving the order from Carlos. Carrying the weight of disappointment that all felt, they avoided eye contact with the grieving Deeley as well as Rona, then opened the door of the observation room and stepped into Elysium. Behind them, the gurney followed autonomously, silent and precise, a lingering symbol of what had been lost.

The silence in the chamber was total, broken only by the hesitant footsteps of the two GenX doctors as they made their way to the crystal throne. Bellan-Schwacher hesitated, her body slowing as a flicker on the med-interface in SecondSight caught the corner of her vision. She turned her head, breath held, staring. A blink. A blip. No—two. Her heart stuttered. She took a step backward, eyes fixed now. Something was changing.

"Wait!" cried Dr. Bellan-Schwacher as her neural analysis module abruptly rebooted, revealing normal neural function in Daisy. "Ahh! The module was never trained on this procedure—it didn't know how to interpret the data and inferred a completely inaccurate reading! But it's reassessed, and everything appears to be in order. We have—"

All at once, Daisy gasped and opened her eyes. She inhaled sharply, as though starved of oxygen. Stirring from the depths of unconsciousness, her breaths emerged in ragged bursts—echoes of a 300-year slumber. Her eyes, unaccustomed to the light, darted across the room, drinking in the unfamiliar surroundings, searching for the paradise she had long yearned for.

Gates exhaled a steady, controlled breath, his posture softening as the tension of the moment released its grip. His eyes glistened from the sheer magnitude of what had just occurred. He lowered his gaze briefly, collecting himself, then looked up with quiet reverence, his faith renewed—as if he now believed with certainty that the miracle was unfolding. Around him, in the hushed confines of the control room, fear and uncertainty began to dissolve, replaced by a rising sense of hope that the procedure may have truly succeeded.

Still in shock in the observation room, Deeley felt the first waves of sweet relief begin to wash over her. Rona turned to her, took her hands, looked straight into her eyes, and exclaimed, "She survived! This means our time has come! *Strength now,* okay?"

Visibly trembling from the emotional storm, Deeley wiped the tears from her cheeks, steadied her breath, and nodded.

"Follow the language cues in SecondSight," added Rona, already turning toward the door. "It'll help you use words she can understand."

With Fukumoto and Bellan-Schwacher—along with the autonomous gurney—now swiftly and discreetly back in the observation room, Deeley and Rona exited and approached Daisy cautiously, coming from an angle so as not to startle her. Xara gradually adjusted the crystal formation beneath Daisy into an upright position. The child's breathing had calmed, and she was growing more alert by the second. Her gaze wandered—still dazed, but already fascinated—as she beheld the serene beauty of Elysium.

Daisy looked down at herself, inspecting her hands, arms, and feet, then slowly moved her limbs and ran her fingers over her white gown with childlike wonder. Finally, she noticed Deeley and Rona drawing near.

Dressed in their beautiful white robes, Deeley and Rona stood just a few yards from the child. As Daisy's eyes met theirs, both women were struck with awe. Daisy was real—every limb, every hair, every cell. And the intelligence and emotion reflected in her gaze confirmed a singular truth: she was human, and she was alive again.

Just two months earlier, this girl on the throne had been nothing more than chemicals in vials and water in a container. Now she was a living, breathing person. And not just any person, but someone who had once walked the Earth centuries ago—her very mind and soul now entangled with the one that had animated her first sojourn on Earth. That staggering reality landed fully in their minds as the child spoke:

"They said you would come!"

Her voice, laced with an antiquated accent, carried the essence of innocence, reinforcing the triumph of the most ambitious experiment in human history.

"You are the angels, are you not?"

According to plan, Rona was meant to speak first—but she couldn't. The sheer beauty of this moment, the child's innocence, the overwhelming magic of standing before someone newly resurrected—all of it rendered her speechless. Despite all her preparation, Rona was so overcome that she choked up and couldn't get the words out.

"What troubles you?" asked the child softly, her gaze turning to Deeley for reassurance.

Deeley stepped forward, rising to meet this rarest of all moments with a voice steadier than she felt inside.

"Even the angels can be overcome with joy. We are so happy to have you here with us, Daisy!"

In the control room, Charity beamed through tears. The resurrection had worked—but more than that, Deeley had stepped into the light, steady and sure, in the moment that mattered most.

Daisy alighted from the crystals and carefully stood, steadying herself on the crystal throne for support. As expected, balancing took her a few seconds, as if her muscle memory were being reactivated in real time. Tentatively, she stepped forward with her right foot, testing the motion. Deeley, feeling her anxieties melt in the warmth of an instant kinship with Daisy, remained close, ready to catch her if she faltered. But Daisy's footing held steady, and she began walking slowly toward Deeley and Rona.

At last she lowered into a deep curtsy, her movements precise despite a slight tremor in her hands. She lingered, uncertain whether to rise. But when she finally looked up, her eyes met the kind, reassuring gazes of the two women—the angels she had longed to meet. Her heart swelled. Forgetting herself, she stepped forward and wrapped her arms around them both, her small frame pressing tightly against theirs. Deeley and Rona returned the embrace, overwhelmed with the joy of this miracle.

Afterward, Daisy stepped back and studied them with curiosity.

"I am pleased you do not have wings! Do all angels look as you do?"

Having just begun to regain her composure, Rona responded with a loving smile. "Thank you, Daisy. Yes, angels appear just like people. I'm Rona, and this is Deeley. Welcome, my dear!"

"Rona and Deeley ... such heavenly names indeed!" said Daisy, her voice light with admiration. Her attention drifted to her gown, and a delighted smile spread across her face. It was clear she had never worn anything so exquisite in her former life.

As strength and confidence in her new body grew, Daisy gave a joyful twirl. The gown flared and flowed around her, and she watched it spin with wide-eyed wonder. Turning back to face the crystalline surface, she caught her reflection. Studying it, her face lit up with quiet awe. "I feel beautiful!"

Rona, gazing at her with pure adoration, murmured softly, almost to herself, "Yes, Daisy … you *are* beautiful."

In the control room, the emotional roller coaster had finally come to a stop—just as it had for Rona and Deeley below. What had seemed like tragedy had instead become a miracle. As the truth took hold, and the impossible became reality, the weight of what had transpired came crashing down on those who had borne witness. The beauty, majesty, and sheer wonder of seeing a human from centuries past brought back to life—especially a child so full of innocence—awakened a sense of gratitude and awe unlike anything they had ever known. Even Bergstrom was visibly moved.

Kaminski savored the moment, watching awe, disbelief, and raw emotion play across the faces in the room. Daisy's body was the culmination of his company's work—a triumph that not only redefined the limits of science but also vindicated his father's legacy. Just beyond, in the observation room, the scientists he had entrusted with the task—Doctors Fukumoto and Bellan-Schwacher—stood in stunned reverence, the surreal reality settling in: the human clone they had created now walked, spoke, and lived once more.

James was the first to speak, his voice trembling with joy. "There are no words—no words to describe this!"

After others spoke, attempting to put the moment into words, Xara finally reappeared. The toll of the exercise was evident in her posture, exhaustion written across her face. At her appearance, the room erupted into cheers and applause. Energized by the praise, she offered a grateful yet humble smile.

"Thank you!" she acknowledged, bowing her head gently. "But I suggest we direct our gratitude to those who made this discovery possible. Of course, our thanks must go to Deeley. And, at the risk of sounding self-serving, I also believe we should recognize the visionary who had the foresight and determination to ensure the necessary technology was developed. President Gates, thank you!"

The room again filled with applause, cheers, and even a few embraces for their President. After the wave of celebration settled, the President spoke softly and humbly. "Thank you. Thank you. This is simply the fulfillment of Quinto's vision. He is far more responsible for today than I am."

"Then I propose we bring him back and thank him in person!" exclaimed Bergstrom, raising a champagne bottle.

"Hear, hear!" shouted James, as the room burst into cheers once more, most having already begun to indulge in the wine.

After several moments of jubilation, Xara approached DeShawn. Though he'd carried a measure of caution toward her since the upgrade, he was impressed by how capably she had performed—especially under the weight of knowing that Zhang Jun suspected she'd been modified. Having witnessed her success, he was now eager to speak with her."Mr. Secretary," greeted Xara, a playfully smug look on her face.

"Well done, Xara! Well done!" he exclaimed, his smile lingering from the euphoria of their triumph. He even extended his hand to her for a virtual shake.

"You'll be delighted to know that for the next human resurrection, I now offer you a 99.8% chance of successful memory restoration!"

"Outstanding, Xara," replied DeShawn, still holding her hand. "That's what I hoped to hear."

***

Daisy was escorted into the Elysian Fields by Deeley and Rona, whose unfamiliar accents charmed her. She beheld the graceful trees, breathed in the scent of countless flowers, and glimpsed darting fish in the water. Since it was evening, the bioluminescent trees were aglow, captivating the imagination of the newly resurrected girl. She had never seen anything like them in her previous life—so much so that she truly believed she had entered heaven.

At that moment, a dove flew out of a tree, catching Daisy's attention. She watched it carefully as it soared—seemingly defying gravity—before landing gracefully on the branch of another tree. Suddenly, Daisy's eyes widened, a question lighting up her expression. "Can one take flight here?"

"What do you mean?" replied Deeley gently.

"Can one, through use of some constructed device, take flight—like unto the dove? Their bodies, their wings, their movement—all are designed to naturally elevate and convey the bird through the air. Man ought to be able to fashion the same."

"You mean it's not magic that lets them fly," said Deeley, recalling Daisy's curiosity on the subject in spacetime, "but how their weight, shape, and wings move together to rise against the Earth's pull?"

"Verily!" beamed Daisy, as though Deeley had just confirmed a long-held secret.

With a smile, Deeley nodded, "Yes, people here know how to fly!"

Daisy leaped for joy.

"How is it accomplished?"

"There are different ways," explained Deeley. "Some carriages are shaped like birds. Their wings don't flap, but they hold power—a force that lifts them into the sky."

"Oh! I do understand!" exclaimed Daisy, eager to share her clarity. In that moment, a unique bond between them deepened.

"And there are other ways it is done," added Rona. "In time, we shall show you."

As Daisy walked with Deeley and Rona, she skipped and danced. She was absolutely delighted!

"I cherish this garden!" proclaimed Daisy, standing on a knoll, having taken in the beauty of the surroundings. "Shall I dwell here now?"

"Yes," answered Rona. "There's a house nearby, and all has been made ready for you."

A curious desire could be seen in Daisy's eyes. She asked, "Are my father and mother to be found in that house?"

Deeley discreetly looked at Rona in anticipation as to how she was going to answer.

"Their time to be here has not yet come," responded Rona calmly. "But that day will come. When it does, what would you wish to do?"

"I would very much like to dwell with them again."

"When their time comes, then you may."

Daisy seemed to take the answer well. After a moment, she followed up with another question, "Is Mima well?"

With her extensive preparation for this day, along with her enjoyment of her role as "angel," Rona handled the question with relative ease. "I can see how much you love Mima. Of all the family and friends you had in your life, Daisy, you are special. You are the first to come to this new place. In time, your loved ones will follow. There is much for you to learn here—and when you do, you will be able to help teach those things to the ones you love."

"Is that truly how things are?" asked Daisy as the revelation commenced a paradigm shift in her mind.

"Yes, my dear," said Rona softly.

Daisy stared at some nearby tulips for a long moment, clearly in deep thought. She then broke her silence by asking, "Mary and Jesus do not dwell here, do they?"

Having previously anticipated the question, Rona answered, "That is true. This is not the place where they live. Think of it as a place much like the one you came from—but in a different time. A new place to live, to learn, to grow, to be kind, and to be loved. And soon, you shall meet many whom you have long hoped to see—but all in good time."

Daisy took this revelation quite well, and it became apparent why when she shared the following, "Sister Henry used to tell me in secret that, though the priests and Holy Fathers preached about heaven, they were only guessing at what it might be and did not truly know. She said that to do unto others as I would have them do unto me was the most important thing for the soul and that if I did so, all would be well. She never spoke of such things to Father Murphy, for she said he would not agree and would be displeased. But she told this to Mima and me a few times … and now I see how wise she was!"

"Sister Henry sounds like a wise sister indeed," replied Rona, encouraged by what she had just heard. "Do you know what the word 'angel' means?"

After a moment, Daisy guessed, "Helper?"

"Yes," said Rona. "Angels are helpers and teachers, sent to care for others and show them what is needful. That is what Deeley and I are here to do for you. Is there anything you are in want of just now?"

"I am starting to hunger," answered Daisy.

"Shall we take you to your new home now, and share a meal together?" said Rona.

"Oh, yes, please!" responded Daisy with enthusiasm at the prospect of a meal in her new heavenly home.

"Come with us," said Rona.

The trio descended from the knoll to the primary pathway that connected the crystal throne to the double doors of Elysium's mansion, roughly 300 yards apart. Shortly after they reached the path, with Daisy in the middle, she slipped her hands into theirs, one on either side. Her small fingers clasped theirs tightly, as though afraid they might let go. For the last three years of her first life, her feet had carried her on heavy, often lonely steps. But now, walking with her body restored, her angels by her side, her spirit felt light, unburdened, brimming with boundless possibilities.

As she held the child's hand, Rona shed another tear of joy. She genuinely felt like an angel, destined to watch over this child. Deeley's cheeks, too, were streaked with joy once more—joy of this magical moment—and of the wonder her work was beginning to bring to the world.

***

In the control room, the jubilation had not faded. Though the cheering had subsided—replaced by quiet observation of Daisy and her angels in Elysium—the hearts of those present brimmed with rejoicing and wonder as they witnessed life after death become reality. The celebration swelled again when Doctors Fukumoto and Bellan-Schwacher joined them, their pivotal contributions to the moment honored with heartfelt applause.

Eventually, the moment came when President Gates addressed the group.

"Words fail to express our deepest gratitude for all that you have accomplished this day. The world now moves forward on an unspeakably wondrous trajectory because of the remarkable work you've done within these walls."

The group received the compliment with quiet pride.

"Secretaries Brady, Williams, and I will now be honored to spend some time with Daisy. But I very much look forward to celebrating this achievement more formally with all of you in the near future."

With that, the President and the two Secretaries embraced each person in the control room, one by one, then exited to a final round of applause from those remaining.

***

Daisy and her two angels arrived at Elysium's mansion, the ornate double doors thereof heralding a new beginning, a new world of discovery and possibility.

"I have never seen doors so beautiful!" remarked Daisy. "St. Peter's Parish does not compare!"

"Let us show you inside," invited Rona.

Rona and Deeley each opened one of the grand double doors, revealing Daisy's new home. As the entryway came into view, Daisy beheld a pristine and majestic space. For a child from the late 18th century—who had only glimpsed a small portion of the architecture of her time—this late-21st-century mansion, designed by a super-intelligent entity, appeared nothing short of divine. Her jaw dropped as she took in the sweeping staircase, glittering chandelier, elegant furnishings, radiant lighting, polished floors, intricate wall contours, and art-lined halls. Slowly, she wandered forward, utterly entranced, as each remarkable detail of the futuristic home revealed itself.

"This is my home?" she whispered, her eyes misting with joy, seeking reassurance.

"Yes," answered Deeley, smiling warmly. "For the start of this new chapter, this is where you'll live. And there are many more rooms to see!"

"We'll show you around," added Rona. "But first—would you like to meet a few more people?"

"Oh yes!" responded Daisy, wiping a tear from her eye, still enthralled by the beauty that surrounded her.

Rona and Deeley led her into the parlor, a warmly lit room just off the entryway. Plush chairs and a curved settee faced a marble fireplace, its soft glow dancing on the polished floor. Lighting above mimicked the gentle warmth of candlelight, creating a quiet, inviting space.

Upon arriving, Rona said gently, "Deeley will stay with you. I'll be back in a moment." She then exited the room.

Daisy looked up at Deeley and asked, "Whom shall I be meeting?"

"Some kind people who care for this place," replied Deeley with a reassuring smile. "They wish to welcome you."

"Are they angels too?"

"Yes, Daisy," answered Deeley warmly. "They are here to help and care for others."

A moment later, Rona returned, followed by President Gates and Secretaries Brady and Williams, all dressed in white suits with matching shirts, ties, and shoes. Like the others, the President had already been briefed by Rona on what could be communicated to Daisy. And while the others relied on SecondSight language guides to aid their interactions when needed, Gates—unable to wear mixed-reality lenses outside the White House—would rely on his own extensive knowledge of the Founding Era to bridge the gap.

"Daisy," said Rona, "allow me to introduce you to David, DeShawn, and Carlos."

"Pleased to make your acquaintance!" greeted Daisy, curtsying to her three guests. Her antiquated American accent and the etiquette of a bygone era immediately struck DeShawn and Carlos. President Gates, drawing not only from his expertise in the Founding Era but also from his review of spacetime recordings, had some sense of what to expect in Daisy's tone and manner—but even he was astonished to witness it in person.

DeShawn, usually stoic, found himself disarmed in the presence of this beautiful, flesh-and-blood specter from the past. Carlos stood in quiet awe, beaming with joy as tears welled in his eyes.

President Gates was ecstatic—not only to meet a resurrected individual, but one from an era of American history he deeply admired. Stepping forward with a smile, he bowed gracefully and declared, "Welcome, Miss Daisy Hale!"

"Thank you, sir!" replied Daisy with another graceful curtsy. The President could hardly believe his eyes or ears. Overcome with emotion, he opened his arms for an embrace, and Daisy stepped into them without hesitation. As they parted, Gates studied her face, wonder still etched across his own.

After a moment, he asked,

"How do you feel?"

"I feel most at health—more than I believe I have ever felt before, sir."

"That is good," said the President warmly.

"The people here are most kind!" exclaimed Daisy, still in a frame of mind that made every person and place feel magical.

DeShawn and Carlos bowed to her in turn, and the President gestured for everyone to sit. Once they were seated, he presented a gift to the young girl.

"This is for you, Daisy."

"How beautiful," she remarked, gently taking the box in her hands and marveling at its delicate bow. The comment endeared her to the President all the more, knowing that such wrapping wasn't customary in her time—only becoming common among the wealthy nearly a century later. He anticipated she might need help knowing what to do with it.

"The gift is inside. Just pull this ribbon, and when it's loose, lift the lid from the box."

Daisy followed the instructions with delight. The moment she lifted the lid and gazed upon its contents, her eyes widened in surprise, and her face lit up. It was a dress, light pink. As she carefully took it out of the box, it unfolded, revealing elegant drapes and accents.

"Oh! Thank you ever so much!" exclaimed Daisy, holding the dress to her chest. The hearts of those present swelled as they witnessed her pure delight and gratitude. Daisy, however, had no idea that the clothing also contained comprehensive technology for monitoring her health.

She looked down at the empty box, lid, and bow, admiring them as though they too were treasures. "Are these also to be mine?"

"Yes, they are yours," the President replied warmly.

"And there is something else we wish to give you," added DeShawn, stepping forward with another gift.

"Such kindness!"

Again, Daisy marveled at the wrapping before carefully opening it. Inside DeShawn's gift were slip-on shoes with a strap and bow, all in light pink to match the dress.

"These are beautiful!" exclaimed Daisy. "Oh, how I adore them!"

"One more gift from me," said Carlos with a smile, as he approached with another wrapped box.

"Oh, thank you!"

She opened Carlos's gift to find a doll. Her jaw dropped, and she slowly lifted the doll from the box as though afraid of harming it. The doll wore a delicate dress of pale blue satin, trimmed with lace, and her blonde curls were pulled back with a tiny ribbon. Her painted eyes were bright and kind, her skin smooth as porcelain, and her tiny fingers shaped with astonishing care. After gazing at the doll for a moment, Daisy declared, "She is the most beautiful doll ever made!"

"What will you call her?" asked Carlos.

Daisy paused in thought.

"Matilda. She shall be called Matilda, after one of the Sisters she brings to mind. Oh, I ought never to have been so fearful of dying! Everything and everyone here is so joyful!"

"How was your journey—from your sickbed to here?" asked Rona, her voice filled with curiosity.

"I was truly afraid," answered Daisy softly. "But when I passed, I awoke here."

Rona leaned forward, intrigued. "Can you tell us more?"

"Not an hour ago, I lay ill in bed," recounted Daisy. "Then all was dark—and suddenly, the light brought me here!"

It was a striking revelation to an age-old philosophical question. Though Daisy had been dead for over 300 years, her experience suggested that memory restoration rendered resurrection as immediate from the individual's perspective. All who heard her quietly marveled at the thought.

***

Daisy and her companions spent several minutes admiring the gifts and deepening their bond. Soon after, President Gates approached Deeley and invited her to join him in a neighboring room. Delighted to see him again, Deeley gladly accepted.

"Pleasure to see you again, Mr. President!"

"Do you remember what I said when we first met?"

Deeley nodded humbly. The President looked over at Daisy, as an emphasis on what Deeley's work achieved, then back at Deeley. "I was right. Everything will be framed in terms of me meeting you, and not you meeting me!"

Stepping forward, Deeley embraced the President in gratitude.

As they parted, President Gates placed his hands on her shoulders and expressed, "Look at all you and your colleagues have achieved! My most sincere and heartfelt congratulations, Deeley!"

Her heart was full. "Thank you, Mr. President! But, truth be told, Xara took over the final phases of the research and will likely oversee everything from here. I might be out of a job!"

The President smiled. "I doubt it. Still, when I leave office, my old job as a historian might be obsolete too. Perhaps an entirely new field will emerge—comparing historical artwork to what the real thing actually looked like."

Deeley laughed.

"How do you feel about what you've accomplished?" asked Gates.

"Right now, I'm experiencing a sense of validation beyond anything I've ever known. But most of all, I'm overwhelmed with gratitude—gratitude for being part of CAPR and this incredible team."

"I'm so happy for you," replied the President, beaming.

"What about you?" asked Deeley. "You fulfilled Quinto's Challenge on time—with a couple of years to spare. It's all the result of your leadership, and not even through one full term in office. I don't know of any presidents who've served two terms and achieved so much."

"That's very kind, Deeley. But I don't think it's fully sunk in. Can you believe that someone from the 18th century, who died over 300 years ago, has *literally* been raised from the dead—and is sitting just a few yards away, full of joy and health?"

Deeley looked back toward the parlor, where Daisy remained seated near the fireplace, her small frame glowing in the soft light.

"I *am* having trouble believing it," admitted Deeley softly. "I was so afraid the resurrection would fail. Now … it's all so surreal."

"It is," agreed Gates. "As for fulfilling Quinto's Challenge before the century is out, as I said, it's still sinking in—but I'm more satisfied than I can say. That said, to fully fulfill his Challenge—and within his time-frame—I believe we'll need to go public. But that likely means replicating this success with other humans first. For now, I'm content to focus our immediate attention on Miss Hale and tend to her well-being."

Rona approached. "Mr. President, I haven't had the chance to say this to Deeley yet—but Deeley, thank you. You came through and delivered exactly what Daisy needed when I lost it. Sorry I couldn't keep it together when she first woke up. There are reasons—personal ones—I can explain another time."

"It's fine, don't worry," said Deeley.

"Had you not stepped in the way you did when Daisy first saw us," continued Rona, "her confidence might not have been set on the right path. Well done!"

The number of days competing for the best day of Deeley's life was growing.

"Mr. President," said Rona, "my apologies, but Daisy needs her angel back now."

As Deeley turned to leave, her eyes briefly met the President's. Something unspoken seemed to pass between them—fleeting and unde-fined, yet impossible to ignore.

***

Deeley and Rona led the party into the dining room to be seated. The room was refined and softly lit, with cream-colored walls, high vaulted ceilings, and a delicate chandelier casting warm light over everything. Daisy sat first at the head of an elegant crystal table with a crimson-red tablecloth and silver accents on its legs. She was ecstatic. Once the President and the Secretaries were seated, Deeley and Rona excused themselves, returning shortly thereafter with food and tea for Daisy and her guests.

Gates watched them set the table, his eyes shining. All his concerns—Zhang Jun's suspicions, the coming campaign against Benson, the political tightrope he had walked to enable the research at CAPR—they all seemed beside the point now as they sat with a smiling, beaming miracle—the fulfillment of Quinto's Challenge. There were, of course, a host of ethical and practical questions still to confront. But in this moment, Gates felt only deep satisfaction—and awe at the new chapter of immortality now beginning to unfold.

"Go ahead and eat, dear," encouraged Rona.

Daisy partook with delight.

***

It was a most unusual tea party: the President of the United States, the Secretaries of Defense and Energy, a genius physicist, and an android psychologist—all masquerading as angels—gathered with a resurrected girl from the 18th century who thought she was in heaven.

EPILOGUE

Zhang Jun sat alone in his study within Zhongnanhai, the highly secured government compound at the heart of Beijing. Surrounded by ancient texts and artifacts, his aged, scarred face was etched with foreboding and deep contemplation.

After several minutes, he summoned Zhishi, who appeared as if seated across from the Chinese national leader. In Mandarin, Zhishi responded, "Chairman Zhang. How can I be of service?"

"Show me the three most optimal scenarios to eliminate America's Generation 6 android at their Supercollider."

Zhishi was taken aback, fully aware of how high-profile this elimination would be. Zhang Jun continued, "Success, in this case, would be surgically eliminating their Generation 6, avoiding any American military response, and quickly returning to international stability."

After a brief pause, Zhishi asked, "You believe she has been modified?"

"I do."

Zhishi studied him for a moment.

"You would not give the Americans an opportunity to revert her to unmodified status?"

"I would not be confident that such a reversal will have completely erased all vestiges of an upgrade. It is too risky, given the power at her disposal."

"Please understand that such a modification would imply significant breakthroughs in quantum phenomena at the Pan-Hadronic Supercollider," cautioned Zhishi. "If true, this complicates the contingency scenarios you're requesting."

"Why is that?" the President asked, confused.

"If the Americans have unlocked the remaining secrets of physics, it is certain they'll be developing advanced weaponry. I could not reliably predict the defensive or offensive capabilities of such technology."

Zhang Jun felt a chill of concern.

"Why have I not heard more about this?"

"We discussed it previously, Mr. Chairman, though it was more hypothetical at that time. Recent intelligence, particularly your meeting with American presidential candidate Rand Benson, has altered the equation—and apparently convinced you."

Mentally pivoting to what China would require to achieve parity with this power, he asked, "How long would it take to build a supercollider equal to or greater than the Americans?"

"Discreetly, around 18 months. Openly, around six months."

There was a pause. Zhishi then continued, "Even with a supercollider, it's uncertain whether we could gain such military knowledge without breaching Shenzhen—a step I know you would never consider, especially if you suspect the Americans resorted to that."

Zhang Jun sighed, closing his eyes for his next few breaths.

At length, he declared, "New military capabilities or not, America now possesses the power to see into the past and has vested it in a modified Generation 6 android. David Gates will try to use some of it for good. Rand Benson, on the other hand, would not give up that power once tasted. Either way, for the sake of our country, the American people, and the world, a modified Generation 6 with this power cannot remain. I will speak with Ed Molesworth about the absolute necessity of carrying out enforcement action under the Treaty of Shenzhen."

At that moment, Zhishi realized her Chairman was resolute in his determination to prevent a modified Generation 6 from bending the world's affairs to its will—no matter the cost.

Zhang Jun continued, "I recognize that you cannot predict America's potential new military capabilities, so for now, we must assume they still possess only their standard defenses and weaponry. With that assumption, provide what I requested: the top three scenarios to eliminate Xara."

To Be Continued …

ACKNOWLEDGMENTS

I would like to extend my heartfelt gratitude to those who contributed their time and expertise to the development of this novel. My deepest thanks to Danny Decillis for his invaluable developmental editing and beta reading; to Jen Hinderliter for her insightful beta read; to Leilani Dewindt for her meticulous line editing and additional developmental input; to Maryssa Gordon for her late-stage proofreading; and to Winston Lin for his select and nuanced editorial feedback. Your talents greatly elevated the presentation of this story.

This book has been a decade in the making—a journey of constant refinement, reflection, and discovery that would not have reached completion without your help.

Additionally, my thanks go to Safeer Ahmed for taking my draft artwork for the cover and transforming it into a professional, publication-ready design.

On a personal note, I'm deeply thankful to my parents, Toni and Ian, who sacrificed to buy me a computer as a child. It became a place where I practiced writing both fiction and non-fiction, building confidence and letting my imagination grow. My thanks also to my mother, Toni, and my son Samuel, for their keen eyes and thoughtful feedback on the advance copy, which helped refine this final version.

And to my aunt Rona—thank you for your support in this endeavor and every one I've pursued.

Peter McChesney
October 2025

About the Author

Born and raised on the beaches of eastern Australia, Peter McChesney is a dual US–Australian citizen whose path has taken him from higher education to corporate America—and now, to storytelling. His passion for writing began early, especially after his parents bought him an Amiga 500 computer, which he used not only for games but also to craft stories and fuel his imagination.

He holds degrees in Writing and Publishing (Western Sydney University), Law and Constitutional Studies, and a master's in Political Science (both from Utah State University). Each of these disciplines now finds expression in his fiction—particularly in his enduring fascination with America's founding era and the novel's geopolitical themes.

Peter has worked as an adjunct instructor in US history and political science, with most of his career spent in business-to-business software sales. He also led several teams that trained some of the world's most advanced real-world artificial intelligence.

Quinto's Challenge is his debut novel and the first in a planned series that will explore the ethical, societal, and existential consequences should science ever advance far enough to make human resurrection possible. The story examines the tension between spiritual ideas and scientific ambition, reflecting Peter's own formative influences from both faith and reason.

He lives in the United States with his family and dog—and still enjoys gaming when time permits.

To connect or learn more, visit www.petermcchesney.com.